GREED

A SINFUL EMPIRE TRILOGY (BOOK 1)

EVA CHARLES

QUARRY ROAD PUBLISHING

A SINFUL EMPIRE TRILOGY

A SINFUL EMPIRE PROLOGUE NOVELLA
AND GREED (BOOK 1)

Murphy Rae, Cover Design

Dawn Alexander, Evident Ink, Content Editor

Nancy Smay, Evident Ink, Copy Editor (A Sinful Empire)

James Gallagher, Evident Ink, Copy Editor (Greed)

Faith Williams, The Atwater Group, Proofreader

Virginia Tesi Carey, Proofreader

For more information, contact eva@evacharles.com

Created with Vellum

Happy families are all alike; every unhappy family is unhappy in its own way.

— Leo Tolstoy, *Anna Karenina*

A NOTE FROM EVA

Dear Readers,

If you've read my Devil's Due series, you know that I don't shy away from dark themes, ruthless characters, and language that will make your eyes bleed. A Sinful Empire Trilogy is no exception. This is **not** a safe series.

Now that I've warned you away...

The underbelly of Porto, with its dangerous men and delicious secrets awaits you!

If you haven't read A Sinful Empire Prologue Novella, just turn the page. If you have already read it, start **HERE**

XOXO
Eva

1

ANTONIO

Hushed whispers filter through the crowd as I approach the casket.

Manuel D'Sousa was a formidable player in our world before cancer ravished the hulking giant, leaving him a hollow shell dusted with mortician's rouge. Even a skilled undertaker couldn't conceal his sunken chest and gaunt features.

As I peer into the satin-lined coffin, the din of the room fades, until there is only his dying directive echoing between my ears.

"After I'm gone, Quinta Rosa do Vale will be yours. In exchange, you will marry my daughter. You will protect her from my enemies and yours—with your life, if necessary."

My gaze sweeps over D'Sousa's lifeless body, stopping at his face, as though waiting for him to come to his senses—to drag himself from the bowels of hell, and grab me by the throat until my eyes bulge from their sockets.

But there is only an eerie stillness about him.

Is this what you really want, old man?

You're leaving me with your prized grapes and your innocent daughter? Me? A man so depraved, he would kill his father with his bare hands, while cursing himself for not having done it sooner.

This is the life you want for your precious child?

Now it's too late to change your mind, fool. Too late for her. Too late for me.

Our fate is sealed in blood.

Till death do us part.

Maybe I'm the fool.

2

ANTONIO

I step away from the casket, into the receiving line, quietly taking note of the tear-stained faces in the room. Normally I don't stand on line for anyone, but it's good for the locals to see me paying my respects.

The D'Sousas have always been well-loved in the valley, especially Manuel's late wife, Maria Rosa, who fed the hungry and championed the underdog. In an ugly twist of fate, she was murdered in the street by the very type of person she took under her wing. The sonofabitch slit her throat in broad daylight.

It happened six years ago, hours before my father drew his final breath. Although the two events were unrelated, people whispered that God had taken an angel, but spared us the devil.

I don't believe in most of that shit, but even I have to admit, the universe works in mysterious ways.

Maybe it can use some of its magic to get this damn line moving.

I glance toward the long, windowless wall where Cristiano, one of my most trusted men, is standing, his sharp gaze scouring every inch of the packed room for trouble. If it's here, he'll find it.

The line begins to thin as it winds beyond the casket. Soon, I'll catch a glimpse of my future bride.

My future bride. Just the thought of it makes the acid churn in my gut. The very last thing I need while securing my hold over the region is a wife.

It's not personal. I haven't seen her in years, and it's been even longer since we spoke.

The last time, she was about ten or eleven, riding a horse that was much too large and spirited for a young girl. She had no trouble controlling the powerful animal. I remember being impressed by her skill. When I praised her, she smiled coyly at me from the saddle, her lively eyes sparkling with mischief.

She's not smiling today, and the sparkle has been replaced with a veil of grief.

Daniela D'Sousa is dressed in black from head to toe, her face scrubbed clean of makeup, like any dutiful daughter mourning her beloved father. But she's not just *any* daughter. She's the D'Sousa princess, *a princesa*, the closest thing to royalty in these parts.

As I inch closer, I see how young she is—and vulnerable, with the glazed expression of a teenager who has been dragged through hell and survived. No doubt the last weeks of her father's life took a toll on her, and now, at just eighteen, she's faced with the daunting task of carrying on a storied family legacy—alone. At least that's what she believes.

While Manuel *never* shied away from tough conversations, in the end, he didn't have the balls to tell his only child he'd bequeathed her to the son of *o diabo*. That task was left to me.

I push aside the thoughts of our *arrangement*, and distract myself with studying Daniela. It's not too taxing.

Her dark hair is pinned neatly to the top of her head, exposing a smooth, elegant neck. Even in mourning she's quite lovely, with all the polish one would expect of a princess groomed to one day become queen.

I continue to watch, as she accepts each condolence with poise and grace. Those who pick the grapes are shown the same respect as those who own the valuable vineyards and port houses. *She's like her mother.*

Someday she'll be a useful asset to me—her kind heart the perfect complement to my black soul. Her soft center balancing my rough edges. *Someday. But not today.*

As Daniela waits for the line to move, she gazes toward the main entrance. When she does, the color drains from her face, and she shudders before exchanging a dire look with a woman standing a short distance away.

The older woman is as pale as Daniela.

Without turning my head, I glance at the entrance, expecting to find a demon lurking.

I find two.

My uncle Abel and his oldest son Tomas darken the arched doorway, casting an ominous shadow over the room. Unlike Daniela, I'm not surprised to see them. They're here for show—to see, and to be seen—much the same reason I'm here. *But I don't like it.*

Abel was my father's younger brother, married to my mother's younger sister, Vera. My father always had the upper hand in the relationship, but the brothers were mostly friendly competitors, often scheming against the other port houses.

My cousin Tomas and I, on the other hand, are fierce rivals who seldom exchange a civil word. It's been like this since we were boys. But like my father, I, too, have always had the upper hand.

One day Tomas will take over my uncle's entire port business, the legal and the illegal enterprises, and our rivalry will grow even more bitter. But with D'Sousa's vineyards in my clutches, my power in the valley will be unassailable. For as long as I'm alive, my cousin will forever be second string.

I catch Cristiano's eye from across the room. He nods. He saw Daniela's reaction, too.

She's afraid of them.

I want to know why.

3

ANTONIO

When I finally reach the front of the line, Daniela doesn't pale, but she draws a heavy breath when she sees me and stands taller, with her shoulders pulled back and pupils dilated. If I held my fingers to her throat, her pulse would be racing. It's a subconscious survival instinct, and I doubt she even realizes she slipped into battle mode.

"*Bom dia,*" she says so softly, her greeting is barely audible over the rustling in the room.

"Antonio Huntsman," I murmur, taking her outstretched hand. The introduction is merely a formality. Everyone in the room knows who I am—including her. "It's been a long time. Do you remember me?"

"Of course." Her brow eases some. "Our mothers were friends."

The best of friends, along with my aunt Vera. Of the three, only my mother is still alive—and that was purely luck.

"Your father was a great man," I acknowledge, sincerely. "You were probably too young to know the details, but while I was away studying, your parents helped my mother. I'll never forget the kindness they showed her. I know it wasn't an easy time for them."

A flicker of something—anguish, maybe—contorts her delicate features. It happens in a heartbeat, and for several seconds I observe carefully to see what else she's hiding behind that stoic mask. But she shows me nothing more.

"My mother lives in London now," I continue. "Otherwise, she would be here. She sends her condolences."

"Thank you," Daniela says, her voice just above a whisper. "How is she?"

"Happy. Very happy."

Daniela's face softens. "I haven't seen her since—" She blinks a few times before continuing. "It seems like a lifetime ago."

There's a resigned wistfulness in her voice that seems out of place from someone so young.

"I adored your mother," Daniela continues. "She would always bring me caramels wrapped in gold foil when she visited. And beautiful ribbons from her travels. I—"

She stops mid-sentence, and for a moment, she appears faraway and unguarded, so fragile she might shatter if she completes the thought. All the talk of my mother must have brought back memories of hers.

My heart is long-hardened, and it takes more than a shaken woman to garner any sympathy from me, but I give her a moment to pull herself together. That I can do.

Daniela wets her plump lips as she fights for composure.

I'm mesmerized by the struggle in her beautiful face. The way the pain whirls in her eyes, darkening the irises.

Her brown eyes are several shades lighter than her hair, with tiny gold flecks that catch the light streaming in behind her. *Expressive eyes.* The kind that hide nothing. *My favorite kind.* Before my imagination gets too far down that path, I remember her father, *my mentor*, is lying in a wooden box, behind me.

"Please give your mother my regards," she adds quietly.

"I will."

With that, Daniela's attention shifts to the person in line behind me, and I get the sense I'm being dismissed. But I don't move. I'm done when I'm done. Not one second sooner. Although it's cute that she thinks she can get rid of me so easily.

The princesa is in for a rude awakening.

"Thank you for visiting my father before he passed," she says, after it becomes apparent that I'm not going anywhere. "I'm sorry I missed you."

Her tone is still exceedingly polite, but cooler, now. She might be happy I visited her father before he died, but she sure as hell isn't happy I'm still standing here.

"Your visit brought him great peace of mind."

If you only knew the half of it.

I nod once and step out of the receiving line, leaving her to greet others—because now, I'm done.

4

ANTONIO

All eyes are on me as I make my way to the rear exit, where Cristiano is waiting. I'm sure the gossips are wondering if I'll stick around to speak with my uncle. As far as I'm concerned, there's no reason to wait to say hello. Respect is paid when it's due. That bastard isn't entitled to a damn thing from me.

On the way out, I pass several of my men who are fanned out across the funeral parlor. I'm vigilant as I cross the room, but I make eye contact with no one.

"Let's get out of here," I mutter under my breath as I stride past Cristiano.

The crowd gathered at the exit steps aside, opening a wide swath for me to pass easily.

Outside, I fill my lungs with fresh air before climbing into the back of an armored SUV.

As the vehicle pulls away, I gaze out the tinted window at the line snaked out the door and around the mortuary. It was like this when my father died too. The only difference is that no one shed a single tear for Hugo Huntsman. They showed up just to make sure *o diabo* was really dead.

Less than a week after we lowered Hugo into the ground, Manuel D'Sousa summoned me for the first time, and delivered a fiery ultimatum. Even now, I remember every word.

"The river of gold and everything along its banks can be yours. But your responsibilities must be to something greater than yourself. You will be called upon to mete out justice and quell unrest, upholding tradition, while ensuring our wine flows freely beyond the valley. If you are not man enough to wear the crown, step aside now, and I'll find someone worthy of the honor."

And just like that, my days of throwing back expensive whiskey and chasing cheap pussy were over. I was twenty-two.

Yes, I had the pedigree, but D'Sousa was kingmaker.

He lived and breathed lush, rich Port—from the vine to the bottle. He knew every detail of the process intimately, and appreciated every aspect. Soon I did too.

Since the beginning, the business—the shadowy parts and the more principled—have filled every corner of my life. Although some might argue that flooding the world market with fortified wine is hardly principled.

"Jesus, I'm glad to be out of there," Cristiano grumbles, settling his large frame into the seat beside me.

Cristiano, Lucas, and I have been friends since we were kids. Lucas, who is at the command center monitoring video feeds we set up in and around the funeral home, is also part of my inner circle. Cristiano and Lucas *are* the inner circle. While there are others I trust, no one else has the kind of access they do. Not even close.

"I hate when you're exposed like that," Cristiano mutters. "Even with all the extra precautions in place. Too damn many people in and out, milling around. It's exactly the kind of occasion one of our enemies would use to take you out. It's not smart."

But necessary. And I'm done talking about it. "Why do you think Daniela was so spooked by my uncle and Tomas?"

He shakes his head. "Not sure. But I'm going to poke around this afternoon. I was starting to worry that you'd want to hang around to see how it played out."

"I saw enough." *More than enough*. She belongs to me, and nobody, *nobody* gets to make her tremble. *Nobody but me.*

"What are the chances they've already approached her about the property?" Not that it matters. She doesn't own it, so she can't sell it, but I want those facts to unfold on my terms.

"We have eyes all over Quinta Rosa do Vale," Cristiano replies, scrolling through his phone. "We'd have known if they showed up. But I guarantee they're planning something."

"Have Lucas sift through Daniela's email and call records, to see if they've contacted her since we last checked. Tell him to drop whatever he's doing—and get on it."

I want answers. Now.

I drum my fingers on the armrest, until even I'm irritated by the tapping.

"I'm going to pay her a visit this week."

Cristiano lifts his head and peers at me from across the console. "Have you changed your mind about waiting to tell her about the betrothal contract?"

"Did you see how young she is?" I scowl at him. "How long do you think I can tolerate a teenage girl's bullshit? Especially a spoiled one?"

He groans. "My sisters weren't spoiled teenagers, but they could torture me without breaking a sweat."

They still torture him without breaking a sweat.

"I already have my hands full with Rafael, and he's away at school."

Rafael is Abel's youngest son. Tomas's little brother. He came to live with me several years ago, after his father's abuse became intolerable. Rafael's a good kid, but every day is a new adventure. Daniela is several years older than him, but after just a few minutes with her, I can already guarantee she'll make my challenges with him seem like child's play.

"It'll be one headache after another if we bring her in now. I have enough problems. And I'm not a goddamn babysitter."

She's not a child, Antonio. No, she isn't, but she's not a woman either.

What she is, is tempting. Too damn tempting.

Something about her vulnerability stirred a desire I can't shake. *A desire to mark her. To spray my seed all over her supple, virgin skin.* That's the truth. It's exactly what was going through my mind when she licked her lips, struggling to keep it together at the funeral home.

One day, I'll tease her until she surrenders—until I demand her surrender. *It'll be brutal and filthy*. No sense in prettying it up to make it sound like something it's not. Wife or no wife, I'm talking about base carnal lust, nothing more.

"She's young," Cristiano admits, propping his elbow on the armrest. "But something about her . . ." He pauses for several seconds, staring into space.

He better not say one fucking word about her innocence being a turn-on. "What about her?" I challenge.

"I don't know. She looks like jailbait, but she seems much older. Something about her eyes. Like they've seen a lot." He draws a breath and blows it out carefully. "Our world can wipe the sheen off the rose-colored glasses pretty quick. Without her mother around, she was probably exposed to some of the dirtier parts of her father's life."

"Her father was sick for a long time, and the end was ugly," I remind him. "That's wariness and exhaustion in her eyes. D'Sousa was careful around her. Up until recently, he sheltered her from everything. Besides, his hands have always been cleaner than ours."

I pause to remember the man I tortured last night, until he

gave up the information I needed. *No regrets. Not a single fucking one.*

Cristiano shakes his head. "Marrying her now is likely to be a huge clusterfuck. But who knows? Maybe waiting will be even worse."

Russian roulette. Not a game for someone, like me, who craves control.

I lean over and adjust the air flow so I can fucking breathe.

"She's not ready to be married to me."

It's perfect, because while I might be more than a decade older, I'm not ready to marry her, either. "I'll make a final decision about the timing, after I spend some time with her."

5

DANIELA

I lift the heart-shaped paperweight from my father's desk, sliding my thumb over the glazed ceramic. I made it for *Papai* in first grade, when my life was all rainbows and unicorns.

He kept the quirky little gift in the same spot on his desk all these years. It sits right in front of a photo of my mother and me, nose to nose, giggling. Her face glowed as she kissed me goodnight in the foyer before they left for the evening. She was stunning, and whenever my father was behind the lens, he captured her beauty in unexpected ways. It's how he saw her—his Rosa.

"What if the travel documents don't arrive?" Isabel asks, before I drown in the bittersweet memories.

Isabel has lived with my family since she was fifteen—more than thirty years. When I was born, she became my nurse, then later, my governess, and after my mother passed, my angel. But through it all, she's always been my closest friend.

"We have almost everything we need already. The rest of the documents will get here. Please don't worry."

Isabel has always been the nervous type, although her

anxiety has been off the charts since the day I told her I'd be leaving the country after my father died. Despite her reservations, there was never any doubt that my friend, her husband Jorge, and five-year-old Valentina would leave with me. I never had to ask.

"I wish we were all traveling together," she says wistfully—for the fourth time this morning.

We've been in my father's office for two hours, managing the to-do list. She gets skittish whenever we spend too long on the preparations. I try to be sensitive, but the clock is ticking louder with each passing day. I'm desperate for us to leave—before we can't.

There's still so much to get done before we go. Some of it necessary, and the rest to appease my conscience.

I had planned on staying in Porto through the harvest—until those animals showed up at the funeral home. They haven't had the nerve to show their faces here yet, but they will.

Abel and Tomas Huntsman—just the thought of them sullying my parents' home makes my skin crawl. Now that my father's gone, it's only a matter of time before they pay me a visit. Isabel knows it too.

With any luck, I'll be long gone when they come looking for me.

"It's not too late to reconsider the travel arrangements, Daniela."

"It's safer to travel separately," I say gently, trying to remain patient with her. "It's one thing if you were to travel to Canada with me to see my great-aunt, but it would raise suspicions if your family came along with us."

She nods and gets up, using her nervous energy to tidy the neat-as-a-pin room.

We've been through every detail, dozens of times. The scheme is complex, but the complexity is essential if we want to disappear.

Parts of it have been in place for years. My father was a

powerful man, with powerful enemies. We always had a plan to flee the country, one we could put in motion at any time it became necessary.

That time has come.

I watch Isabel fuss with the drapes on the window that overlooks the sprawling vineyards on the southern end of the estate. The ones that have been in my mother's family for more than three hundred years. The conditions on the south side create a perfect microclimate for growing grapes unlike any others. It's those grapes that transform ordinary Port into something extraordinary.

They're the most important vineyards in the entire country, a World Heritage site, and now, my responsibility. *Mine.* It's almost laughable.

"Don't worry," my father assured me more times than I can count. "You'll have plenty of help when I'm gone."

Despite my father's promises that he tied up all the loose ends and put safeguards into place when he learned he was dying, it's always been clear to me that no one would fall in line behind a young woman. Unlike my father, I believe that the unflinching loyalty people have always shown our family will die with him. It might be different if I had been born a boy—it might have all been different.

"If you still intend on riding, you should get going," Isabel says, collecting some paperwork from the desk, and organizing it into folders. "The morning's slipping away, and you need to shower and be ready to receive guests."

Guests. *Ugh.* It's been a week since the funeral, and I'm long past tired of opening the house to visitors paying condolence calls, but I won't shame my family by shirking tradition. Besides, my father deserves the honor.

I glance at my schedule and sigh heavily. I really can't afford to play—but I'm already dressed for it. I woke up determined to spend some time with my horses today and threw on riding clothes first thing. There won't be many more opportunities with Zeus and Atlas. The horses are one of the many reasons leaving Porto is so painful.

The doorbell rings, startling me. I glance at Isabel. "Are we expecting someone?"

"Not at this hour," she says cautiously. "But people keep sending flowers and food. So much food." She waves her hands in the air. "I've been giving it to the staff to take home to their families, but we still have more than we can eat."

"Send it to Santa Ana's. They must know some families who will appreciate the food. We shouldn't let it go to waste."

We really shouldn't. But roasted meat and vegetables or a rum-soaked cake showing up on the doorstep is the least of my concerns. Abel and Tomas, on the other hand—that's something to worry about. I'm sure when the doorbell rang, it crossed Isabel's mind too.

We stare at each other silently as a single pair of footsteps approaches. If it were food or flowers, Jose, my father's butler, would take it directly to the kitchen without bothering us.

Not waiting for the inevitable knock, Isabel gets up and pulls the heavy French door open.

"Pardon me," Jose says in an apprehensive tone. "Antonio Huntsman is here to see Daniela."

6

DANIELA

My stomach roils, and I shut my eyes for a few seconds. *Antonio Huntsman. As though I don't have enough problems.*

I'll never understand why my father liked him so much. Not just liked him, but supported his rise to power. *Papai* could have squashed the entire Huntsman clan like a bug, but he didn't.

"*I don't have the luxury of destroying our world, to exact that kind of revenge—even in your mother's name.*"

That was his final word on the subject.

My father never invited Antonio to our home, until the end —at least not when I was here. But his trust in him was an affront to my mother—and to me—and painful. *Excruciatingly painful.* Like picking the scab off a fresh wound. *My scab. My wound.*

Although he had a soft heart when it came to us, nothing was more important to my father than preserving *our world*. I understand the imperative too, but a small part of me will never forgive him for not destroying everything the Huntsmans hold dear.

No, Antonio wasn't involved in what happened that day, but

as far as I'm concerned, the men in that family are monsters. It's in their genes. And if the gossip is true, this one's no different than the rest. *Maybe crueler.* But if I have to choose, I'd rather take my chances with him—just not right now.

I glance at Jose, who's still waiting patiently for some direction from me. "Please tell him I'm indisposed. Thank you."

He hesitates before nodding. Not many people want to tell Antonio Huntsman to get lost, but the staff who work inside the house are loyal—sometimes to a fault.

Isabel turns to him. "I'll go," she says. She must have seen the same wariness in Jose's eyes that I saw.

"Maybe I should see him and get it over with," I grumble, although it's the last thing I want to do.

When I start to stand, Isabel motions for me to stay seated. "You're not dressed for visitors. I'm going to tell him you're not seeing guests right now. I'll invite him to come back. He won't make a problem in your father's house."

Maybe not. But it's not my father's house anymore. It's mine. "Thank you."

"Who shows up unannounced at nine thirty in the morning?" she mutters, breezing into the hall.

Antonio Huntsman, the arrogant bastard who does whatever he wants. That's who.

To a large extent, he's always been this way. Good-looking, rich, with a powerful father—a trifecta that never required him to learn humility.

It doesn't have to be that way. Money and power don't have to suck every drop of humanity from your soul—but they often do.

As much as it pains me to admit now, when I was younger, I had a huge crush on Antonio, and although he barely knew I existed, he was always nice to me.

When I was nine, he intervened when some boys were being mean to me and my friends at the Feast of the Immaculate Conception. He put an end to it pretty quick. Those boys never bothered us again. Neither did their friends.

There were a few other small things too, but he was so much older that our paths seldom crossed—unless he came to visit with his mother, which was rare, but always a special treat. *I thought so, anyway.*

But from the rumors I've heard in the last few years, there's nothing kind about Antonio now. *I guess the apple doesn't fall far from the tree.* That old saying isn't for nothing.

When curiosity gets the best of me, I creep into the hall where I can hear the conversation in the foyer, but still remain out of sight.

As I inch closer, the voices become less garbled.

"I'm sorry, *senhor*, but as I said a moment ago, *Senhora* Daniela is not seeing anyone until the *customary* calling hour."

Isabel's voice has an edge. She's a stickler for protocol, and he must be giving her a hard time. *Good luck, Antonio.*

"The customary calling hour?" he hisses.

He won't make a problem in your father's house. File it under famous last words.

"Yes, *senhor*. Visitors are free to drop by to pay their condolences, but not until the appointed time, as has *always* been the custom."

Oh Isabel, teaching a lesson in manners is not the way to deal with the likes of him.

"I'm a busy man. I don't have the time or the patience for arbitrary customs. Tell Daniela I need to speak to her. I won't ask politely a second time."

A second time? You didn't ask politely the first time. Good Lord, he's even more full of himself than I remember.

I've heard enough. I might not fare any better, but it's not right to leave her to deal with him.

I take a deep breath and force myself from the safety of the shadows.

7

DANIELA

"Good morning, *Senhor* Huntsman," I greet him as I enter the sunny foyer. Even though my stomach is somersaulting, my voice is steady and clear.

Antonio gazes over Isabel's shoulder, but doesn't say a word as I approach. Probably because he's too busy raking over my form-fitting riding clothes like he can see right through them. It's openly lewd and entirely unrushed, as though he doesn't give a damn if anyone catches him looking.

"*Bom dia*," he drawls in a buttery timbre, when I stop beside Isabel.

Although I feel my cheeks warming, I lift my chin and force a smile. There is no way I'm going to let this jerk see that he's embarrassed me in my own house.

"I realize this isn't an ideal hour to pay a visit." Antonio peers into my eyes, holding my gaze steady. "But I won't take up too much of your time."

I don't shy away but I take a quiet breath, replaying his words in my head one by one, looking for something resembling an apology. All I find is arrogance. But unlike Isabel, I don't bother to waste my breath teaching manners.

"Why don't we talk in my father's office."

Not that we need to talk. I know exactly why he's here. He wants the grapes—or more likely, the entire estate. He owns plenty of premium real estate throughout the valley, but men like him aren't satisfied until they have everything. Although it's not just that. Quinta Rosa do Vale, *my* legacy, is the ultimate jewel for his kingdom. It will put all the power in one man's hands, cementing *his* legacy forever—even I know this.

But nothing is forever, Antonio. If that's what you believe, you're a fool.

When you're powerful, they stand in line to knock you down. That's why my father always had so much security around us. *Not that it saved my mother.*

Antonio follows me down the hall without a word, staying a few steps behind, even when I slow my gait. It's not an act of deference. He's not a deferential man. He's a pig.

When I peek over my shoulder, his eyes are glued to my skin-tight breeches. I don't have the self-assuredness to sway my hips in an exaggerated manner that lets him know *I know* he's looking, or the pluck to flip him off. My experience in dealing with men like him is virtually nonexistent. So instead, I pick up my pace to get to the destination as quickly as possible.

Isabel follows, too, and I'm sure I'll hear about what a *porco* he is later.

When we're just inside the office, Antonio turns to her. "I need a word with *Menina* Daniela," he says, referring to me in the way someone might refer to a younger girl, and dismissing Isabel as though it's his damn house and he's the king.

With one simple sentence—that's all it takes—he seizes the power in the room.

I glare at him for a second or two—not more. I'm not sure what I expect to accomplish with a mean look, but it doesn't matter. He doesn't even notice.

In truth, I don't care if he calls me *menina*, *senhora*, or *dona*.

Although it's not surprising that he chose the one title that would diminish me. But what does bother me is that I can't find the words, or the courage, to tell him to speak to the staff politely or leave. That's what my parents would have done.

I glance at Isabel, trying to convey my apologies through my eyes—like a coward or a helpless girl might do. "Why don't you get us some coffee? *Por favor.*"

She pulls her mouth into a tight, thin line as she turns toward the door.

"Nothing for me. I won't be here long. Shut the door behind you, *por favor,*" Antonio instructs, drawing out the words *por favor* to mock me. It wouldn't surprise me to hear that he never says please.

His behavior is appalling by Porto standards—even for an arrogant bastard.

Not only is it customary to accept food and beverages when paying a visit, it's an insult to the host to turn down refreshments. And no man, with *good* intentions, would *ever* suggest being alone with a woman he's not related to in some way. These are dated customs, but much about Porto is last century. No one knows this better than Antonio Huntsman, who has used the old ways to accumulate power.

Isabel is fuming, her forehead etched with lines that seem to have become a permanent feature since we first learned my father was terminally ill. Between the wrinkles and her graying hair, she looks so much older than forty-eight.

"It's okay," I assure her. "I'll take care of the door."

She hesitates, with a pointed look at Antonio and then at me.

I nod and flash her a small, reassuring smile. Isabel might be a nervous Nellie, but she'd protect me with her last breath.

As her footsteps disappear down the hall, I gauge him carefully. The son of *o diabo*. He looks every bit the part.

There's no way in hell I'm shutting that door.

Despite what my father believed, I find Antonio Huntsman terrifying—especially now that we're alone. His bespoke suit, tailored to within a half-inch, might suggest a certain kind of refinement, but his dark, soulless eyes say something else entirely.

"It's nice to see you again." I can't even force a smile.

His mouth twitches at the edges. "Is it?"

Without waiting for a reply, he saunters over to the south window and surveys the estate like it belongs to him. "I've never stood at this window," he murmurs. "It's a breathtaking vista."

Enjoy it, because it's the last time you'll see it from this room.

"Do you still have that feisty stallion?" he asks, gazing into the distance.

The question takes me by surprise. My horse seems like an odd thing for him to remember.

"Zeus. Yes, but age has mellowed him. He's not so feisty anymore."

Antonio glances over his shoulder at me. "The first time I saw you on him, I thought I'd have to jump the fence and rescue you. But you had that horse wrapped around your finger. Either you were fearless, or you hid your fear well."

"I wasn't afraid." *I didn't know fear then. I was sheltered and protected in every possible way. There was no reason to be fearful.* "Most people think the key to handling an animal of that size is to hide your fear. But you can't hide it. Animals smell fear. The key to controlling a spirited horse like Zeus is to have no fear."

Antonio turns and faces me, with an intensity that's unnerving. "That's how you control men, too. I can't remember the last time I was afraid, but I can smell fear from a mile away."

The way he says it—his tone so matter-of-fact, but his words fraught with danger—sends a ripple up my spine.

In this moment, he reminds me of my father's fiercest guards. The ones who have folded the brutality of the work seamlessly into their lives. The ones who would put a bullet in your head while asking about your family.

I slide my sweaty palms along my breeches, as discreetly as possible. *Hopefully he can't actually smell fear.*

"What can I do for you, *senhor*?"

With a few long strides, he's practically on top of me. So close I could touch the stubble on his jaw without fully extending my arm. His proximity is unsettling, but not enough to stop me from admiring his long, inky lashes, and the strong cords in his neck.

"You called me Antonio when you were a child. It seems silly to start calling me *senhor* now, *Daniela*."

He draws out each syllable in my name in a way that makes the hair on the back of my neck prickle.

"What can I do for you, Antonio?" I motion for him to have a seat, while I step toward the chair behind the desk.

"This is a social call, not a business meeting. Why don't we sit near the fireplace?"

All week I've been entertaining men claiming to be paying condolence calls, but who were really only interested in the vineyards. Sitting in my father's chair gave me the courage to tell them *no*, even when they became insistent. *I need that courage now.*

"I'm more comfortable here," I reply, easing into the chair, with my spine steely against the firm leather back.

Antonio scratches his temple and smiles. It's not a genuine smile, but more like the way lips might contort when someone is struggling for self-control.

While waiting for him to take a seat, I lace my fingers together tightly, so my hands don't shake. As the seconds pass, I become more and more convinced that he doesn't plan on sitting.

While I adjust my bottom on the seat, looking for some of the courage that was here just yesterday, Antonio splays both hands on the desk and leans over, his mouth an inch from the top of my head.

"I don't give a damn where you'd be more comfortable. We'll sit by the fireplace." His edict is issued in a stern whisper, which makes it seem even more menacing. "Don't make me say it again."

8

DANIELA

I grew up in a world where there is plenty of tough talk and no shortage of tough actions to back it up, but no one speaks to me like that—not in this house. At least they didn't when my father was alive.

I swallow hard and try to calm my pounding heart. But I don't move. I'm not sure I can move.

He steps back, still towering over me. "I'm a guest," he says in a voice as tightly restrained as his movements. "In your home. And as ridiculous as it is, it appears that you're in charge of the estate now. My comfort, not yours, is something that should concern you."

I'm normally quite patient, and good manners have been drilled into me since the moment I took my first breath. But I've had my fill of his insults. *More than my fill.*

I chew on the inside of my cheek, holding my tongue, before I say something I'll regret. If I don't want this to escalate, I need to keep myself in check, because clearly no one checks him.

This is your house, Daniela. Act like it.

I can't grind the heel of my riding boot into his balls like he deserves, and I'm not foolish enough to think I can toss Antonio Huntsman out on the street. But I do need to show some kind of authority, otherwise he'll continue to humiliate me.

If he wants the property, he's certainly going about it in a strange way. Maybe he thinks he'll wear me down until I agree to sell it, just so he'll leave.

That's not happening. I'll burn everything to the ground before I let anyone named Huntsman have my mother's vineyards.

From the corner of my eye, I see him glowering at me. I can almost feel the burn on my scalp.

The one thing I'm sure about is that he's not going anywhere without a fight.

Let him make an offer for the property, and you can politely refuse him. It might get a little testy, but then he'll leave—just like the others.

He's not like the others, a little voice in my head warns. But I can't come up with a better idea.

I raise my chin. "Well, I certainly don't want you to be uncomfortable."

It's not my intention, but the words tumble out like an exaggerated eyeroll that I doubt he appreciates. Antonio doesn't say anything, but there's a growing intensity vibrating off him, and I wouldn't be shocked if he grabbed a fistful of my hair and dragged me over to the sitting area near the fireplace.

Before he makes a move, I stand and step away from the safety of the antique desk that embodies my father and everything he valued. The safety is merely an illusion I've been clinging to since he died. Nothing is safe around Huntsman. Certainly not me. Even my father's sturdy desk can't change that fact.

"The door," he says, pointedly, with his brow raised.

Something inside me snaps.

Fuck you! I want to scream in his face. *Fuck you!*

Don't stoop to his level, good sense chides. I won't, but I'm done being a doormat.

"This is still my father's house," I huff, indignantly. "He's been dead just over a week. You might not feel as though you need to show any respect now that he's gone, but I still do."

Antonio tilts his head ever-so-slightly to the side, and stills. His face is unreadable.

My little tirade surprised him. To be honest, it surprised me.

He doesn't say another word about the door. Not a single one. It feels like a victory, and defying him is strangely intoxicating.

Once we're seated a safe distance apart, I clutch the win tight and find my voice.

"We really don't know each other—not as adults, anyway." I look directly into his dark eyes, without flinching. "You paid your condolences at the funeral home. If this isn't a business meeting, what is it?"

Antonio sits back, with his broad shoulders filling the chair. He crosses one leg over the other, an ankle resting casually on a knee, like he has all the damn time in the world to toy with me.

Sitting there, he looks like any other handsome businessman in a conservative striped tie and shoes polished to a high sheen. Aside from the scruffy jaw, there's not a single sign of wear on him—not an errant thread or even a small scuff. His brightly colored socks are unexpected, though. They're all the rage with dark suits, but they seem too whimsical for such a dangerous man.

There's a glimmer of amusement in his eyes when he catches me checking him out. Suddenly my earlier victory seems inconsequential.

"Let's get something out of the way—since we're both *adults,*" he says, mimicking me. "I'm not interested in the grapes or the vineyards. This is exactly what I say it is: a social call. If it were something else, I wouldn't hesitate to tell you."

I don't believe a word out of his mouth, but I nod.

"Now that your father's gone, who's in charge of the day-to-day operations?"

Social call my ass. "I am." I keep my head high and ignore the smirk he's not trying very hard to conceal.

"As you know, my father didn't die suddenly. When he was diagnosed with colon cancer at the end of last year, he knew it was only a matter of time. He put in safeguards, and shored up the workforce so that there are only trusted people in high positions. The vineyards are well-established, with a manager who has been with us for two decades. He knows every vine as well as he knows his children. And with Isabel's help, I've been running the house since shortly after my mother died."

And I don't have to justify anything to you. But I did. Rattling off a laundry list to bolster my credibility, as though he might take everything away if I can't convince him I'm competent.

"It's a lot for someone who only recently turned eighteen."

Since my father's illness became known, there's been a lot of public speculation about how an eighteen-year-old *girl* would be able to carry on a family legacy. The mayor of Porto, suggested during a television interview, that I might need to find a suitable husband to help me. No one raised an eyebrow when he said it, although I suspect my mother rolled over in her grave.

"I've heard the gossip too. But no one needs to worry about me. I'm quite capable."

Antonio doesn't say anything as he adjusts the lower portion of his tie so that it doesn't crease as it drapes over his belt buckle, but when he glances up, I see the incredulity in his eyes. It's probably the most ridiculous thing he's heard all day —or ever.

While he's not entirely wrong, his self-righteousness makes me want to scream.

When the others came looking to buy the vineyards, they at

least pretended to show me a modicum of respect. They spoke politely, and brought fancy pastries, flowers, and silk scarves to woo me. Huntsman brought his condescending attitude.

"Have there been many inquiries about the property?"

I flash him a small, impertinent smile. "I thought this was a social call?"

He glares at me, the way a parent might warn a naughty child before she's sent to time-out. But at this point, I'm too irritated to fall in line for him, even though I have no doubt he'd be happy to punish me if I continue.

"It is," he replies tersely, nostrils flaring. "I'm just making conversation. And trying to gauge how much pressure you're under."

So you can step in like some hero, and offer to buy the vineyards for a song.

"Why is that?" I demand more forcefully than is polite.

His jaw tics, and the silence is uneasy. Antonio doesn't seem so amused by me anymore. Given his stony eyes, I should probably be more nervous, but getting under his skin feels like another victory. It's almost as tasty as the last.

"I'm getting the sense you don't trust me, Daniela." He says it so quietly, the silence is virtually undisturbed.

Trust. Such a weighty word. I sit with it for a minute, maybe two, mulling it over. "Should I trust you?" I ask finally.

The words wobble out with a soft, but uncertain landing. They sound sincere, without a hint of sarcasm—like maybe I want to trust him.

Deep down, I long for someone with his kind of power and knowledge to guide me. I'm in over my head. But it doesn't matter what he says, or how desperately I need someone like him on my side. I'd never trust him. Not in a million years.

Antonio presses his lips together until they all but disappear.

Should I trust you? My ridiculous question flails in the silence, as I search frantically for a way to snatch it back.

"I'm not here for the grapes or the vineyards." His tenor is unyielding, but the edge is mostly honed. "I don't like to have my motivations questioned, or to repeat myself."

His stormy eyes drill into mine, boring deep, until I'm certain he's seeing more than he should—more than I want to reveal. I'm so flustered, I look away. It's not a tactful move, or discreet. There's no doubt that Antonio is fully aware of how uncomfortable I am. How uncomfortable he makes me.

"I came to check on you," he continues, in a sober tone that's abandoned all of its sharpness. "But no. You shouldn't trust me. I'm everything you believe me to be. Probably worse."

9

DANIELA

I shiver as a chill blows through the room, rubbing my arms to warm myself.

"You shouldn't trust me. I'm everything you believe me to be. Probably worse."

What kind of man says that about himself—without shame or apology? *No one.*

His expression is virtually unreadable, like a skilled poker player biding his time. Although, I don't feel as though he's playing me. Not about this. I think he meant exactly what he said.

I draw a quiet breath. The no-holds-barred admission is startling, but in an odd way, the frank honesty is disarming. Like everything else about him, it rattles my bones, leaving me off-balance.

And because I must be the most foolish woman in the entire valley, it also draws me to him in ways that I don't want to be drawn to him. I can't explain it. But it's true.

Antonio Huntsman is danger wrapped in a handsome package, with masculine ridges and angles along a powerful frame. Underneath, barely concealed by the refined wrapping, is the worst kind of danger. I know it. I know it in my marrow. I know it in every cell of my being. Yet some element of that danger is attractive.

God forgive me.

I raise my eyes in his direction. He's watching me. Studying me like a novelty. I suppose I am. The girl who can't make up her mind about the elusive Antonio Huntsman—the country's most eligible bachelor. Like the devil he is, I'm sure he senses every conflicting emotion warring inside me.

"Have there been many inquiries about the property?" he asks, again.

Inquiries about the property. Yes, that's where we were before I started thinking about kissing the bad boy until he weakened my resolve, and I gave him *everything.*

He's not a boy, Daniela. Don't make that mistake.

I glance at his face, unsure how much to divulge about the property. Although I'm certain he knows all about the men who came calling this week. I doubt anything of consequence happens in Porto that he doesn't know.

"The vultures began circling before the body was cold," I confess, painting a more visceral picture than my stomach can take.

Antonio smiles gently—as gentle as danger smiles. "I'm sure they did. It must be tiresome. What have you told them?"

"The same thing I've told you. The property is not for sale, and neither am I."

He looks down at his trousers, smoothing the lightweight wool over his thigh. My pussy flutters as his fingers skim the thick muscle. It's unexpected. And unwelcome. And entirely human.

"Marriage proposals?" He gauges my reaction with an eagle eye.

From men of all ages. More than I care to count.

I shrug.

"Did you order a tiered chocolate cake or a white one?" He says it with such a dry wit that I smile. *A real smile*. It's been so long, I'm surprised the muscles still act voluntarily.

This side of him is charming, although I'm not foolish enough to let my guard down completely. But I'll play.

"A white cake, of course."

"*Ahh*. Of course. I should have known. A traditionalist. A cake as pure as the bride." His eyes twinkle at my expense. It's another subtle dig at how young I am—how inexperienced.

Hopefully my face isn't as red as it feels.

Fortunately, he pulls a phone from his jacket pocket and glances at the screen, sparing me some embarrassment.

"I'm happy to hear that nothing's for sale," he murmurs, still preoccupied with the screen. "When the time comes, I'm sure you'll hold out for a high price. That's what girls like you are taught from the womb."

He scowls at the phone, ignoring me as though I'm not even here.

Girls like me. He didn't say it in a nasty way—and he's not entirely wrong either. Although *girls like me* don't set their price, because they don't have complete freedom to choose who they marry. Some have no freedom.

But I do. And I'm definitely not for sale, and with any luck, I won't have to sell the property either. Eventually, I want to come back to Porto. Someday, when it's safe again, I want to come home.

My chest tightens, welling with emotion I'm having trouble controlling. It's almost as though the reality of leaving Porto, of leaving *home*, hits me now, for the first time. I've been so wrapped up with my father's deteriorating health, then the funeral, and the vineyards, and the preparations to leave, that I haven't stopped to think about, to *really* think about what leaving will mean not only for me, but for all of us.

The sacrifice is enormous—especially for Isabel and Jorge.

I'll add it to all the other things they've done for me that I can never repay.

You can't have a meltdown now. Not in front of him.

I cough to cover a sob that's threatening to spill out into the room, but it only calls attention to my distress.

Antonio lifts his head and opens his mouth as if to say something, but instead, he gives me a moment to collect myself.

"I apologize," I murmur. "It's been a long few weeks."

"Don't apologize. Raw emotion is honest. Being honest with me always pays off. *Always*."

I simply nod, because I don't trust the words to come out without wobbling. I don't care one iota about being honest with him. With any luck, our paths will never cross again.

"Now I'm going to be honest with you. I need to make a call."

Thank God. I start to stand, thinking he's leaving, but he shakes his head. "Don't get up. I'll only be a minute."

So much for God's mercy. At least I'll have a small break from him and his intensity.

10

DANIELA

Antonio walks over to the window on the far end of the room and looks out so that I can't catch more than cryptic bits and pieces of the conversation. Although it doesn't matter. I'm not interested in his call.

I'm focused on his back. Wide at the top, tapering gently into a perfect vee.

His suit jacket fits like a glove. The luxurious fabric stretches across his broad shoulders in a way that makes my mouth water.

It's true. I wish it wasn't, but I won't kid myself.

He holds the phone to his ear with his left hand, while the right is high on the window jamb. The set of his arm, with his long fingers against the wood, evokes a memory. My eyes glaze over, and I feel the fluttering between my legs again.

I'm mesmerized by those strong hands.

Just like that day.

When we were tweeners, my friends and I stalked Antonio and his buddies, Cristiano and Lucas, like they were celebrities. Although my crush was one-sided, it didn't stop me from scribbling "Daniela + Antonio" inside hand-drawn hearts in my notebooks.

It was a harmless crush—until the day we caught him kissing Margarida Pires, in an alley on the edge of the square. Margarida was my friend Susana's older sister. She was beautiful, with hair the color of spun gold, and round, full breasts that men of all ages stared at for too long.

Susana, Elisabete, and I were on the balcony outside my family's apartment in the city, spying on Antonio and Margarida. Susana and Elisabete couldn't stop giggling at them kissing, but I was hypnotized by the way he touched her, and how she responded.

Margarida's back was flush against the stone building, and his right hand was braced above her head. They were pressed against each other, like lavender stems between the pages of a book.

Antonio brushed his lips and clever fingers over her skin, whispering so only she could hear. When he buried his mouth in her neck, Margarida's eyelids fluttered closed, and her head fell back, her bruised lips forming a perfect O.

I could almost hear her gasps—almost feel her pleasure, like it was mine.

"Hey," one of my guards called to them, when he caught us spying. "Get a room if you don't want an audience."

They looked up at where we were crouched on the balcony, behind the iron rails. Margarida turned away, but Antonio jerked his chin in our direction with a shameless grin on his gorgeous face.

Another guard shooed us off the balcony, so I didn't see any more. But that didn't stop my eleven-year-old imagination from conjuring all sorts of scenarios involving passionate kisses and declarations of undying love.

That night, I replayed their kisses over and over, and as the pressure grew, I rolled on my tummy and squirmed against a decorative pillow, humping the firm bolster until my whole body shook.

Every time I saw him after that, every time his name was

mentioned, I imagined his lips on mine. I dreamed that all his kisses belonged to me.

Then my mother was murdered.

After that, I never imagined kissing anyone. Not that there was much opportunity for meeting boys. My father holed me away for my safety, and the little girl with dreams of passionate embraces and romantic love became just a short chapter in my saga.

But then a few months ago, Antonio visited my father here. I watched him arrive through my bedroom window. He wore a tailored suit that hugged his body like the one he's wearing today. He was older than the boy I remembered, and more serious, but still breathtaking.

As much as I wanted to, I couldn't pull myself away from the window—away from him, with his full lips and dark, wavy hair combed off his face, the ends gently grazing the back of his collar. His gait was tall and proud, like it had always been. But from a distance, there was a roughness about him that hadn't been there before. It added some mystery that made him even more enticing.

And even though I shouldn't have, even though it desecrated my mother's memory, I sat in my room while he was downstairs with my dying father, and fantasized about kissing him again.

That night, after the lights were out and the house was quiet, my fingers teased the wet, swollen flesh between my thighs, whispering his name in the dark as I writhed on the mattress.

"Aside from having good people in place, do you have a plan for the harvest?"

His deep voice startles me. *Plan?* It's all I hear, sending a wave of terror through me.

11

DANIELA

"For managing the harvest," he explains, eying me carefully.

For managing the harvest. Relax.

"Yes," I reply, a little too breathy. "It's in place." I was so wrapped up in my little fantasy, I didn't notice him end the call, and the word *plan*—

You need to pull yourself together, Daniela.

"There's nothing extraordinary about this year that should make the grapes more or less valuable than last year," I add, still reeling.

Antonio shrugs and lowers himself into the chair. "Such a pragmatist. I like to think every year has the potential to be a vintage year, right up until the end. But you're probably right."

He seems less agitated, now, and since he's going to find out anyway, maybe I should plant some disinformation. I've already done this with a few people who work here so they won't be alarmed when the time comes.

If I lay the groundwork with Antonio, he won't be surprised when he learns I'm not in Porto, and he can shut down the inevitable gossip right away. The less gossip, the quicker I'll fade from everyone's mind.

My heartrate ticks up as I prepare to lie, but not enough for him to notice. "Actually, we're so organized for the harvest, that I'm going to visit my father's elderly aunt in Canada. She's my only living relative. They were close, but he didn't tell her he was dying because she was too frail to travel. I'll tell her in person. It was my father's final request."

He eyes me warily. Maybe that was too much information in one fell swoop. Like a staged story. I make a concerted effort not to squirm—it's not easy.

"You feel it's wise to leave the country so soon after your father's death?"

"It's what he wanted." *Well, it's what he would have wanted, if he'd been close to his aunt.*

"Who's traveling with you?"

"I'm traveling alone," I say confidently, having practiced this response in my head many times. Someone, even if it was only David the vineyard manager, was sure to ask.

"*Alone?*" He sits taller in the chair, white-knuckling the narrow, upholstered arms. "Have you ever traveled anywhere alone? Have you even been to the market without a shadow?"

No, I haven't. Still, he's insufferable.

"I would ordinarily travel with Isabel. But she's moving to be closer to her husband's family. They have a young daughter and feel it would be best to raise her farther outside the city."

"I don't give a damn about Isabel," he snaps. "She doesn't look like she could protect herself, let alone you. I'm talking about trained men. Guards."

I'm not sure how to respond.

You should have kept your mouth shut and let him find out when everyone else did—after you were safely out of the country.

I don't know what made me think I could manipulate him like I'm a covert spy for the Portuguese Security Intelligence Service. *This was a huge mistake.*

"I'm taking a direct flight, and my aunt's friend is meeting me at the airport," I tell him carefully. "I wasn't planning on taking any guards. No one will know me there, so I thought it would be safe. But you make a good point. I'll reconsider my plans."

Hopefully that's enough to placate him.

"I'm surprised you're not concerned with what people will say about a woman traveling alone, considering you were too afraid to close the damn door in your own house."

He's testing. *Stay strong.*

I look directly into his eyes. "I understand that the Canadians aren't as concerned with unchaperoned women as we are in Porto."

His nostrils flare, and he snarls like an angry dog as he stands. "You seem to be coping fine."

I stand too, still wondering why he came, but thrilled to be *almost* rid of him.

As we cross the room, he stops and lifts the photo of my mother and me off my father's desk.

While he gazes at it, I bristle. It takes great effort not to yank it out of his hand so he doesn't dirty my mother with any more Huntsman DNA.

"How old were you when this was taken?"

His voice is whisper quiet, almost reverent, and I relax a bit.

"Five."

"Were you a dancer?"

I shake my head, lulled by something in his voice. "No. The white leotard and purple tutu was my favorite outfit. It had tiny beads that sparkled. I wore it as often as my mother allowed."

Why did I share that special memory with him? Why?

He squeezes my wrist in a gesture that feels intimate and overwhelming—strangely comforting and completely out of character. It's quick, and there's no time to wrest my arm away before it's over.

Antonio places the photograph back in its spot behind the

little heart and turns toward the door without sparing me another glance.

The silence is thick and chewy, and there's a noticeable shift in his demeanor before we reach the door. It's like the sudden wind change that occurs before a storm, sending animals scurrying for shelter. Not an innocent cloudburst, but a brutal storm with vicious winds and grapefruit-size hail that destroys everything in its wake.

It's coming. I feel it. But it's too late to hide.

12

DANIELA

Just before the doorway, he stops abruptly, and hands me a card. "You can reach me at this number day or night, if you need anything." He leans in as he speaks, his smooth, full lips grazing my ear.

I leap back, but he reaches for my arm, yanking me toward him, and swivels, until I'm pinned between his body and the wall. For a split second, I feel like Margarida, and to my horror, my body reacts just as I've always imagined hers did.

"I don't want to be overheard," he says gruffly. "You were the one who insisted on keeping the door open." He slips the card into my waistband, and his fingers linger too long on my bare skin. "Call if you need anything. That includes protection from my uncle and my cousin Tomas."

Protection from my uncle and my cousin Tomas.

My vision blurs, as the blood rushes from my head. If he says anything else, I don't hear it above the fear clawing into my chest.

Why would he say that about his uncle and Tomas? What does he know? *Nothing. Don't be foolish, Daniela. Keep your mouth shut.*

"I don't know what you're talking about." My voice is shaky. There's no way he missed it.

His eyes are glued to me—soaking up all my discomfort.

I'm worried that he'll see something in my face and press me for information, so I lower my gaze and study the pattern on his shirt to calm myself.

"I have two pieces of advice that I would take to heart if I were you. Don't attempt to sell the property right now. It's never a good idea to make decisions of that magnitude while you're grieving."

He pauses, but I don't dare look up. Before he's done giving me advice, I'll have counted every white-on-white swirl dotting his shirt front.

"Don't ever lie to me. I can spot a liar anywhere, even a good one, and you are *not* good," he taunts. "It never ends well for those who lie to me. *Never*."

With that warning, he lowers his head, using his solid body to back me flush against the plaster, where he crushes his mouth to mine, coaxing my lips open with his tongue.

In seconds, my knees buckle and I'm clinging to his shoulders just to stay upright.

"Have you ever been kissed, *Princesa*?"

His voice is husky, and although I feel the ferocity throbbing inside him, he uses a gentle thumb to sweep a loose strand of hair off my cheek.

The combination—tender and fierce—is dazzling, stealing my breath as it sends shivers skittering *everywhere*.

Suddenly I'm too hot, panting like an animal. *No, I've never been kissed before. Not like this.* Somehow, I manage to shake my head, as his fingers glide through my braid, loosening the thick plait.

"We better make it memorable, then," he murmurs against my throat, before his lips are on mine again, and all I know is his warm, velvety mouth and the strong hand that cradles my head.

He's dangerous, common sense whispers. *He's dangerous*.

But I'm paralyzed. Helpless to save myself. I don't even try.

I don't want to be saved.

He inches closer, and my back arches off the wall to meet him.

Our bodies are fused, and my hips sway against him without any sense of self-preservation. It's as if I don't understand exactly where this is going. *But I do*.

He's dangerous, common sense whispers, louder this time.

My head spins and spins, incoherent thoughts chasing each other until I'm dizzy.

I might be naïve, but even I recognize the hard shaft wedged between us as arousal. But instead of being intimidated or frightened by something I know so little about, I'm a hot, tingly bundle of nerve endings, lost in the scent of his spicy cologne. *Danger be damned.*

His large hands cup my ass, securing my body firmly against his, until the throb between my legs consumes every thought—every action I take.

I need relief. It's all I can think about.

When I wiggle against his cock to soothe the ache, he groans. It's the raw, guttural sound of a man wrestling temptation. It's arousing. And heady.

A bold sense of power surges through me, and I do it again. And again. And again.

The intensity sizzles dangerously between us. I'm too caught up in him—too tangled in the curls of pleasure—to think about where this is going, or how it'll end. All I know is his skillful mouth and practiced hands. His hard muscle and masculine scent.

It's as though I'm possessed, and no longer have control of my mind or body.

Antonio's lips are bruising, demanding my surrender, as his fingers dig deeper into my flesh, holding me still against his solid body.

Without warning, he sinks his teeth into my bottom lip, and although I whimper from the pleasant zing, it jolts me out of my stupor.

What are you doing, Daniela? He's the enemy. How much do the Huntsmans need to take from you? You stupid, stupid girl. How much?

Overcome by a sharp attack of conscience, I force my head to the side. "Get off me," I croak, pushing at his chest. "I don't want this."

"Liar," he taunts, softly, caging me with his muscular forearms braced on the wall, above my head.

He's right. *I do want this.* I spent years wanting this very thing, but I can't disrespect my mother's memory any more than I already have. I won't do that.

"Get off me. Now!"

He doesn't budge.

"Not until I'm finished with you." His voice is low, rough and tight, edged with menace. "You'll learn that in time. It'll be a pleasurable lesson, if you don't fight me."

It'll be a pleasurable lesson, if you don't fight me.

The panic hits hard, landing with such force it's paralyzing. *He's not going to stop.* History is about to repeat itself. *I don't want to die.*

Terror swirls in my head, until my thoughts are nothing more than a labyrinth of fears.

I can't die. Please. No. No.

A scream withers in my throat when Antonio takes secure hold of my chin, forcing me to meet his eyes.

"You have nothing to worry about—not today. Deflowering virgins isn't my thing."

He pauses, his features hardening into something grotesque

as the light fades from his eyes. "I'm not a man who has the patience to teach inexperienced girls how to swallow cock. I play with women. *No exceptions*. And I prefer when someone else has taken the time to break them in properly."

I squeeze my eyelids together to block out his filthy words, and so I don't have to look into his face, where a tempest rages that's as black as his soul. But Antonio is not having it.

"Look at me when I speak to you."

My heart hammers until the pain in my chest is almost unbearable, but I do as I'm told. At least I try. When it takes me a few seconds to focus, he tips my chin higher until we're peering at each other, with only a breath between us.

"Our fate—yours and mine—is entwined for eternity. For now, you're safe, *Princesa*. But when I come back, it'll be for more than a kiss."

He releases his hold on me, turns, and walks out.

I don't move a muscle. I'm not sure I even breathe, until the front door latches.

What just happened?

Nothing. It was nothing. Don't think about it. Within a week you'll be gone, and it'll all be behind you.

I adjust my braid, but the ribbon is missing. It's not caught on my clothing, or on the floor. I look near the desk, but it's not there either. It's the least of my concerns. But searching for it makes a fine distraction, so I don't have to think about what almost happened here. What I wanted to happen—until I didn't.

I glance out the window, cupping my elbows. In the distance, a black car is leaving the property through the front gate. It has to be him.

You can come back, Antonio, but I won't be here when you do. I hope you enjoyed the kiss, because that's all you're ever getting from me.

13

ANTONIO

Thiago, my longtime driver, is waiting with the car outside D'Sousa's front door.

"The helipad?" he asks, as I climb into the vehicle.

"Yes." *Before I go back into that house, peel off those skin-tight riding breeches, and fuck her against the wall like an animal.* One damn kiss, and I'm still having trouble getting my body under control, like I'm a goddamn teenager.

She's trouble.

"I have a meeting in an hour."

"Traffic's light," Thiago tells me, as he engages the privacy screen. "We'll have you back in plenty of time."

When the screen is all the way up, I call the villa. It's not much of a villa, but more of a cave equipped with state-of-the-art technology. It's accessible only to Cristiano, Lucas, and me.

"I'm on my way back," I mutter, knowing they have me on speaker.

"We expected to hear from you sooner. Problems?"

"She's leaving Porto, just as we thought. She concocted a whole bullshit story about a trip to Canada to tell her father's elderly aunt that he died."

"The aunt with end-stage Alzheimer's who no longer speaks or recognizes anyone?"

Cristiano is clearly more amused by her recklessness than I am. If we didn't already know about her great-aunt, it would have taken us less than ten minutes to figure out. It won't be hard for others to verify her story either.

Daniela is out of her league. While parts of her plan are solid, most of it's amateurish, with gaps big enough to drive a tank through.

"Since her father had only one aunt, yeah—that would be the one."

"Did you learn anything else?" Lucas asks impatiently.

Her mouth is warm and sweet, and her hair smells like the orange blossoms that perfume the procession route on Good Friday. But more importantly, I learned that her gorgeous little body tests my self-control in ways that are dangerous.

I don't share any of this with them.

"She's a terrible liar."

"Anything useful—like why she's leaving?"

"No," I reply sharply.

We discovered her plan to move to the US a week ago. We've managed to cover a lot of ground in that time, but it pisses me off that we still don't know her precise motivation for fleeing the country. She doesn't strike me as the kind of person who would shirk her responsibilities here, just to have a fling in the US. Something's chasing her.

"You still think Abel is behind her leaving?" Cristiano's voice is tight. He knows my uncle. Abel is capable of anything —including killing his wife.

"One hundred percent," Lucas spits out, before I can reply.

"I agree. But we shouldn't rule out anyone. Abel and Tomas could be a red herring." Whenever there's a problem, we always look to them first—with good reason, especially in this case.

Daniela showed us her cards at the funeral home. She's

afraid of them. I crack my knuckles to relieve some of the building pressure. "If we allow ourselves to get lured by the obvious, we could get screwed. I trusted Manuel D'Sousa, but I don't pretend to know everything he had his hands in."

"Were you able to install the listening devices?" Lucas asks.

"Only in the office. One under the lip of her father's desk, and the other in the sitting area."

"I'll activate them now."

"She's adamant about not selling the property. I don't get it. From what we know, she appears to be leaving the country—indefinitely. She's gone to a lot of trouble to cover her tracks. Why hold onto something that's going to be that kind of albatross?" *Because she doesn't really want to leave. Because this is her home.*

"She's inexperienced," Cristiano says, quietly, "and probably driven more by emotion than practicality. Sounds pretty normal for someone her age."

Maybe.

Although it wasn't my idea, I'm not unhappy she's leaving. If I was, she wouldn't be going. It's that simple.

"Who's she planning to leave in charge of the estate while she's away?" Cristiano asks.

"She trusts the vineyard manager to take care of business. I'm sure her father told her to lean on him."

David is trustworthy, and she can lean on him all she wants, but he works for me now. That was settled long before Manuel died.

"Did you learn anything that would have us deviate from any aspect of our plan to deal with her?"

"No," I reply, firmly. "We're sticking with the original plan."

I can almost hear the collective sigh of relief from them.

With D'Sousa gone, every asshole is going to make some kind of power play to test my resolve. *Let them.* It's our chance to see if the loyalty in the valley is to me, or to my uncle, or to someone else.

"We're prepared for whatever the bastards throw at us, but it's not going to be easy. I can't afford distractions."

And Daniela is one huge fucking distraction. She proved that today.

Thiago stops at the traffic light, and I glance at the car idling beside us. We're in an armored Mercedes, and Thiago is as capable a soldier as he is a driver, but this is a precarious time. An assassination attempt in the middle of the day would be bold, even for my most brazen enemies, but stranger things have happened.

"Where are we with the apartment in the US?"

"I rerouted some emails, and connected her with our Realtor in Fall River. She sent some pictures of the apartment, and Daniela agreed to take it furnished. Our team will occupy the first and second floors of the three-decker. They'll live on the third."

"What about the guy who forged the travel documents?"

"Leo," Cristiano replies. "I sent Alvarez to talk to him this morning. Apparently, he's a little prick with a big mouth. He essentially confirmed everything we know about her travel plans. Alvarez said that he didn't have to push to get the information. *Leo* couldn't keep his mouth shut about how he set the D'Sousa *princesa* up with fake passports, ID cards, and everything else she needed to set up residency in the US."

I've heard enough. "Eliminate that fucker, before he talks to anyone else. Make sure you get everything you need before he takes his last breath."

This whole thing is a clusterfuck, not to mention a huge time suck. But Daniela needs to grow up, and I need to deal with the shitstorm here. While I do, it's better for all of us if she's tucked away in a corner of the world where no one will find her—until I'm ready to bring her home.

"Lucas, is it going to screw things up, or can you work around it if *Leo* isn't in the picture?"

"I'll reroute the server, and if she contacts him for anything else, I'll provide it."

"Good. Get rid of him. I don't want to share the earth with that fucker for one more day."

"I'll make sure there's not a trace of her at his place," Cristiano answers, before I can say anything else about it.

"I'm getting off, so you can get back to work. We're almost at the helipad. I have a meeting with the Minister of Agriculture in my office, and then I'll be down."

After I hang up, I sit back and take a swig of water, gazing at the turbulent river below. There's a storm brewing inside me too.

14

ANTONIO

You're going to drive me insane, Daniela, even before I taste your sweet little pussy. If I didn't have a war to fight, you wouldn't be going anywhere.

You belong here. In Porto. Deep down you know it, and that's why you don't want to sell the property. The fertile vineyards, the lush valley, and the ancient city—reigning over the empire is your destiny—and mine.

For now, I'm going to give you some time to play. Something you never had the chance to do under your father's watchful eye. It'll be my wedding gift to you, before I bring you home and drop you into a gilded cage, where you'll spend the rest of your days as my obedient wife.

Until then, develop your passions, take some classes, dance in clubs, and sip those fruity drinks that young American women love so much. You can have your fun away from the glare of the spotlight, but under my protection.

Enjoy, pretty girl, but not too much, or I'll drag you home and drape your tight little body across my knee, until your ass is the color of Vintage Port. Then I'll fuck you until your screams echo off the stucco walls.

I pull the red ribbon from my jacket and smooth the satin between my fingers before bringing it to my nose. The faint scent of orange blossoms, sweet and pure, brings my dick to life.

We'll meet again, Princesa, and when—

Boom!

The car jerks sideways. I jerk with it.

Thiago brakes, and the vehicle skids to the right.

What the fuck?

I glance out the window, struggling to stay upright in the seat.

A rig is alongside us—inches away. Even a reinforced car is no match for something that size. We're caught between the monster truck and the edge of the narrow road.

The river. Fuck.

The truck swerves and sideswipes us, again.

We land on the shoulder, spinning, the Mercedes teetering on the edge of the embankment.

My fucking phone is nowhere to be found.

I grab the seat in front of me for leverage and fumble for the button, lowering the partition between us.

"This is an attack!" I bark, as Thiago fights to control the vehicle.

Boom!

Fuck!

"We need reinforcements," he yells, as we take another hit and tumble into the steep ravine.

"Call the villa. Press the SOS button on the steering wheel," I shout over the noise.

Thiago doesn't respond. Not even when I scream his name the second time. Or the third.

Time slows as we bounce around the interior, weightless.

While the car rolls, I claw my way to the front, and cling to the steering wheel. My vision is blurry, dotted in black. I grope for the button and press. But I can't hold on.

The car bounces, sending my head into the windshield.

Can't see. *Need to stay awake.*

Stay awake.

Stay awake.

Fight, Antonio.

Fi—

I hear my father's booming laugh from inside the gates of hell as the river swallows me.

GREED

A SINFUL EMPIRE TRILOGY (BOOK 1)

1

DANIELA

SIX YEARS LATER

Getting through customs takes longer than expected, and by the time the taxi stops in front of the Moniz Law Office, light is breaking over the horizon.

"How much is the fare?" I ask, opening my wallet.

Before the driver answers, his phone rings. "One moment, please," he mutters, holding up a finger to silence me.

What's one more lost moment? It won't change anything—not for me. Although lingering at the curb isn't a good idea.

I adjust the hideous sunglasses from Dollar Mart and lower the brim on my cap before turning my face toward the sidewalk. It's not much of a disguise, but at this hour it's enough to get me from the car to the door without being recognized.

Once inside, I'll sign the paperwork transferring the property and return to the airport in time to catch a flight back to the US. If all goes according to plan, I'll be home before the end of the day, sleeping in my own bed tonight.

My own bed, *yes*. But Fall River isn't home. It's a safe harbor. The place where everyone important to me—everyone who's left—is awaiting my return. The gritty American city has been my refuge for the past six years, but it's not home.

I sigh deeply as the light creeps across the sky—purple hues melting into gold, casting a celestial glow on the ancient city, softening centuries of wear.

While I wait for the driver to end the call, I soak in every nuance, committing the smallest details to memory. It might be years before I see the sun rise over Porto again. *This could be the last time.*

As I untangle my emotions, a small box truck pulls in front of us.

The taxi headlights shine on the rear of the vehicle, illuminating the chain and padlock securing the roll-up door. From this angle, it's the single defining feature. The truck is so unremarkable it could fade seamlessly into the landscape, coming and going without catching anyone's attention.

My stomach roils as I study the grimy license plate.

Memorizing a series of numbers won't do you one bit of good if you're abducted.

I grab the door handle, prepared to bolt. But before I do, a delivery man emerges from the truck with three bags of sandwich rolls. He jogs across the street and drops the bread on a bench outside a shuttered coffee shop.

I draw a breath to quiet the trembling inside.

This might be home, but it's not safe for me here—and it might never be. I can't even begin to think about testing the waters until after Quinta Rosa do Vale officially changes hands, and the deed is sealed and recorded as a matter of public record.

After that, I'm not worth anything. Yes, I'll be millions of dollars richer, but money isn't what they want from me. It's the priceless vineyards. It's always been about the vineyards.

"How do you want to pay?" the driver asks, pointing to the charge on the taximeter.

"Euros. Thank you," I murmur, handing him some bills before getting out.

My eyes dart up and down the deserted street before I climb the steep steps into the building.

This is it. After I sign the papers, we'll be safe. No more looking over my shoulder. Despite the freedom ahead, a muscle in my chest contracts painfully.

I'm not sure the price of safety has ever been so high, but this isn't just about me. If it were, I'd never give up Quinta Rosa do Vale. They'd have to pry it from my cold, dead hands.

Inside the shallow entryway, I pause to offer a small prayer. Not to God—he doesn't seem to want any part of my dilemma—but to my parents, *to my mother*, who I hope will forgive me for what I'm about to do. In my shoes, she would do the same thing. At least that's what I tell myself when my conscience pricks sharply. Although it never dulls the pain. *How can it?*

When I sign those papers today, I'll be spitting on the graves of my ancestors. With a simple stroke of the pen, I'll convey more than three centuries of my family's blood, sweat, and tears to a stranger.

A stranger.

I still don't know the identity of the buyer. Attorney Moniz has been dealing with the representative of a trust. *The Iberian Trust.* But someone's hiding behind that trust—that's for damn sure.

The bile rises in my throat as I imagine the possibilities. In truth, a complete stranger is preferable to some of the alternatives my mind conjures.

I shove the cap and sunglasses into my tote, but I don't bother to even finger-comb my hair. Who cares if I look like hell? *Nobody*. In less than an hour, I'll be nothing more than a tragic footnote in the history of the region.

When I step into the lobby, a young woman in a smart blue dress is at the reception desk. I don't remember her, but it's been six years since I was last here. *Shortly after my eighteenth birthday.* I'm sure a lot has changed. *Like I have.*

She looks up as I approach. "Good morning."

"Good morning. I have an appointment with Attorney Moniz. Daniela D'Sousa," I add, just above a whisper, as though my name alone might summon demons from the rafters.

"Of course, Ms. D'Sousa," she says kindly. "He told me to send you right up when you arrive. Do you know where his office is located?"

"Is it still at the top of the staircase, across from the library?"

"Yes." She nods, adjusting the brooch on her silk scarf. "I think he might still be on a call, but if the door is open, go right in and take a seat."

I turn toward the stairs, but a sense of unease stops me in my tracks. "Is Attorney Moniz alone?"

Moniz assured me the buyer wouldn't be here. *"It's too early for the civilized to do business, and it will be easier for you this way."* But circumstances can change, and I don't want to be caught off guard.

"At this hour?" The receptionist's blonde head bobs up and down as she smiles reassuringly. "Can I bring you some coffee or tea?"

"Tea would be wonderful. Thank you."

I breathe a small sigh of relief and find the stairs. Pedro Moniz, my father's lawyer and old friend, made this long, tortuous process, mired in arcane Portuguese property law, as easy as possible for me.

Although there was nothing he could say or do to blunt the heartache.

The paintings in the stairwell are the same ones that have hung here since I was a child. The Douro Valley's most important churches, port houses, and vineyards captured on canvas for all to admire.

I squeeze the railing and lower my gaze before I get to the painting of Quinta Rosa do Vale.

It's a stunning piece of art, painted right before harvest, when the grapes were plump, their purple skins pulled tight over the sweet flesh.

I can't bear to look at it.

One foot in front of the other, Daniela. It's almost over.

When I reach the top, Moniz's door is open, but the lights are off. Apart from the hissing and groaning of a radiator awakening, it's quiet. *Too quiet.*

Maybe he's finished with the call. Or perhaps he's taking it from one of the other rooms.

The receptionist said to go in and have a seat.

I clutch my tote and step timidly across the threshold into the dark office. At first, it appears I'm alone. But as my eyes adjust, I notice a man at the window in the far corner of the room. He's gazing at the sunrise with a phone to his ear.

As the shadowy figure comes into focus, the hair on the back of my neck rises. Even with his back to me, even in the dim light, even after all this time, I recognize him immediately.

A warning blares inside my head, and I turn to flee. But the doorway is blocked by the man who sat behind me on the plane—the hulking giant who looks like he plays American football for a professional team.

I can't breathe.

"Excuse me, please," I plead, as though he might let me by if I'm polite.

The hulk doesn't utter a word or spare me even a small glance, and he doesn't budge. But I'm desperate to leave before the man at the window notices me, and I attempt to muscle my way through.

It's a waste of energy. He's an unmovable force.

When I pivot to find an alternate exit, Antonio Huntsman is there, eyes flaring, almost daring me to run, again.

2

DANIELA

I freeze in my tracks, a cornered animal with little hope for survival.

He's still too, intensely focused, like a predator who could be easily triggered.

It's been years since I've seen him in person, but the younger version of this man still haunts my dreams—more often than I care to admit.

The last time we were this close, he stole a kiss. That's what I tell myself, because it's easier than admitting I gave it to him—that I wanted that kiss.

Twenty minutes after the reckless kiss, his car was forced off the road, into the river. When I left Porto, he was in critical condition, and it was unclear whether he would survive.

But it's hard to kill the devil.

He doesn't look any worse for wear. In many ways, he looks the same. Maybe more confident. The intensity still vibrates off him in a way that signals danger. *Beautiful danger. Irresistible danger.* The kind that beckons, not with a word but with a smoldering gaze.

Standing here, with his hand buried in his trouser pocket, he's a photographer's dream.

Venomous snakes always hide under pretty skins.

I continue to hold myself as still as possible, only swallowing to clear my airway.

"Our fate—yours and mine—is entwined for eternity. For now, you're safe, Princesa. But when I come back, it'll be for more than a kiss." Those were his last words to me.

The door clicks shut behind me, cutting off more of my air supply.

"Where's Moniz?" I gasp, my voice barely audible.

"I gave him the morning off." Antonio gestures toward one of the chairs near the desk. "Have a seat, Daniela."

His commanding tenor raises gooseflesh on my arms.

He knows you're here to sell the property. He wants it.

Sit and hear him out, or stand and fight. Those are my choices.

My soul shrivels at the thought of a Huntsman owning my mother's vineyards.

You're not in a position to be sentimental. Especially now. Don't waste time pretending you won't sell to him. You'll do what you need to do so you can get back to Isabel and Valentina.

Maybe I can negotiate something, because between him and the guard stationed outside the door, I don't think fighting is going to get me far.

I lower myself to the edge of the seat, using the chair's sturdy arm for support. "I assume this is about the vineyards."

He shakes his head, unbuttoning his suit jacket before propping himself on the corner of the desk, where he can lord over me like a king.

"I have a plane to catch and no time for games. What is this about?"

He doesn't reply, but he looks me up and down, suggestively, his eyes lingering here and there without a tinge of shame. It's much the way he leered when he visited after my father died. It's still appalling, but this time, I don't blink.

Six long years have passed since that visit, and in the interim, my life has shifted, dramatically. Instead of having an entire staff to help me with tedious chores, I'm now the maid. Rather than a lavish wing to myself, I share a bedroom with a child. Not a single person treats me like I'm from an important Portuguese family—they don't even know, and if they did, they wouldn't care.

Some might see this fall from grace as a tragedy, others as my comeuppance. I don't have the energy to conduct a thorough analysis. At the end of the day, I do what's necessary to keep food on the table and a roof over our heads. It's a simple, sometimes grueling life, but it's kept us safe.

When Antonio completes his lewd appraisal, his dark, piercing eyes meet mine. It's a look designed to intimidate. And it does. But despite the intermittent tremor in my left eye, I don't shrink—that would only empower him.

The old radiator gurgles in the corner. Otherwise, the room is deathly quiet. The air between us so heavy, it's practically weeping. Antonio's scrutiny is hard and threatening, without a glimmer of humanity.

My hands are beginning to ache from being clasped so tightly, but at least they're not shaking.

I don't know his intentions, but I can guess. This is about the vineyards. *It has to be.*

There's a binding contract on the property. *You're too late, Antonio.*

Although it's never too late for wealthy, powerful men to get their way. It's either handed to them at the very last minute, or they snatch it from unwitting hands. There's rarely a penalty for that kind of behavior, so they walk away unscathed and emboldened. And they do it again, and again, because the greedy are insatiable.

I glance at him. His expression hasn't softened—if anything, it's more menacing. More determined.

Antonio is about to make my life a living hell. It's written all over him, twisting in his sharp features, scraping through the vast silence—metal against metal. I feel it in my bones. A chill so pervasive that a hot bath and layers of spun wool won't cure it.

"Why are you here?" I ask softly, my voice straining under the stress.

He doesn't reply. He hasn't said a single word since he told me to have a seat. For now, he seems content to let my anxiety build.

The wait is making me jittery. Inside, the threads are spooling tighter and tighter. Soon they'll snap, and my emotions will spin out of control. I can't allow it to happen.

I know pain. Torn flesh, bitter anguish, heartache—I know the demons intimately. Even more, I know how to battle through the suffering.

Yes, I might end up bloodied and scarred, but Antonio Huntsman can't throw anything at me I can't handle.

I sit up taller and dig in my heels. "What do you want?"

This time, there's not a shred of softness or deference in my tone. It's insistent and demanding, leaving no doubt that I'll ask again, and again, until he answers the question.

His gaze narrows, zeroing in on mine with laser focus. "It's time to come home, Daniela."

His voice is firm. Uncompromising. And while I doubt anyone ever says *no* to him, his jaw is set, as though he's bracing for a fight.

This isn't at all what I expected. I assumed he got wind of the sale and would demand I breach the contract with the buyer and sell him the property instead.

The butterflies in my stomach swirl frantically while I try to form a coherent response that won't back me farther into a corner.

"I don't understand." I choose the words carefully, feigning ignorance, although it's not much of a stretch. I really don't know where he's headed.

"Porto is your home. You belong here. This is your legacy."

It takes me long moments to wrap my head around it. But when I finally do, it feels as though my soul has been exposed to the light, filleted with surgical precision.

Porto is your home. You belong here. This is your legacy.

If I didn't know better, I would think the bastard is privy to my dreams—my ridiculous fantasies. The ones I never share with anyone. Not even Isabel. Dreams that are so far out of reach, the edges are fuzzy.

He knows the property is changing hands today. Of course he does. Despite Moniz's efforts to conceal the sale, that shouldn't come as a total surprise. But he also knows what's in my heart. He knows how much I want to keep Quinta Rosa do Vale, how much I want to come home, back to my old life, and he's using that knowledge to play me in the cruelest way.

He wants me to come home. *Bullshit. He wants the vineyards. Don't let him lure you off the path. It's not safe.*

I look straight into his eyes. All these years of hiding have taught me to lie without squirming. "My home is in Canada now, with my great-aunt. She needs me." It's the same lie I told last time to throw him off my trail. But I went directly to the US, without ever setting foot in Canada.

Antonio wraps his long fingers around the beveled edge of the desk and angles forward ever so slightly.

"Really?"

His tone is smug. So smug I'd like to slap him across the face hard enough to make my palm sting.

"What does she need? Someone to water the flowers around her grave?"

He knows she's dead. Why would he bother with my relatives? Why?

I lower my eyes, giving myself a few seconds to regroup.

3

DANIELA

If he knows about my great-aunt, what else does he know?

I imagine him digging into the past, unearthing secrets meant to remain buried forever.

I'm so worked up I can't think straight, and a few measly seconds isn't enough to clear my head.

It doesn't matter who buys the property. *But it does. No, it doesn't. Not anymore. You're out of options. He knows the deal is almost done, and he's not going to allow the sale unless it's to him. Remember who you left back in the US. That's your only concern now.*

"I've entered into a sales agreement with a buyer," I blurt when the voices arguing inside my head become too much. "We've been working on the sale for several years, but I'm willing to sell you the vineyards, if you can persuade the buyer to let me out of the contract."

I despise myself right now. My cowardice. My unwillingness to fight for something that rightfully belongs to me. But I hate him even more. I hate him with every fiber of my being.

"The employees need to be treated fairly," I add, modulating my voice to hide how much I loathe him. "A strong severance package, or better, they'll be allowed to keep their jobs. The contract I came to sign protects everyone who works at Quinta Rosa do Vale. That's all I care about."

"That's all you care about? You don't care if I torch the house you grew up in, or the vineyards your family nurtured for generations? The vineyards that provide grapes to make the Port that keeps the entire region afloat? And you don't care about money for yourself? Is that right?"

What a prick.

But I can deal with it. My new life has made me stronger and, to some extent, tougher. It's taught me how much the human spirit can bend to survive. The universe already taught me that lesson once, but I was too young to grasp it fully at the time. Now I could write a thesis on it.

I'm a survivor. Plain and simple. Antonio Huntsman's bullying doesn't even nick the surface.

It takes some doing, but I gather the courage to respond.

"I can live without your money. And the region will manage without Quinta Rosa do Vale's grapes. But if you want to burn the property to the ground, be my guest. I'm not going to stop you. To be clear, I'd rather see it in a mountain of ashes than with your family."

His closely groomed beard doesn't hide the tic in his jaw.

"Tough words from a woman confined to the four corners of this room. If I were you, I'd be pleading for mercy instead of trying to piss me off."

In the US, I'm a woman struggling to make ends meet, like so many others. There's nothing unique about me. But here, I'm still a D'Sousa. And I'll be damned before I beg a Huntsman for anything.

"You're going to do what you want to do," I reply coolly. "You're going to take what you want to take. Pleading for mercy doesn't work with men like you." *I've seen it firsthand.* "I'm not getting on my knees for the likes of you."

He crosses his arms over his broad chest and sits back. But his scowl doesn't recede.

"Work it out with the buyer. I'll sign whatever you want," I assure him, standing. "But I've got a plane to catch, so if you'll excuse me."

"Sit down," he growls. "We're done when I say we're done. Not one second sooner."

His voice is low, laced with simmering rage.

I don't sit. Not because I want to challenge him—although I do—but my better sense tells me he's too angry to push any further. I don't sit because the stress and the jet lag are catching up with me. My body feels like it's running seconds behind my brain.

"You will sit in that chair by your own accord, or with my assistance, but you will do it."

He shifts his leg, and I collapse into the seat before he makes good on the threat.

His father had no reservations about raising his hand to a woman. *Children learn what they live.* I highly doubt Antonio Huntsman is above manhandling me.

"I don't know what more you want from me."

I sound beaten, and in many ways, I am.

"You're in a better position to work it out with the buyer," I explain, although he knows it. "You have more influence, more lawyers, more money. I have nothing but the property—that I've already agreed, in writing, to sell."

"The buyer? Iberian Trust?" He peers down at me with an expression that seems less hostile now.

I nod.

"That trust belongs to the Huntsman portfolio."

At first I don't understand what he's talking about. I'm exhausted. I haven't slept well in weeks, and I didn't sleep a wink on my overnight flight. My brain churns slowly as it tries to make sense of it. Then it dawns on me. It was here, in front of me, all along.

I should have known. *Moniz should have known.*

The question I have for him is within easy grasp. It's right there, but when I open my mouth, nothing comes out. It's as though my tongue has been immobilized, swaddled in layers of dusty cotton.

It takes considerable effort, but eventually I manage to eke out the words without choking. "You're the buyer?"

Antonio shakes his head. "I'm not a buyer. The paperwork is a sham. Quinta Rosa do Vale already belongs to me." He reaches down and takes a lock of my hair between his fingers. "As do you."

I jerk away from his touch, but his grip tightens until my scalp screams. At first the pain is welcome, cutting through a growing numbness. But soon the throb becomes too much, and I'm forced to sit still while he fingers my hair. *Still, but not quiet.*

"What the hell are you talking about?" I snarl, the hatred eclipsing the fear in my heart.

"Both you and the vineyards have been mine since the moment your father took his last breath. And Daniela, you will get on your knees for me. Make no mistake about it."

4

DANIELA

The bastard isn't talking about kneeling in prayer. *What a monster.*

You expected something different from the son of o diabo?

No. Not really. But the foolish girl inside remembers Antonio differently. At least she wants to remember him differently.

If you listen to her, she'll lead you to danger. It's true. She will.

"I want to speak to Pedro Moniz."

Antonio releases his grip on my hair and sits back, his long fingers drumming on the desk. "Moniz is my attorney. It's unlikely he'll talk to you about my business matters. Not if he wants to live long enough to play with his pretty young wife tonight."

Oh my God. Moniz was in on the whole thing. It was an ambush. I walked right into the trap without even a whiff of their scheme.

How could my father's closest friend have sold me out like this? I've known him all my life. He was at my birthday parties and at the church for my First Communion. He would come on

Christmas and eat at our table and share our wine. He held my hand while my father passed.

Papai trusted him. He told me to trust Moniz too. *"Pedro knows everything about my business matters. Don't hesitate to go to him for advice. He'll guide you wisely, Daniela."*

The traitorous bastard guided me, all right. Straight into the wolf's lair.

I should have known better.

Pedro Moniz belongs to my father's world—Antonio's world. The old boys' club that controls *everything* in Porto. I'm a woman. A *young* woman. *And clearly naive.* Even if Antonio wasn't a threat, Moniz would never betray the silent oath that binds powerful men—*not even for me.*

"Quinta Rosa do Vale already belongs to me. As do you."

My heart is pounding so hard I'm certain he can see it through my jacket. *I need a plan.* A foolproof one. And I need it now.

I dig into my tote for some balm and glide it over my lips as he watches quietly. Chapped lips are the least of my worries, but it buys me a little time.

Maybe, *maybe*, he owns the property—I'll need to see proof—but this is the twenty-first century, and human beings cannot be owned like pets. *Not even in Porto.*

I can't come up with a viable plan. *Nothing.* All I can do is draw this out, hoping that something will come to me—before it's too late.

"I have no idea what you're talking about."

His eyes blaze as he speaks. *The victor with the spoils in reach.* "Your father bequeathed me the property on the condition I marry you. It's time for me to make good on my end of the deal."

Every inch of me is numb. Inside and out. It's almost as though he's speaking in tongues, using words and phrases no mortal can comprehend.

I'm a pawn in a deal. Chattel for barter.

My father arranged my marriage—*to a Huntsman.* The very people responsible for my mother's torture and death. *Papai* loved her with every piece of his heart. Every single one. And he loved me. I'm sure of it.

I glance up at Antonio. His eyes are soft, and I see what looks like pity in his expression. But no regret. There's nothing that even resembles regret or remorse, and he's certainly not seeking forgiveness. Men like him never seek forgiveness. Not even with their last breath.

If I want to be free of him, I need to appeal not to his heart or conscience, but to his practical sense. Because in the end he'll do what's best for him.

"You don't want to marry me."

The corner of his mouth lifts slyly. "Not any more than you want to marry me. Maybe less."

Could he be more of an asshole?

"Here's the truth, Daniela. Even if frivolous emotions were part of my nature, I would never marry for love. When I take a wife, it will be strictly a business decision. You were offered to me with a priceless piece of property." He shrugs. "Why not you?"

I swallow hard, my insides quivering.

His tone is emotionally bankrupt. Devoid of all passion—let alone anything approximating love. It's chilling. Even if he wanted me just for sex, it would feel more humane. This is a cold, calculated business decision. *One I had no voice in.*

I don't know what my father was thinking.

Papai knew my pain. He never invited Antonio to our home while I was there—not until he was dying, and then only that one time. My father knew the risks involved with marrying into the Huntsman family—especially when he was gone and couldn't protect us. I can't believe that, in the end, he chose this for me. That he would take this kind of risk. I don't believe it.

"My father would never arrange a marriage between your family and mine."

The words come from my mouth, but I almost don't recognize myself speaking. It's as though I'm standing outside my body, watching the events of my life unfold. *Disassociating.* I've never had therapy, but I've learned a lot about trauma. The last time I experienced something like this, I was twelve. *Maybe I haven't toughened up.*

"We're going to have serious problems," he warns, "if you don't start trusting my word."

"We already have serious problems." My voice is flat and hollow, reflecting the defeat I feel inside.

Antonio raps his knuckles on the polished desk. "The circumstances are unique, and I imagine this news comes as a shock."

A shock? A shock is when wet fingers touch a live wire. This is ripping my beating heart from my chest and stomping on it.

"I'll humor you, today," he adds, like he's doing me a big favor. "But this will be the last time I provide evidence to back up my word. And it will be the last time you accuse me of being a liar."

He hands me a laminated sheet of paper from the desk. "That should address your concerns."

I stare at the page. At first, the individual letters are all I see. The black lines and swirls blending into one another. Eventually I begin to make out words.

It's a simple contract. One sheet of paper, front and back, signed by Huntsman and my father. My heart clenches at *Papai*'s familiar scrawl.

Near each signature, there's a small mahogany spatter. I draw a deep breath to steady my trembling hand. The stain is a drop of each man's blood. I'm certain of it.

A blood oath.

My chest aches.

Unless this is another sham, I'm screwed.

Antonio would never go back on his word. Not on a blood pact he made with my father. To do so would bring great dishonor to his name. No one would trust him to keep a deal of any significance. It would make it impossible for him to continue as a serious leader.

Valentina's sweet face appears before my eyes—and Isabel, ringing her weathered hands. *Don't worry.* I'm not surrendering. Not yet.

"You coerced a dying man into a blood oath? That's low, even for someone named Huntsman."

The rational part of my brain knows he didn't force my father into anything. Even on his deathbed, my father wasn't the kind of man who could be pushed around easily. But I want to believe *Papai* was threatened. I *need* to believe it.

Antonio doesn't flinch as he takes the paper out of my hand and pulls out his phone. He scrolls for a few seconds before holding the screen inches from my face.

I gasp at my father sitting in a chair—his deep voice is unmistakable. And strong. My eyes well as I listen to him trade me away as though I'm a basket of grapes.

How could you do this to me? I always tried to be a good girl, a good daughter. I took good care of you, right until the end. Why would you do this to me?

Antonio and my father memorialized the contract so no one could quarrel with it. *Papai* signed of his own free will. There's nothing to suggest otherwise, only an abundance of evidence to support a consensual agreement.

He approached Huntsman with the marriage arrangement.

It's a punch to the gut. The kind that catches you unaware. I want to curl up in a ball and sob for days. But I can't afford to be soft. I need to be as heartless as he is if I expect to have any say in my future.

Antonio plays the video again, but I've heard enough. I shove the phone away and find the nerve to peer into his vacant eyes.

"I'm not marrying you."

5

DANIELA

Antonio's gaze skims my body, not in a sexual way, but as though he's taking stock of my appearance.

I'm wearing some of my best clothes, but they've been laundered many times. The black blazer has taken on a bit of a shiny hue, and it's frayed at the seams. It's meager, especially when compared to the fine suit Antonio is wearing.

"Why not?" he asks gruffly. "It's not as though you're such a prize. I was promised a *princesa*, and yet, here you are, looking like the beggar's wife."

The tears sting the back of my eyes. *Don't you dare give him your tears.*

I blink a few times to clear my vision, and gear up for a fight.

"I'll go to the police. Or the UN. You can't kidnap a woman across international borders. There are laws that even you can't disregard."

"You came to Porto of your own accord. I won't dignify the *I'll go to the police* with a response. We both know that will get you nowhere. The UN?" He chuckles. "Clever. There's only one problem. You left a trail of bodies behind, Daniela. Do you want to spend the rest of your life in prison? Maybe you've forgotten, but the prisons here aren't as cushy as those in the US."

I shake my head. "Threaten all you want, but I haven't killed anyone."

"The man who forged your travel documents died mysteriously around the time you fled the country. Then there's Isabel's husband. Although I don't believe his body has been recovered—yet. I'm sure there are others the authorities can connect to you."

I bring a shaky hand to my mouth. Jorge, Isabel's husband, started drinking heavily a year ago, and about six months ago, right before he disappeared, his behavior changed radically. He turned sullen at the drop of a dime, and belligerent without provocation. In my heart, I knew he was dead, but I always assumed it was the result of a bar fight. I never imagined—

I can't bear to look at him. "You murdered Jorge?"

"Not me. But he was drinking too much, and talking too much. He was willing to sell some of your secrets. Sounds like a perfect motive for murder. Did Isabel help you? How about her daughter—Valentina, right? Do they have the death penalty in the US for accomplices?"

I lunge at him like a savage with nothing to lose. But he captures my wrists before I can claw out his eyes.

"Save your scratching and biting for the honeymoon, *Princesa*. And your energy. You'll need it."

"Let go of me, you bastard." The words emerge with great contempt, but it's only a small slice of the hate in my heart.

He yanks me closer, securing my hands behind my back and caging my legs between his. "Listen carefully," he murmurs, right above my temple. "Because I'm not going to say it again. No one—*no one* attacks me without paying a hefty price. That includes you. You've been warned."

After I've digested his warning, he lets me go.

I step back and sink into the chair.

I don't care what he claims. He killed Jorge—or had him killed. And Leo, who painstakingly put together all the travel documents for us. *Why?* Did their deaths have something to do with the property? With me? *Are they dead because of me?*

I glance at him while he scrolls through his phone. *How can someone so beautiful on the outside be so ugly inside?*

Maybe they're not dead. Maybe he's manipulating me.

"You're right about one thing, Daniela. There are laws. But here, I make the laws. Don't make the mistake of thinking otherwise."

A shiver runs through me. I won't make that mistake. I can't afford to die. My heart twists. *I don't want to die.*

Somehow, I need to get out of Porto and back to the US—to Isabel and Valentina. And more important, I need to warn them, because they might not be safe either.

"I'll sign whatever you need. You don't want to marry me. You said so yourself. I have obligations to attend to in the US."

"Obligations? Like cleaning bathrooms? The *princesa* scrubbing piss from toilet rims. How charming."

I shove down the lump in my throat. Until now, I've never been embarrassed about cleaning other people's messes. After all, for years someone cleaned mine. But as much as I hate to admit it, his taunting stings.

"It's not glamorous, but it's honest work. Unlike what you do."

"I do what your father did, and what your grandfather before him did." Antonio glowers at me. "It's what allowed you to wear the pretty dresses and jewels, and keep show horses. Spare me the sanctimony."

The image of my father signing me away is imprinted on my brain. He proved himself as ruthless as any of them, taking his parting shot from the grave. *Like a fucking coward.*

Did he secretly blame me for my mother's death, and this is

his revenge? His beloved Rosa was murdered while I was spared. I didn't fight hard enough. *I didn't fight at all.*

You can fight now. You're not twelve anymore.

"Don't you have more questions for me?" He tips his head to the side. "Perhaps about Quinta Rosa do Vale. You have my attention. Now would be a good time to ask."

I do. But more than anything, right now, I want to get out of this room. The rest will have to wait. The longer I'm here, the less likely I'll be allowed to leave.

I pick up my tote and hook it over my shoulder as I stand. "I don't care what kind of proof you have. Video can be manipulated easily. I'm not buying any of it."

His jaw clenches. I'm five feet five, but he towers above me, a vein in his neck pulsing.

"Your father gave me the vineyards in exchange for the promise that I would marry you and ensure your safety. I intend to honor that promise."

Ensure my safety. He gave me to the beast, to save me from the ogres.

Maybe my father's intentions were nothing more than misguided, *maybe*, but it doesn't matter. In the end, they're all monsters.

"Manuel D'Sousa is dead. I'm his daughter. His blood. I'm releasing you from your promise. You can have the vineyards, but you don't need to be saddled with me."

I'm inches from the door when he grabs me from behind and shoves me against the wall roughly, using his hips to pin me there. Before I can react, his lips are on mine.

I use my fists to ward him off before his mouth makes me feel things I don't want to feel.

He captures my wrists, and in one effortless move, he secures them above my head. "You can fight me all you want. But just like those juicy grapes, you belong to me."

His cock is hard, and every time either of us draws a breath, it grazes my belly, reminding me of *everything* the arrangement entails.

I don't want to have sex with him, especially here, like this —I don't. But I'd be lying if I said my body wasn't reacting to his swollen cock. The pulsing between my legs is impossible to ignore. *Like last time. And just like last time, my arousal makes me feel ashamed and traitorous. My mother's memory deserves better. I deserve better.*

"You'll give me *everything*. And if you have an ounce of brains in that pretty little head, you'll learn to like it. I warned you that when I came for you, it would be for more than a kiss."

"Please," I beg, knowing it will get me nowhere. But I'm desperate, and I don't know what else to do. "Please don't."

"Don't what, Daniela? Don't fuck you against this dirty wall? Don't lay you across that desk and torment you until everyone in the building hears you beg for my cock?" He brushes his nose against mine. "Maybe you'd like that."

Without thinking, I spit at him.

He doesn't flinch, but his words get uglier.

"Did you let your boyfriend, Josh, lick that tight little pussy? *My* pussy. He's lucky I didn't kill him for touching what's mine."

The panic inside me is welling, seconds from exploding all over the room. He must sense it too.

"I've never forced a woman to do anything she didn't want to do—not sexually. But if you continue to push me, you'll be the first. I'll redden your ass until you can't sit for a month, and then I'll fuck you in ways you can't even begin to imagine."

I look him straight in the eye. "You're a monster."

"I am. Here's a little piece of advice for you, *Princesa*. Don't poke monsters. Because we'll devour you without a shred of mercy—and toss your bones into the gutter."

He releases me, then uses a tissue from the desk to wipe his cheek.

"Cristiano will take you to our home in the valley." Antonio drops the tissue into the trash, his eyes never leaving mine. "I strongly recommend that you don't try to run. There are guards all over the property—and the punishment for defying my order will be more than you can bear."

I'm out of time. He's not going to let me leave Porto. I need to think of something.

"If you expect me to live here, I need to go back to the US to tie up loose ends and pack my belongings."

"You have nothing to tie up." He fingers my blazer. His disgust is palpable. "You need to pack more of this? Cheap clothing from a discount store? Or did you buy this used?"

I feel his sneer in my marrow, but I don't respond.

"I don't want that garbage in my house. Everything you need will be provided for you."

"I'm your prisoner?" My voice wobbles. *Stop it, Daniela. Stay strong. Strength is the only thing men like him respect.*

"I've been gone for six years," I continue, my head high, "but the D'Sousas have lived in the valley since the beginning. Not everyone has forgotten me. And they certainly haven't forgotten my family. Holding me captive will just make you more enemies."

He squares his shoulders, glowering at me.

"My prisoners aren't given soft, clean beds to sleep in, and warm food to fill their bellies. But holding you captive, even in luxury, only buys me more capital—much more. If I'd keep the D'Sousa *princesa* against her wishes, there's no end to what else I might do, if it suits me."

The D'Sousa princesa. Fuck him.

But he's right. Of all the things Antonio needs to stay on top in his rough-and-tumble world, being feared is perhaps the most vital.

I need to come up with something—anything, at this point. Think, Daniela. Think. Remind him how unpleasant this is going to be for him.

"I'm more trouble than I'm worth. The land is the real value."

"I decide what has value, and what doesn't. But hear this clearly: Under no circumstances are you going back to the US. Your life is here, by my side. It can be an enviable life or a miserable existence. It's your choice."

He takes my hair between his fingers and brings it to his nose before letting go.

"I don't give a damn what kind of life you choose for yourself, but you're not going anywhere that I don't sanction."

His words fall with a loud thud as he opens the door and stalks past the guard in the hall.

I wrap my arms around my midsection.

What am I going to do about Isabel and Valentina? They're in trouble without me. *Penniless.* But for now they're safer in Fall River. *Aren't they?*

6

DANIELA

"*Senhora*," a tall man with broad shoulders calls politely from inside the doorway, "we need to be on our way."

Cristiano. Growing up, there were three of them: Antonio, Cristiano, and Lucas. They were thick as thieves, and while everyone crushed on Antonio, they would have gladly settled for one of the other two. *Except for me. I was only ever interested in the ringleader.*

"I need your phone," he continues.

My phone? "You can't have my phone."

"My orders are to take your phone. And I will." He speaks so calmly it doesn't register as a threat, but I have no doubt he means it.

"My hope is that you'll hand it over," he continues. "We all follow orders. It'll be much easier on everyone if you do as well."

"Before I give you my phone, I need to let my roommate know where I am. She's expecting me home tonight. She'll worry and call the police. In the US, the authorities take missing women seriously." I add the last part, hoping it will incentivize him to let me place the call. I can't just disappear—like Jorge. Isabel will be frantic.

"Give me her contact information," Cristiano says with that same cool demeanor, as though nothing rattles him. "I'll make sure a text or email is sent from you, letting her know you've been delayed."

He doesn't miss a beat, as though they abduct women all the time and are used to dealing with the pesky details. *Maybe they do.*

As I pull a pen and scrap paper out of my tote, it occurs to me that this is nothing but a ploy. He already knows how to reach Isabel. I'd put money on it.

"You don't have my roommate's contact information? I don't believe that for a second." I glare at him, waiting for a response.

"There's very little information we don't have about you, and those directly inside your orbit. It sounds like you already figured that out," he says pointedly. "It's for your safety. But I thought it might be less overwhelming for you if I didn't rub it in your face."

"How sweet of you to think about overwhelming me while you're holding me against my wishes."

"Your phone, *senhora*." He holds out his hand.

I think about making Cristiano wrestle it from me. It's clearly not his preference. But he'll do it, if necessary. I can see that too.

It's not worth it. Better to bide my time and wait to pick a fight I might actually be able to win.

I check my messages and email one more time, then sneak a peek at a photo of Valentina. *It's going to be okay* is my silent promise to her. *"You'll both be fine until I get home."* It's the last thing I said before I kissed them goodbye.

"When I get this back, I expect every photo to be there."

But for those photos, I have little else of any value. I steel my spine and slap the phone into his outstretched palm harder than necessary.

He doesn't blink.

"How are your sisters?" I ask as we descend the stairs. "And your mother? I remember how she would sing at Mass on Christmas Eve. The voice of an angel. She must be so proud of the man you've become."

He doesn't say a word, but when I glance at him, there's a flash of humor in his expression. I feel like kicking him in the shin to wipe away the amusement.

As we get to the lobby, the traitor in the sophisticated blue dress is nowhere to be found.

"Where's the receptionist? Preparing to kidnap the next victim?"

"There's a car waiting out front," he says, ignoring my sarcasm. "They're expecting you at the house."

"Who is *they*?"

"I'll introduce you when we arrive," he replies, evading any meaningful response.

I don't waste another breath asking the bastard any more questions about who is expecting me. Although I can't help but wonder what kind of people would be willing to hold me captive.

7

DANIELA

Cristiano and the burly guard lead me to a black sedan pulled up in front of the building. It's daylight now, but early. No one is around who might be willing to help me. Still, marching me out the front door demonstrates how confident they are that they can quash any problems if I cause a scene on the street.

Once I'm in the car, Cristiano nods at the guard on the sidewalk. "I've got it from here," he informs him before getting into the front passenger seat.

The man behind the wheel is the cab driver who picked me up at the airport. *Another setup.* One thing after another. *How could I have been so stupid? How?*

I squeeze my eyes shut to prevent the tears that are threatening.

The effort Antonio put into getting me here is staggering. His power is formidable. I'm familiar with this kind of unchecked authority. My father had it—although maybe not to this degree. *I'm not sure anymore.* Regardless, even though I recognize the power, it's unnerving to be the target of such a bold display.

The driver makes a right and then a quick left. We're leaving the city.

"Cristiano will take you to our home in the valley." Your home, not mine.

"Where are we going?" I ask from the backseat, although I suspect they're taking me to Antonio's family home.

"The valley," Cristiano replies, as though the Douro Valley is a specific location, like a restaurant or a store, rather than a vast region where a majority of the vineyards are located, including Quinta Rosa do Vale. Although I doubt we're going there.

"Cristiano, your obtuse responses try a woman's patience. For all you know, I have a knife in my bag and I'll stick it in your back when I tire of your evasiveness."

His shoulders stiffen. "You boarded a plane in Boston and went through security with no issues. You landed, stopped in the ladies' room, and then went directly into the cab we arranged, and to Moniz's office."

So much for not overwhelming me with how closely they've been monitoring.

He glances over his shoulder at me. "If we even suspected you were carrying a weapon, you wouldn't have been allowed anywhere near *Senhor* Huntsman. We've been ordered to keep you safe. But don't do anything foolish, because no one will hesitate to protect Antonio—at whatever cost."

It's a clear warning: *When it comes to protecting Antonio, we shoot to kill.* I don't doubt it.

When the car stops for a bus to pass, I try the door handle. It's locked. Probably just as well. I doubt I can outrun the two men in the front seat, even with a head start. Besides, there's a high price to pay for running. I've already been warned. Antonio Huntsman doesn't seem like a man who gives second chances.

I glance at my watch. It's already been the morning from hell, with hours left to go.

My father arranged a marriage between me and Antonio Huntsman. He took a solemn blood oath, and he didn't have the balls to look me in the eye and tell me any of it.

Marriages are made between important families all the time, especially here, and land is often a dowry. I know this.

The bride, and even sometimes the groom, have no say in any of it. My parents had an arranged marriage. It worked out better than most, but still.

You don't marry your daughter off to your enemy.

My father saw it differently, though. Even after we buried my mother. Even when he sent me away to recover. Even with all the time he spent alone, grieving, drowning in profound sorrow, not knowing if I would survive the tragedy, as he called it, he never stopped believing what was best for the region was best for us.

He wanted Antonio to keep me safe. *What bullshit.* What he wanted was to keep the grapes safe, and the vineyards out of the hands of an eighteen-year-old girl. He didn't trust me to manage any of it. Or more to the point, he didn't trust me to do right by his precious valley.

My father believed, with all his being, that Antonio Huntsman was born to rule the region, to move the valley forward in a way that would ensure it continued to prosper into the next generation, and beyond. He refused to see him as the enemy. *"Hugo Huntsman was the enemy. Abel and Tomas Huntsman are enemies. Antonio is not our enemy."* He said it more times than I can count.

Are you happy now, *Papai*? You didn't have the courage to face me on Earth, but one day you'll have to face me, and if you ever make it to heaven, you'll have to face my mother and explain your actions to her. You can tell her what you did to me, and Isabel, and Valentina. She'll look at you with the revulsion you deserve.

Isabel and Valentina. Despite my assurances to them, they won't fare well for long. Isabel has been on pins and needles since Jorge . . . disappeared. She doesn't have the confidence to speak English in public or to venture far from the apartment alone. She's never held a job in the US—she was too afraid that the immigration authorities would discover her documents were forged.

Valentina just turned twelve. She can't work. Besides, she needs to be a girl—we've always wanted that for her. We don't have extra money for trendy clothes or electronics, but we do everything possible to ensure she doesn't grow up too fast, and that her life is happy and carefree. Until Jorge started drinking heavily and disappeared, it was a happy childhood, free from the worries that burden adults. *The kind every girl deserves.*

Stop, Daniela. Ruminating about the past is not going to get you out of this mess. You need a plan forward.

8

ANTONIO

I lean back in my office chair, the rolled leather armrests flexing beneath my hands.

This is exactly where I sat when I issued the order. *"Bring her home. I want her here within the week. Use whatever means necessary to make it happen."*

Three simple sentences, strung together and spoken without a whiff of emotion. Although even then I knew there would be nothing simple about it.

Within the week. The words hung in the air, heavy and somber, while the blood pounded in my ears. I'll never forget it.

I'll also never forget how Cristiano and Lucas gaped at me from across the conference table that day. Faces wary. Shoulders slumped.

Having Daniela in Porto would be life-changing—for me and, to some extent, for them too. Her life would also be upended, but at the time, I had too much on my mind to consider anyone beyond the valley.

The consequences of that order still weigh heavily on me, and the real trouble hasn't even started. Aside from a handful of trusted people, no one knows she's here or that I've acquired the property.

A seismic shift will rock the region when our competitors realize that Quinta Rosa do Vale is mine, and that I hold all the cards—every single one. I snatched them up right under their noses.

When the news gets out, at best it will require extinguishing dozens of small fires. At worst it'll be all-out war, family pitted against family. It could result in a black eye on the entire Port industry, with irreparable damage costing billions. It keeps me up at night, and I'm sure it weighs heavily on Cristiano and Lucas too.

I put it off for as long as I could, but the second my blood stained the betrothal contract, it was inevitable. We would marry, and I would be responsible for her safety. The fallout be damned.

For the first five years she was in the US, we monitored her closely. She had guards shadowing her—discreetly, of course. But otherwise I let her spread her wings.

It bought us time to prepare for a siege.

During those years, we made sure every port house got their fair share of D'Sousa grapes. Lucas also continued to plant disinformation about Daniela's whereabouts—and cover her tracks so no one would find her. It worked.

But six months ago, something changed. Someone started looking for Daniela, and they were getting close. Her name started popping up in search engines, again, and in dark corners of the web—all encrypted, layer upon layer, so deep Lucas and his team still haven't been able to trace the footprints.

We still don't know who has their sights on her, but from the cryptic bits and pieces we could put together, it was clear they knew she was in New England. They hadn't tracked her to Fall River, but it was only a matter of time. At that point, I had no choice. I could no longer keep her safe with an ocean between us.

In the last six months, we've made Daniela's life hell, putting up one obstacle after another, hoping to wear her down so she'd come back of her own volition. But we underestimated her.

Despite how hellish we made it, she toughed it out. *Princesas* are normally more fragile—but not her. Even Lucas was impressed by her resiliency.

We were mere hours from drugging and kidnapping her across international borders when Moniz finally got her to agree to come to Porto to sign the paperwork.

There's a quick rap on the door, and I look up as Lucas breezes in. "What took you so long?"

"Sorry. I was waylaid. We have a situation with missing cargo."

"You are fucking kidding me."

He shakes his head. We don't discuss cargo in detail anywhere but the villa, where we're not vulnerable to eavesdropping. But his scowl tells me we have a big fucking problem.

"How did it go at the lawyer's office?"

I glower at him. "Have you heard from Cristiano?"

"They're en route. He'll call you on his way back from the valley."

I nod. "I want to go to the docks tonight and chat with those motherfuckers myself about how they *lost* cargo. It's not like it got up and walked away." Well, it could have, but I guarantee it didn't.

"You don't need to get your hands dirty. We can take care of it."

Missing cargo. The rage coils in my chest, like a venomous snake, waiting for any opportunity to strike. "I'm not afraid of getting my hands dirty."

"Antonio." Lucas looks pointedly at me. "We don't know

everything we're dealing with yet. We don't know anything. It might be a trap." He shakes his head. "It's dangerous."

It's dangerous. It was Cristiano who said those exact words six years ago, when I insisted on paying a condolence call to Daniela without taking guards with me. I blew him off.

Manuel D'Sousa had just died, and there was lots of unrest while people jockeyed for power. On the way back to the helipad, a large rig forced my car off the road into the raging river. Fortunately, when the car hit the water, the doors opened. If it hadn't been for that safety feature, my driver and I would have both been a casualty of the river.

It was touch-and-go for more than a week, but in the end I fared significantly better than the sonofabitch driving the rig. Although, even after days of gruesome torture, he never gave up the name of the person who sent him after me.

Apparently death was a better option than giving us the name of the bastard who hired him. That narrowed the pool of suspects significantly. Although not enough to retaliate—not yet, anyway.

"Unless you have something more pressing, I'm going back downstairs to see if I can locate the cargo."

"Do it. I'll be down in a few minutes to help."

We have so damn much on our plate right now—the last fucking thing we need is this shit.

When Lucas closes the door behind him, I go over to the window and gaze across the Douro River. It's still early, and aside from a shopkeeper sweeping the sidewalk outside his café, there's little sign of life in the hilly neighborhoods beyond the river. The peaceful aura surrounding the sleepy city—*my city*—is deceiving, but for a minute I let myself pretend that the worst kind of evil isn't skulking in the shadows.

I might not be a good man, but even I don't play in the worst of the devil's playgrounds.

Don't kid yourself. You were prepared to allow an innocent woman to be drugged, stuffed on a plane, and trafficked across the ocean.

I was.

It wasn't my first choice, not because it was such a despicable thing to do but because it was too risky. If something went wrong, we couldn't count on help with the cleanup—not like here.

But payback is a bitch, and Daniela D'Sousa is gunning for my balls now. After today in Moniz's office, there's little doubt she's going to make my life a nightmare.

"I'll go to the police. Or the UN." The UN—I hadn't anticipated that one. Fortunately, I can think on my feet.

We've learned enough about Daniela over the past six years to know she's strong-willed and determined. I went in prepared for a battle, and I got it. No surprise there.

Not much came as a surprise today. Even in cheap, rumpled clothes, fresh off an overnight flight where she was packed like a sardine in economy, she was gorgeous. Her body is curvier than when I last saw her up close. She's a woman now—there's nothing left of that girl I kissed in her father's office.

I watched from afar as it happened. The team in the US sent regular updates, sometimes with photos or videos. And just last year I personally delivered a few cases of Port to a friend who owns a club in Charleston, South Carolina. After the visit, I had the pilot divert my plane to a small airport outside of Fall River. I rented a car and parked down the street from where Daniela lived—and waited for her to get home from her second job.

It was well after eleven when she got off the bus and trudged the four blocks to her house. There were six inches of dirty snow on the ground, and the temperature was in the single digits. Her coat didn't look anywhere near warm enough to ward off that kind of bitter cold.

As she trekked down the dimly lit street, the wind howled,

stirring something primal in me. It took everything I had not to get out of the car, toss her over my shoulder, and bring her home.

It's not that it was such a dreadful life, but it wasn't the one she was born to live.

What did come as a surprise, in the lawyer's office, was how easy it was for her to slip under my skin again. I'm older now too. Smarter. At least I like to think so. But I reacted to her today the same way I did six years ago. My brain. My body. My goddamn emotions—it all went to shit quickly.

I'm not someone who has made it this far because I'm a hothead. I can be. When it's just Cristiano, Lucas, and me in the villa, I often let down my guard, and if a particular situation warrants me acting out of control, I will. Otherwise, I make decisions with a cool head and ice water in my veins—unless Daniela's in arm's reach, pushing my buttons.

The damn woman knows how to get to me, and she's not afraid of rousing my worst instincts. She's a problem. *A huge fucking problem.*

But that's about to change.

I run a Port empire, the ancient city, and every corner of the surrounding valley with an iron fist. Nothing stands in my way —not for long. Taming the D'Sousa *princesa* is the least of my worries.

You want to go to war with me? *Good luck, Princesa.*

9

DANIELA

Once we're outside the city limits, there are no cars on the road. By European standards, it's still quite early, and the valley is rural, far less densely populated than the city of Porto. It's the ideal location to hold a prisoner.

When the car turns in to an unmarked driveway, I'm not quite ready. The ride has been at once too long and too short for someone like me, faced with the unknown.

The driver slows as he approaches a set of security gates. Before we come to a complete stop, armed guards flank the vehicle.

Growing up, our home was heavily guarded, but not like this. We didn't visit the Huntsmans' often—at least I didn't—but I don't remember their house having this level of security either. Antonio must have more enemies than my father, or his. *Or maybe the times are more dangerous.*

One of the soldiers exchanges a few words with Cristiano. When they're done, he glances at me in the backseat before motioning to someone in the guardhouse. The gates open, and we proceed up the long cobblestone driveway.

"This is Antonio's home?"

Cristiano nods. "I believe he expects it to be your home too."

And I expect a knight in shining armor to swoop down and rescue me from the evil villain, but that's not happening either.

While the setting is vaguely familiar, this is not where Antonio grew up. I'm a bit surprised. He's an only child, and I assumed, with his mother remarried and living in London, he would have taken over the property. It's been in her family for ages.

Add it to the ever-growing list of things you've been wrong about today.

As the nervous energy begins to take root, sitting still is becoming difficult. I stare out the window, distracting myself with the scenery and trying to get the lay of the land.

It's still too early in spring for lush plantings, but the property is exquisite. Although it's not the budding camellias that hold my attention but the guard posts that ring the perimeter. They appear to be the highest points on the estate. While they're some distance apart, escaping without being seen will be difficult.

Difficult but not impossible. Even a fortified estate has weak spots. They're often discovered by children playing or teenage sweethearts eager to be alone—*or by a mother and daughter wanting to pick wildflowers on a sunny day without an entourage of armed men tagging along.*

Not now, Daniela. You need to stay focused on the surroundings. It could be the difference between freedom and captivity.

The house is on a hill, set back from the road. From a distance, it's little more than an amorphous blob on the horizon. But as we get closer, the three sprawling stories begin to take shape.

It's not a house at all, but a castle, with warm taupe trim that pops against the creamy stone exterior. The four square turrets, one on each wing, are straight out of a fairy tale.

I guess it shouldn't be surprising that the man who fancies himself a king would live in a castle.

The driver pulls up under an ivy-covered portico, and Cristiano gets out. When the lock clicks, he opens my door.

"How long has Antonio lived here?" I ask as we walk to the entryway.

"He's owned it for some time. The grapes used to produce Huntsman white Port are grown here."

Cristiano holds open the door, and we're greeted by an older man with a warm smile, who Cristiano introduces as Victor. He wasn't gray then, but I vaguely remember him as the Huntsmans' butler.

"It's an honor to meet you again, *senhora*," he says. "I met your parents on several occasions and admired your mother's work with the poor. The people of the valley owe her much gratitude. Your father too. He was a great man."

He was a great man. I once thought so too.

I bite my tongue and smile. It's a small, pathetic curl of my mouth, but under the circumstances it's the best I can do.

"Hello, Victor. It's very nice to meet you too. Thank you for your kind words about my parents."

"We've been very excited about your arrival. I hope everything is to your liking. If not, please let me know, and I'll take care of it immediately."

I want to cling to his arm and beg him to help me. But that's not how it works. Victor's here because he's loyal. Antonio would never allow anyone inside his home, where he sleeps, unless he fully trusted them. That's how it was in my father's house, and I guarantee that's how it is here too.

Cristiano excuses himself after telling me that he'll be available if I have questions.

My mouth is bone-dry as I watch him walk away. "When will I see you again?" I call after him before he disappears out the door.

He stops and turns. "You're in good hands. Victor can call me if you need something that he can't help you with. He knows how to reach me."

I want to beg him to stay, although I don't know why. He hasn't been exactly forthcoming, and in the short time we were together, he threatened me more than once. Victor seems like he'll be more sympathetic to my situation.

I take a step toward him. "Please don't forget to contact Isabel."

"It's already been done," he assures me, kindly.

I nod and pull back my shoulders as the door closes behind Cristiano. Reality is setting in, and I'm feeling a little teary.

"Please don't worry, *senhora*," Victor clucks. "We'll take good care of you. You have my word."

I feel my head bob up and down as though it has a mind of its own.

"*Menina*," Victor calls crisply, motioning to a young woman who has been standing at the edge of the room since I arrived.

"Paula is new to the house," he explains after he introduces us. "*Senhor* Huntsman doesn't normally have female guests here for any extended period of time."

I'm sure Antonio only keeps his female guests around until he's satisfied. I have no doubt they're long gone by breakfast.

"The upper residence," he continues, "is normally staffed by men, but we wanted you to be comfortable, so we assigned Paula to the wing where your suite is located."

He's treating this as though I'm an important houseguest, here for a vacation in the countryside. It's nearly impossible to keep secrets from the indoor staff, especially from someone like Victor, who's clearly in charge of running the house. *How much does he know?*

"She'll be up to speed in no time," he adds, "but if you would be so kind as to give her some grace while she learns your routine, we would be most appreciative."

"Of course," I reply, and smile at Paula, who I need to win over quickly. *She could be an ally, if I play my cards right.*

"You've traveled a long way. I have fresh coffee and a little something for you to eat before we give you a tour of the house and show you to your room so you can rest."

I don't want coffee. I don't want a little something to eat. I don't want a tour of the house. And I couldn't care less about my room. But it would be rude and ungrateful to say so, and I need to gain both Victor's and Paula's trust if I ever expect to get out of here.

"That sounds wonderful. Thank you."

Wonderful is a gross exaggeration, but the sooner I learn the layout of the house, and the routine, the sooner I can make an escape plan.

10

DANIELA

Ninety minutes later, we arrive at the third-floor suite that will be my prison until I can convince Antonio to let me go back to the US, or until I take matters into my own hands.

We enter through a spacious sitting room with a Persian rug that looks like it would feel heavenly under bare feet. The walls are the palest blue, embellished with creamy panels and gold leaf trim. Three enormous windows overlook a garden with a bubbling fountain.

It doesn't look at all like a cell.

"Most of the fireplaces on this floor have been converted to gas so they can be used by anyone without too much fuss." He walks over to the mantel and holds up a small object. "The remote is here. You shouldn't have any trouble with it."

I follow him into a bedroom that's large and airy, and every bit as lovely as the sitting area. Victor crosses the room and opens a set of French doors that lead to a balcony with a bistro table and two wrought-iron chairs.

"The view of the river from here is something," he says, almost to himself. "It's a bit cool at this time of year, but on a warm day, the tiles absorb the sunlight, and it can be a pleasant spot for afternoon tea."

As I peek over the railing, I don't imagine myself enjoying tea, not on this balcony anyway. But the drop to the ground is too far to contemplate, unless a prince taps on my window one night. Unlikely, since princes seem to be in short supply here.

By the time we finish touring the dressing room, I'm speechless. I don't know if it's the designer clothing hanging neatly along an entire wall, or the well-equipped bathroom with a soaking tub and walk-in shower, larger than the bathroom I share with Isabel and Valentina. But either way, I'm completely overwhelmed.

It's been a long time since I've been in rooms this luxurious. Even the houses I clean for wealthy families aren't this lavish.

The guest suite is stunning. Immaculately renovated, with no cost spared to make visitors comfortable. No one would argue that point. But I'm not a guest. I'm a prisoner.

Antonio can dress it up any way he chooses. He can call me his fiancée, wife, mistress, whore, whatever suits him, but I'm being held against my wishes. That makes me a prisoner.

I glance around the room, chiding myself for admiring the bookshelf nestled in the corner behind a tufted chair and ottoman.

Not all prisons are austere, with iron bars and concrete walls. Some cages are gilded, surrounded by saltwater pools and flowering shrubbery. Lavish surroundings can trick the mind into believing it's free. But even great opulence can't fool the soul. My confinement will be luxurious, but I will be confined.

"Is there something special you would like me to prepare for your lunch?" Victor asks, pulling me out of the malaise.

"I'm not fussy. I eat anything. Please don't go to any trouble for me."

"Cooking for you is an honor. Is there anything you need before we let you rest?"

I shake my head, but there is one thing. "What time will Antonio be home?"

Victor's brow furrows. "I'm not expecting *Senhor* Huntsman today."

What? I feel my lungs deflate. *How can I negotiate with him if he's not here?*

"Victor, would it be possible for me to speak with him?"

"You'd like to speak with *Senhor* Huntsman?"

His smile is stiff, and I can tell I've put him in a bad position.

"I'm sorry, but I do need to talk to him, please."

The polite, soft-spoken man hesitates for a long moment. *He's preparing to tell me it's not possible to reach Antonio. I'm sure it's a lie.*

His Adam's apple bobs before he utters a word. "I can reach Cristiano," he says finally, pulling a phone out of his back pocket. "He'll know if *Senhor* Huntsman is available."

While Victor speaks to Cristiano, I think about how I might be able to steal his phone for an hour to call Isabel. I need to keep my eyes open for an opportunity. I glance at Paula. It might be easier to take her phone. *Maybe she'll lend it to me.*

"Cristiano would like to speak with you," he says kindly.

My hand shakes—part fear and part fury—as I take the phone. From the corner of my eye, I see Victor shoo Paula out and move to the edge of the room to give me privacy.

I don't bother with niceties. "I want to speak to your boss."

"I have no boss." The voice is deep and smooth, with an icy glaze that makes me shiver. "I'm a busy man. I expect you to save your neediness for my bed." He pauses. "But since you just arrived, I'll make a concession. What can I do for you, Daniela?"

You can get me some rope so I can strangle you.

"I hoped we would revisit the *arrangement* once I was here, but Victor says he's not expecting you today."

"Victor isn't at liberty to discuss my comings and goings."

Fuck you.

"We need to talk. I want to do it as soon as possible. I'm a prisoner here. I won't put up with it forever."

"You'll put up with what I say you'll put up with—all of it. And if I were in your shoes, I would remember who I was speaking with, and I'd think twice before I opened my mouth. You're in no position to make demands on me or my time."

My head is about to explode.

"You would do well to remember who you're speaking with too." I don't raise my voice, but my tone is firm. "I'm a human being. Not a cat you keep in the barn to chase mice. My family is as important as yours in this valley. I won't allow you to treat me like an animal."

I stop for a breath and brace myself for his response. But there's nothing.

"When can we talk?"

Still nothing.

It takes me much too long to realize he's gone.

11

ANTONIO

What the fuck?

I toss the phone back to Cristiano.

How dare she demand to talk to me. How dare she demand anything of me. In front of the staff, no less.

She grew up in this world. She's not some innocent who doesn't understand the dangers of challenging me publicly. She's a grown woman who knows damn well it weakens me every time someone, *anyone*, questions my authority and I don't act. It invites other people to test me, too, with more than a sassy mouth.

Damn woman.

I should go to the house and teach the *princesa* a lesson she won't forget.

"Antonio," Lucas calls, yanking me out of my head, but not out of my foul mood.

"What?" I snap.

He glances at me from across the table, but he knows better than to call me out on my temper. Although his expression says plenty.

"The maid, Isabel, is in a panic about Daniela staying longer than planned."

"I care about this why?"

I know why I should care about it, but I'm aggravated, and I want to take it out on Daniela's ass. But she's not here, so Lucas is bearing the brunt of my ire.

"Why?" He raises his brow. "Because panicky people do rash things. What if she goes to the police? We have people on the ground in Fall River who could get caught up in an investigation. I don't like it."

He's right, of course. But I'll be goddamned before I tell the insolent bastard.

I draw a deep breath. "What exactly did you say when you contacted the maid?"

"I sent a text as Daniela and explained there had been a small delay with the paperwork. I also told her that between the poor reception and the time difference, speaking by phone would be difficult."

"So what's the fucking problem?"

"She texted back that she's nervous for the kid, and she's worried about Daniela's safety. I have a dozen texts from her since then."

"Pull our people out. Then if she goes to the police, there are no issues." I glare at Lucas. "But she's not going to the police. She has forged documents. She's too afraid of the INS tossing her in jail."

"They'll be out by the end of the day," he mutters, banging on the keyboard.

"Keep one or two people behind to watch the house," I add, "in case someone comes looking for Daniela. Everyone else is done."

"We should be absolutely sure," Cristiano says, staring straight ahead, elbows on the table and hands steepled near his chin. "That team was carefully curated. If we let them loose, we might not be able to pull them together quickly, if something happens."

"I'm absolutely sure. Daniela's here. We have no reason to keep tabs on the maid or the kid. I'm certainly not going to risk our people to protect them. They're not my responsibility."

"Do you care who we leave behind?" Lucas asks.

Someone with a fucking brain. "Use your judgment. But make it someone with a strong stomach. Isabel has a young daughter, but if she becomes too big of a problem and we have to get rid of her, we will. The kid too."

12

ANTONIO

The silence in the room is so thick it could choke a horse.

I'm sure Lucas is steaming, although his head is down, but I feel the sear of Cristiano's eyes on me.

"You have something to say?"

He doesn't respond.

I very rarely go after a woman, and I have *never* touched a hair on a child's head, but Daniela has me so out of sorts, so pissed off, that I'm willing to take my revenge wherever I can find it.

"You have something to fucking say?" I bark at Cristiano like an irascible prick.

Without thinking, I slam my fist on the table, sending everything flying, nearly toppling Lucas's open water bottle onto his keyboard.

I need to calm the fuck down before I do something stupid that can't be cleaned up with a few paper towels.

I roll back my chair and go to the bank of windows that overlooks the Douro River and the city beyond.

Running the region takes a clear head. Decisions made in

anger are often bad decisions. I can't let her get to me, or everything I care about will end up in rubble.

I rub circles over my eyes before turning to my two friends, the closest thing I have to brothers. "How can we reassure the maid so that there are no problems?"

The cords in Cristiano's neck soften.

Lucas is dark like me, not just his hair and eyes, but in all ways. Cristiano is blond, with clear blue eyes, and a true sense of humanity. Although when the occasion calls for it, he can be ruthless too.

I've seen him plunge a knife into a man's stomach without batting an eyelash, even knowing it would be a slow, painful death. But unlike me, he carries those sins with him. It's a luxury I can't afford.

"We might want to have Daniela call to reassure her that everything is fine," he replies. "Lucas can put a time delay on this end, and we'll monitor the call and shut it down if Daniela says too much. But I agree with you. We shouldn't make the situation with Isabel bigger than it needs to be."

He agrees with me. I almost laugh.

"I'll think about it." She's going to have to earn a phone call, and right now the only thing she's earned is my belt on her gorgeous ass. "In the meantime, get Daniela a new phone. Without internet access. We'll hold on to it until the time is right."

This is the clusterfuck of all clusterfucks. I'd kill D'Sousa myself if he wasn't already dead.

Why didn't I just tell him no, I don't want to marry your daughter? Why?

Because I wanted those vineyards, and everything they represent, that's why. And more than that, I owed him. I owed him big.

I turn to Cristiano. "Tell the foreman at the docks I want a meeting tonight."

"Are you sure you don't want us to handle it?"

"This is my city. I won't be sidelined. In case you've forgotten, I'm a capable soldier."

"I haven't forgotten. But it's not just that—"

"What is it, then?"

"I'm in no position to give out relationship advice, Antonio." He shakes his head. "But you have a woman at your house who we lured across the Atlantic under false pretenses. She believes she's a prisoner, and in many ways, she is. A few times today she appeared to be on the verge of a spectacular meltdown. Tough way to start a marriage."

Lucas snickers from behind the monitor, but I ignore him.

Cristiano knows a turbulent, drama-filled marriage is the very last thing I want. My days are hell. I don't want to go home to hell every night too. That's the reason she's at the house in the valley, while I'm staying at my place in the city. It'll be that way until she adjusts to the idea of becoming my wife.

But just because I don't want to live in turmoil doesn't mean I won't. I'll have the fight every night for the rest of my days, if necessary. But if she makes my life hell, her life is going to be hell too.

"You think it'll make her feel better if I go to the house tonight? Maybe I'll grab a nice bottle of wine from the cellar and pick up a big bouquet of flowers on my way home. What kind of flowers do you think she likes? Roses? Camellias?" I turn toward Lucas. "What do you think?" The sarcasm is more scathing than the situation warrants. But I can't stop myself—or at least I don't want to stop.

"If I go tonight, it'll make things worse." *Although it's hard to believe that's even possible.*

"Daniela's jet-lagged, and she needs a good night's sleep and a few days to come to grips with her new life." *And if we're under the same roof, neither of us is sleeping.* She has a hot little body, and she knows how to push my buttons. I don't trust myself when it comes to her.

"I don't know, Antonio. I spent an hour with her, and I don't think coming to grips with her new life is in the cards. Not without—"

I swivel to face him. "Not without what?"

"Effort. It's going to require some effort if you don't want your life to be one drama after another. She's different than the women you're used to. Some of those women would do anything to marry you. She's not like that. And she's been away a long time, living in a place where the customs are dramatically different from ours. Daniela's tough."

"Not tougher than I am."

"No. But if that's how you play it, it's going to be hard on the staff. Holding Manuel and Maria Rosa's daughter against her wishes will be brutal on them. She's already won Victor over."

Christ. "How?"

"Just by being herself."

"I won't tolerate disloyalty from anyone. I don't give a shit who it is. Trust me, with the right incentive, she'll fall into line." *And I'm just the man to provide that incentive.* "Once she's had a taste of my wrath, she's not going to want to incur it again."

There's a gleam in Cristiano's eyes as he places a cup at the base of the espresso machine. He doesn't believe a goddamn word of it.

13

ANTONIO

The evening at the docks proved useful. Not only did it take my mind off Daniela, but we got some answers.

Two assholes who work for me sold the missing cargo to a Russian oligarch with ties to the Bratva.

Most of the people who work for us are loyal. They keep their mouths shut and their hands out of the coffers. But the Huntsman organization is large, and while we make every effort to ferret out the bad seed, every now and then someone slips through the rigorous vetting. It can't be helped.

Those two thieves were publicly punished. When I finished interrogating them, we stuffed their dicks in their mouths and strung them up on lampposts outside the warehouse. It was gruesome, even by my standards, but it had to be done. There won't likely be another diversion for a long time.

After that, you think I would have slept the minute my head hit the pillow, but I was up half the night thinking about the *princesa* tucked away in the valley. Neither my mind nor my body gave me a moment's peace—not even after I jacked off, twice, imagining Daniela naked and on her knees, milking my cock with her sassy mouth. It's become my favorite fantasy.

I glance at the time and curse softly before calling Victor.

He answers on the second ring. "Good morning, Antonio."

"Good morning. How's our guest?" *The one who already has you wrapped around her little finger.*

"I haven't seen her since she arrived. I sent up a tray for lunch, but she didn't eat a morsel. And for dinner I sent her a wide variety of food, hoping something might appeal to her. But she didn't touch it. Paula finally persuaded her to have a biscuit and a cup of tea. She hasn't left her room."

"She had a long trip. I'm sure she's tired." *And stubborn.*

He's uncharacteristically quiet before clearing his throat. "Last night, when the tray came back to the kitchen untouched, I sent Paula back upstairs to see if *Senhora* Daniela would prefer something lighter. When she returned, she told me Daniela appeared to have been crying."

I'm not surprised to hear it. I expect there to be lots of tears shed before we reach an understanding. Maybe after, too. I'm not entirely immune to Daniela's suffering, but I've found the best way to get people in line quickly is to instill a little fear in them—or a lot. It almost always works.

"I don't want to speak out of turn," Victor continues. "But I have the company of those who work on the estate. We share meals together, and we talk and laugh. I can come and go as I please. But if it were not for that, it would be lonely here without you and Rafael, now that he's in London. I don't know the circumstances of her visit, nor do I need to know. But if she's a friend, and not an enemy, perhaps you might allow her some company. It would be good for her."

Like Cristiano and Lucas, Victor and I go back a long way, and he rarely feels the need to keep his opinions to himself.

Victor was my parents' butler. Growing up, he saved me from more than one of Hugo Huntsman's beatings. It was Victor who contacted me when my father was spinning out of control. He was afraid my mother would wind up dead. She almost did. His phone call saved her life. For that reason alone, he gets the privilege of sharing his opinions with me—up to a point.

"She's been there less than twenty-four hours. I doubt she's lonely yet."

"I'm sure you're right. But women aren't like us."

I could ignore him, but he's like a dog with a bone when he gets something in his head. "What about Paula? I thought that's why we brought her up from the caves."

"Paula," he huffs. "I'm not sure she has the brains to be a personal maid, let alone a friend to someone like Daniela D'Sousa. She comes from a dignified family. Paula doesn't know the difference between a soup spoon and a dessert fork. I don't know who recommended her for the position."

My head is starting to throb. "Let's see how today goes."

"The thing about women is life's much easier when they're happy. *Senhora* Daniela doesn't seem like someone who is so hard to make happy."

"I'm done with this, Victor, and I strongly suggest that you be done with it too. What else is happening at the house?"

"Nothing to speak of," he replies with a resigned sigh. Clearly he wasn't ready to stop nagging me about Daniela. "The crew is gearing up for the planting," he continues. "I'm preparing their breakfast now."

When my mother's cook Alma started working full time at my apartment at Huntsman Lodge, Victor took over the kitchen while still running the household. He loves being in control of *everything*, and he's resisted hiring a new cook. At some point, I'm going to force the issue.

"With Daniela staying at the house, will you have time to oversee the staff and feed the crew, especially once the season is in full swing?"

"My hair is graying, but I'm not an old man," he replies with some indignation. "Besides, Daniela doesn't seem as though she eats very much. I can manage. Should we expect you this evening?"

I want to give her another day or two—give myself another day or two. But a part of me knows he's right. I can't leave her languishing forever. I need to deal with her.

There's also another part of me that wants to see her, *that burns to see her*, although that part can't be trusted to make good decisions. Not when it comes to her.

"I'll be there by eight."

14

DANIELA

I've been locked in my suite for more than twenty-four hours. There's no actual lock. I can come and go as I please. Victor made that clear when he gave me a tour of the house. But I haven't found the gumption to venture much beyond the bed.

You need to do better if you expect to get your hands on a phone to call Isabel.

A shower might make me feel better, but I suspect there are cameras hidden in the suite, and I'm not letting them see me naked. I've used the toilet, because there was no choice, but each time I tented myself with a sheet so that no one watching could see anything. They know what I'm doing, but I'll be damned if I allow them to strip me of all my dignity.

I've searched the room carefully, and I haven't found any cameras. *That doesn't mean there are none.* They can be difficult to find. My father was experienced at spotting a plant, but even he used trained men to sweep our house regularly for recording devices.

As I skim the room, a knock on the door startles me. I glance at the clock on the bedside table. One o'clock. *Relax. It's just Paula with lunch.*

I open the door to the hall.

"Good afternoon," she says shyly, glancing at my unkempt clothes.

"Come in. Please."

"Victor made fresh bread to go with your soup," she says, placing the tray on a table in the sitting room. "It's still warm."

"Thank you."

"I'll straighten your bedroom and bath while you're having lunch."

"You don't need to clean up after me. I'm happy to do it."

The young maid looks confused and more than a little flustered, and I remember: *This is her job. I'm her job.*

None of this is her doing, and I won't make her life more difficult. It's not fair, and I need her help—although not with cleaning.

"But if you have time to straighten the room, that would be lovely."

She smiles as though she won a prize and turns to go into the bedroom.

"Paula, is there a flashlight on your cell phone?"

She nods.

"May I borrow it?" I can barely keep the excitement from my voice. "I dropped an earring near the bed, and I can't find it. It might have rolled into a dark corner under the frame."

"I don't have it with me. We're not permitted to have our cell phones while we're on the property. Security holds them. But I'll look for the earring while I'm straightening your room. If I don't find it, I'll bring up a flashlight later."

We're not permitted to have our cell phones while we're on the property. The words are crushing, but I manage to keep it together.

"Thank you. How long have you worked here?"

"In the house?" she asks.

I nod.

"Two weeks."

"Do you know if there are cameras in this suite?"

Her eyes dart around the room, and she takes two steps back away from me.

She's paler than the cream wainscoting, and her eyes are wide, darting around the room like a scared rabbit. I suppose that's my answer.

"I worked in the caves, putting labels on Port bottles," she says, a bit out of breath. "And I helped clean up after meals during harvest, and washed glasses in the tasting room. Then Jacinto picked me to work in the house. I-I don't know about cameras."

"That's okay, Paula," I say, as gently as possible. "Please don't worry. I was just curious." I smile at her. "I'm happy you're here to help me."

She nods and gives me a small smile, but she's still a bit gray. I'm sure she's worried about being caught talking about surveillance. That's the kind of thing that can get someone fired, or worse.

"Oh," she says. "I almost forgot to tell you. *Senhor* Huntsman will be joining you for dinner this evening."

My heart pumps harder, but a sense of relief settles over me. It's as if my body is engaged in a tug-of-war with itself, a push and pull, like all things with Antonio.

But there's no doubt—the news lifts my spirits. Not because I'm dying to see him, but because right now my fate rests in his hands.

I look down at my dingy, wrinkled shirt and my faded pants that could use a good scrub. I've been wearing these clothes since I left for the airport two days ago. I slept in them on the plane, and then again last night. I've washed my face and brushed my teeth, and although my hair is combed, it's greasy. Oh, and I stink.

I need to figure out a way to ensure some privacy so I can shower. I can't go to dinner like this.

15

DANIELA

I don't know where dinner is being served, so I follow the voices to the kitchen, where someone can point me in the right direction.

The moment I set foot in the room, the conversation stops.

Victor goes back to the pot on the stove, while Antonio glares at me.

"Hello," I say casually. "It's nice to see you."

He doesn't reply, but there's a flicker of annoyance in his eyes. He stalks toward me, and when he stops a foot away, he wrinkles his nose.

I stink. I'm well aware of it. And now he is too. *It's humiliating.*

"I changed my plans for the evening to come to the valley and have dinner with you so you wouldn't have to eat alone."

I hope he's not looking for gratitude, because I'm fresh out of thank-yous for assholes.

He gestures to my clothes. "You have a closet filled with *clean* clothes. Is this some kind of statement?"

I shake my head, feeling like a child who has come directly to the table after making mud pies in the garden.

"We dress for dinner here," he instructs in a tight voice. "Just like your father's house. Some meals are more formal than others, but they all require bathing."

"I apologize," I murmur, smoothing my blazer.

He doesn't deserve an apology. But this isn't who I am, and I'm embarrassed. Although not as embarrassed as I would be if there were guards monitoring me in the shower.

"I'll dress for dinner next time."

He steps closer, gripping my arm above the elbow so tightly I can't move. "*Next time* is right now. I suggest you go upstairs and shower quickly, because the staff is on until dinner is finished, and they've already had a long day. This isn't the US. They're not paid overtime."

I feel the color rise in my cheeks. With Antonio still holding my arm, I glance at Victor, begging silently for forgiveness.

He smiles kindly and winks at me with both eyes.

I look up at Antonio. His gaze is dark and threatening, not inviting questions or comments. *But I need to know. I have a right to know.*

"Are there cameras in the bathroom?" I whisper, my heart racing.

His brow crinkles, and he blinks a couple of times. "No."

"Do I have your word?" Not that it matters. I clearly don't have a choice.

He drags me to the bank of windows across the room from where Victor is mincing parsley, out of earshot.

"You're hurting me," I hiss, but he doesn't loosen his grip on my arm.

"Is that why you haven't showered or changed your clothes since you arrived?"

I nod. "I'm not—"

"Did you sleep in those clothes?"

I lift my chin. I'm not going to let him make me feel any smaller than I already do. This is all on him.

"I didn't have another option. I'm not an exhibitionist, and we both know that photos of me naked would eventually find their way to the internet."

He doesn't say the words, not even in a roundabout way, but I see the regret in his face. It's gone as quickly as it came, but it gives me a sliver of hope. I had started to have doubts that he had any humanity. *But his conscience is still there.* It's buried under a mountain of sins, but the heartbeat is detectable.

There's hope for me.

"You have my word," he says unequivocally.

Maybe I'm foolish, but I believe him. He'd have no qualms about telling me there are cameras and I need to suck it up.

"There's no surveillance in your suite," Antonio continues. "It will remain that way as long as you don't give me any reason to have it installed."

He couldn't leave it at *"There's no surveillance in your suite,"* like a decent man would have done.

One small pang of regret does not a decent man make.

"I won't be long," I murmur, scowling at where his fingers still squeeze my arm.

Antonio slowly removes his hand, and we glance at the welts on my skin. They're a fresh, vivid red. Tomorrow there will be bruises.

Acid tickles my throat. The insults I want to hurl are on the tip of my tongue. But I won't be reduced to the animal he's pushing me to be.

I stay quiet and let my eyes spew the fury.

To his credit, he doesn't look away. He takes all my anger, my disgust, every drop of it—until I'm tired of looking at him.

When I'm done, I turn and walk across the room and through the doorway with my head high.

He can go straight to hell.

16

ANTONIO

Are there cameras in the bathroom?

It was a whisper, but I'm sure Victor heard every word. I'm also sure an image of my father came to mind when he heard the fear in her small, timid voice.

It was bad, although not as bad as the marks I left on her skin. Marks not put there for pleasure—mine or hers, or as a calculated punishment to teach a lesson. I have no problem marking her in either of those ways. But the welts on her skin are the stain of a raging, out-of-control man.

Like my father.

I've seen angry, red handprints before. On my mother's smooth cheek, her neck, arms—anywhere my father could reach. It always started with an open hand. Then his fists would fly, and before he was done, he might kick her, or beat her with some shiny object that caught his attention.

Violence begins with a whimper, not a roar.

I've spent a lifetime evading Hugo Huntsman's shadow, ridding myself of his stench. In less than thirty-six hours, Daniela has managed to coax the rage to the surface. To dredge up the pain I keep buried, *the rage*, stir it ruthlessly, and send me back to the edge of the abyss.

She's not entirely to blame. My father's DNA is a powerful force, rotten to the core. The roots are deep and clawing, their tentacles insidious. True escape is not part of my destiny.

Darkness is my destiny. I accept it. But I will not be Hugo Huntsman. I'd rather be dead.

Without a word to Victor, I go to the library and pour a whiskey, emptying the tumbler and pouring another before putting down the bottle.

This is not the life I want. Not for me, and not for her either. She's an innocent woman who doesn't deserve to be saddled with a monster.

But it's not so simple. I vowed to marry her—to keep her safe. A drop of my blood sealed the oath. Honoring that promise will require sacrifice—from both of us.

It might have been easier to have married her right after her father died, when she was young and more malleable. But I had a war to win, and power to solidify, and she was little more than a child. Beautiful and barely restrained, even then, but much too young for my tastes. Now she's been out of the country, living in the US, where arranged marriages and other old ways of our world don't exist—at least not in the open. It's hard to walk away from that kind of freedom once you've tasted it.

But she will. I'm not going to give her a damn choice.

Daniela's spirit needs to be broken. *No.* Not broken. I don't want that either.

Her fire makes my blood hot—and my dick hard. I've spent more time than I care to admit thinking about fucking the little hellion. I want her passionate. *I want her hungry.* I want her blood to burn the way mine does. But that passion needs to be better controlled. I need her compliant. Obedient. It's for her own good.

Most women who grew up like Daniela already understand

the danger that lurks in the shadows, waiting for an opportunity to pounce. They learn, as teenagers, to balance their safety with their desire for freedom. Mothers, older sisters, and wise aunts pass on this life skill, much the same way they teach about fashion or babies.

But Daniela has no sisters, no aunts, and her mother died when she was twelve. She had the maid, but the dangers Isabel knew were far different from the ones awaiting her young charge.

Her father taught her nothing. He sheltered her from anyone and anything that could do her harm. He protected her, but in the process he denied her important life lessons.

I don't know any more about teaching a woman how to balance safety and freedom than her father did. Maybe less. My instincts are the same as his: Take away all autonomy, any meaningful choice, and confine her to the house, unless she's well-guarded or with me. But unlike Manuel, I can't keep her cloistered forever. At least I prefer not to. She's an adult now, and she deserves more—at least an opportunity to earn more.

I'm prepared to give her some measure of freedom, but first she needs to submit to the rules and stay within the boundaries I construct. It's the only way to ensure her safety in this dangerous world.

"*Senhor*," Victor calls from the doorway. There's a brittle politeness in his voice that's not normally there. "Where should I serve dinner?"

"We'll eat in here. Near the fire."

He strides into the room and takes the candlesticks from the mantel. It takes me a few seconds to realize they're for the table. I'm here for dinner and to set a tone. It's not a romantic evening.

"Candles aren't necessary. Between the lamps and the fire, we'll have plenty of light."

He nods curtly and replaces the candlesticks before leaving

without a word. As much as I'm sure he'd like to, Victor knows better than to question me further.

I light the kindling in the fireplace and gaze into the flames as it catches. No matter how much sadness fills her warm brown eyes, I can't be soft with her. Not even when we're alone. Not yet. Maybe not ever. That part is in her hands.

Why didn't I stay in the goddamn city tonight?

17

ANTONIO

When I turn around, Daniela's in the doorway, wearing a fitted skirt with a soft red wrap draped around her shoulders. Thin lines mar her brow, but her head is high and her posture regal. *Not like a* princesa *but like a queen.*

"Come in."

She hesitates before stepping into the room. *Can't blame her for being wary.*

As she moves, the light bounces off the gems dangling from her ears, bathing her face in a pearly glow.

She's gorgeous.

I suck in a long breath as my eyes rove down her legs to a pair of high-heel slides.

I can blame oaths and contracts until I'm blue in the face, but this is why I didn't stay in the city.

"Red is beautiful on you," I murmur, taking a step toward her.

"Red is beautiful on everyone."

Her lips curl as she gazes at the fire, but the smile doesn't reach her eyes. "Although it's not so beautiful when applied directly to the skin."

It's a small slap to remind me I'm an asshole. I should have known she wouldn't let the manhandling slide. A part of me is happy she's calling me out, but as much as I deserve it, I can't allow her to question my behavior.

I glance at her arm. The color has deepened, and it'll be a dark-purple hue by tomorrow. *She's entitled to the small slap.* That's what my better angels whisper.

No one's around, so I choose to ignore the slight. But I know better. Tiny infractions, if not nipped in the bud, turn into something bigger and, ultimately, more dangerous.

If you can't control your woman, how can you control the entire region and a multibillion-dollar Port industry? That's what my enemies will conclude right before making a power grab.

Daniela is going to fight me every step of the way. Nothing will be easy.

Easy is boring, Antonio. Easy is all the women who came before her. The women who were happy to spread their legs. The ones who wanted nothing more than to be your wife. The women who couldn't capture your interest for more than an hour or two. She's not like them.

No, she's not.

I reach over and take a loose wave between my fingers. She lowers her eyes but doesn't pull away.

Sometime after she left, while I was still healing, I wandered through the D'Sousas' house to see what kind of upkeep the property would require. I spent longer than necessary in Daniela's room—trying to get a sense of the woman who would one day be my wife. At least that's what I told myself.

But the truth is, I was recovering from a near-death experience. My enemies got to me because I was reckless and arrogant. I felt young and stupid, and my lungs were still weak from the ventilator. I'd been in bed for weeks, unable to work out, and for a while I couldn't even make it to the bathroom without stopping to rest. My pride was wounded and my body weaker than it had ever been.

Being in Daniela's room infused me with a renewed sense of strength—of purpose. It made me feel alive. I promised to marry her. To keep her safe. I was with her right before the attack, and her bedroom was steeped in her essence, reminding me how sweet she tasted, how her hair smelled of orange blossoms, and how hard my cock had been from a simple stolen kiss.

I drank her in. Learned everything I could about her—and took it with me.

In the shower that night, I braced my shoulders against the stone and fucked my fist while I fantasized about her. Her pouty lips on my cock. Her eyes filled with lust as she smiled shyly from her knees. Her sweet smell carried by the steam. With my eyes shut and the water beating on me, I pumped fast and rough until I was spent.

Just thinking about that night makes me hard.

When it was time to bring her back to Porto, I had Victor stock the bathroom with toiletries I remembered from her room. Brands she couldn't afford while she lived in the US. I'm not sure if I did it for her, or for me.

"Your hair is damp." I rub the curl between my fingers, dispersing a faint citrus scent into the air.

"I didn't want to keep you waiting any longer than necessary."

"You mean you didn't want to punish the staff any more than necessary. You don't give a damn about making me wait." My words are sharp, but my tone is light.

Her cheeks pinken. "That's not true."

"You're not the innocent girl I met with in your father's office—you're a beautiful woman." *Who's going to be the death of me.* "While you've proven to be quite wily, you're still a terrible liar." I pause. "Don't ever forget what I said about lying to me."

I tug on her hair gently, but it's enough to make my point.

She pulls her lips into a tight, disapproving line, but she doesn't say anything.

"Would you like a drink?"

"No, thank you. I haven't eaten much today. It's probably better if I wait. I'll have wine with dinner."

One choppy sentence after another tumbles out in a breathless voice. She's nervous. *As she should be. Isn't that what you want?*

Daniela watches as I pour myself another whiskey. She's quiet, but I suspect the noise inside her head is loud and frenzied.

"I apologize for the way I came to dinner earlier. I wasn't sure—please don't punish the staff, especially Victor. He's not a young man, and he's up early. I'd be more than happy to serve dinner and to clean up when we're done—or at least clear the dishes. I'm used to it. We don't have help at home."

This is your home. And you're not a goddamn servant. Stop acting like one.

"What about Isabel? Isn't she a maid?" It comes out gruffer than I intend.

Daniela narrows her eyes, shooting daggers at me. "Why did you kill her husband?"

She awaits my response with her chin up and shoulders squared. As nervous as she is, she has a streak of courage inside her that won't be kept down. Even though it makes my life more difficult, it's hard not to admire her mettle.

"Why?" she demands in a whisper.

I didn't, but I would have. The sonofabitch contacted us and offered to share Daniela's location for the right price. He also wanted a lot of money in exchange for secrets he claimed to know. He deserved to die, but someone else got to him before we did.

"I've already told you once—I didn't kill Jorge. But don't

spend a second mourning him. He was only too happy to sell you out, and not just you, but his wife and daughter. He was the worst kind of scum."

The color drains from her face. "Is—is that how you found out where we were living?"

"We've known where you were the entire time." *And although it took awhile, someone else found you too.*

Daniela blinks several times before the wheels begin turning. No doubt she has more questions, but I'm not ready to give her more answers.

"If Isabel isn't your maid, what role does she play in your life?" I know all about Isabel. More than I care to know. But aside from redirecting the conversation, I'd like to hear about the relationship from her mouth. It might provide some insight into how to deal with Isabel, who is still too damn anxious for her own good. Plus, it might give me some ammunition to keep Daniela in line, if we need it.

She steps closer to the fire and holds her hands inside the decorative grate, warming them.

"She's had many roles. Isabel came to live with us when she was fifteen," Daniela says in a hollow voice. "My mother intervened to protect her from being trafficked. I'm surprised you don't know the story."

Oh, I know the story. Not just hers but dozens like hers.

"Since my mother died, she's been more of an assistant than a maid. She's always been like a member of the family." Her voice catches as she says the word *family*.

I pour some water and hand it to her.

"Thank you," she says, taking the glass.

When she presses her glossy lips to the rim, my cock twitches like I'm fourteen. *Christ*. I avert my eyes and take a swig of whiskey.

"Let's go back to Victor for a moment," she says softly.

"Please let him go to his suite at a reasonable time. He needs to rest."

"Why do you care so much?"

"He's not young. And he's gone to a lot of trouble to make me comfortable. The better question is, Why don't you care?"

Aside from my mother, who essentially has an unlimited pass, no one would dare question me using that tone. Not even Rafael, or Cristiano, or Lucas. *No one.*

"Watch your tone, *Princesa*. I won't repeat myself."

I add a log to the fire, and then another. "We all have our roles in life. Some we've chosen and some that have been chosen for us. Victor is free when I no longer need him this evening—after coffee has been served, and every dish has been washed and put away." I turn to her. "Your role is to enjoy the food he's prepared and to be good company for me while we have dinner—and later."

Her chest rises and falls, and I half expect her to tell me to go fuck myself. *That I won't let pass.*

Daniela slides her tongue over her fuckable lips and gazes into my eyes. "I'm the one responsible for dinner being delayed. Punish me instead."

Punish me instead. It takes every bit of self-control I can muster to not move.

I'm jonesing to give her what she wants. To punish her in ways that'll have tortured whimpers and helpless cries tumbling from that sexy little mouth.

While I'm fantasizing about defiling her gorgeous body, she's watching me intently. Taking stock of the animal. She doesn't bat an eyelash. It's as though she sees into the depths of my twisted soul, but instead of recoiling, she thumbs her nose at the beast. She's nervous but not afraid—there's a difference.

I don't need her skittish. It's the last thing I want. But a little fear is healthy. Instilling a sense of it in her would go a long way in helping to keep my promise to her father. I'll enjoy the hell out of it too.

I might be a monster, but I'm not a liar. The thought of her uneasy, quivering in her high heels, has my cock pressing against my zipper. I want her apprehensive. Wet. Conflicted. Gooseflesh dotting her flawless skin. Every time she bites her lip, every hard swallow, every shiver—I'll relish all of it.

Every morsel of her discomfort, every bite of shame, is mine.

When it comes down to it, I'm not much different from my father.

18

DANIELA

After what feels like an eternity, Antonio moves within inches of me and runs a callused thumb over my mouth, parting my lips.

"Be careful what you ask for, *Princesa*. Because there's nothing more I'd like right now than to punish you."

His eyes are pitch black, and his buttery timbre doesn't conceal the warning in his voice. Even with the fire a few feet away, and a cashmere wrap covering my shoulders, I shiver.

And he doesn't miss it.

There's a glitter in his eyes. Not a warm shimmer, but the glint of an icicle hanging from the eaves of a charming Victorian. It's magical, until it snaps and pierces your chest.

He drops his hand from my mouth, and I draw a ragged breath.

"Besides, I did punish you," he says with some complacency. "You have a sassy mouth, but a soft heart. You feel bad about Victor now, but tomorrow when you see the dark circles under his eyes, you'll feel even worse."

What an ass.

Victor rolls a cart in with our dinner, sparing me from responding in a way guaranteed to buy more trouble.

Antonio gestures to a chair and remains standing until I'm seated. The good manners are all for show, but I'm not impressed. With the right training, any dog can learn a clever trick.

As Victor transfers the dishes and fusses with the table, I have a little time to think some more about how to get out of this mess.

While showering, I went through the options. None of them good—at least not in the short term.

Plotting an escape might take weeks, maybe longer. Since I know nothing about his timeline, we could be married before an opportunity presents itself.

I can play along with his marriage plans until I gain his trust, and then beg him to send Isabel and Valentina money. It could work, but it's too soon to know. Plus, it'll take time to convince him that I'm fully on board—unless I expedite the process by having sex with him. *Ugh.*

My last option is to simply offer to trade sex for money for Isabel. *Double ugh.* Besides, I doubt Antonio needs to barter to find a woman to have sex with him. *But you need to try. Maybe, but not yet.*

As revolting as it sounds right now, if we marry, I'll end up having sex with him anyway. I have no illusions about it. Why shouldn't it be on my terms? Women have used this ploy successfully throughout history—men too. I glance at the red imprint on my arm, and my stomach churns. This isn't how I expected my life to turn out.

I'm not proud of toying with prostitution—that's essentially what it is—but I don't see a better alternative. Even if Isabel can sell what's left of the jewelry, it won't keep a roof over their heads for long. They're going to need money to live—to eat. They're in the US because of me. I made the choice to flee six years ago, against Isabel's better judgment. I'm responsible for them.

I need to proceed on all fronts. I don't have enough time to let things play out.

It could be worse, Daniela. He could be a stranger. An unattractive stranger who smells of stale booze and hasn't seen a dentist in years.

I glance at his unshaven jaw, then to the way his sleeves are rolled to just below the elbows, the white, crisp cotton hugging his sun-kissed forearms.

How many times have you dreamed about his hands on you—his mouth? Too many to count.

When he reaches for the bottle of wine, the cords in his forearms contract, and I feel the tug of arousal, taunting me. I don't want sex with him. *I don't.* My brain doesn't, anyway. My traitorous body is another matter entirely.

The struggle between what my brain knows and what my body craves—what it's always craved—is making me dizzy. It's been that way since—forever, it seems. Since my mother died, anyway. Before that, my brain and body worked in tandem. They both wanted the same thing. *Him. Only him.*

What could you possibly have known about sexual desire?

I might not have known it by that name, but I knew about the longing. The tingling between my legs that came on at night, when I lay in my bed and fantasized about him kissing me. The ache that could only be soothed with friction. I knew all about those things. They were my dirty little secrets.

You were a child. The same age as Valentina.

But what about all the dreams and the fantasies that came later? What about last year? Or last month, when you woke up panting after dreaming about him, wanting nothing more than to slide your fingers into your pussy, even though Valentina was asleep in the bed a few feet away? You weren't a child then.

It's only when I remember Valentina that good sense prevails—at least for now.

I can't just do nothing. *What if I can't escape? What if I'm stuck here forever?* I need to do something. It's honestly that simple.

"You need to eat," Antonio says gently. "Starving yourself isn't going to do you any good. You need a clear head. Otherwise you'll start making bad decisions. That would be unfortunate."

He doesn't say unfortunate *for you*, but it's implied.

"If you'd like me to eat," I say casually, "maybe we could have dinner without any more threats. Otherwise my stomach won't be able to tolerate food."

I smooth my napkin in my lap without looking at him. The suggestion wasn't snarky, but I'm sure it won't sit well with him.

19

DANIELA

"Do you have everything you need upstairs?" he asks, after a few minutes of silence. While he never agreed to stop the threats, the question and his tone make me think he might have taken my request to heart.

"Yes." In some ways, much more than I need. In other ways, I'm missing important pieces.

"In a day or two, you'll have access to a credit card and a bank account. You should feel free to order anything you need—although you can use it for whatever you'd like. It's not limited to necessities."

"An allowance. How civilized." I didn't mean to say the last part. The last thing I want right now is to goad him.

He takes a drink of wine and places the glass on the table carefully.

"It's not an allowance. Allowances are for children. You're not a child. There's no limit on what you're permitted to spend—although I would expect that you would consult me before making a substantial purchase."

I don't ask him to clarify *substantial*, because I don't intend on making any purchases. I'm sure the card and bank account will be monitored, so they're of little use in hatching a plan.

"The house is lovely," I say, changing the subject to something more neutral.

He seems taken aback by the compliment.

"I mean it. It's stunning."

He nods and picks up his fork. "A house this size is always a work in progress, and we're still renovating, but the bulk of the work is finished."

His features are softer, his expression less severe. For a few seconds, he resembles the Antonio who saved me from the mean boys growing up. This version of him is less intimidating, more approachable. That Antonio might have insisted we honor a betrothal contract, but he would have never allowed Isabel and Valentina to become destitute.

"I love the turrets," I add, hoping to keep his intensity at bay for a little while longer. I need a break from being anxious.

"Have you been up to the top?"

I nod. "I got the VIP tour of the house. The view is spectacular."

The corners of his mouth curl. "You should see it during a storm."

There was a cyclone raging inside me at that time, but that's not what he means.

"Victor only took me to the one with the gym. Do you use the others?"

"I keep a racing simulator in one, and the other two are empty. You're welcome to use them if you need some extra space."

I don't plan on being here long enough to need more space. "You still race?"

"Not as often as I'd like, but I keep a car and a pit crew at the ready. The simulator keeps my skills sharp."

With all his responsibilities, I'm surprised he'd take the risk. "Even with sharp skills, racing is a dangerous sport."

"With any luck, it'll make you a young widow."

I gasp softly. So softly I'm not sure he noticed—although he doesn't miss much. His tone was too glib, as though some part of him doesn't care if he lives or dies. It's unsettling. Even with all I have at stake, I don't want my freedom that way.

"I won't pretend that I want to be here. Or that I want to marry you. But I certainly don't want you to die to stop the marriage from happening."

He cocks his head, as if waiting for me to say more.

"For most of my life, I didn't see you as the enemy," I add softly. "I don't wish you dead." *Not yet, anyway. Hopefully not ever.*

Antonio pours us each more wine. "Your heart's too soft, Daniela."

"I'm tougher than you think. Under the right circumstances, I could put a bullet in a man's head."

He glances at me, and a small smile plays on his lips. "A bullet in a man's head, just like that."

Go ahead, underestimate me. That can only work to my advantage.

"Believe what you want to believe."

He chuckles. "You're adorable, *Princesa*. Do you even know how to fire a gun?"

No. My bravado is going to seem even more ridiculous now. But there are circumstances under which I could fire a bullet—or take one. But I'm not sharing those with him.

"I've never fired a gun," I confess reluctantly.

He nods. "At some point, you should learn to handle one. I don't intend on you ever needing to use a weapon, but I'm not a fool. Once we're married . . ."

Antonio looks down at his plate while taking a forkful of rice. He never completes the thought. He doesn't need to. I can finish it for him. *Once we're married, you become the best way for my enemies to hurt me.* Although, in this case, *humiliate* is a better substitute for hurt. For him to be hurt, he'd have to care about me.

That's what happened with my parents. They were angry at my mother, but they killed her to destroy my father, whom they despised. In many ways, it worked. He was never quite the same without her.

Antonio's features have darkened again, and he seems to have pulled away. Having him emotionally unavailable isn't helpful to my plan.

"Don't worry about teaching me to use a gun," I quip with a healthy dose of sarcasm. "Even if you force me to marry you, I won't kill you in your sleep. Food poisoning's not off the table, though."

A ghost of a smile plays on his lips, but it doesn't materialize into anything real.

"I'm not afraid of dying in a racing accident," he admits, taking a drink of wine. "I use the simulator to stay on top of my game because I hate to lose."

Of course. Better to die than lose.

I liked it better when we were discussing the fairy-tale turrets. I've had enough of death talk. Besides, I'm more likely to win him over if he's not in a sullen mood.

"As nice as this house is, it seems awfully big for one person. Don't you get lonely here?" *Like a real person—the kind with a heart and soul.*

"I keep an apartment at Huntsman Lodge. It's where I stay most of the time. When my cousin Rafael came to live with me, I wanted him to have some space outside the city. I bought the house then."

Years before my father died, I remember hearing that Rafael was living with Antonio. There was all sorts of gossip, including that they were actually brothers instead of cousins. I even heard someone speculate that Antonio was Rafael's father. It all sounded far-fetched.

"I'd heard Rafael was living with you. Did something happen at your uncle's house?"

"My uncle is a monster, but you already know that."

He studies me for a long moment, and my heart pounds harder with each passing second.

"Isn't that why you left?" he asks, still gauging my reaction. "You were afraid of him."

Antonio lays his fork at the edge of the plate. He's expecting a response. If I change the subject or evade the question, I'll in a sense be saying, *Yes, I'm afraid of him*. Then there will be follow-up questions and relentless probing. I can't afford that.

I look straight into his searching eyes. This might be one of the biggest lies I've told in my life—and I've told many at this point. But as Valentina would say, I need to hit this one out of the park.

"I was alone and afraid of everything, then. Your uncle was but one of many worries. I was worried about you too." *And rightfully so, as it turns out.*

I can't tell whether he believes me or not, but he cuts a bite of beef and doesn't say a word.

I need to change the subject—anything is safer than follow-up questions. Antonio's not a fool.

"I was a bit surprised when Cristiano brought me here. I expected you to have taken over your family's estate." It's a bit out of left field, but it'll do.

"My mother isn't in Porto often, but it's her house." He shrugs. "I have no interest in it."

"I remember the little playroom under the stairs. Is it still there?"

He shakes his head. "There was a fire. The house burned down to the foundation. I had it rebuilt for my mother so she could start over. But it looks very different."

"How awful. Was anyone hurt?"

"No."

"Still, to lose a beautiful house and everything inside that you've collected over a lifetime."

"Nothing was lost. Nothing worth keeping, anyway. Everything of value was moved out before the first ember was lit."

He set fire to the house he grew up in. *Jesus.*

20

DANIELA

I wrap my shawl tighter around me as he pours us more wine.

What about the house I grew up in? Up until now, I haven't had the courage to ask. David, the vineyard manager, emailed weekly updates about the property while I was in the US. But I suppose those were all lies too. My stomach twists painfully.

I still don't quite have the courage to ask about the house, but I have so many other questions.

"The employees at Quinta Rosa do Vale—what happened to them?"

"Anyone who was willing to stand in front of me and sign an NDA was welcome to stay."

A nondisclosure agreement—how civilized. Although I'm sure it's not the contract that keeps the employees in line. But having to sign it in front of this man must have put the fear of God into them.

My shoulders tighten at the thought of what he put the employees through. Good people. Honest and loyal. He didn't have to treat them like they were criminals.

"Do they know you own the property?"

He shakes his head. “Only David. The others know I have an interest in the property. Your father and I met many times at his office in the vineyards. We walked the grounds often, and he introduced me to many of the workers. Everyone assumes I have not only a personal interest in seeing your father’s vineyards thrive, but as the current president of the Douro Port Wine Foundation, I have a professional interest as well.” He glances at me. “Their assumptions are correct. Whether or not I own the vines is beside the point.”

They met at the vineyards. My father kept an office there that he went to every day he was well.

I’m not surprised he didn’t destroy the vineyards, but what about the house? I take a sip of wine, letting the alcohol warm my throat. *Ask him. I’m not ready.*

“Did you sell my horses?”

“Atlas and Zeus have been well cared for. The stable manager stayed on.”

A small sigh of relief escapes into the room. I didn’t think he’d destroy the horses, but this is a man capable of terrible things.

“After we’re married, you’ll have an opportunity to see them.”

The news about the horses gives me hope and a shot of courage.

“My parents’ house—is it still standing?”

When he doesn’t meet my eyes, my stomach clenches. I’m sure the house is gone, with everything in it. If he had no use for his childhood home, he certainly had no use for mine.

After several long, excruciating seconds, he responds. “It’s still standing. At some point, Cristiano will take you there so you can see for yourself.”

My body unclenches, one muscle at a time. It’s almost too good to be true.

I walked away, and I was prepared to sell the house, but it gutted me to do it. The sense of relief is overwhelming.

"You would let me visit the house?" The swing from low to high feels almost euphoric, and before I can catch myself, I blurt out the question like a child might.

Antonio leans across the table and traces the contour of my face with his fingertips. "There's very little I'm not prepared to give you, *Princesa*, if you can be trusted."

With my skin burning from his touch, he lowers his hand and pulls a piece of crust from the bread. "If we're going to go through with the marriage, and we are," he says, glancing at me warily, "I want you by my side. I'm not interested in a pet to keep locked in a cage—unless you force my hand. Then you'll get what you deserve."

He dips the corner of the bread into the rich sauce on his plate. "But I want more than that," he adds, so softly I'm not sure I heard correctly.

For a moment, I see something human in Antonio. Not vulnerable. Not soft. But unmistakably human.

"When will the marriage take place?" I ask, to remind myself that despite flashes of humanity, he's still a bad man.

"I haven't chosen a date, but I expect we'll be married within a month."

Within a month. It's not that much time to get him to change his mind, or to escape. "Will I have input into the date?"

"No." He shakes his head. "The timing will be based on several factors that are out of either of our hands. You're welcome to work with the wedding planner, as long as you stay within the parameters I set. Her name is Nelia. We can set up a conference call with her, or a video chat."

I couldn't care less what food and beverages are served, or whether the flowers are fresh or dried, but I'll need to engage in the process if I expect him to believe I've come to terms with the arrangement.

A month. Maybe less. There's no time to waste. You need to accelerate the plan. You can't wait to signal you're willing for the relationship to become physical.

Maybe. What have I got to lose? *Aside from your dignity?*

I push away the nagging voice, pick up my wineglass, and smile at Antonio over the rim. It's my best attempt at flirting. But it's more awkward than sultry, and I feel my cheeks warm.

Before I can continue the embarrassing attempt at a femme fatale act, Victor brings in a tray with espresso and flan, along with a small bowl of almonds, chocolate truffles, and a large bunch of deep-purple grapes.

"Dinner was delicious," I gush as he prepares the table for dessert.

"Thank you," he beams, almost sheepishly. "Paula has prepared your room for the night. Is there anything else you need before I give her permission to retire?"

"No, Victor. Thank you. Please tell her I don't need her first thing in the morning if she has things to do. I'll come down for breakfast."

He flashes me a warm smile. "I'll prepare you something special."

"You don't—"

"Indulge an old man. It's my pleasure to cook for you."

Antonio takes in the conversation but doesn't offer a kind word of his own. He also doesn't tell Victor that he won't be needing him again this evening.

My mother taught me that a measure of a person is how they treat those around them who have less—less money, less power, less authority. This is especially true of staff, particularly inside staff, who are privy to intimate details of family life, and all the secrets.

What kind of person would be so callous as to punish an older gentleman, who has been with his family since he was a boy, in order to teach me a lesson?

The irritation is bubbling inside, but I hold my tongue —for now.

"Good evening." Victor nods and leaves the room.

"Would it have been so terrible to tell him to leave the dishes for tomorrow?" I ask after Victor closes the door behind him.

Antonio stares at me for several seconds, as if deciding whether to share his thoughts, which I'm sure will include a lecture about minding my own business.

"The kitchen and the house are within Victor's purview," Antonio begins cautiously. "He knows what I like and what I won't tolerate. Otherwise, he's free to do as he pleases. I don't interfere with how he does his job. If he wants to leave the dishes for tomorrow, he will. You don't need to worry about Victor's beauty sleep."

My mouth falls open while he speaks. "So that *until every dish is washed and put away* was for my benefit? Just to torment me?"

"For the most part. You're quite beautiful when you're tormented. Flushed and vulnerable. I like it so much, it makes me want to torture you more often."

As much as I hate to admit it, the spark in his eyes makes my nipples bead.

"That's twisted." My voice is breathless—sultry—and genuine. It's not at all part of any contrived scheme to seduce him.

"You have no idea how twisted I can be, *Princesa*."

21

DANIELA

Every nerve in my body tingles at his voice—or maybe it's the predatory gaze that has me on alert. I'm not sure if he's warning me, or if it's a threat, or something else. Whatever it is, it's not innocuous. That I do know.

I should be wary of a man who thinks I'm beautiful when tormented, but there's something about his smooth, husky voice that's alluring. I don't think the torture he's referring to is the kind reserved for terrorists. It sounds dark and dangerous, although not lethal, but raw and primal—filled with the promise of pleasure. *Twisted pleasure*. The kind I've fantasized about—*with him*.

God help me.

I reach into the dainty bowl for an almond. Maybe chewing something crunchy will distract me from my throbbing pussy. Before I'm able to fish one out, he swats my hand away. It's playful, but *nothing* with Antonio is a child's game.

Are the almonds just for show? Did I violate some arcane dining etiquette?

It's been a long time since I finished a meal with dessert *and* fruit and nuts. At home, we eat fruit often—whatever is on sale, and Isabel usually prepares a simple dessert on Sundays, but unless it's Christmas, we don't have them together—with almonds, no less. Nuts are expensive. Maybe my table manners are rusty. "Did I do something wrong?"

"No," he assures me, dismissing my concerns with a single word. "But the almonds are for the Port I want you to try."

Of course. It's been so long since I've sampled Port, I'd forgotten.

Whenever we had a Port tasting at our house, my father had his butler set out a variety of accompaniments, and we'd play a game. Guessing how a particular Port might taste after eating caramel, chocolate, nuts, or even cheese. Each coaxes a different note from the Port, changing the way it tastes on the tongue. I got quite good at it, but my father was the master.

"May I have some grapes, or are they for the Port too?" I ask with some cheekiness as he gets up and goes to the far end of the room.

"Not yet. Don't be so impatient. Good things come to those who wait, *Princesa*. Haven't you ever heard that old adage?"

"Many times. But I live by the motto *tomorrow is promised to no one*. If you take too long, I'm going to eat a grape and an almond."

Antonio shakes his head, but he seems more relaxed than he has been all evening. I am too—relaxed enough to admire how beautiful he is, with long, lean muscle taking up every inch of his sculpted body. He must spend plenty of time in that gym upstairs.

I'm so focused on the way Antonio's trousers hang on his hips that I don't catch what he does to make the bookcases swing open to create what looks to be a passageway. I'd be lying if I said I wasn't just a little delighted by the trick.

"How did you do that?"

He disappears without answering the question and comes out with a silver tray that holds a bottle of tawny Port, a small decanter with what appears to be a younger Port, and four glasses.

"Is there a room back there?" I ask with much too much excitement in my voice.

Antonio's face lights up at my question, and I see the boy who grinned and cocked his chin at my friends and me when we caught him kissing Margarida Pires in the alley.

For a few glorious moments, I forget he's holding me captive. I forget he plans to enforce a betrothal contract he made with my father. And I want him to kiss me the way he kissed me at the house after my father died.

"King Carlos had the castle built with several secret passages to protect the royal family," he says, dragging me from my fantasy. "But Nate Turner had several more put in when he lived here."

"The British spy?"

Antonio nods as he pours ruby liquid from the decanter into two of the glasses.

"First try this," he says, bringing a grape to my mouth.

I hold my breath while he feeds me from his fingers, avoiding his gaze and trying not to read too much into the intimate gesture. But it's hard.

When he takes his hand away, I chew the grape carefully to distract myself from the flush at the back of my neck. "Where did you get grapes at this time of year?"

"We do have markets here."

I roll my eyes, taking another grape.

"They don't taste familiar?" he asks.

"They remind me of D'Sousa grapes, from the oldest vineyard, but not as sweet." I don't say not as tasty, because it seems rude. But they're a bit like the lackluster grapes from the supermarket at home, rather than the sweet, flavorful grapes grown in the old vineyards.

"They are D'Sousa grapes."

I wrinkle my nose. "Really?" They don't taste at all like I remember. "It's still too early to plant new vines, let alone have anything to harvest from the established ones."

"They were grown in a greenhouse." His eyes light up. "We tried to reproduce the grapes from the vineyards that belonged to your mother's family. We even used some of the soil from the property."

"Why?" I ask cautiously, even though I know the answer has to do with money.

"It would increase production of our most sought-after Port. But more importantly, if we were successful, it would ensure that if anything happens to the vines, all is not lost. Those vines are an important piece of our history."

Of my history. But it's a fair statement. "It's been tried before."

"Without success. But we have a good team on it. I'm confident that one day we'll be able to cultivate a similar variety."

"Nothing grown in a greenhouse ever tastes like it came from the earth. Plus, the greenhouse can't mimic the microclimate that makes those grapes special." It comes out sounding more churlish than I intend. I certainly didn't mean to insult him, or discourage any attempt to preserve the vines. "What I meant to say—"

"Shhh," he says. "I agree with you, but we have to try. Taste this."

He slips a toasted almond between my lips and puts a glass in my hands. Then he sits back and waits for me to taste the Port.

I take a sip while he watches intently.

"It's extraordinary." I meet his gaze before taking another sip. "I mean *really* extraordinary."

He nods. "I think so too." His voice is bursting with pride but not a trace of arrogance.

"How old is it?"

"Fourteen months." Outwardly, he's controlled, but I can almost feel the excitement rumbling inside him. "I'm hoping it will be declared a vintage."

I smile. It's not an ordinary smile. This one involves my entire body, heart, and soul. Vintages are few and far between. Some port houses, centuries old, have only a few declared vintages in their history.

"Huntsman, or more widespread?"

"The biggest vintage declaration to date," he says, almost reverently. "If it happens, it will involve many houses, some that are long overdue. Everyone's bone-tired, and frazzled. The drought and the fires that took some established vineyards last summer made the season especially hard on everybody." There's genuine sorrow in his eyes and a real sense of loss in his voice. "We need this," he adds from somewhere distant.

My heart clenches. Not just because of what a vintage means for the battered region, but because he showed me a piece of his soul. A piece that's not ugly or selfish, but distinctly human.

This is not a greedy man who wants a good year for himself and to hell with everyone else. This is a man who truly cares about the valley and the industry that keeps it humming. But perhaps more than anything, this is a man who carries the burdens of the region on his shoulders.

It's still impossible for me to reconcile, but my father had his reasons for choosing Antonio. Not just to protect his vineyards, but me too. I hope that one day I can find it in me to forgive him.

"Quinta Rosa do Vale?" I ask cautiously. The fires didn't reach us, but the drought caused problems. As with everyone else, it seems, the year before last was a special year. I want to know how special.

"She shined. Even among the stars, Quinta Rosa do Vale

was the brightest. The Port you sampled is made from her grapes. A single vintage."

I stop myself from leaping to my feet and throwing my arms around him, but it takes some doing. "Antonio." I'm smiling so hard my cheeks hurt, but still, the tears threaten. "Thank you."

I thank him because although those vineyards no longer belong to my family, they were tended by them, reared for generations in the way that precious children are reared. I won't be spiteful about their success. I want them to continue to thrive.

"We shouldn't get ahead of ourselves," he warns. "The institute hasn't declared anything yet. Not formally."

"You have influence. Especially as president of the foundation."

"I do. But I won't cheat. That would cast a pall on the history of the region and diminish the value of any vintage that came before or after."

It's an interesting declaration—stunning, almost.

I believe the apt term is *honor among thieves*. The man who would kill another, and force a woman to marry him, won't tip the scales on declaring a vintage. *This is why my father's trust in him never wavered.*

I eye the Tawny Port that we haven't tried yet. I pour some in a glass and take a spoonful of flan, bathing it in the rich caramel before bringing it to his mouth. "It's your turn."

22

DANIELA

His eyes flicker with dangerous sparks as he snatches my wrist and sucks a drop of caramel from my skin before tasting the custard.

I feel his mouth on my flesh, long after it's gone, and the heat filters through me until I'm almost panting.

Without warning, Antonio pulls me into his lap. "It's easier to enjoy you from here," he murmurs, lifting a glass to my lips.

I don't resist. Not him. Not the sweet, fortified wine. None of it—and I'm afraid this isn't part of some scheme I've concocted but what my body wants—*and maybe my heart too.*

He takes a sip from the glass after I've had my fill.

"It's your turn again, *Princesa*," he says in a voice so husky, so rough, it makes me hope that my turn will hold something besides a spoonful of silky custard and a sip of Port. Something not so sweet, but intoxicating. Something forbidden.

His lips brush mine, and I relax into the gentle sensation, my body melting into his. When I'm boneless, he takes my bottom lip between his teeth, nipping and tugging before letting go.

"Ahh," I gasp, tingling from my breasts to my core.

My eyelashes flutter closed as my face tips upward, drawn to him like the warm sun.

"*Princesa*," he groans, before his mouth crushes mine, swallowing the gasps as they spill from my throat. His tongue explores, unrestrained, demanding, and skillful.

I'm lost in sensation so potent, so visceral that I'm struggling to even breathe.

As I fight to remain afloat—to remain present—his rich, masculine scent rouses something primitive. Something foreign. Something almost unspeakable. But I don't let shame drown me. Instead, I inch my palms across his shoulders, and enjoy the hard muscle under my fingers.

The kiss goes on, and on, and on, luring me deeper and deeper into his spell.

I want him. *I've always wanted him.*

He slides his large hands over me, petting and teasing, until I'm light-headed and needy. *So needy.*

For long, dangerous moments, I forget that sex is part of a plan to help Isabel and Valentina. I forget that I'm his prisoner. I know nothing but his mouth and his hands—and the way he uses them to make me feel things that I've read about only in books.

Antonio threads his fingers through my hair, pushing it off my face. "Your skin is flushed. So gorgeous." He lowers his mouth, and I pull his head down, leaving him with no doubt about what I want.

He cups my breast, his thumb circling the nipple through my thin blouse. The pace is maddeningly slow, unrushed by my desperate whimpers.

The kiss deepens, consuming any remaining good sense. *Consuming me.*

I shift on his lap, and he grunts, pulling his head back and cupping my ass with a strong hand.

"You're tempting, Daniela. *So* tempting. I need to taste you. I want to lick your sweet pussy." He slides his hand deeper into my hair, tugging my head back. "Would you like that, *Princesa*?"

The moan caught in my throat reminds me that sex is all I have left to barter with—all I have left to advance my plan.

I can't squander this moment—*I can't.* But I'm not sure how to proceed. Do I want to make a trade now, or use sex to build trust? *I can't think clearly with his mouth and hands on me.*

"I think you'd like my mouth on your pussy," he murmurs when I don't respond.

Once I give him what he wants, there's nothing left to trade.

What do I want?

I can't force myself to even think about it. I'll never be able to look in the mirror again if I admit the truth. It doesn't matter how bad I want his kisses. Or his touch. Or how much I want him to taste me. Nothing matters but—

"What do you want?" he murmurs, his warm breath against my ear.

He's coaxing me to tell him what my body needs. He wants me to talk dirty. *Doesn't he?* "I-I-I don't know," I confess in a shaky breath.

Antonio pulls back, his hands still threaded through my hair. "Don't lie to me." His voice is still blanketed in lust, but there's a harsh edge now. And his gaze is ruthless.

"I know the difference between a woman who's aroused and eager to play, a woman who's nervous, and one who's willing to suck my dick because she wants something." He has my hair in a firm hold now. "What do you want? I won't ask again."

I draw a breath, and then another, as the shame spreads like an itchy rash, inflaming every cell of my body. *This is about the people you love. This is your life. Fight for it. Take control, or cry in the corner, like a sheltered* princesa, *because life's become too hard. Too degrading.*

"I have a deal for you," I blurt ungraciously.

He raises his brow but doesn't give anything away. "A deal?"

I nod. Feeling braver and more confident than my half-baked scheme should allow.

"I'm listening."

23

DANIELA

All of a sudden, money for Isabel and Valentina isn't enough. I want my freedom. But there's little to no chance he'll let me go back to the US. If I take the risk, I might end up with nothing.

"You can do whatever you'd like to me"—I swallow the bitter pill—"sexually. Before the wedding. I won't complain. In exchange for my—my cooperation, you'll deposit the money that you planned on letting me spend into my bank account in the US for Isabel. I'm the sole breadwinner. Without me there, they have no source of income."

"And what will you do, walk around bare-assed?"

I can't tell if he's game, or if he's angry, or indifferent. His expression gives nothing away.

This is humiliating—carved so deep, I'll never get the stench off.

"There's enough clothing in the guestroom closet to last me a lifetime. I don't need material goods. I need the peace of mind knowing that they have food and a place to live."

He stands, dumping me off his lap. I lunge for the edge of the table so I don't fall on my face.

"You're willing to let me fuck you before the wedding?" he asks, his voice tight. "How generous." The words whorl with biting sarcasm. "You think I'm going to wait to have you until some arbitrary date? Why would you think that? You've already spread your legs for a man you weren't married to."

Bastard. Like he hasn't fucked anything and everything within a hundred-mile radius.

"What makes you think I'm going to wait for my turn?" he asks, stepping closer.

I don't respond. It doesn't require a response, nor does it deserve one.

He studies me while the gooseflesh rises on my arms. "Whatever I like, huh? Oh, *Princesa*, you'll rue this day."

My knees wobble, and I clutch the back of the chair to steady myself.

"My own personal fuck toy, and it's not even my birthday or Christmas."

It sounds so crass from his mouth, I feel like I'm going to vomit.

I can't do it. There's got to be another way. Think, Daniela. Think.

"You might not like the cards fate has dealt us," he says with a bitterness that makes my stomach coil. "I don't like them either." He looks at me pointedly. "I'm not a good man. I've been up-front about it. But I came here this evening with good intentions. You came to play me. Remember that while I give you everything you asked for—and more."

What have I done? "Please. Be reasonable."

"It's too early to beg, *Princesa*," he sneers. "And don't waste your breath. Begging won't get you anywhere with me tonight." He takes a lock of my hair, rubbing the strands between his fingers.

"I made a mistake. I need more time."

He lets go of my hair, like it's coated in poison, and slams his fist on the mantel.

"Do you think I care whether you need more time? I own you like I own your family's vineyards. You'll spread your legs and twine them around my waist anytime I ask. How many men have fucked your tight little pussy?"

I won't be part of this filthy game.

"How many men have been inside that cunt? Answer me."

"Why do you have to be so vulgar?"

He pauses for a heartbeat. "I'm plainspoken, and I don't pull any punches. A woman willing to trade sexual favors for money is in no position to call anyone vulgar."

Asshole.

I pull my shoulders back. "I've given myself to one man."

"Josh." He spits out the name like sour milk. "The man who owns your heart. Isn't that why you really want to go back to the US?"

"We're not even together. I don't know why you'd say that."

"And yet you don't deny it." He grabs my wrist and pulls me to him, scaring me now.

"What are you doing?"

"Giving you what you asked for."

My insides are trembling. *This was your stupid, stupid, stupid idea, Daniela.*

"I told you. I changed my mind."

"You don't get to make an offer and then pull it back once the other party agrees. That's not how it works. Maybe you can play games with boys like *Josh*, but with me, a deal's a deal."

I was foolish to try to play him. But this is the kind of deal I should be able to walk away from at any time.

"Why are you doing this? There are other women who would be happy to have sex with you as often as you'd like, in whatever way you'd like."

"For all intents and purposes, you're my fiancée. Are you suggesting I take lovers?"

No. "I don't care. Yes. That's what I'm suggesting."

He grabs my chin and positions it so I can't escape his raging eyes. "Within a month, I'll have a beautiful young bride, and I don't intend to satisfy myself with whores while you sit around fantasizing about a boy named Josh who you will *never* see again."

He releases my chin, and I hobble back, out of his reach.

"Although, who knows? Maybe you'll end up being the biggest whore I've ever fucked."

I dig my heels into the rug so I don't lunge at him and beat him with my fists.

"I want your pussy. Your smart mouth. Your tight little ass. And I'm going to have them."

"No." I shake my head. I thought I could go through with this, but he's made it too ugly. I'm not sure I can do it—not even for Isabel and Valentina.

He pulls out his phone and places a call.

"Deposit five thousand American dollars into Daniela D'Sousa's bank account in the US. Then text the maid, as Daniela, and tell her the money is for food and rent." He smirks at me. It's a gloating smirk, like he's won everything—and he has. Or, at least, he's minutes away from it. "Do it now."

24

DANIELA

Five thousand dollars for food and rent.

He hangs up and tosses his phone on the table, then rubs a palm over his unshaven jaw.

"You do realize I didn't need to transfer a single penny. I could have torn off your clothes, splayed you on that table, and fucked you without fulfilling any promise. Do you think anyone would come if you screamed?"

No. I don't think that.

"I did my part. Now it's your turn," he purrs, stepping toward me.

I'm shaking, inside and out. But he's right. He did as I asked—and he was more generous than I expected. With what I already have in the bank, five thousand dollars will get them through at least a couple of months. That should give me enough time to get back to the US.

This was my idea, and I won't risk having him take the money back.

It's just sex, Daniela. You don't have to give him your soul.

While I'm giving myself a pep talk, he cradles my cheek in

his hand. "I'm going to punish you for trying to manipulate me," he murmurs, inches from my head.

I shiver at the threat.

"I have a lifetime to use your body. I'm not going to fuck you tonight."

A small whimper escapes. "Thank you," I whisper, my voice raw and hoarse. Not that I should have to thank him for respecting my boundaries, but I made a deal. And I would do it again.

"You're maddening," Antonio murmurs, "but exquisite." He drags a finger around the curve of my ear to my collarbone. "Your skin is so soft." He lowers his head and drops a kiss on my throat. "And it smells delicious."

I close my eyes, squeezing them tight. Not because I'm afraid, but because I'm so conflicted.

Antonio brushes a gentle hand over my hair before sweeping his arm across the table, shoving the dishes and utensils to one side. A cup teeters before toppling over the edge, spilling black coffee on the antique rug. But he doesn't seem to notice as he lifts me onto the table and nudges my knees apart.

"I won't fuck you tonight. You have my word," Antonio promises, standing between my legs. "As much as I'd like to," he mutters under his breath.

A sense of relief washes over me as my inner thighs press against the outer edges of his. I don't know why I believe him, but I do.

He lowers his gaze, following his fingertips as they trace the bruise blooming on my arm. The mark he put there. "Does it still hurt?"

"No."

"That will never happen again. You're not a punching bag. I'll never lay my hands on you unless I'm firmly in control of my emotions. You have my word on that too."

It falls short of an apology, but I suspect it's more than most people get from him. In a strange way, I believe this too. At least I want to believe it.

Antonio lifts my chin and sweeps his mouth over mine. “You’re mostly safe with me.”

Mostly.

His kisses move from gentle to rough and insistent, and I feel my hands clutch his shoulders, my fingers sinking into the tight muscle.

My reserve melts away, slowly at first, until the heat between us eviscerates every good instinct standing between me and ruin.

In my mind, my conscience bites. *I should listen.* I know that everything about this is wrong and that I shouldn’t enjoy it so much. Maybe he’s right. Maybe I am a whore. But as my tongue slides against his, I don’t care.

Isabel and Valentina are taken care of, for now. Tomorrow, I’ll plan an escape.

Tonight, I’m going to forget he’s holding me captive. I’m going to forget that his family tortured my mother and slit her throat. Tonight, I’m going to focus on the boy I fell in love with before everything went to hell. I’m going to enjoy his hands and his mouth. His kisses. I’m going to enjoy all of it. *God forgive me.*

He draws back, dipping his finger into a glass of Port. His eyes darken as he paints my lips with the ruby wine in the same way I might apply a stain. Although his finger is thicker than mine, stronger, and he’s not careful to stay within the lines. But still, not even a swipe of Chanel gloss could make me feel this beautiful—this alluring.

When he’s done, he sucks every sweet drop from my mouth. He’s thorough and meticulous, and I’m panting softly, small gasps slipping out into the thick air.

He inches closer, reaching behind me for a bottle and refilling the glass. As he moves, my skirt hikes up, and my legs edge farther apart. When I tug at the hem, he pushes my hand away.

"This isn't the time for modesty. Let the cool air lick your pussy. It's overheated, isn't it?"

I respond, not with words but with a small mewl.

"Are you wet for me?" he murmurs, dipping his finger into the Port again. "I'll bet you are." He traces a finger over my throat and between my breasts, his warm mouth following, lapping the luscious droplets from my flesh.

I'm hot. *So hot*. And my heart hammers as he sucks the liquid from my neck. Tomorrow there will be a bruise there too. *But this is different,* I tell myself. He's in control now—I feel it—not only of himself, but of me too.

Desperate to soothe the throb between my legs, I tighten my thighs around his and slide a hand over his broad chest.

His heart is pounding, too, powerful and steady. Instead of backing away, instead of heeding the warning that this is quickly getting out of hand, I lift my hand to his scruffy jaw and explore the sharp contours of his face.

Antonio rests his hands on my hips, his eyes boring into mine. He doesn't move as my fingers travel along his skin—not at first.

"What are you doing?" he asks, his raspy voice enveloped in a lustful haze.

I shake my head. "I don't know."

He takes my hand and brings it to his lips. I purr when he places a small kiss on my fingertip, and while I'm soaking in the blissful moment, he lowers his mouth and bites into the soft flesh.

"Ouch!" I cry out from the surprise, not because the sting is painful. I jerk my hand away, but he doesn't let go—not before he brushes his lips over the bite mark.

"Some women find a little pain heightens their enjoyment.

Some men too," he says, his fingertips skating up my inner thighs, searing the sensitive skin as they go.

"Do you enjoy pain?" I ask cautiously.

His thumbs move in a steady rhythm, sweeping closer and closer to my panties, until they graze the lace-edged gusset. "With you? I could enjoy almost anything."

His thumbs slide under the lace, and I let my eyelids flutter closed. "Look at me," he demands softly. "Yes. I enjoy pain. Inflicting it, mostly."

25

DANIELA

My heart stops, but his fingers don't, and I'm too aroused to press him about the kind of pain he likes to inflict.

"So wet," he murmurs. "So tempting. So innocent. I'm going to take your sexy panties," he whispers above my ear. "Did you wear them for me?"

I gasp as he slips the underwear down my legs, slowly, stopping only to slide off my shoes.

"Before the night's over, I'm going to soothe that little ache between your legs. You'll feel so much better," he coos.

Shame washes over me. But I don't want him to stop.

"But first." He grazes my lips, gently, and tugs at my blouse. "Take off this pretty flowered shirt for me. Show me what's underneath."

Suddenly I feel shy, and I hesitate. Antonio doesn't urge me on. He doesn't say or do anything. He's patient, with all the confidence of a man who knows I'll eventually do as he asks.

I swallow hard and avert my eyes while I pull the shirt over my head and unfasten the hooks on my bra. My mother's locket dangles between my breasts, and I take it off and lay it on the table, hiding it under my wrap so I don't have to look at it while he debases me.

When I had sex with Josh, he always took off my clothes. He never required me to hand them over. Antonio's doing this because it adds an element of humiliation, like parading me through the streets while I carry the white flag of surrender for all to see.

The worst part is that I don't mind—not really. There's something about it that's sensual, stirring the need in me beyond anything I've ever experienced.

He holds out his hand, and I place my clothing into his outstretched palm. He doesn't give them a passing glance as he drops them at his feet.

"So beautiful," he murmurs, cupping my breasts. He makes small, tight circles around my nipples. They bead for him, gladly, as though pleasing him is more important than anything else. Maybe even more important than what I want.

Don't I want this? Isn't this what I fantasized about on the long bus ride home from my night job, and later, alone in my bed?

The thoughts bleed away as he pinches a nipple, making it impossible to think about anything but the erotic sensation. *"Ahhh."*

"Did you feel that between your legs, *Princesa*?" he asks, smearing my nipples with the ruby Port before lowering his mouth to a hard peak.

My back arches, and I brace myself on my hands while he lavishes attention on my breasts.

"I want your skirt," he whispers, reaching for the zipper. When he does, his hard cock presses against my bare pussy, and I jump back.

"I gave you my word. We're just going to play a little."

He stands back, eyes burning, and watches as I squirm out of what's left of my clothes without totally exposing the wet flesh between my legs. My efforts are of little use, but I squeeze my knees together as soon as I'm finished.

"I don't think so," he murmurs, moving my legs apart as he steps between them. He's large and looming, and I don't know what to expect next as he hands me a glass of water. "Take a few sips."

I hold the glass with two hands, trying to keep it steady.

Antonio is still fully dressed, making me feel more naked. More vulnerable.

His fingers play on my mound while I drink. It's hard to swallow. Hard to even breathe.

After a few moments, he takes the glass out of my hands and sets it aside.

"Just feel. No judgment. No self-doubt. No shame. Let me make you feel good."

"Yes." My head bobs, but the movement is so small it's barely perceptible. "Yes," I repeat. Although it wasn't a question. He wasn't asking for permission.

I'm not sure how I feel. I'm aroused, unsure, nervous. And then there's the part of me that wants to tear open his shirt and feel the heated skin under my fingers.

Antonio hooks his leg around a chair that's been shoved to the side and drags it closer, all without taking his hands off me.

He lowers himself to the edge of the seat and places his palms on my inner thighs, pushing them apart until it's almost unbearable.

I'm exposed. Completely on display—*for him.*

"Stroke that pretty little cunt for me. Show me how you touch yourself."

I draw a breath. Not sure of how to proceed. *I can't do it.*

"I've never—" I'm too embarrassed to even form the words.

"Haven't you ever made yourself come?" he probes when I don't finish my thought.

"Never in front of anyone."

"Do you have toys you play with? A vibrator?"

I shake my head.

He takes my hand and moves it between my legs, drawing my fingers through the slit.

"You're going to get comfortable making your body sing for me. We'll practice, but right now I can smell your arousal. It's all I can think about. I don't have the patience to teach tonight."

I'm mortified, and the arousal he thinks he smells is starting to slip. He must sense it, too, because he slides his fingers over my mound and strokes my pussy.

Although I shut my eyes to hide, his touch feels good. *So, so good.*

"Open your eyes. I want to see your pleasure."

I do as I'm told, but it's starting to get to be too much, and my chest is tightening. It's those damn conflicting feelings again. *Get out of my head,* I want to scream. *Get out of my head!*

"You're so wet, Daniela," he murmurs, coating his fingers with the evidence. "I knew you would be."

This is new to me. The filthy commentary. The unabashed openness and discussion. Josh and I had sex mostly with the lights out. He never said a word until it was over, and God knows, I never did.

Fear is starting to creep in. I don't know if it's the newness of it all or that I don't mind his dirty talk. That I don't mind the shame. But the apprehension is growing, and he senses it.

"It's okay," he reassures me. "You can pretend this is whatever you want. Whatever you need to free your inhibitions."

He rubs my belly to calm me, his fingertips skating over the soft skin. "You can make me into some monster if that soothes your conscience. But we both know you want this as much as I do."

I don't say a word. I don't bother to deny it. Because it's true.

When he slides a finger into me, my walls squeeze it, and he pushes in another, rubbing my clit with his palm.

The sensation sends small zings through me, and I squirm into his hand for more.

He pulls away, leaving me with nothing. "I decide how much you get, *Princesa*. Your job is to just feel and enjoy what I give you."

I'm hot and sweaty. Confused. Agitated. And I'm about to jump out of my skin when he lifts my feet one at a time and drops a small kiss on each heel before placing it on the arm of the chair. His elbows rest on my inner thighs so that I remain open to him.

Embarrassment, *not shame*, begins to wedge its way in, and because I can't close my legs, I close my eyes.

"Keep your eyes open, Daniela. Don't make me say it again." His tone is threatening, and I'm certain there will be consequences if I don't obey.

"I'm going to lick your gorgeous cunt, and you're going to watch until your legs tremble."

His face disappears, and I feel his flat tongue make a long sweep over my quivering pussy.

Oh God.

He does it again, and again, and again, circling the swollen bud when I least expect it, licking until I writhe on the table. Until there are no doubts left inside me. No shame. No embarrassment. Until all I know is his mouth and my throbbing pussy.

It's then that he pulls away.

26

DANIELA

"No. *No*. Please don't stop." The plea comes from me, but the voice belongs to a woman I don't recognize. A woman caught in the voluptuous curl of lust. A desperate woman, with passionate needs and desires. *It can't be me.*

Antonio skims his hands across my belly, tonguing the sensitive skin, moving lower and lower, slower and slower, until I whine, because *I need more*. More of his mouth, his tongue, the rasp of his whiskers. More of his hands, his fingers—*and God help me,* I want his cock.

Only when he's ready does he go back to eating my needy wet flesh. He adds two fingers to the party, and the sounds that come from me are feral and reckless.

I grip his head between my hands. I pull his hair. But he ignores my urging, keeping to his own rhythm until my thighs tense.

Then he pulls away.

It's cruel and punishing. And my cries are louder, more desperate this time.

"Please," I beg without a trace of shame.

"Please what, *Princesa*?"

I don't want to say it, but I will. My pride and all decorum are buried under the achy need he sparked. "Please—fuck me."

His mouth twitches, and there's a smug sense of satisfaction in his eyes. *I don't care.*

"Mmmm," he moans. "I wish I could, but I gave you my word."

"I don't care about your promise." I pout like a child who's just been told she can't have chocolate before dinner.

He lowers his head again and coaxes the little pearl onto the tip of his tongue, blowing on it gently. It's sublime. I wriggle and buck off the table, but the scream and the orgasm die together before they materialize.

"What?" I gasp. *"No!"*

Antonio stands and unbuckles his belt. And as though it's something I do every day, my fingers slide down my belly while he tugs at his zipper.

"Don't even think about it," he warns, swatting my hand away from my pussy. "You're lucky I don't put you to bed with your hands bound so you can't rub that greedy little cunt."

Bind my hands? He wouldn't. Would he?

Antonio frees his cock from his pants, palming it while I watch. It's steely and smooth—*and big.* His hand moves from root to tip, and I'm riveted by how comfortable he is with his body.

His cock gets longer and thicker as he pulls, and a fat, milky bead forms at the center of the dusky crown.

I want to taste the creamy little drop. I want to lap it up and let it dissolve on my tongue. But some part of me feels too shy, too inexperienced, to lean over and lick.

While I'm contemplating a move, Antonio steps closer and rubs his swollen cock over my clit. I whimper. Every nerve ending in my body sways faster and faster, building the momentum to push me off the edge.

The slide of flesh against flesh is both excruciating and

exquisite. I need the release. *I need it.* But with the tiniest shift of his hips, or a slight change in pace, he dangles the orgasm just beyond my grasp. It's pure evil.

Just when it feels within reach again, just as I'm about to take it, he pulls away, leaving me frantic.

I grope for him, but he slips his hands behind my knees and lifts my bottom off the table, opening my legs at just the right angle to create a cradle. He nestles his cock on my pussy and lets it lie there for several seconds, throbbing, while I pulse under him.

His eyes are black and hooded. His breath comes in heavy gasps and spurts. He's close too.

"This is what you deserve," he mutters, sliding me back and forth along his length, bringing my knees together until my pussy embraces his cock. It's like I'm a doll he's playing with. A toy. *A fuck toy.*

But I don't care about any of it. My sole reason for living right now is the orgasm I'm chasing. The one he's held out of reach for too long.

I'm close. "I'm so close," I whimper.

Antonio wrenches himself away. He swipes a hand across his mouth and begins to pump his fat cock. I've never watched a man pleasure himself. It's arousing and lewd, and I can't stop staring.

His head falls back. His features tighten. His face is flushed and sweaty, contorted as though in pain. He's tormented. And beautiful. Achingly beautiful as he pulls his proud cock roughly.

I feel the eruption as it happens—as it wrenches itself from his muscular body.

His tortured grunt echoes inside me. It's all I hear as he sprays his seed on my stomach, my breasts, and my mound.

My thighs clench, but the orgasm is now well beyond my grasp. I'm confused. And frustrated.

I don't understand.

"You. Are. Mine," he growls, daring me to question his right. Daring anyone to question it.

While I'm still reeling, he steps back and adjusts his trousers, tucking in his shirt. His breathing is still erratic.

"You were lucky that all you bought yourself was a little edging. Next time, I'll tie you to the bed and edge you until the need is wound so tight, it's unbearable. I'll be merciless," he adds just above a whisper.

There's an eerie calmness about him as the threats emerge, one after another, each more lethal than the last.

"A manipulation is no better than a lie. In many ways, it's worse. If you *ever* try to manipulate me again, I'll toss you to the guards and let them have at you. When they've had their fill, they'll take you deep into the caves and drop you into a real prison. The accommodations are far less luxurious than here."

I sit up and grab my shawl to cover myself. My eye catches the sparkle of my mother's locket, and shame floods me.

I'm a disaster. Sullied by his cum. So furious I could scream.

I can't stop the tears. They gush unrestrained. The sadness and anger and embarrassment. A whirling storm, tearing through me, leveling every wall I've erected to protect myself.

He tosses my shirt at me. "Clean yourself up."

I'm shaking uncontrollably. "You are a despicable human being."

"I am." He steps closer, almost in my face. "How does it feel to have begged a despicable human being to fuck you? I'm guessing not so good."

He starts toward the door, then turns. "And don't barter with your body like a common whore. It's beneath you."

Something inside me shrivels and dies. And, for a fleeting moment, I want the rest of me to die with it. *No, Daniela. You're a survivor.*

I hold the shawl against me, shielding my nakedness from him.

"My body is all I have to barter with, you bastard. You've taken everything else from me. *Everything*," I screech, my voice shaking as much as my hands.

Antonio stops short of the doorway, but he doesn't turn to face me. It's as though he's waiting for me to hurl more vitriol at him before he leaves. But I have nothing left. I'm empty. Shell-shocked by his behavior.

After a few moments of silence, he squares his shoulders and walks out, leaving me on the table with the rest of the leftovers.

27

ANTONIO

My damn phone has gone off three times in the last fifteen minutes, but I was too busy *teaching Daniela a lesson* to even glance at it.

What a fucking joke. If anyone got schooled tonight, it was me.

When my mouth was on her pussy, I didn't give a damn who was on the phone, or whether the world around me was imploding. All I cared about were her whimpers and moans, and the way she trembled when I licked her wet, pink flesh.

At least I didn't shove my dick into her like she wanted. *After I promised I wouldn't fuck her.* I was half a second away from burying myself balls-deep inside her. *After I promised, repeatedly, that I wouldn't.*

She said she didn't care about the promise. Maybe not today. But one day, when it matters, she'd remember I wasn't strong enough to keep my promise to her.

If I had half a goddamn brain, first thing in the morning, I'd put her on a plane, send her back to the US, and be done with her.

"What?" I growl when Lucas answers.

"About fifteen minutes ago, we learned that an ambulance was on its way to Abel Huntsman's house. It's there now. Thought you'd want to know."

Christ. "What happened?"

"Not entirely sure. Sounds like he had a stroke. We'll have more information once the EMTs are outside the house."

We don't have surveillance inside my uncle's house. It's swept regularly, and if we were caught, it would be World War III—or worse.

"I'm on my way to the villa. Cristiano with you?"

"Yeah. We're here for the duration."

I disconnect the call and head to the garage, where Thiago is waiting.

This night just keeps getting better and better.

Dinner was a roller-coaster ride. One minute, Daniela was all excited about a vintage year for the valley, and the next, we were at each other's throat about a feckless pussy named Josh.

I don't give a shit about her having sex with Josh. *Not really.* Although I'm beginning to think it bothers me more than it should.

I didn't expect Daniela to be a virgin. It's important to some men in our culture, mainly the older men, but not to me. I was fourteen the first, and last, time I popped a cherry. *Clara Freitas.* She was sixteen. I wasn't a virgin, but my experience had been with whores—women my father paid to make me a man.

Before we were even dressed, Clara invited me to have dinner with her family. "How about Sunday then?" she asked after I declined the first invitation.

"You're a nice girl, but I don't want to have dinner with your family. I'm not looking for a girlfriend."

She started to cry, with the wet blood still smeared on her thighs. There wasn't a lot of blood, but mixed with semen it looked like someone had been hurt. And they had been.

"You took something from me that I only had to give once," she

said, sobbing. "It's gone forever. Why would you take something of such value that you only wanted for a few minutes?"

She wasn't wrong, and I didn't like the way it made me feel.

Even as a teenager, playing with virgins was unnecessary. There were plenty of experienced girls—and later, women—who were willing to let me into their beds for the night. And when they wanted more, they were better equipped to shoulder the disappointment—because there was never more.

I've never lied to a woman to get her into bed, or promised anything I didn't deliver. That includes Clara Freitas. But I've stayed clear of innocents ever since that afternoon with her. *It's not worth the hassle.*

No, it's not important that Daniela's not a virgin. It would complicate our situation even more.

What is important, what has me so pissed off I could gut someone, is that she tried to play me like I'm a chump. Manipulations and lies are fraternal twins, each carrying the same deceitful gene.

She can't be trusted. Plain and simple.

It might be my problem, but it's about to become her problem too—and she's not going to like it.

I fucked up tonight. Let my personal needs take precedence over my business. Something I never do. I should have responded the first time my phone went off—or at least glanced at it, for Chrissakes.

The worst part is that I knew there was a problem—no one who has my number would call and text three times in the span of fifteen minutes unless there was an issue. *A huge issue.*

What if it had been a cargo problem, or another emergency that needed my immediate attention?

The stakes are too high for too many people. I can't afford to be distracted by pussy. Not even a sweet one that quivers deliciously on my tongue.

28

ANTONIO

"Any news?" I ask as soon as I set foot in the villa.

"They called the priest," Cristiano says soberly.

It's not that he gives a shit whether my uncle lives or dies, but every time a major player dies, the ground shifts, and things in the valley become unstable—and dangerous. I hate my uncle, too, but he's a big player in our world.

"We're sure it's Abel?"

"We have eyes on the hospital, inside and out. It's definitely him."

"Tomas?"

"He went in the ambulance with your uncle."

Sucking his cock, I'm sure.

"I'm going to call Rafael." I turn to Cristiano. "Contact Luis. Have him get the plane ready for a quick trip to London and back."

"When do you want the flight to leave Porto?"

"As soon as possible. I want Rafa here before the sonofabitch dies. Abel's taken plenty from that kid, but he's not taking away his right to say his piece while the old man is still breathing."

Rafa came to live with me a few years after his mother disappeared. He has dyslexia, and instead of getting him the instruction he needed, his father beat him for being stupid. He pummeled him at every turn. As far as Abel was concerned, the kid couldn't do anything right. Although it's as likely Rafa was punished because he was my aunt's favorite. She loved both her boys, but Rafael was the baby.

Things got so bad that my mother decided to petition for custody. I couldn't allow it. The last thing I needed was for her to get caught in the crosshairs. My uncle wouldn't hesitate to kill her. He'd already murdered one Adriano girl. He wasn't going to kill her sister too. Not while I still had a pulse. Besides, she'd already raised one asshole. She didn't need to raise another.

Breaking the news to Rafael is the last thing I want to do right now. I don't care how much of a monster Abel is—he's still Rafa's father. It doesn't matter how cold your blood runs. It still affects you when your father takes his last breath—for good or bad.

"Hey, old man," Rafael teases when he answers the phone. He doesn't really sound surprised to hear from me. We talk by phone or video-chat at least once a week. He'd prefer to text, but I won't allow it. You can't tell shit about how someone's doing from a text.

"I'm shocked you aren't tucked between the covers with some warm milk," he adds with a snort. "It's long past your bedtime."

I roll my eyes. "I'm happy to meet you in the gym, anytime, anywhere, my friend. Mano a mano."

He always laughs, but he's yet to take me up on it. That's how I know I'm still on top.

"Do you think we can catch up tomorrow? I'm kind of busy right now."

"I have bad news. It can't wait."

I hear him suck in a breath. "What's wrong?" There's genuine concern in his voice. *Empathy*. "You okay?"

My chest swells. I'm not proud of many things I've done in my life, but I'm proud of the young man I helped raise.

"I'm fine." I pause, deciding the best way to break the news. *There isn't one.*

"Your father suffered a stroke. I don't know much else, except that they've called a priest. The last rites aren't administered at the drop of a hat. They must be reasonably certain he's going to die."

Rafael doesn't miss a beat. "Shit happens."

There's no empathy now. I can't say that I blame him. But this is not how it's going to play out.

"That's it? Your father's dying, and that's all you have to say?"

"Pretty much. I've got a hot babe in my bed, and she misses me. I'll catch you la—"

"Don't you dare hang up."

"Cut me a break."

"Tuck your dick back into your pants and get rid of the babe. You need to come home. Tonight."

"Why?" he asks defiantly.

"Because he's your father, and you need to go and see him. The plane's on its way to London."

"Don't waste the fuel. I'm not getting on that plane."

"You *are* getting on that plane. And you *are* going to that hospital. Because you're a man, and sometimes men are required to do things that are unpleasant." My voice is even, but firm. I give Rafa a lot of rope now that he's a young man, but this is nonnegotiable.

"He's your father. You need to make some kind of peace—for yourself. I don't care what you say to him, but you do it while he's alive. Otherwise, you'll regret it someday."

"Do you regret not making peace with your father?"

Oh, I made my peace with that sonofabitch. "We only know how we'll feel with the benefit of hindsight. Then it's too late."

"Tonio—you're my father. My real father. The only one I need."

I would be honored to be the kid's father. But I'm not. I'm his cousin. His guardian. But I don't say any of it, because Rafa would see it as a rejection. And he's already had enough rejection to last ten lifetimes.

"The plane will be there in two hours. Plan on going straight to the hospital, unless he dies while you're en route."

"Forget it."

"Listen carefully," I say in a tone that I know will grab his attention. Rafael gets very quiet. "You're too damn old to be challenging me at every turn. It was fine when you were a kid, but you're not a kid anymore. If you ever expect to work for me, to be anywhere near my men, you'll learn to speak more respectfully."

"I would never disrespect you in front of anyone," he assures me with great sincerity. I believe him. "This is you and me. Like it's always been. Family. *Real* family."

I don't say any more, because I want him to feel like he can come to me about anything—say anything. But he needs to be respectful.

"Is my brother with him?"

"I believe so. I'll send a couple of my men to meet the plane when it lands back in Porto, and you have guards with you. This isn't a good time to have a showdown with Tomas, but you don't need to put up with any shit from him either."

For a few seconds, I contemplate telling him I'll go along so he doesn't have to face those bastards alone. It would be the easiest way to manage the situation—for both of us. But easy doesn't mean good. If I go with Rafael, he'll think I don't have faith in him to take care of business, and he'll start to lose confidence in himself. We worked too damn hard to rebuild the confidence his father stole from him for me to throw it away now.

"What am I supposed to say to a dying man who I hate with every fiber of my being?" he demands. "*'I hope you rot in hell for murdering my mother and spreading filthy lies about her running off with another man.'* Is that what I'm supposed to say, Antonio?"

My heart clenches for the tortured little boy I hear in his voice.

"If that's what you want to say, say it. This visit isn't for him. It's for you. It doesn't matter what words you use. None of it matters. He can't hurt you anymore."

I don't regret the words, but in my soul I know they're a lie. Bad genes follow you forever. Boys who grow up with abusive fathers, without a lick of honor, suffer for a lifetime. That's the truth. It's my truth, just like it's Rafael's, but there's no way in hell I'm sharing that with him.

"Send the babe home. Pack a bag and get on the plane. Plan to stay a few days. I miss your ugly face, and there's someone staying at the house I want you to meet."

"What, you got yourself a live-in babe?" He snickers, like it's a far-fetched idea.

"Something like that."

"I was kidding. You serious?"

"We'll talk when you get home."

29

ANTONIO

After we say goodbye, I toss my phone aside and run my fingers through my hair. Between Daniela and Rafa, my balls have been busted pretty good today.

"You're going to introduce Daniela to him?" Cristiano asks, looking up from his laptop.

"I don't want to wait any longer to tell him that we're adding another member to the family. He'll keep it quiet."

"I'm not worried about him. What about her? She gave me an earful the other day."

I rub my hands over my face. I've tried to teach Rafa that women aren't objects put on Earth to satisfy men's needs. And now I have this woman staying in my house—against her wishes. I wouldn't put it past Daniela to spill her guts to him. Not that he could do a damn thing to help her.

Maybe I'll do a little bartering.

"How are we doing with a phone for Daniela?"

Lucas lifts a phone off his desk. "All set. Safeguards are in place. You want it?"

"Yeah."

He tosses it over.

"How did dinner go?"

I glare at Cristiano. "The house is still standing. But that's only because she'd never risk Victor getting hurt."

How did dinner go?

Daniela's torn—about everything. I felt the indecision swirling inside her all night. She sent nothing but mixed signals—hot, cold, happy, angry...sometimes within the span of seconds. The only time she wasn't battling was when my hands and mouth were on her.

She'd deny it vehemently, but she kissed me, dug her fingers into my shoulders, and let her tongue tangle with mine. She swayed into my cock, grinding her pussy against the bulge until it took everything I had not to sink my dick into her. But when she bucked off the table, hair matted to her damp skin, eyes unfocused, whimpering my name, that's when I knew it was more than just a deal for her. She can pretend if it helps her sleep at night, but she wanted me as badly as I wanted her.

But even with combustible chemistry, getting her to the altar is going to be hell.

"Did you learn anything about why she left?" Lucas is hyper-focused on this. He believes it has something to do with the bastard who ran me off the road the day I visited her. I don't agree. It was too much for someone to coordinate in the course of a visit. I wasn't there long enough to put something like that in motion.

"I didn't learn a thing about it. At least nothing I believe. But I'm not sure it matters much anymore."

"Loose ends. I hate them," Lucas grouses.

"Anything new from the hospital?"

"He's stable, but it's not looking good."

"We need to put out some feelers and take the temperature. As word starts to leak, there's going to be some jockeying."

"Already on it."

"Tomas still at the hospital?"

"Yep."

My uncle is the brains behind their entire operation. He never handed over any of the reins, because he knew his oldest son is an idiot.

"We need to keep tabs on Tomas. He thinks he's a fucking genius, but no one else believes that. Someone will approach him and offer him what looks like a sweet deal."

"The Russians," Cristiano says soberly.

"That's exactly what I'm thinking. But I don't rule out the Camorra. Either way, we can't let it happen."

The Camorra are well entrenched in Porto, as are the Georgians, but they're small contingencies that rarely cause us heartburn. The Russians, on the other hand, want a foothold along the Atlantic within easy reach of our European neighbors, and of the US. They can talk a good game, but they don't give a damn about our Port, or what the industry means to the people who live along the Douro.

The region will implode if they get their tentacles into the valley.

30

ANTONIO

"Hey," Rafael chirps, sauntering into my office. He seems more at ease than he was on the phone last night. Probably because the hospital visit is behind him.

"Rafa." I come around the desk and embrace him. He's my height, a man, but a part of me will always think of him as a boy.

"How did things go at the hospital?" I ask, motioning for him to take a seat in front of the desk. I sit in the chair beside him, angling it so I can see his face. Rafael has a habit of making light of anything that causes him heartache, but his eyes don't lie.

"It pretty much sucked. Right up there with having my wisdom teeth out—if they hadn't given me anesthesia." He throws his head back, closing his eyes.

I don't say anything. I sit patiently, waiting for the pain to tumble out.

"I didn't feel a thing, Antonio. *Nothing.* Not even hatred anymore. He was so pathetic lying there. Just a feeble old man. I can move past the way he treated me, but I'll never forgive him for what he did to my mother. He deserves no mercy. Not from God. Not from anyone."

No, he doesn't.

"Did you see your brother?" I ask when the silence feels too heavy.

"Yeah. He's still an asshole."

"He is. But that should never stop you from doing what you need to do. I'm proud of you for going to the hospital."

He grabs a ball of rubber bands off my desk. "*Pfft.* So what's all this about a babe in residence?"

He's done baring his soul. Now the ball's in my court.

I take a deep breath, sit back, and stretch out my legs, trying to make this appear casual and light. I don't want to add any more weight to his shoulders.

"I'm getting married in a month. The bride has moved to the top floor. I don't think she'll cramp your style, but don't parade around bare-assed outside your suite."

It takes a lot to shut Rafa up. But it's hard to form words when your jaw's on the floor.

"*Whoa.* Back up, stud muffin. *Bride?* You're getting married? Did hell freeze over?"

I chuckle. "Probably. And yes, I'm getting married."

"This is kind of sudden, don't you think? I didn't even know you were seeing anyone. Why am I just hearing about this?" His antennae are up, and he looks a bit slighted.

"You didn't hear about it because, unlike you, I don't kiss and tell. But it wasn't sudden. We were betrothed more than six years ago, and it's time."

He flops back in the chair. "*Dude.* I'm sorry."

"Why?" I probe, even though I know the answer.

"*Betrothed* is just a fancy term for arranged."

"In our world, yes. But the arrangement wasn't made for me. I was a party to the agreement."

He nods and is quiet for several seconds, as though he's processing the new information. "Is she hot? Do I know her?"

"First, I suggest if you want to stay on my good side, you don't refer to my fiancée as hot. Second, yes, I'm sure you know her—or at least know who she is."

"I'm getting gray here waiting for her name."

With every person I tell, it becomes more real. *It is real. Like it or not, you're marrying her. I am, and if she'd just behave, I wouldn't even mind.*

"Rafa, I'm sharing this with you because you're an important part of my life. Other than Cristiano and Lucas, no one else knows this information. And no one can know until I'm ready to divulge it."

He snickers, making light of the moment. It's what he does when he's nervous or uncomfortable. "What, did you kidnap the president's daughter?"

Not quite—but damn close. "I want your word."

"You don't need to worry about me. I'd take a bullet for you, man."

"I don't need you to take a bullet. Just keep your mouth shut."

"You can trust me."

"I know." I meet his prying gaze. "I'm marrying Daniela D'Sousa."

Rafael's eyes widen, and he whistles long and low. "*Wow.* The D'Sousa *princesa*." He shakes his head. "Isn't she a little young for you?"

I glare at him, and he lifts both hands, palms facing me. "No judgments. I just remember her as an annoying little kid."

"She's older than you."

"Barely." He laughs. "She finally got her hooks in you."

I don't think she sees it quite that way.

"She's always been into you."

He has my complete attention. "What are you talking about?" I ask carefully.

"Daniela and her friends. They would always come up to me and ask, *Is Antonio in Porto? Is he coming to the feast? Have you seen him?*" He grimaces. "God, they were so annoying. The boys and I would say, *Yeah, he's here*. We would tell them that even if you were out of the country. One of us would say, *I saw him earlier near the rides*. Or something like that. They would walk around in circles, for hours, looking for you."

I sit back in the chair and feel the smile bloom—inside and out. Just thinking about the little mouthy hellion—who last night acted like she could barely stand the sight of me—stalking my every move makes me laugh.

"She finally snagged you, huh?"

"That's one way of looking at it. Although now that she has me, I think she'd like to throw me back." My tone is playful, but the words ring true.

"That's women for you," he says, shaking his head, like he's an expert. "So you haven't told your mom?"

"No. Not yet. And if you talk to her, keep your mouth shut."

"She'll be ecstatic. Maria Rosa was one of her best friends. My mom's too," he adds quietly.

My mother will be many things, but ecstatic isn't one of them. There's nothing I can do about it. She'll have to deal with it, like everyone else.

"Alma and Victor don't know?"

"Victor isn't stupid, but he would never ask. If Alma knew, my mother would know."

"Is that why Daniela's staying in the valley, to keep her away from Alma?"

"That, and we're not married."

His eyes light up, and his shoulders begin to shake. "Yes, because you wouldn't want to have sex with someone you're not married to," he taunts. "Tell me, Antonio, what does it feel like to be a virgin in the twenty-first century?"

Little bastard. "It's not about me. It's about respect. She's not like some *babe* you handcuff to your bed. She's going to be my wife. Not that what happens between Daniela and me is any of your damn business."

"I'm just giving you a hard time," he mutters sheepishly, dropping the rubber bands on my desk. "Is the wedding going to be a big shindig?"

I shake my head. "Small. We'll have a big celebration at some point. Maybe in the fall, after the harvest." He leans over and ties his shoe. I wait until he's done before continuing. "I'm hoping you'll stand at my side in the church, with Cristiano and Lucas."

All the teasing disappears, replaced by a wave of emotion so enormous it touches my soul.

"I would be honored." His voice catches as it fades away. "More honored than you can imagine," Rafael murmurs, almost under his breath.

This is more than standing with me as a best man. It's elevating him publicly in the eyes of everyone in the church—and beyond, because everything that happens in that church will filter out into the valley. It's a cherished spot for a kid who spent too long wondering if he had any value aside from being a punching bag.

"How long are you staying?"

"I have exams." He shrugs. "I need to get back to school tomorrow—or the next day."

"Let's have dinner together tonight. You can meet Daniela as an adult and see if she's still annoying."

31

DANIELA

Before I went to bed, I left a note for Victor explaining that it was late and not to expect me before lunch. I still don't have an appetite, but I promised I'd come down for a midday meal. Fortunately, I don't have to worry about running into Antonio. He left after he was done with me last night.

I have to be more cautious around him. Smarter and more calculated. I need to remember that even when my old feelings for him creep in, he doesn't share any of them. *He never did.*

He's planning to marry me—and use me for sex when there's no one better available. I don't care what he says. He's not looking for a real marriage. He wants to fulfill his end of a grand bargain.

Yes, he'll buy me pretty clothes and jewels, and all the trappings of a luxurious life. *A lonely, empty life.* Even if it wasn't *his* family who killed my mother, it's not a life I would ever choose. Not even with a handsome man who plays my body like a master.

I need to get out of here before we take vows. Escaping after we're married might be easier, but it will embarrass him. He'll never stop hunting me once I have a ring on my finger.

The clock ticks louder with each passing day, but I'm no closer to leaving.

I shut the suite door, praying that somehow the tide will turn in my favor. I'm due. *Long past due.*

As I take the stairs to the kitchen, I hear some laughter and stop to look out the open window on the second-floor landing. There are several people—staff—milling around and having lunch, or a cigarette break. Paula's there, too, sitting on the tailgate of a truck bed. Her feet are dangling as though she doesn't have a care in the world, laughing with a young man about her age.

It reminds me a little of the dinner breaks we took at my night job. We would gather outdoors when it was warm, relaxing for thirty minutes before it was time to go back to mopping and scrubbing. I won't miss the work, but I'll miss my colleagues and the shared camaraderie.

As I continue down the stairs, I can't stop thinking about the people outside.

This place feels so formal, not just the decor, but there's a stodgy air about it. A stark contrast to the playfulness outside.

Victor has run a household for ages. He's polished, but there's also a bit of fun about him. Everyone else I've encountered who works in the house, including Paula, is reserved and cautious. Maybe it's just around Antonio—*and me.*

"*Bom dia, senhora,*" Victor says brightly, as I enter the kitchen. "You're looking well."

"*Bom dia*, Victor."

"Where would you like to have your coffee? The breakfast room is normally what I'd recommend, but it's being painted."

"Would you mind if I had lunch in here?"

"Mind? It would be a pleasure," he says, motioning for me to have a seat at an elegant quartz counter with a thick beveled edge.

"I'm so sorry about dinner last night." I apologize as he

places a small vase of flowers to my left. When I glance at his face, there are no dark circles under his eyes, or any other sign of missed sleep, which makes me somewhat relieved. *But still.* "I ruined your evening and made you work much later than necessary."

"Nonsense." He waves his hand, dismissing my concerns. "I enjoy a little life around here. Now that Rafael's away studying, the house is quiet, like a mausoleum with so many lovely things to look at, but not much of a soul."

Soulless. That sounds about right.

"On my way downstairs, I noticed that there were picnic tables and a couple of trucks outside. The staff were having lunch and seemed to be enjoying themselves."

He tips his head to the side. "Right below the staircase on the second floor?"

I nod. "Yes."

Victor grins and shakes his head. "As soon as the weather permits, they're outside every day. Young fools. Although not all of them are so young," he says, smiling wistfully. "But they're all foolish."

"I don't understand."

"Start with this," Victor says, setting down a plate of melon slices, strawberries, and fresh cheese. "It's light and will prepare your stomach for something heavier."

"Thank you." I glance at him before taking a sip of coffee. "Are you going to tell me why they're foolish?"

"There's no surveillance in that small area. That's why they're huddled together."

My heart stops. I place the cup back on its saucer, with a small tremor in my hand. "They think there's no surveillance, or there isn't?" *I have to know.*

He shakes his head. "There isn't. But it wasn't an oversight, like they imagine. When the spy lived here, he set up the security system that way. In an emergency, even if the system was breached from the outside, he could escape the property undetected. When Antonio bought the house, he left it that way on purpose."

Complex exit strategies that ensure safety are the price one pays for a glamorous life and unchecked power. "I guess when you have a lot of enemies, being able to leave under the cover of night is a good thing."

Victor chuckles. "You're a breath of fresh air. And just the woman Antonio needs in his life. I hope you'll stay awhile."

A sense of sadness creeps into my soul. Nothing to do with Antonio. I hate misleading Victor. *There's no other way.*

"Powerful men have formidable enemies," Victor continues. "But that's not why he left the area without cameras, and unguarded. Antonio grew up surrounded by a large household staff. He played with the children—Cristiano and Lucas are still his closest friends. His mother is very dignified, like yours was—she's always been that way. But Lydia Huntsman ran a warm, informal house. The boundaries between staff and the family were lax unless her husband was there. Antonio's father was more formal, more exacting, unforgiving." Victor's voice trails away.

I suspect he didn't have much affection for Hugo Huntsman. *Not difficult to imagine.*

"Antonio favors his mother," he continues. "He has his moments, as we all do, but by and large he treats the staff as though we're human, with human needs and dreams. When Rafael was living here, this"—he waves his arm around the room—"had the pulse of a home. Antonio insisted on it."

Victor freshens my coffee and places the pot back on the stove. "But even now, he's generous and fair, although he'd be upset if he knew I mentioned it. That area, outside, is where staff can have a smoke, share a kiss, or just laugh without the fear of being watched and judged. But to think that Antonio doesn't know about the lack of surveillance is simply ridiculous."

An area without surveillance. I could probably get there—if I'm allowed to go outside—but then what?

A phone rings, and Victor retrieves it from a countertop not far from the stove. It was there yesterday when I came into the kitchen too. It probably wouldn't be difficult to *borrow*, although it's probably password-protected. In some ways that's a relief. I don't want to steal from Victor.

But an unguarded location. *That might be my way out of here.*

After a few words with the caller, Victor hands me his phone and disappears without a word.

32

DANIELA

"Hello," I say softly.

I'm sure it's Antonio or Cristiano. Who else would it be? But I'm polite, in case it's someone who deserves my respect.

"Good morning." *Antonio.* "I trust you slept well?"

God, he's insufferable. "Considering your disgusting behavior last night, I'm surprised I slept at all. But so sweet of you to ask."

"Given your impertinence, I assume Victor's no longer in the room." He doesn't raise his voice, but his tone is threatening.

"That's correct."

"Abel Huntsman had a stroke last night. The doctors don't expect him to survive."

With any luck, he'll suffer plenty before the devil comes to claim him. I suppose I should extend some sort of condolence, but I can't bring myself to do it.

"My cousin Rafael is home from school for a day or two. He's on his way to the house. His room is also on the top floor. It's in a separate wing, but you might run into him. I didn't want you to be alarmed to see a stranger up there."

"Thank you for letting me know about Rafael. He was a young boy the last time I saw him, and I doubt I'd recognize him now."

"He'll be joining us for dinner tonight. I want the two of you to have some time to get reacquainted before the wedding."

The word *wedding* makes me bristle. But I'm grateful not to be alone with Antonio tonight. He'll be on better behavior if another person's there—even if that person is named Huntsman.

"What time is dinner?"

"Eight o'clock."

I half expect him to tell me to take a shower, but he doesn't—at least not yet.

"Daniela?"

Here it comes. "Yes?"

"Rafael has a lot on his plate, and he doesn't need anything more. He knows we're getting married, but he doesn't know the circumstances under which you're here, and even if he did, he couldn't help you."

Don't worry. I wouldn't waste a breath expecting Rafael Huntsman to help me.

"You'd like me to play the adoring fiancée? Is that what you're getting to?"

Antonio scoffs, and I expect a cutting retort, but there's only quiet on the other end. I'm starting to learn that he wields both a sharp tongue and looming silence as weapons. I'm not sure which is worse.

"I don't want any trouble tonight," he says finally. "Since you love deals so much, I'm going to offer you one."

Lucky me. I don't say anything.

"Do you want to hear it?"

I'm done with him and deals—or at least I should be. "I don't know. Do I?"

"If you can get through this evening without giving me heartburn, you can call Isabel in the morning."

The man is full of surprises. *Sometimes wonderful ones.* My pulse surges, and I sit back in my seat. *He's going to let me talk to them. Don't get too excited yet.*

"Do we have a deal?" he asks, knowing full well I'd never refuse.

"Valentina will be in school in the morning. I'd like to video-chat later in the day, when I can speak to both of them. And I don't want there to be a time limit on the call."

"Then you better be on your best behavior, because you want a lot of things. But I'll agree to it, *if* you behave."

You're going to have to do better than an off-the-cuff agreement. "I want your word."

"Why? Will you ruin the evening if I don't make the promise?"

"You claim to be a man who honors his word." I pause for a breath. "And if you change your mind, or if this is a game, or some sort of punishment to break me . . ." My heart twists. "I don't think I can take another blow, Antonio. I need your word."

He's quiet again. Although this time the silence feels more contemplative than punishing. I just handed him another weapon to use against me, but it's true. My psyche is fragile.

"I don't want to break you. As infuriating as you can be, I admire your grit. Your resiliency. Your courage. The way you take a punch and throw it right back." He pauses for a beat. "What I want is for you to come to terms with our arrangement, like I have. I want you to accept it, and maybe one day embrace it. I want you to learn to obey without every second being a struggle. Your safety depends on it."

"My safety?" The most pressing threat to my safety is him—but he's not the only threat. I don't kid myself about that.

"We both know your father wouldn't have given you to me if he didn't believe you were in danger. No question, it might have simply been the mounting worries of a dying man. But it's unclear, because he refused to elaborate. I don't claim to know what was in his heart."

"Protecting the vineyards was in his heart. Not protecting me. Don't kid yourself." The hurt is woven into every word—each syllable raw and aching, laying my pain bare for him to weaponize. I need to learn to keep my mouth shut.

"There were other ways to protect the vineyards. He could have chosen any one of them. Your father loved you," Antonio says, gently, his humanity bleeding through. "He made that clear at every opportunity, Daniela. Don't ever doubt it." His tone is tender, akin to a warm embrace.

I don't know what moves me most. His words about my father's love, or Antonio putting aside his stern demeanor, trying to lift my spirits.

It feels wrong to take advantage of his mood. The rare compassion should be nurtured, if it will ever be expected to grow. But I have other responsibilities, and I can't worry about his soul. I need all my energy to fight for my own soul.

"There is something additional I'd like included in the deal."

33

DANIELA

"Don't get too greedy, *Princesa*."

There's no bite in his tone, so I forge ahead. "I'd like to take a walk outside. Get to know the grounds a bit, and breathe some fresh air."

"Nothing's stopping you from going outside, as long as you stay away from the vineyards. The workers there are more likely to recognize you. Very few people know you're here, and aside from Victor, no one knows your last name. They'll eventually put it together, but by then it won't matter."

This is your problem, not mine. If I see someone I know, they might be willing to help me escape. *No one's going to risk his ire to help you.* "I don't care who knows I'm here."

"You should care. You're at some risk until we're married. You may leave the house, but if you do anything to call attention to your identity, you'll have to deal with me—and you won't like it."

The biggest risk to my safety is you. "Fine. But I want to take a walk without guards following me like I'm a criminal."

He doesn't say no immediately, but I can tell he's not excited about the prospect of me roaming the grounds alone.

"My mother never had guards traipsing behind her in broad daylight while she was on our property. I doubt yours did either."

"Maybe you should use a different example. It didn't end well for your mother."

The acid churns in my stomach.

And whose fault is that? I re-bury the thought so it doesn't accidentally come out in a snit.

"There are military instillations that aren't as heavily guarded as this place. How about if I walk with Paula? I'm sure she'll report back if I commit some sin." The last part comes out surlier than intended.

"That's fine. But you're asking for a lot for someone who hasn't spread her legs for me."

The crass comment is Antonio's way of slapping me for my surliness, and it stings enough to make me blanch. But I cover the pain with sarcasm.

"I thought that's what I did last night."

"I'm quite sure that was for you, not for me. Although, next time, when you're not being a little manipulator, maybe it will end better for you."

Really? That's what you think?

"My mother never said a word against my father unless they were alone. When it was just the two of them, she had carte blanche to speak her mind."

"If you're going to complain about last night, save your breath. You got what you asked for. I went to the house with good intentions."

All good intentions went out the window the day you lured me across the ocean and imprisoned me.

"I'd like us to have the same understanding my parents had. Does that work for you?" I ask sweetly.

"Within reason. What is it you want to say that requires a pass?"

"The Americans have a term they like to use. I'm sure you heard it often when you studied there."

"The Americans have a lot of terms they like to use. Which one are you referring to?"

"Asshole." I draw the word out, being playful with my tone. But I'm not playing. I can't allow all his behavior to go unchecked. If I knew I could escape tomorrow, I could tolerate anything. But I might be here for a long time, and I won't let him degrade me until I'm completely destroyed.

Antonio doesn't respond immediately, so it's impossible to know what he's thinking. I take a sip of coffee while I wait to see if he's angry or amused.

"You never told me, *Princesa*. What do you fantasize about when you stroke your pussy? Tell me."

I have my answer. He wants to embarrass me. He expects me to call him a pig. But he's going to get a dose of truth instead.

"For the last six years, I've shared a room with a little girl. I worked two jobs and picked up extra shifts when I could. There weren't many opportunities for self-exploration, especially in the last year. I think you saw to that when you made my life harder than it needed to be. Not everyone lives in a castle with lavish amounts of privacy."

"Pity."

It's an obnoxious reply, but from the tone it's clear I took some of the wind out of his sails.

"If my lack of sexual experience doesn't appeal to you, let me go, and find someone who enjoys your filth."

"I think you enjoy my filth," he murmurs. "You were aroused last night, soaking wet, and the filthier it got, the more aroused you became. What you need is permission to be a dirty, dirty girl, and a lover who knows how to coax it from you. You need a man who knows how to satisfy needs you don't even know you have."

I've had a man who knew how to satisfy my needs. It's on the tip of my tongue, but I don't say it. It's not true, and he'll sense it. But more important, Antonio is not above having Josh murdered.

"Don't you have an empire to run?"

I can almost picture his smug little smile. "I do. Not now, but at some point we need to discuss the wedding."

"You were vague when I asked yesterday, but what kind of timeline are you imagining?"

"A few weeks. A month, perhaps. But it's more than an imagining. It's a certainty."

For you, maybe. I won't be here.

34

DANIELA

Armed with the information Victor gave me at lunch, I spend the better part of the afternoon planning an escape, with an occasional trip to the second-floor window to conduct reconnaissance.

I have a few euros left, and one hundred and four American dollars. Although it won't take me far, it's a lot more money than I normally carry. I also have a US government-issued ID. But no passport or phone. Cristiano confiscated them at Moniz's office. Fortunately, he didn't take my purse. Otherwise, I'd have no money either.

The passport is the biggest problem. I can buy a burner phone once I'm out of here, but passports are harder to come by.

I caress the antique locket hanging between my breasts, letting my fingertip trace the tiny hinge. My mother wore it near her heart, too, with a picture of her mother tucked into the left side, and a picture of me on the right.

I unclasp the solid gold charm and open it carefully. After she died, I slipped *Mamai*'s picture inside, over my grandmother's.

In the last few years, when money got tight, I sold all my jewelry, and with a heavy heart, most of my mother's. But I kept the locket, even though it would command a good price. My mother wore it all the time, and I couldn't bear to part with it. *I still can't.* Although I might not have a choice.

The knock at the door startles me, and I close the locket and tuck it inside my shirt. "Come in."

"Do you need anything?" Paula asks from the doorway.

"I don't. Thank you. But come sit with me for a few minutes. I could use the company."

Paula comes inside and sits at the edge of the love seat, like a timid fawn. Poor woman. She hasn't quite figured out how to be a personal maid, especially to someone like me, who's informal and doesn't need help at their beck and call.

"I saw you outside during lunch today, on the back of a truck with a young man."

The color drains from her face—all of it.

"It's okay. You're not in any trouble," I assure her. But she doesn't relax.

I feel terrible for bringing it up, and if I had any decency, I would stop questioning her. But I don't. *I can't.* That area, without cameras and guards, might be my best hope to get out of here, and she knows about it. I have to pick her brain, even if it makes me a despicable bitch.

"Is he your boyfriend?"

She nods.

I smile softly. "Is it a secret?"

She shrugs. "My mother knows about him, but not my father."

Ahh, of course. "Fathers are always the last to know. Right before husbands," I tease. But she doesn't laugh. Or smile, even.

"Paula, I'm not going to tell your father about him—or anyone else. You understand that, don't you?"

She nods, but it's not convincing.

"Then why is your face green, like you're about to vomit?"

Her shoulders shake gently as she begins to cry. I get up for a box of tissues and sit on the small sofa beside her.

Her father might be traditional, and strict about her boyfriends, but this is more than that.

"Please tell me what's wrong. Maybe I can help."

She balls a tissue between her hands. "I'm not allowed to date. When I worked in the tasting room, Raul and I saw each other all the time—but then I came here." Her shoulders roll forward as they slump. "Raul sometimes comes to have lunch with me."

"You don't need to be so nervous. That's what *amorzinhos* do. They do everything they can to be together." Not that I have much experience with the kind of love that makes sweethearts take risks. My relationship with Josh wasn't like that.

"Please don't tell—*Senhor* Huntsman. I beg of you."

"I won't say a word. But why would *Senhor* Huntsman care about you and Raul? I can't imagine he'd tell your father." Although Antonio certainly supports the misogyny of the old ways.

Her brow wrinkles. "It's not about my father." She pauses for a few seconds. Her hands tremble as she reaches for a fresh tissue. "Raul works in the vineyards. He's not supposed to be here. If *Senhor* Huntsman knows, he'll be fired—maybe worse." She starts to cry again, and I squeeze her hand. "He takes care of his mother and his brothers and sisters. Working at the vineyard pays well."

I can't believe I've pushed her to tears. If it weren't for Valentina and Isabel, I'd stop now, but I can't.

"I'll keep your secret. I promise. Please don't worry."

She sits quietly.

"Tell me about the area outside where everyone has lunch," I ask, hating myself as the words form on my tongue. "They seemed so happy and carefree. I'm jealous."

"What do you want to know?"

I shrug. "Are there people out there every day?"

"If it's not too cold or raining." She shakes her head. "Just at lunch. More in the summer."

"Who do the trucks belong to?"

"John and Carlos."

"Do they park them there all the time?"

She hesitates, glancing at me before she answers. "Usually. So that there's a place for everyone to sit. It's permitted. And they like to show off their big trucks. They treat them like children, covering the truck beds so they don't get dirty."

Covered truck beds? I smile.

"Do John and Carlos live on the property?"

"Carlos lives with his wife nearby. John lives in the city, but he only goes home on Fridays. Gas is expensive to come and go every day."

Fridays.

"I'd like to start taking walks, and I'd love if you came with me so that I don't get lost. Do you have time tomorrow?"

"Of course," she replies. "The property is so beautiful, especially now. The camellias are starting to bloom."

"I don't want to keep you from your work, but you have my promise that I'll take your secret with me to the grave."

She nods. "Thank you."

When the door clicks shut, I flop back on the sofa. *Friday.* I need to figure out how to hide in that truck on Friday without being seen. Tomorrow, when we go outside, I'll see if I can investigate a bit. Getting into John's truck will get me to Porto, which would be ideal, but even if it has to be Carlos's truck, at least I'll be out of this place.

But even if I can stow away, what then? I have no documents. I'll never be able to board a plane.

I can take a freighter from the docks. Melissa, at my old job, said she was saving money to do this. When Tori questioned her, she assured us it was a thing—in the US.

Do they do it here too?

There's another knock at the door. Paula must have forgotten something. Either that or she needs more reassurances.

"Come in," I call, standing and smoothing my skirt.

The door opens, and a young man is in the doorway. He's quite handsome, although he hasn't fully grown into his body.

"Hello," he says with a smile. "I'm Rafael Huntsman, and you don't look like a little girl anymore."

35

DANIELA

He has a disarming way about him, and I laugh. "Rafael. It's so nice to see you. I almost didn't recognize you without that FC Porto cap you always wore."

He chuckles. "It was signed by members of the championship team. Of course I always wore it." His grin spans from ear to ear. "You remember my hat?"

I nod. "I never saw you without it, except at Mass."

It's a little awkward, because although we know each other, it doesn't seem right to greet each other with a hug, or a kiss on each cheek, in the traditional way.

"Please come in. Have a seat."

"I won't stay long. I just came to say hello."

I don't know if it's because he's so much younger than Tomas and Antonio, or if it's because I remember him as a little boy, but Rafael doesn't scare me in the way his brother does. Maybe because he doesn't look much like him.

Rafael resembles Tomas, but only marginally. He favors his mother's side of the family more than the Huntsman side—like Antonio. Maybe that's why there was so much gossip about him being Antonio's son. *And his brother.* Unlike Antonio and the other Huntsmans, who have dark-brown eyes, Rafael's are crystal blue, like a pristine lake, and they sparkle with fun.

Antonio's eyes once sparkled with fun too.

Rafael makes himself comfortable in a chair near the windows. "I'm still having trouble imagining Antonio married —especially to you."

I open my mouth, pretending to be aghast. "Are you insulting me?"

"No," he replies with great exuberance. "Not at all."

"To be honest, I'm having trouble imagining it myself." *More than you'll ever know.*

He gazes at me, grinning again.

"Are you going to share what you're thinking?" I tease. "I can always use more reasons to smile."

"I was thinking about the last time I saw you. You were with your little girlfriends, looking for Antonio." He shakes his head. "Always looking for Antonio, like I was chopped liver."

Yes. I remember. It touches something inside me. "Those certainly were simpler times. But had I known that you would eventually take off that silly cap, and that all your teeth would grow in, I might have chased you instead."

He laughs. "I bet you never thought you'd end up here. Or maybe you did."

I dreamed about it, but in my dreams, I was a cherished bride, not a prisoner. *Oh God.* I hope he doesn't share the story with Antonio. *That's all I need.*

"Rafael, this is our little secret. Antonio doesn't need to know I was an infamous stalker in my youth."

His eyes twinkle, but he makes no promises.

"Where did you go?" he asks. "There was a lot of speculation when you left Porto."

"Across the Atlantic, to take care of family. My father had an aunt in Canada. She was old, and very sick." *It's mostly true. Although the family I was taking care of wasn't a Canadian aunt.*

He eyes me carefully, but doesn't press for more details.

"How long are you staying?"

"I leave tomorrow," he replies. "My exams start next week."

"As happy as I am to see you, I'm sorry you had to come home under these circumstances."

Rafael lifts a brow. "My father?"

I nod.

"Nothing to be sorry about. I'm not close to my father. We haven't spoken more than a few words in years." His chest expands as he draws a ragged breath. He might blow it off, but I don't believe the estrangement is as easy as he pretends. Especially now, with his father dying.

"Living with Antonio is the best thing that's ever happened to me," Rafael murmurs. "He's going to make a good father one day." Narrowing his eyes, he points a finger at me. "Don't you dare tell him I said it."

Good fathers are selfless, and loving. Rafael must have a low bar for what it means to be a good father.

"I need to get a workout in." He sighs, slapping his hands on his thighs.

As he stands, I notice his phone sticking out of his gym shorts. He's an adult—a man—I'm sure Antonio doesn't monitor his phone.

I stand on tiptoe and place a kiss on each cheek. "Thank you for stopping by."

"We'll talk more at dinner," he says softly.

Ask him, Daniela. Now!

"I know this is unusual, but would it be possible for me to borrow your phone?"

He tilts his head to the side, looking a bit surprised.

"I don't have a computer yet, and my phone service is unreliable. I'd like to check my email."

"Sure. You can use it, but I can lend you my computer, if you prefer."

"The phone is fine. I promise I won't snoop."

"Not too worried." He hands it to me. "I'll stop by on my way back from the gym to get it. The password is V-E-R-A."

I almost gasp. *Vera. His mother.* My heart clenches.

Sadness creeps into Rafael's face the moment he realizes I made the connection. All I see is the little boy with his soccer cap and missing front teeth, crying for his mother—like it was yesterday. I reach over and touch his arm.

Vera Huntsman disappeared about a year and a half before my mother was murdered. Her husband claimed she ran off with a man, but I heard my parents talking one night when I was supposed to be in bed. My mother believed that Abel sent her away, or had her killed. An almost paralyzing fear gripped me, and I ran straight to my room and hid under the covers, as though I was next.

"Thank you," I murmur, clinging to the phone.

"Have fun," he says, his easy smile back.

"I promise to leave a little money in your bank account."

"If Antonio trusts you enough to bring you into his house, I can trust you too."

When he leaves, I collapse with my back against the door.

Get to work, Daniela.

36

ANTONIO

"Victor said you wanted to see me," Daniela says, sashaying into my office. "I hope this is about my call to Isabel. I more than upheld my end of the bargain during dinner with Rafael last night."

Much to my surprise, she did. Dinner couldn't have gone better. Anyone watching would have pegged us for a loving family or caring friends sharing a meal.

"Good morning. Even when the door's open, people normally knock before they barge in."

Her hair is in a high ponytail, and she's wearing black lounge pants that drape over her hips in a way that makes my cock take notice.

"You can borrow this computer." I hand her a brand new laptop that will eventually be hers. "It's all set up to video-chat with Isabel. Cristiano thought the larger screen would make the chat more enjoyable."

"Thank you," she says earnestly.

"You can sit at the conference table. I won't bother you."

Daniela stands in the center of the room with her body

rigid and her mouth open. "You're going to be here, listening, while I talk to them?"

"I am. And the conversation will be on a slight delay. You won't notice it, but if you say anything about your situation, the call will end without any goodbyes, and you'll lose the privilege to have another."

She clutches the computer to her chest and starts toward the table. "You can listen all you want. You can't steal my joy."

"I'm not trying to steal your joy," I say quietly.

She mutters something under her breath, but I don't call her on it.

"I realize this isn't easy on you, Daniela, but it's a complicated situation. I'm juggling a lot of balls, and keeping them in the air the only way I know. I'm sorry you have to bear the brunt of it."

She stops in the center of the room with her back to me, as if waiting for more. Some part of me wants to tell her more. But I'm not sure how. Other than Cristiano and Lucas, and one or two others, I don't confide in anyone about business matters. There's too much at stake—*that's precisely why you need to read her in. Maybe.*

"As I've told you, no one knows that Quinta Rosa do Vale is mine. The moment word gets out that you're here, it will begin to dawn on my competitors that they need to act quickly if they want a chance at the vineyards. The stakes, and the risks, become enormous then—not just for you and me, but for the entire valley. I need to control the flow of information for as long as possible. I expect you to cooperate."

Daniela turns to face me, still embracing the computer.

"All that surveillance you had on me for so many years—it was all a huge waste of money. Because you didn't learn a thing about me. Not anything of importance, anyway. I would never breathe a word about my situation to Valentina—or Isabel.

They would be sick with worry. Do you think I want that? Everything I do is for them. They're my family."

For a few long moments, we lock eyes. Daniela keeps her head up, and the courage she exudes as she probes under my skin is something to behold.

She pivots without another word and walks to the far end of the table, where she goes to some trouble to set up the computer so that she doesn't have to look at me, and so that I can't see the screen. It makes me smile.

She earned this call, and she can have it any way she wants, for as long as she likes. That was the agreement.

Last night went smoother than I ever thought possible. Rafael likes her, and she seemed to genuinely like him too. He went to meet friends at a club after we finished dinner, and invited Daniela to tag along. No such invitation was extended to me. I've played the parent for too long to be invited to the party.

"Come with me," he said to her before he left. "My friends will love you." He was talking to Daniela but side-eyeing me for a reaction.

I cleared my throat, but I couldn't hide the amusement. Nothing would make me happier than for the two of them to be close. Rafael could use a soft touch to temper my firm one. I was confident that she wouldn't go. I'm not exactly sure why, but I knew she'd say no.

"You're not married to the old man yet," he goaded. "There's time for one more fling."

She laughed. "I'm not much of a party girl. I'd just spoil your fun."

The entire exchange was good-natured, and tongue in cheek. But it reminded me that she was young, actually closer in age to Rafael than she was to me. Although she's so much more mature than him.

It also reminded me that although I had let her go to the US to spread her wings and enjoy herself, she hadn't had any fun. At least not the kind that I had imagined for her.

The joyful cries from across the room pull me from my morose thoughts.

"Lala!" a young girl shrieks through the computer.

"Valentina, my love. I've missed your sweet face. I can't wait to hug you to pieces."

Daniela's voice is filled, *filled*, with emotion. I don't know what I expected, but the unrestrained passion slays me.

I don't catch what Isabel says because I'm staggered by the pure joy and happiness I hear in Daniela. It's almost crippling.

What the fuck am I doing keeping her here? She'll never belong to me the way she belongs to them. And she'll resent me for every second of her life.

Grow some balls. This is the way it has to be.

What I still don't fully understand is the extent of her loyalty—and her love for them. The bonds between them. I don't get it.

Are Daniela and Isabel lovers? It's crossed my mind, but I've dismissed the thought each time.

They're discussing whether Valentina should be allowed to tweeze her eyebrows. The answer is a resounding *no*.

If I were a decent man, I'd give her some privacy. But I'm a selfish, greedy bastard, and the longer I listen, the greedier I get. The animated conversation gives me a glimpse of her that I've never seen, and I learn some things too.

Apparently, Daniela's a whiz at long division and knows how to conjugate French verbs. Blueberry crepes are her favorite breakfast, and she only eats the brown M&M's.

When Valentina tells her that some girls were mean to her and Jamie at lunch, Daniela tells her to ignore them. "*You're so much smarter and prettier than those girls. They're jealous, and they want to make you small and ugly like they are. But they can't, unless you let them. Don't let them steal your goodness.*"

Listen all you want. You won't steal my joy. I guess that's how she deals with me too—the ultimate bully.

Isabel and Daniela talk around the edges about paying bills and buying groceries. Isabel is anxious, but Daniela redirects the conversation whenever the hand-wringing starts. She might have helped raise Daniela, but it's clear that Daniela is the person in charge now.

Before they hang up, Valentina reminds her that they need to go shopping for a confirmation dress.

"Don't worry," Daniela assures her. "You'll have a gorgeous dress and a pair of new shoes to match. I haven't forgotten.

"I need to say goodbye now," she continues, the sorrow in her voice palpable. "I don't want to take advantage of my host."

Interesting. I didn't put a time limit on the chat, and it's unlikely she cares about taking advantage of *her host*. She's kept up a good front. Maybe she's taken all she can of the ruse. I think even Isabel has been assured that Daniela is safe and will be returning to the US soon.

"I miss you both so much."

Just one song, Valentina chirps, and starts singing, urging Daniela to sing too. And she does.

Her voice is sweet and slightly off-key as she dances in the chair.

"I'll call again as soon as I can. Isabel, answer your phone, even if you don't recognize the number. My service is spotty here, so I don't know what phone I'll be using."

After some kissy noises, the room gets deathly quiet.

I glance over at the conference table. Daniela's face is buried in her arms. I can't tell if she's crying.

I feel powerless, which is not a feeling I have often—or at all, anymore. There's always *something* I can do. But not about this.

There's nothing I can say or do to make this better, or to change her fate—or mine. It takes everything I have not to turn over my desk and stomp out of the room, destroying everything in my path.

After a few minutes, she gets up and walks out without a word.

My stomach burns with all the things I could have said but didn't.

And as if this day hasn't already been a fucking nightmare, I'm visiting my uncle this afternoon.

37

ANTONIO

"*Boa tarde*," I say in a clipped tone as I enter Abel Huntsman's hospital room.

"Good afternoon," Tomas replies, drawing out the greeting while he picks his jaw up off the floor.

"How is he?"

Tomas eyes me as though he's unsure how to respond. "It doesn't look good."

I don't extend any condolences, because I'm not sorry the bastard is on his deathbed. Instead, I nod and step over to the bed to assess the situation for myself.

"I'm surprised to see you here," he says, probing around the edges. What he really wants to say is, *What the fuck are you doing here?* But he doesn't have the balls.

I saw what I came to see and step away from the decrepit man in the hospital bed. Abel dying is a mixed bag. Tomas isn't capable of running the company, and it's going to cause a great deal of instability in the region, and perhaps an attempted power grab from outside. It has the potential to become a real thorn in my side.

"He's still my uncle," I reply sharply, not that I owe the

dumb fuck a response. "And even if he wasn't, I'm the president of the foundation. It's my job to make sure there are no wrinkles in this year's production."

Tomas taps his foot against the faux wood floor, not like he's jonesing to throw a punch, but like he's a nervous little bitch.

"Give us a moment, please," I tell the young nurse, fiddling with one of the wires attached to a monitor.

After she scurries out, I turn a hard gaze on my cousin.

"Do you need help running the company?"

If he were almost anyone else, I would broach the subject with more sensitivity. No one likes their competency called into question. And men, especially, hate asking for help.

"From you?" he scoffs. "I'm all set."

Bullshit. "What provisions are in place to secure Premier's holdings if he dies?"

"If you're asking if Rafael will get his hands on any of the property, the answer is *no*. Not the lodge, the vineyards, not a bottle of Premier Port, not a single goddamn grape. My father saw to that the day the little traitor went to live with you."

This is his little brother he's talking about. What an asshole.

"That's not what I'm asking. Rafael doesn't need a fucking thing from you. That time has long passed."

"No, he doesn't need us, because he has you to hold his hand and turn him into a huge pussy. I'm surprised you let him come to see my father without you. That must have been so hard. I bet you were chewing on your nails the whole time."

I take a step closer to Tomas, and he steps back, almost stumbling on a chair. There's nowhere to go without getting past me. We're the same age, but I'm taller and stronger. He's not going anywhere unless I let him.

"Rafael is a man. He doesn't need me to protect him from a sniveling coward who gets his little-girl feelings hurt at the drop of a hat."

After a few seconds, I step back, and he slithers into the

center of the room so he can't be boxed in again. *Yeah, that'll save you from me.*

"We're all set. Premier is on top, as always."

With my grandfather's blessing, my father took the Huntsman brand for himself. The Premier brand was left for Abel. But in his hands, Premier has never been the *premier* Port.

"Not on top," I say with all the smugness he deserves.

He opens his mouth as if to respond but then thinks better of it. "My father needs peace and quiet. It's time for you to leave. And you don't need to come back."

I glare at him from several feet away. "I come and go as I please. Always have. I don't recall ever needing your permission for anything."

He sneers.

"Any word on your mother?" I bring it up every time I see him, because I know it's like pouring salt into an open wound.

He buries his hands in his pockets. "No word."

"You still looking for her? Because I've got some good people on my team—the best. I'm happy to help. Offer still stands."

He shifts from one foot to the other. "My mother got involved in things she should have kept her nose out of. And then she ran off when she got caught."

"If you couldn't convince her to stay in her lane, it was your fucking job to protect her. She was your mother, and you let the bastard murder her. Or maybe you did it. Maybe you were so jealous of the way she fawned all over your baby brother that you killed her."

"She took off," he barks defiantly. "I don't know how many times I need to tell you that."

"It doesn't matter how often you repeat bullshit. It doesn't make it true. I don't believe you." I take a step closer. "What I do believe is that there's a special place in hell for men like you.

Men who fail to protect the women who are important to them. She gave you life. I don't know how you live with yourself."

"You're a fine one to talk. How many people have you killed while they begged for their lives?"

"I look at myself in the mirror every single day. I never shrink. And you know why that is? Because I didn't murder my mother, or stand around holding my dick while someone else killed her."

His eyes are bulging. With any luck, he'll have nightmares about his mother for a week. My work here is done.

"You're a big talker," he taunts. "But the day's coming when you won't be able to live with yourself. The world's changing, and outside of the region, no one gives two shits about you."

With one long stride, I'm in his face. "If you *ever* lay a finger on my mother, or anyone else I care about, I'll kill you. But it won't be quick. I'll keep you suffering for a *long* time. You're good with hurting helpless women? We'll see how big of a man you are when I dip you in acid, inch by inch, and strangle you with your small intestines when I get bored of your screams."

I don't even glance at my uncle before I walk out.

38

DANIELA

When I get back to my room after dinner, there's a cell phone on the nightstand. I should be thrilled, but as I approach it, my imagination starts to run wild.

Is this some kind of trick? A test of some sort? Victor didn't mention he left a phone for me. Neither did Paula. Antonio hasn't been here since yesterday morning—I haven't seen him, anyway.

Nothing happens here without Antonio's knowing. Certainly no one would give me a phone without his blessing.

I glance at the phone, but I don't touch it. Not right away. Not before forcing myself into the bathroom to get ready for bed.

When the water is warm, I rub some cleansing gel into my face until it's squeaky clean, and then I pat on some moisturizer. Yesterday and today were only marginally useful in understanding the comings and goings in that outside area, right below the window.

When we took a walk this morning, I managed to steer Paula out a side door that leads to the small area. No one was there at the time, and the information I gleaned was only a bit helpful, not like the treasure trove I got from searching the internet on Rafael's phone while he was using the gym. *That was a useful hour.*

It seems that cargo freighters run from the port of Porto all the time. Not a big surprise. Many of those freighters carry passengers for a fee that's far less than the cost of a plane ticket. If I'm lucky, I'll find one that doesn't require me to show a passport. Ships with lax rules are usually more expensive, and many of them involve characters and accommodations that are less savory than those that play by the rules.

It is what it is. The accommodations here are lovely, but the character with the big cock is pretty unsavory too. At least some of his behavior leans that way.

The first thing I need to do when I get out of here is to get a burner phone to contact Isabel, and then I need to sell my mother's locket. It makes me sick to part with it, but there's no choice. I need money to travel.

What's less clear is how to get out of this fortress. Carlos's or John's truck seems like the best way out. But nothing is simple.

Carlos uses a soft cover to protect his truck bed. If I get locked inside, I can cut my way through the tarp to get out. The downside of sneaking into his truck is that he lives only a few miles away. I'll still need to get to the city to get to the docks. *How will I do that?*

If I can manage to get into John's truck on a Friday, I can get to the city. But his truck bed has a retractable cover, and I don't know if I can cut my way out if I get locked inside. By law, those kinds of covers can be sold in the EU only if they have safety latches inside, like trunks. But not everyone follows the law. It's a tough situation.

I learned more about truck beds and their covers from my internet search than I wanted to. However—

Oh my God.

That's what the phone on the nightstand is about. I deleted the search history, but Antonio knows I used Rafael's phone. He's taunting me.

While I'm brushing my teeth, the phone rings.

Just ignore it.

But it's difficult to ignore. Every shrill ring is a stark reminder of Antonio's rage—and of the penalty he'll exact for breaking his rules.

When I'm at wit's end, the ringing stops.

Thank God.

I breathe a giant sigh of relief. It's not as though I'm completely off the hook, but maybe for tonight I'll get a reprieve.

After I change into a nightgown and crawl between the sheets with a book, the ringing starts again.

My pulse races as I stare at the phone. I can't avoid him forever.

39

DANIELA

"Hello." My voice sounds small and hesitant.

"Good evening," he says in a low, silky timbre. "I see you found your new phone."

I hold my breath, bracing for a stern lecture filled with the promise of punishment. But he doesn't sound angry—at all. Quite the contrary. "New phone? The phone is for me?"

"Since the chat with Isabel went off without a hitch, I thought you might like a phone so you can be in touch with her more often."

My heart leaps. I won't be able to take the phone with me when I leave, because I'm sure it can be tracked, but I can talk to them every day while I'm stuck here. Although it means keeping up the ruse with Isabel that everything's fine. *It's worth it to hear their voices.*

"Thank you. I can't tell you how much I appreciate being able to talk to them."

"Don't get too excited. The phone is closely monitored, and there's no internet access. If you want to video-chat again, you'll need to ask."

Why couldn't he just say 'you're welcome'? Why does every kindness have to come with a small slap?

"Where are you?" he asks softly.

Where am I? Really?

"Out shopping and getting a manicure." There's a touch of humor in my voice to offset the sarcasm. "Oh wait, I'm not allowed to leave the property. I'm in my room. But I'm sure you already know that."

"Where in your room, *Princesa*?"

"I'm in bed," I reply cautiously.

"Hmmm," he murmurs.

I should have told him I was curled up in a chair, reading. What if he wants phone sex? So what if he does? Daniela!

"Thank you again for the phone. But it's late, and I was almost asleep. Can we finish this conversation tomorrow?"

"You don't sound like you were almost asleep. You squeaked like a little mouse when you answered, but now you sound wide awake."

I don't bother to argue, because he's right, and he knows it.

"I left something else in your room. Maybe that's why you're in such a big hurry to get rid of me. Did you find it?"

"I don't know what you're talking about." I scan the room, but there's nothing that appears new. "No. I don't see anything."

"Go to your dressing room, and on the top shelf, above the lingerie drawers, there's a leather case. Bring it back to the bed. But before you do, take the key that's on a red ribbon from your panty drawer."

"You were in my closet? In my drawers? When?"

"I was. And does it matter when?"

I don't respond, because all I can think about is him rifling through my things. *They're not really your things. You're just borrowing them while you're here.*

"Do as I ask, and stop worrying that I touched your underwear."

It's unsettling to know he was in the room where I sleep, without me knowing, although I don't pretend to have much privacy here.

"Daniela?"

"I'm going," I mutter, climbing out of bed. *A case and a key. What are you up to, Antonio?*

On a high shelf, above the lingerie drawers, there's a blush-color leather case about the size of a hatbox. It wasn't there this morning.

I stand on a small step stool and pull down the case. It's not particularly heavy. Whatever's inside doesn't weigh a ton.

When I'm leaving the room, the gold lock catches my eye, and I remember that I'm supposed to retrieve a key too. Under different circumstances, this might be fun, but I don't trust him. Although I have to admit, I'm curious to see what's inside.

I open the top drawer and find a key with a red ribbon looped through it, exactly where he said it would be.

"I have it," I tell him when I get back to the bedroom.

"Took you long enough. Did you remember the key?"

"Yes," I reply, holding it up as though he can see through the phone. "It's right—"

I freeze when my eye catches the cherry-red ribbon. *This is my hair ribbon. The one I was wearing the day he visited Quinta Rosa do Vale, after my father died. The one I could never find. Isn't it?*

That's ridiculous, Daniela.

He's saying something, but I'm too busy examining the ribbon for any sign that it's mine to pay attention to him. *I'm not certain about the ribbon.*

You know it's yours.

"Is—is this the ribbon I had in my hair when you visited after my father died?"

"It is. I'm in a benevolent mood today. I'm giving back some of the things I stole from you."

I don't say anything. I'm still trying to wrap my head around the idea that he took my ribbon like a schoolboy and kept it for six years.

"Don't overthink it, *Princesa*. Open the case."

My head is fuzzy as I pull the round case closer and insert the key. Even as I do, I can't keep my eyes off the ribbon.

Because I have no idea what to expect when I open the case, I pull back the lid carefully.

What in the name of fresh hell?

The inside of the case is multitiered, like a jewelry box, but much larger. I rifle through the contents, finding a variety of sex toys in silk pouches, two sizes of batteries, condoms, an assortment of lube, and antibacterial soap.

You have got to be kidding me.

I don't say anything. Neither does Antonio.

All I can do is stare at the box in horror, and at my ribbon, becoming more and more agitated as the seconds pass.

"See anything you think you might enjoy?"

Fuck you.

"Why did you leave this for me? What exactly do you think I'm going to do with these things?"

"Daniela, you're young and inexperienced, but you haven't been living in a cave in the Arctic. You know damn well what those toys are about. But if you have any questions about how to use or care for them, the instructions are at the bottom of the case."

"I know what they are. But if you think for one minute—"

"You said that you haven't explored your body in years. You accused me of stealing your opportunity to have those experiences. I'm giving it back," he adds softly.

I swallow hard. I did say that he'd robbed me of the experiences. It is true—mostly. There's little opportunity for self-love when sharing a room with a child.

"The items in the box are for you to enjoy. I chose them

myself, but you can choose other things that suit you better, or that you might want to experiment with."

I'm about to die of embarrassment.

"I intend to learn your body—and your mind—every corner of both. I intend to explore every whimper, every sigh, every moan. You might never know yourself as well as I'll soon know you, but you need to explore, to learn what gives you pleasure. Every woman needs to know her own body intimately."

So good of him to tell me what every woman needs. "Do you intend to watch?"

"Do you want me to?"

"No," I say without hesitation. That's the last thing I want.

"Then I won't. Those toys are for you. Aside from one or two things, we'll rarely use toys when we're together. I think you'll find my cock is more than enough for you."

I roll my eyes, even though I suspect it's true.

"Choose one of the silk bags—any one—and take out the toy."

40

DANIELA

I pick up a silver pouch and take out a pink vibrator from a Swedish company. It's curved and smooth and firm, the size of a cock. I've wondered about vibrators. But it's the kind of thing Isabel frowned on, and somewhere along the line, her way of thinking became mine.

"I'm not a whore," I whisper. *Trading sex for their survival doesn't count.*

"True exploration begins without judgment." He pauses, and I hear his breath catch.

"And you are a whore. *My* whore. Just like you're *my* woman. *My princesa*. Soon *my* wife, and, perhaps one day, a true partner. I'll take you roughly, without permission or apology. I'll mark you with my teeth, my hands, and my seed. But I'll also take care of you. That includes giving you more pleasure than you think you can take. And when I'm done, and you're curled up under the covers, warm and sated, I'll watch over you while you sleep."

Something about his words—his deep, buttery tenor—is arousing. The flush creeps up the back of my neck, and I'm grateful he's not here to see it.

"I have no interest in these toys, or any others." *Liar.* "You can take them back. I won't be using them."

He doesn't say anything for a minute or two.

I finger the ribbon while I wait for a response. I don't know exactly what it'll be, but there will be one. I guarantee it.

"I'm not giving you a choice, Daniela. Each morning, before you get out of bed for the day, you'll choose a toy and play with it until you orgasm. *Every* morning. It's not up for negotiation."

I can't believe we're having this conversation. *I hope you're happy,* Papai. *This is what you did to me.*

"I'll know if you defy me," he continues, like the asshole he is. "If I even suspect, I'll start requiring photos with the toy inside your pretty pink pussy. If you manipulate me, I'll send someone to take a video of you writhing on the bed with a vibrator pulsing against your clit. Then after he brings me the video, I'll slit his throat, because no one lives after seeing your pussy."

The thought of anyone watching me come—not a lover, but a random person—*a man* not of my choosing, but of his, is repulsive. I blink back the tears. "Why? Why are you doing this to me?"

"Because you need it. Because someone has been whispering in your ear that sex is shameful. That pleasure is the devil's work. It's all a lie, Daniela. A *huge* lie. Those days are over. Now I'll be the only one whispering in your ear, coaxing you to take every drop of pleasure. I'm going to whisper louder, and louder, until the only voice you hear is mine."

"You don't know anything about my morals or beliefs."

"I know you're burdened with old-fashioned, pious beliefs. I think you're a passionate woman who needs permission to enjoy her sexuality. I could give you that permission, but at this point, I'm not sure it would be enough. So I'm taking it one step further. I'm *demanding* your compliance. And we're going to start now. *Right now.*

"Take the vibrator out of the gold pouch. That's a good toy to start with—straightforward and not too intimidating. It's already been cleaned, but you'll need to clean it again after you use it. Read the instructions."

"Antonio. *Please.*" But even as I plead with him, I remove the vibrator from the gold pouch. It's purple and not as intimidating as the pink one.

"Take off your clothes," he commands, ignoring my pleas. "All of them. Don't talk. Don't think. Just listen to my voice—and feel. Let me guide you to a place where there's only pleasure. And more pleasure."

"I can't," I whisper. "It's too much, too soon."

"Should I send someone to assist you?" he asks in the same way a porter would ask if I need help with my bags.

"No," I gasp. I don't think he'd actually send anyone to *assist* me, but he's not above coming to do the job himself.

"Tell me when your clothes are off and you're lying on your back, in bed."

It's okay. He can't see you naked. He can't see anything.

I pull the nightgown over my head and fold it neatly, wasting time. When the last wrinkle has been smoothed away, I get into bed. My limbs are tight and heavy as I slide them over the mattress.

"I'm in bed," I say softly.

"Put the phone on speaker, and place it on the pillow beside you."

"What if someone hears?"

"No one will hear unless you have the volume turned up all the way. Just relax," he murmurs in that smooth timbre. "Focus on the sheets under you. How do they feel against your skin?"

"Soft. Cool."

"*Mmmm. Soft.* But not as soft as you. I wish I was there right now, *Princesa*, running my tongue over your soft, luscious flesh."

My breathing is shallow and quick. Everything about this

feels so dirty. But I don't hate it as much as I thought I would—or should. *I don't hate it at all.*

"Rest both palms on your breasts," he murmurs. "Rub circles, wide, then tighter and tighter until your nipples are hard and peaked. Use a gentle touch at first, barely skimming the silky skin. Then firmer." His tone is even. His voice whisper-soft, and cajoling. "Are your nipples firm little peaks?"

"Yes."

"Squeeze them. Hard. Then let go quickly."

His voice is hypnotic, and I've surrendered to the spell, doing as he asks. *"Ahhh."*

"You're such a good *princesa*. So beautiful. When you stroke your breasts, do you feel the throb in your pussy?"

"Yes," I whisper into the dark room.

"Let your hands roam over your ribs, and across your belly. Go slow. Enjoy the velvety skin under your fingers, and the flutter and pulses enveloping your core. Don't rush. Take your time, pretty girl."

His breathing is choppy. *He's aroused too.* I imagine him stroking his thickening cock, like he did the night he punished me. I wet my lips as my back arches off the bed.

Everything is happening in slow motion around me, but a frenzy of sensations are building inside.

"Spread your legs for me, *Princesa*. Let your knees fall to the side. Do you feel the cool air on your pussy?"

"Yes." I do feel it—the cool air licking my bare pussy, making it quiver.

"Are you wet? Check for me."

I slide two fingers over the sensitive flesh. "*Mm-hmm*. Very wet."

"I like you wet," he murmurs. "Bring your fingers to your mouth, and suck on them like you would my cock. Make them nice and clean. Enjoy every drop of your sweetness." His cadence has slowed even further. He's demanding, but patient. "Tell me how you taste."

I stop thinking about every command. Stop the negative internal chatter. The judging. I just listen and obey like a well-trained pet. It's easier. *And it's what I want.*

"A little salty," I croak from somewhere deep inside my chest.

"That's how I remember you. A little salty to balance all the sweet. You're delicious, *Princesa*. I need to taste you again. It's all I think about."

I swallow hard, starting to feel overwhelmed by all the sensations.

"Spread your juices all over your pussy—make it nice and slick for me."

I'm so aroused, the lightest touch of my fingertips causes a sultry moan to escape into the quiet room.

"The sound of you pleasuring yourself makes me rock hard. If I was there, I'd use my dick to smear the juices all over your cunt. I'd slap it against your clit while you begged to come. Would you like that, *Princesa*?"

I don't answer. I just squeeze my eyes tight. Not to shut out his dirty talk, but to savor it.

"Take the toy and turn it on a low setting. Then place it flat against your pussy."

"Oh," I gasp, arching off the bed. Even on low, the vibrations are powerful, sending zings of pleasure through me.

"That's it. Move it up and down your slit. Slide the head over the swollen little nub."

My hips buck as I drown in pleasure.

"It feels good, doesn't it?"

"Yes." *So good.*

"Turn it a little higher. Not all the way up yet. How does it feel now?"

"Good." The word tumbles off my lips.

"Just good? I want it to feel amazing. Turn it up a little higher."

"Oh God."

"Is your belly tightening?"

"Yes."

"Turn it higher. All the way up."

I moan loudly as I writhe against the mattress. I'm so close.

"Let go, Daniela. Just feel. Surrender to the sensations. You're safe. Let go. Let me hear you."

My legs shake. And my jaw falls slack as I submit fully, not just to the orgasm—but to him.

"I want to feel you come, *Princesa*. I want to feel your pussy throbbing around my cock."

"Ahhhhh," I cry as the muscle in my stomach balls, almost painfully. The orgasm rips through me, shattering every wall I've erected, leaving me limp and gasping for air.

It's quiet as I catch my breath. Only my heart thumping.

He's gone.

I reach for the phone. I don't even know when he hung up. Something inside my chest contracts, leaving an ache.

I'm alone. In some ways more alone than ever.

Bastard.

I hate you, Antonio, for making me feel things I don't want to feel. I hate you.

I fling the vibrator across the room. It bounces off the chair and lands on the rug, barely making a ripple.

It's almost Friday. When you're gone, he won't be able to play his games with you anymore.

I bury my face in the pillow and cry myself to sleep.

41

ANTONIO

I'm in a Douro Port Wine Foundation meeting, ready to tear my hair out while I listen to board members whine incessantly about trivial matters, sounding more like spoiled toddlers than CEOs.

Tomas is seated at the table, too, shooting me mean looks from time to time. *What a pussy*. I don't know whether he expects me to piss my pants at his scowls, but all he gets from me is a smug smile.

It's a good thing there are no pressing matters on the agenda today, because all I can think about is Daniela and that damn vibrator sending her over the edge last night. Her voice was breathy and dreamlike, and those little moans and gasps are addictive. If I'm not careful, they're going to be my undoing.

Talking her through the experience hadn't been part of my original plan. I meant it when I told her the toys were for her. But *damn*, I'm not sorry about the way things turned out. Although it only made me hungrier for her. That part doesn't thrill me. Wanting something too much can lead to disaster—especially where women are concerned.

My phone lights up, and I smile when Gray Wilder's name appears on the screen. He's returning my call from last night.

I grab the phone and step out while some blowhard is complaining about the quality of the rubber hoses he purchased in bulk. He actually brought one with him so we could see for ourselves. I was three seconds from grabbing that hose and flogging him with it.

Gray's always had impeccable timing.

I met him while studying in the US. Two cocky rich boys who bonded over fathers who were monsters. We each had one. *Had* being the operative word. In the end, they both got their just deserts.

"Hey." My relationship with Gray is not as tight as my relationships with Cristiano and Lucas, nor does it have the firm roots, but we share a unique friendship—at least from my perspective.

"Hey, you ugly sonofabitch, what's good?"

I laugh out loud. Gray doesn't care who I am. He never feels the need to defer to me, *ever*. He'd tell me to fuck off in a heartbeat, and has, many times. Around him, I'm never hampered or weighed down by the responsibilities of my position. I can put aside the crown Manuel D'Sousa placed on my head more than twelve years ago, and just be. It's liberating.

"It's all good on my end. And you?"

"Can't complain. How's your mom, and Rafael?"

"My mother's well. She's so busy these days she doesn't even have time to stick her nose in my business. And Rafael is biding his time with babes and booze, but from his grades, it seems he's opening a book here and there too."

"Sounds familiar."

"Sounds like a lifetime ago. How are your brothers?"

"Chase is elusive, as always. I've given up trying to figure him out. And JD is pussy-whipped like you wouldn't believe."

"That's what he said about you when he called a few weeks ago, begging for a case of my best Port."

Gray laughs. "All true, man. All true," he confesses, although he doesn't sound one bit sorry. "Did you call last night to shoot the shit, or is something up?"

"I'm always happy to shoot the shit, but I called because I'm going to be in the US in about a month, and I thought we'd come down to Charleston. Maybe I can finally meet Delilah. I'm beginning to think she's a figment of your imagination."

"Trust me, she's real. But more importantly, who's *we*?"

"My wife," I reply hesitantly. Not because I don't trust Gray, but because the word still doesn't roll off my tongue easily. "Or at least she will be then."

"You're getting married? *Jesus.* When?"

"Less than a month."

"*Less than a month.*" He whistles. "Is this some kind of shotgun wedding? Because I don't remember getting an invitation. Her daddy already polish his rifle? That's never a good sign."

I scoff. "It's going to be a very small event. Mainly for show. Once the harvest is over, we'll have a big celebration for family and friends, and I fully expect you and Delilah to come. Maybe spend a week or two with us after."

"Another good man falls. Congratulations."

"Thanks." It comes out awkward, maybe because it's still new, or because congratulations feel like the wrong sentiment when you're forcing a woman to marry you.

"I didn't even know you were dating anyone, you sly dog. Tell me about the unlucky bride."

He means it as a joke, but it needles me more than it should. "The marriage was arranged some time ago, so it's not exactly sudden. I'd appreciate your discretion, for the time being."

"Don't give it another thought. Tell me about the bride. Is she good with it?"

I know what Gray's getting at, but I'm not having the discussion with him. His world is different from mine.

"She's a decade younger than us, quite pretty, and has a good heart. Loves the region, maybe as much as I do. It's in her blood, like it's in mine. She'll make a suitable partner."

Gray is quiet for a moment. "*A suitable partner.* God, you're such a romantic," he quips finally. "Do you even like her?"

"Yes. I like her." *More than I care to admit.* "Romance isn't part of the equation. In my world, marriage isn't about love. It's about building alliances."

Gray's quiet again, like he's trying to wrap his head around it, or maybe it's pity I hear in the silence.

"I understand marriage is hard work, even when you're in love," he says carefully. "Are you sure you want to do this? Because you sure as hell don't sound like it."

"I'm sure. It's complicated, and I have a lot on my mind. That's all." Starting with the way the men sitting in the conference room, right now, are going to go ballistic when they find out not only about the marriage, but about Quinta Rosa do Vale. *Especially about Quinta Rosa do Vale.*

"I don't pretend to understand the nuances of your world, and I'm the last person to judge anyone. As you know, my family's pretty fucked up. All I'm going to say is if you're coming to the US, you better make damn sure you stop in Charleston. You'll stay with us. Maybe take your new bride down to the club, after hours."

My dick twitches at the thought of having Daniela in the dungeon, or the stable, or any one of those well-equipped rooms. "I'm not sure she's ready for the club, even after hours."

"That's what you get when you rob the cradle. But at least you'll have someone to push around your wheelchair in a few years. And wipe the drool off your face."

"You're an asshole."

"Right back at you, baby."

After we say goodbye, I brace my shoulders against the wall.

Daniela might be ten years younger, and she looks it, but in many ways she's an old soul without the carefree spirit of a young woman.

I understand marriage is hard work. Especially when the bride has to be dragged kicking and screaming to the altar.

Although Victor claims she's acclimating, coming down for meals, and taking walks with Paula. Only time will tell. For now, I'll give her some space to adjust. But it's not easy. I want her—bad—especially after last night.

Fortunately, for the next week I'll be traveling around the EU, representing the foundation's interests. Otherwise, she'd become a permanent fixture in my bed, sooner than advisable. The timing of the trip couldn't be better.

42

DANIELA

It's Friday, again—finally. With any luck, things will go better today than they did last Friday.

This morning, I sent Antonio the final *done*. That's what I text him after I play with the toys. The first morning, it felt shameful to text him, but then it became routine—all of it. And while I'd never admit it to him, I've been so anxious the orgasms have been heavenly, helping to wash away some of the stress.

Antonio's been away for a week, and other than my morning text, we've had no contact. We're supposed to have dinner tomorrow, but I won't be there. Because today is *the* day.

I pray.

I'm ready. More than ready. But I was ready last Friday too. The night before, I packed a small backpack with a toothbrush, deodorant, a change of underwear and socks, a paring knife from the kitchen, a pair of scissors, a hand towel, and my wallet.

But it rained all day, and no one went outside at lunch or during breaks. Both Carlos and John had their truck beds locked down tight the entire day. When they pulled out after work, I slid onto my bedroom floor, with my back against the bed frame and my knees pulled to my chest, and sobbed.

I was so close, *so close*, to reuniting with Isabel and Valentina, but because of the damn weather, my dream was out of reach for at least a full week. Yes, I could have climbed into the back of Carlos's truck in the interim, but stowing away in John's truck will get me to the city, where I need to go.

Waiting an entire week was painful, but it allowed me to study the comings and goings of the outdoor area for a bit longer. Clear patterns emerged as I observed day after day.

Carlos and John unlock their vehicles and open the tailgates at the midmorning coffee break. The covers are only ever pulled back far enough to expose about a third of the truck beds. After the break, the tailgate gets put up, and the covers are adjusted to protect the entire bed.

The trucks are left unlocked, and whoever gets to lunch first opens the tailgate and retracts the covers partway. This is a recurring pattern. Unless it rains, little varies day to day with regard to that area and the people who come and go during breaks. After observing for more than a week, I don't anticipate any surprises.

The other things that I can count on are that Victor prepares dinner on the other side of the house beginning midafternoon, at the latest, and the majority of the staff complete their duties on the upper floors by the afternoon break.

My best chance to climb into John's truck, unseen, is between three o'clock and four thirty.

It's 3:10, now. I'm meeting Paula at the side door in five minutes for a walk. Except for the day it rained, we've been taking a daily walk. I've learned a lot about her, and I'm sorry that we won't have the opportunity to become close. She's somewhat anxious, but she has a good heart. She's a lot like Isabel, except much younger.

After a quick glance around the room, I grab the backpack that I always take with me on these walks and shut the suite door for the last time. *I hope.*

On my way downstairs, I pause at the second-floor landing and peek out the window. No one is outside. My stomach does a somersault or two before I tear myself from the glass.

Paula's waiting when I get to the bottom of the stairs. I'd love to say goodbye to Victor, but that's impossible. This morning at breakfast I told him how much I appreciate everything he's done to make me comfortable. I was careful not to raise his suspicions. He's an angel, but his loyalty is to Antonio, not to me.

"Are you ready?" I ask, flashing Paula a warm smile.

"I'm ready," she chirps. "It's a beautiful day." She hands me a water bottle, which I stuff into the backpack. If she notices that the pack is fuller today, she doesn't mention it.

The door shuts behind us with a louder-than-normal thud. At least it seems that way to me.

When we get to the break area, no one is there. *Not a soul.*

My heart rate ticks up.

Now, Daniela.

I take a big breath. "Paula, I'm so sorry to do this to you. I meant to mention it earlier. I was so hot last night. I don't know if it was the room, or if I had a fever."

"Are you feeling better now?" she asks with some concern, making me feel like a complete heel.

I touch her arm. "Totally better. But my sheets were drenched with sweat. I would have changed them myself, except I don't know where you keep the laundered linen. Do you think you could go up and change them?"

"Now?" she asks, her brow furrowed.

"Yes. I'm sorry. I think it would be a good idea if you did it now, so that you're finished with all your work by the end of the day."

"I can stay later if you need me."

She's such a good soul, who doesn't deserve to be lied to, but it's for her protection as well as mine. The less she knows, the better for us both.

"Absolutely not. As I told you—you work hard, and I want you to have the weekend off. Victor gave his blessing. I'll be okay out here. I won't walk too far without you."

"Of course." She nods.

Paula's been a bright light in this ordeal. I want to hug her, but if I do, I'll tip my hand. "If I don't see you before you leave, have a wonderful weekend."

"Thank you. See you Monday," she calls over her shoulder, walking toward the house.

I stand for a minute, quelling the rising panic.

Have I missed anything? Have I crossed every t and dotted every i? Only hindsight will tell if I was careless.

Go, Daniela, go. Now.

Without wasting another second, I climb into the truck bed and slip under the retractable hood. I creep on my belly until I can't go any farther. *I hope it's late enough that no one comes out and decides to open the cover all the way.* I haven't seen it happen yet, but there's a first time for everything.

If one of the staff finds me, I've prepared a ridiculous story about playing a trick on Paula, hiding and then jumping out when she least expects it. *Surprise!*

That story would never fly with Antonio, *not a chance*, but no one on the staff would ever question me, even if they doubted the veracity. *Except the guards—they would question me.*

Paula assured me that unless they have any reason to be suspicious, the guards never check staff vehicles on the way out, only on the way in. They'll definitely contact Cristiano or Lucas, or maybe even Antonio himself, if they find me hiding in the back of a truck. I shudder at the prospect before shoving it away. I can't let my fears get the best of me now.

I lie on my side and rest my head on the backpack, with my back flush against the cab, trying to make myself as small as possible. I try not to think about all the things that could still go wrong before I'm off the property.

And I pray.

43

ANTONIO

I'm in my office at Huntsman Lodge with my assistant, Cecelia, reviewing next week's schedule when Lucas's name pops up on my phone. We just spoke fifteen minutes ago. Lucas isn't a big talker, by any measure. *There's some goddamn problem.*

"Give me a second," I tell Cecelia, picking up the call. "Yeah."

"Daniela was seen getting into the back of a truck in the break area on the side of the house."

What the hell? I lean back in the chair, pressing my tight shoulders into the firm leather. "Whose truck?"

"Amos Correia's kid, John. He does landscaping, and a few odds and ends around the property."

"Hold on."

I turn to Cecelia. "I need to take this call. Then we'll get through everything you have for me, if it takes all night." Cecelia nods and gets up.

I was gone for a week, and she's been trying to pin me down all day about my damn schedule. I'm sure she's annoyed at the interruption. I don't pay her to be annoyed, but I keep the thought to myself, because she's highly skilled, and more important, she's trustworthy.

"Any idea where she might be going?" I ask when the office door clicks shut.

"John stays with his parents during the week, but he has an apartment in the city that he goes to on the weekend. Porto would be my best guess."

That's where I'd go first if I was on the run. "How long has she been in the truck?"

"Less than fifteen minutes."

"Did she have help?"

"Cristiano's on it."

"Is Correia's kid involved?" John better make his peace with God if he's helping her escape—*from me.*

"Also unclear. We're sending a guard to pick him up."

The more people who know, the bigger the problem becomes. Not to mention it's a direct assault on my authority.

"Don't pick him up. And tell Cristiano not to bother interrogating anyone."

"What do you want us to do?" he asks, as though he's confused by my instructions.

"I'll be down in ten minutes. Hold tight until then. But let her go."

"That's it? Just let her go?"

"That's it. Not one fucking thing more."

I end the call and toss my phone on the blotter, rubbing my temples to ward off the throbbing in my head. I have a business to run and more responsibilities than I care to have. I don't have time for this kind of distraction. That's what she's been, a huge distraction. I'm sick and tired of her bullshit.

I've had more than enough.

I get that she's still adjusting to a new life with limited freedom, but I wasn't the one who went to her father. He came to me.

She feels her golden wings have been clipped? *Too fucking bad.*

The more I think about it, the more pissed off I am. I'm not an angel, but I've made her surroundings as comfortable as possible, and I've been willing to bend on things like phone calls to her damn maid in the US, and walks on the property without a guard. I should have thrown her in one of the empty towers and let her sleep on the cold floor without any outside communication until the wedding. Then she couldn't have pulled this crap. Although, even then, she probably would have found a way. I don't put anything past her.

You want to go back to the US, Daniela? Back to cleaning toilets? Go for it. I'm done playing games.

I activate the intercom at Cecelia's station. "I'm off the phone. You have exactly five minutes to review any pressing business with me."

44

DANIELA

It's almost 8:15, well after sunset.

The truck's been parked for more than two hours. Shortly after the engine was turned off, someone got out of the cab, slammed the door shut, and engaged the lock.

After about thirty minutes of silence, I used the credit card light from my wallet to search for the safety latch that will unlock the retractable cover. I think I found it, but I'm trying not to get too excited. I could be mistaken, and even if I'm right, it might not work.

If it fails, I'll attempt to cut my way through the cover. Although I might not be successful. Either way, I'll have to wait for the middle of the night to try something so risky.

Waiting until dark is hard. But necessary. If John, or anyone else, sees me climb out of the truck, there will be less of a chance they'll recognize me if it's dark out.

Fifteen more minutes should do the trick.

While I wait, I review the plan again. *Buy a phone, call Isabel, sell the locket, get to the docks, and find a freighter that will take you —anywhere. Call Isabel, again, with the final plan.*

It seems so simple, but the potential for disaster looms until I'm on that ship heading out of Portugal.

I glance at my watch, like I've been doing every five minutes since the truck pulled out of Antonio's driveway.

Eight twenty-nine.

I'm nauseous, as I crawl along the truck bed to the safety lock. Before I engage the lever, I pull out the credit card light one more time to read the directions posted near the lock. No reason to make a mistake now.

I follow the illustrations precisely until I hear a small pop.

Thank you, God. Thank you.

I creep along toward the tailgate, dragging my knapsack alongside me. As I stick my hand out of the truck to unlatch the gate, I freeze. *What if it's alarmed? Don't risk it.*

I yank at the cover from inside, pulling as hard as I can, but it doesn't open more than six inches. Not enough for me to squeeze through. After a few more minutes, I get on my knees, still scrunched down, and use my body to create momentum as I push the damn thing open. *There's no way I'm going to get trapped here. It's not going to end like this.* But in my heart, it feels like a real possibility.

After several tries, it opens enough for me to slither through. The sense of relief is palpable as I climb over the tailgate. I move quickly but carefully. The last thing I need is an alarm to blare.

As soon as my feet touch the ground, I take off without stopping to get my bearings. I just run. And I run. And I run—until I'm wheezing and can't run anymore.

I slip into a small alley, doubled over. After a minute, I walk around in tight circles, hands on my hips, trying to catch my breath.

While gasping for air, I run through the list of things that need to be accomplished before I reach the docks.

You've already done the hard part.

After a few sips of water, I walk for about twenty minutes through the oldest part of the city until I come to a neighborhood market where I might be able to purchase a cheap phone.

The market is almost empty, although this is a touristy part of town, and I'm not too worried about being recognized.

I find the prepaid phones immediately. But because I need international calling, they're not cheap.

When I get to the register, it occurs to me that I don't have enough euros to buy the phone, and I can't use my bank card. Although, why not? It's an American bank, and by the time Antonio can track the purchase, I'll be long gone.

"Do you know where there might be a pawn shop in the area? Somewhere that buys jewelry?" I ask, handing the card to the young clerk.

She shrugs. "I've seen them around. But I can't remember where."

"What are you selling?" a gruff male voice asks from behind me.

45

DANIELA

I turn my head to get a look at the stranger. He's about forty and doesn't look like someone I want to share my personal business with. "Not selling anything today. Just checking prices."

He nods, eyeing the gold chain around my neck—the one that holds my mother's locket. "There's a high-end pawn shop a mile down the road. Take a right on Fonte Taurina Street. You'll see it as soon as you turn the corner."

"Thank you," I say, finishing my purchase.

"I can give you a ride."

The clerk hands me a receipt with a concerned look. She needn't worry—there's no way I'm taking him up on the offer.

"That's very kind, but I can use the walk."

"The shop will likely be closed by the time you get there, if you walk."

Then I'll find another one. I'm not getting in a car with this guy. Something about him makes me uneasy.

"That's okay. It's not that important."

I don't spare him another glance as I hurry out of the store and up the street.

If you expect to find the shop open, you have to run, Daniela. I'm tired and don't know if I can run anymore. But I do, although it's more of a jog than a sprint.

I don't stop to call Isabel, because then I'll never make it.

It's a good thing that I'm wearing yoga pants and a sweatshirt. Otherwise, people might be alarmed at a woman running down the road. This isn't the US, where it's not unusual to see joggers on the sidewalk at all hours of the day and night.

Once or twice I glance over my shoulder to see if the man from the market followed me. I don't see him, and there are too many people on the street for him to try something. The amount of pedestrian traffic is a double-edged sword as I enter a more residential part of the city. While it makes me feel safer in some regards, there's also more of a chance I'll be recognized.

When I get to Fonte Taurina, I turn the corner, and the shop is there, on the right, like the man said. But it doesn't look open. *Shit.*

I walk up to the door, looking over my shoulder as I ring the bell. I wouldn't be all that shocked to see Antonio stalking toward me. *Stop, Daniela. Don't feed the anxiety.*

"Good evening," a pleasant woman's voice says through an intercom.

"Good evening. I have an antique locket that I'd like to show you."

"You need an appointment."

An appointment? *Oh God.* "My mother is dying. She's in the US. I need to get there tonight, and I don't have the money to purchase a last-minute plane ticket." I've become quite the liar. It's not something I like about myself, but it's a necessary evil. "Please," I beg.

"I'm sorry. I can't help you tonight. If you'd like to make an appointment for ten o'clock tomorrow morning, maybe I can help you then."

Make the appointment, just in case you can't find another open shop.

"If you don't have anything earlier, ten o'clock will be fine."

"What's your name?"

"Danielle DeRosa." It's the name that Leo set me up with before I left Porto, and it's on my ID.

I cross the street and duck into an alcove in front of a shuttered boutique to call Isabel. My fingers tremble as I input her number.

You need to keep it together for her sake, and Valentina's.

"Hello," she says. My heart jumps at her voice. *This is going to happen. Soon you'll be with them. Stay calm.*

"It's Daniela."

"Is everything okay? You don't sound okay."

"I'm fine. Isabel, please listen carefully. I don't have much time. Go to the bank and withdraw all the money in the account." *Wait.* I can withdraw cash here too. Maybe I won't need to sell the locket. My heart clenches at the prospect of being able to keep it—at least for a while longer.

"I'm sorry. Not all the money. Leave seven hundred and fifty dollars in the account." *Is that enough? From my research, it should be more than enough to get me out of the country.*

"Take my mother's diamond ring to the pawn shop and get as much as you can for it. Then come back and gather all our important papers, and pack a few things for you and Valentina." *Next comes the hard part.* "Then take the bus to Boston and check in at the Hampton Inn near the airport. You'll need to take the subway there."

"What are you talking about?"

I already hear the anxiety in her voice.

"I know this is out of nowhere, but you need to be strong, Isabel. Valentina can help translate for you at the bus station and in Boston. But please don't burden her too much. She's still a child. And don't tell her what I'm about to tell you. I mean it.

Promise me." Isabel would do anything to protect Valentina, but when things are bad, she sometimes lets her anxiety spill out all over the place until everyone around her is drowning in it.

"I promise." Her tone is already shaky and garbled, and I haven't even started.

"Antonio Huntsman was at Moniz's office when I got there."

She gasps.

"He's been holding me prisoner, but I managed to escape."

She starts to sob.

"Isabel, please don't cry. He didn't hurt me. Not once. If you can't be strong for me, do it for *Mamai*, and for Valentina. I know you can do this."

"They're going to kill you, Daniela, so that you don't tell anyone what happened. Valentina's at that age where—" She can't bear to finish the thought. Isabel was kidnapped and trafficked. It's always been her worst fear for Valentina. "They'll take the vineyards."

She doesn't say that they'll kill her, too, because she cares more about what happens to me and Valentina than she cares about herself. And the thought of my mother's vineyards in Huntsman hands makes her as sick as it makes me. I fight back my own sobs.

"Listen to me," I say as calmly as possible. "Antonio doesn't know anything about what happened. My father made a betrothal contract with him. They signed in blood. He gave Antonio the vineyards in exchange for marrying me. He saw holding me captive as complying with his part of the agreement."

"No!" she says sharply. "No. They are liars. Your father would never give you to them—or the vineyards. Don't believe it."

I don't bother to burden her with the video evidence. "It doesn't matter right now." A small sigh twists from my chest.

"I'm fine. We're all going to be fine. Please do as I ask, and wait for me to call you again. I don't have a passport, so I need to find another way out of the country, and as soon as my travel plans are settled, I'll call you."

"What if you can't get out?" she asks, each syllable quivering with stress.

"I can. Freighters carry passengers all the time. I just need to get to the docks to figure out how it works."

"Daniela!" she shouts. "That plan is foolish. The docks are too dangerous."

"Someone I worked with at the mill has done it. Not everyone can afford plane tickets to travel. It's a new thing." The calling time on this phone is limited, and I can't waste it arguing with her.

"Please go. Take the papers and Valentina, pack a few things, go to the bank before it closes, and the pawn shop, and then get on the bus to Boston. Don't waste any time. They know where we live, and eventually they'll show up there." I hate to tell her this, but I need to light a fire under her. "Tell Valentina we're going on a surprise vacation. Make sure she doesn't tell her friends anything." I squeeze my eyes tight at the thought of Valentina so abruptly, without even a goodbye, leaving her friends. *I didn't want this life for you, sweetheart.*

"May God be with you," Isabel murmurs. "May your mother watch over you."

"I love you, Isabel, and that little girl. There's nothing on this earth I love more." *Not even my life.* "We'll be together soon."

I end the call and find an ATM, but I can withdraw only five hundred euros. I'm not sure if it's a limit on the machine or if it's a limit set by my bank. There's only one way to know.

A few blocks away, I find a bank with an ATM and try again. While it spits out the money, a tear trickles down my face.

Maybe the bad luck is behind me.

46

DANIELA

When I arrive at the port, I wander aimlessly for a few minutes. It's almost eleven thirty, and there are more people milling around than I expected. Although I don't know why I had any expectations. I've been here only a couple of times as a child. And only to the area with the cruise ships, never to the working section of the docks.

"Can I help you?" a security guard asks.

I draw a large breath. *Here we go.* "I'm looking to purchase a ticket for a trip on a cargo ship."

"Vacation?" he asks, sizing me up.

"Yes." I smile brightly.

"Where you headed?"

"Somewhere warm, I hope. Although I read it's best to be flexible if you're catching a ride on a freighter."

"Those tickets have to be bought in advance," he says with a wrinkled brow. "You can't just come down here and hop on a ship. We don't allow it. What if you were a terrorist?"

"I'm not a terrorist. Or a criminal of any kind," I assure him.

"No exceptions."

I've come too far now to let a security guard stand in my way. I swallow hard.

"I understand. Do you mind if I walk around a bit to get the lay of the land? I'll come back tomorrow and purchase a ticket for some time in the future."

"I'm not going to stop you from walking around. Just don't wander into any restricted areas. And I wouldn't go too much beyond that red light." He points to a light on a warehouse along the pier, some distance away. "It starts to get dangerous when you get too much past that point. Unsavory characters."

No shortage of unsavory characters in the world. Some of them live in castles.

Without another word, he walks away to harangue a couple kissing on a bench.

What am I going to do now? If I can't get on a freighter, I'm screwed. Even the train requires papers or a passport.

"Hey."

I glance up, and a young man is leaning against a pole a few feet away. *He's talking to me.* When I don't acknowledge him, he beckons with two fingers. But I don't move.

"I'm not going to hurt you," he says, walking toward me.

Unlike the man in the convenience store, this guy doesn't seem very menacing. He has a baby face, and even the leather jacket and baggy jeans can't hide his scrawny frame.

"I heard you talking to the guard." He holds out a bag of croquettes. I'm starving, but I shake my head. "You sure? They're not warm anymore, but they're delicious."

He's not going to poison you. What about date-rape drugs? Are they just for drinks, or can they go into food too? I'm not taking any chances.

"They look scrumptious, but no thank you."

He nods and takes a bite, and for a second I wonder why he came over to talk to me. "I need to go." I turn and start to walk away.

"If you want to get on a ship, I can help you."

I stop in my tracks and take a breath before stepping toward him. "You know of a cargo ship that carries vacationing passengers?"

He nods. "More than one, actually."

"I'm interested, but I need to hear more." This could be the answer to my prayers, or a trap.

"Do you have papers or a passport?" he asks, studying me carefully.

I have an ID, but it's issued in the US. I'll still need a passport to travel. "No. I'm a Portuguese citizen, but I don't have papers."

"That's okay. It'll cost you extra, but I know a ship where they look the other way, as long as you have money."

"How much money?" I ask, holding my breath.

He shrugs. "It depends how far you're going, and how generous the captain feels today."

I glance at the man. He's a little rough around the edges, but he seems like a nice enough guy. It's not as though the docks are deserted. There are plenty of people around. But more than that, I don't have a better option. I don't have *any* other option.

"Let's go talk to the captain." My insides are shaking, and the bravado in my voice surprises me.

"Let's go," he says, walking in the direction of the red light the guard cautioned me about. "By the way, I'm Joey."

"Nice to meet you, Joey. I'm Rosa," I add without missing a beat. He doesn't give me the creeps like the guy in the market, but I don't know him, and there's no way I'm giving him my real name.

As we get closer to the ominous red glow, I start to get anxious. Joey doesn't look like he could fight off unsavory characters or whatever trouble might lurk beyond the red light. "The guard warned me not to go beyond this point. He made it seem dangerous."

"Yeah. I heard that. But there's no way you're getting on a ship without papers, unless you venture farther into the port. Besides, he was talking about you walking around alone. You're not alone anymore."

I side-eye the stranger with his gangly frame. *It feels like I'm still alone.*

47

DANIELA

Joey whistles, and a young man peers over the side of the ship.

"Captain around?" Joey yells up to him.

The man nods.

We stand on the edge of the pier, the diesel fluid competing with the smell of brackish water. It's nauseating. My stomach's empty, but I'm glad I didn't eat one of those greasy croquettes.

"Do you know the captain well?" I ask before taking out the water bottle from my pack. I'm still not comfortable with any of this. It's not at all what I'd envisioned when Melissa described her vacation travel. *People embellish.*

"We're not drinking buddies, but I've known the captain a long time. He can be intimidating—got to be to take those tankers out on the open ocean, day after day. Nerves of steel. But he's a good guy when you get to know him."

Maybe. "Do you know other people who have traveled with him?"

"Plenty. You worried?"

Scared to death. I shrug.

"You don't need to worry. The ship's solid, the crew competent, and the captain knows what he's doing. You'll be basking in the sun before you know it."

Before I can ask any more questions, a man comes into view, unhooks a rope from the top of a ramp, and jogs down toward us. He's in his forties, maybe, tall and muscular with a suntan. I don't know if it's because of his size, or because he has such a stern look, but he's intimidating. Joey was right.

"Good evening," he says, sliding his hands into his pants pockets.

"Good evening, Captain. I'd like you to meet Rosa. She's interested in an adventure, but her passport was stolen."

The lie trips easily off his tongue. I never said my passport was stolen, but I suppose he had to say something.

"No papers?" the captain asks, turning to me with hardened features.

"No."

"Where are you from?"

"I'm a Portuguese citizen, but I've been living in the US for many years." *And I should have never left.*

He nods. "Where you going?"

"I read it's best to be flexible about location and departure when traveling on a cargo ship. I'm willing to be adventurous." *God, I sound like a moron.*

The captain scratches a sideburn as he glances at Joey. He seems to be weighing the decision. "We're leaving for Barcelona tonight, and we go on to the Middle East from there."

"Barcelona sounds wonderful." It's perfect. I won't have to be on the freighter for too long, but it will get me out of the country. "I'll get off the ship there. What time do you leave?"

"In a few hours. I'm shooting for two o'clock, but it's likely to be closer to two thirty. There's a lot of traffic in the port tonight."

"That sounds perfect. How much is the fare?"

"Without documents, one thousand euros."

A thousand euros. A plane ticket to Barcelona would cost only a small fraction of that, and a train ticket even less. But I'm not getting on a plane or a train without documents.

"Would you be willing to take seven hundred and fifty euros?" I should have offered him less, because if he agrees, I'll be out of euros. *That was foolish, Daniela.*

"Sorry." He starts to leave.

My heart plops into my stomach as he turns.

"Maybe she has something else of value," Joey pipes up.

The captain pivots. "Like what?"

Joey cocks his chin at me. "Do you have a watch or jewelry, anything?"

"I have some American dollars."

"No use to me," the captain mutters.

My watch is a piece of junk, but I hold my wrist out to him.

"That's not worth anything," he grumbles. "What's that around your neck?"

My heart breaks, but I keep my head up. "It's an antique locket. I'm sure you can recoup your money if you sell it." I take the necklace off and open the locket, using my fingernails to pry the pictures out carefully. He's not getting these photos. I don't care if I have to swim to Barcelona.

"I'm not sure it's worth two hundred and fifty euros, plus the trouble of selling it." He gazes at me. "But you seem like a nice girl. I'll take you to Barcelona."

I smile at him, even though the longer I stand here, the more nervous I am.

My anxiety about being caught and dragged back to Antonio has melded with the concerns about getting on the ship alone. It's all a jumbled mess, and I don't know what worries me most.

"Thank you," I say softly. Because no matter how unsure I am, I have to take my chances with the captain.

"You'll need to board now and settle in before we pull out.

But you can't come aboard until I have the cash and the necklace. Your watch too."

This is extortion, but it's his freighter, and I can either ante up or find another way out of the country.

As I dig in the backpack for my wallet, the knife blade winks at me. It's not large, but it has a sharp point. *I have scissors too.* Hopefully I won't need to use either, but having them makes me feel a little better.

I give the captain my jewelry and the cash. He counts it and hands Joey what looks to be fifty euros. *So much for seems like a nice guy.* Not a good Samaritan at all, but an opportunist.

"What's the money for?" I ask Joey.

"I connect travelers with ships." He shrugs. "Like a travel agent."

I guess everyone needs a side hustle.

"Have fun," Joey calls, striding toward the main entrance, probably in search of another desperate soul.

"Follow me," the captain says.

I glance up at the ship and out toward the ocean, then at the tiny photos in my hand. With fear in my heart, I follow him up the ramp.

48

ANTONIO

After spending the better part of the afternoon and the evening working on things that I've neglected since Daniela arrived, I came up to my apartment to change into a pair of jeans and a T-shirt. At least that's the excuse I gave Cristiano and Lucas. The truth is, I was driving them crazy and making it difficult for them to focus. And somebody has to focus.

We have a shipment expected to arrive in the UK tonight. The same type of goods that went missing a couple of weeks ago. There were traitors in the ranks, and we flushed them out, but they weren't working alone. Neither of them had the brains to be masterminds. That's for sure.

But we can't afford to have any more cargo taken right under our noses, especially so soon. We're all on pins and needles until it arrives and is transported to the final destination.

Daniela picked the perfect day to run. *Goddamn woman.*

Despite the cargo concerns, I've been having a hard time keeping my mind off her—keeping my rage in check. The risks she's willing to take for freedom are unfathomable. She's naive but not stupid. The trouble she could find is chilling, even to me.

I made every mistake when it came to Daniela. I should have married her right after her father died. Before she tasted real freedom.

Her escape is not going to be like last time. No one's covering her tracks to save her from reckless choices. She's going to have to suffer the consequences of her decisions. *And she deserves what she gets.*

I'm not going to lose a wink of sleep over it. My conscience is clear.

I turn off the racing simulator. I figured I'd work with it while I was up here killing time. Thirty minutes is normally enough to clear my mind and relax me. *Not today.*

My phone rings, and I reach for it immediately.

When I see Sonia's name on the screen, a sense of disappointment hits me—hard.

You are a stupid, stupid bastard, Antonio. She's not calling. What the fuck is wrong with you?

I swallow my anger, my pride, and all good sense, and take the call.

"I didn't expect to hear from you tonight. What's up?" Even as I ask, I know why she's calling.

"Booty call."

Despite my dark mood, I laugh.

Sonia and I have a complicated history. My mother not so secretly hopes I'll marry Sonia and give her some grandbabies to spoil. That's never happening.

"I couldn't sleep," she says, quietly. "Went out for a walk, ended up at the lodge."

"You're here, now?"

"In the lobby."

"I'll be down in a minute. Don't go anywhere."

Ordinarily I wouldn't deal with Sonia at this hour. She's the type of woman who shouldn't be encouraged to show up whenever the mood strikes her.

But I need a distraction.

49

DANIELA

I *have to get in touch with Isabel,* it occurs to me when I'm halfway up the ramp. "Is there cell service on the ship? I need to make a call."

The captain shakes his head. "No service anywhere around here. You can email or text—maybe it goes through—but that's the extent of it."

"I need just a moment, please."

I text Isabel: *I'm getting on a ship to Barcelona. Stay at the Hampton Inn in Boston until I call you.*

It's almost seven thirty in the evening, her time. Maybe she'll get back to me right away. I'd love to know if they're on their way to Boston.

"I don't have all night," the captain says roughly.

"Sorry." I slip the phone in my pack as we walk up the ramp. The image of pirates and gangplanks comes to mind as I take each tentative step.

When we get aboard, the ship is clean. For some reason, it makes me feel better. We pass a few crew members who nod at the captain and mostly ignore me.

"Passenger quarters are down here," he says, descending two short flights of stairs.

"Are there any other passengers on the ship?"

"A few. But everyone's asleep by now."

At the end of a long, dim hallway, he uses a key to open a steel-gray door. Then steps aside so I can enter first.

I freeze in the doorway. The room is empty. He shoves me inside and slams the door shut behind us.

"I don't understand."

He stands in front of the closed door. Fleeing isn't an option. *What am I going to do? You have a knife.*

When I reach around for my knapsack, he grabs my wrist and drags me to the wall, pinning me there with his large body.

"What are you doing?" I cry, struggling against him to free myself. But he's too big and too fast.

"What do you think I'm doing?" he growls, tossing my backpack aside.

I want to cry or scream or something when it lands on the floor well out of my reach.

He shackles me to the wall like he's done this before.

I'm going to be trafficked. Sold to the highest bidder.

Stay strong, Daniela! Isabel and Valentina are counting on you. Don't let them down.

"Please let me go. Please. I can get you more money."

"You'll sell for a pretty penny. You don't have the kind of money it takes to buy your freedom. If you did, you wouldn't be here."

"I do have it."

I don't know if it's better to tell him who I am or reveal my connection to Antonio, or both, or if it will just make matters worse for me.

Could they get any worse?

I lift my chin. "My name is Daniela D'Sousa. My father was Manuel D'Sousa. My mother was Maria Rosa."

"My name is Vasco da Gama," he sneers, then laughs, his hand on the doorknob.

"I'm engaged to be married to Antonio Huntsman," I blurt out, because I can't let him leave. Once this ship is out on the ocean, the danger increases.

He pauses and turns to face me. "Is that so?"

"Yes, and Antonio will pay to get me back." *I hope. Unless I pushed too far. He might be done with me. The captain doesn't need to know this, Daniela.* "You don't want to make an enemy of him."

He grins. "Antonio Huntsman's bride-to-be. Well, well. If it's true, you'll earn more money for me than I thought." He starts to leave again.

"Please don't go. Let's discuss this. Please."

The captain comes back and crouches next to me. "Don't worry, I'll be back. And when I do, I'm going to fuck you real good. Break you in for your new life. You don't have a hole I'm not going to stick my dick into." He smiles, and I notice his teeth have a yellow cast. "And if you really are the D'Sousa girl"—he takes a lock of my hair, and I flinch—"I'm going to enjoy it all the more. I've never fucked a *princesa*. Is your cunt velvet lined? Does it taste like honey?"

A sour taste tickles my throat. What a vile human being. But I don't say anything that might make him carry out his threats now.

He lets go of my hair. "I have to leave before my crew figures out where I hid you. Because they'll want to fuck a *princesa* too. But you're mine first."

Without another glance in my direction, he grabs my knapsack and turns out the light, leaving me in the pitch dark. I hear the lock turn and his heavy footsteps retreating.

What have I done? What have I done? There's no way I can escape.

Marrying Antonio doesn't seem so bad now—maybe it

never did. Maybe the part I couldn't live with was being separated from Isabel and Valentina. *And the risks if the secret ever came out.* That was part of it too.

What will come of them if I don't survive? *I abandoned them.* I could have married him and sent money. They would have been fine. But I wanted to be with them. *You were selfish.*

I was. I wanted a life I was never going to have—not after Antonio lured me back to Porto.

Does he know I'm gone? *He must.* Are they looking for me? *Probably. But they'll never find me. Especially once the freighter leaves Porto.*

I slump onto the floor and cry, and cry, until there's nothing left.

Maybe some people are put on this earth for no other reason than to suffer.

I want my mother. *I need her.* The need is childlike and primitive, but my whole body aches for the comfort of her embrace.

My shoulders shake, and sobs of despair fill the tiny room, but there's not a single tear left to shed.

I did this to myself. I had no choice. I didn't.

The engine hums, and the ship sways. With every shift of the vessel, even the slimmest hope for rescue evaporates.

It's not long before my mind and body begin to slip away. Drifting farther and farther into a dark abyss.

I'm not afraid anymore. I'm awake, but calm. A hollow shell.

Alone in the dark, I don't think about Isabel or Valentina anymore, or about anything, really. I simply exist—like a discarded trinket, or an empty bottle of vintage Port. Once loved and cherished but having outlived its usefulness.

I'm not sure how much time passes before I hear footsteps.

There's nowhere to hide. No weapons. *Nothing*. My heart rate doesn't even tick up. I'm too exhausted.

I wet myself. I didn't feel the urge, but I feel the gush. It's an involuntary act. My body giving up.

The footsteps get closer and closer. When they stop, the lock turns, and my eyelids flutter closed.

As the footsteps enter the room, I shrink.

The fight is gone.

50

DANIELA

My feet are unshackled first, and I'm yanked upright by the arm.

A familiar scent slowly breaks through the stench of concentrated urine. My heart clenches.

Antonio.

It's your mind playing tricks.

A sliver of hope slices through the despair, but I don't open my eyes right away. My spirit won't survive the blow if I'm mistaken.

When my hands are free, I slowly open my eyes. *Just a tiny peek.*

"Antonio," I gasp, tears falling again.

He doesn't say a word as he drags me up the stairs and off the ship. *It's still docked. I thought*— I don't try to understand it.

Antonio doesn't even look at me. The vitriol that surrounds him is like a shield. A black cloud so dense it's impenetrable. But I have to try. I *want* to try.

"Thank you for saving me. I'm so sorry."

I'm starving for a human connection. A small touch to remind me I'm alive. I reach for him as we get to the pier.

"Don't you dare," he growls, swatting my hands away. He's rough, but the sting on my skin is nothing compared to what I feel in my heart.

Without a word, Antonio shoves me into the backseat of a waiting car and slams the door. He doesn't get in. At first I'm scared of what's going to happen to me, but Cristiano slips into the passenger seat, and I relax a bit. *He won't kill me.* At least that's what I tell myself.

Cristiano hands me a bottle of water over his shoulder. He doesn't look at me either. But I don't feel any rage from him.

"Do you have something I can sit on?" I ask, embarrassed that I peed myself, especially now that I'm going to get it on the car seat too.

He shakes his head but doesn't turn around.

"I'm sorry," I murmur. "Thank you for coming." It sounds so ridiculous, but my emotions are on a wild ride, and that's what spills out.

As we drive through the deserted pier, I remember Isabel is waiting to hear from me. She's going to be beside herself if she doesn't hear anything, and she's going to frighten Valentina.

"I realize I'm not in any position to ask for favors," I say earnestly. "But please contact Isabel, like you've done in the past. Tell her the plans have changed and to go home. Please don't say anything to worry her."

Cristiano doesn't respond at first, and I worry about what's going to come of them in Boston. They can't afford to stay in a hotel forever.

"That was done shortly after you spoke with her," he says finally.

"Thank you."

I stare out the window, seeing nothing. Errant thoughts, mere fragments, run through my mind, chasing one another. *"That was done shortly after you spoke with her." What does that mean? Did they know where I was all along?*

My pulse begins to race. "Were you tracking me?"

He doesn't reply. And I don't ask again.

As the car exits the pier, the driver makes a sharp right. He isn't headed toward Antonio's house in the valley. "Where are you taking me?"

Cristiano doesn't respond, but he raises the privacy screen so there can be no more questions.

51

DANIELA

After winding through the city for several miles, the driver takes a left into Huntsman Lodge. While I've been by it hundreds of times, I've only been inside a handful, when it was open to the public during celebrations.

The driver doesn't pull up to the main building but takes a utility road around to the back of the sprawling complex.

When the car stops, the lock clicks, and Antonio opens the door and hauls me to an elevator on the loading dock. It's just the two of us on a descent that seems to go on forever.

He doesn't look at me. Not once.

"Not a word from you when we get inside," he spits out, the venom nearly choking me.

I don't know why we're here. Or what it means for me. But I don't ask. Instead, I press my lips together, biting down on the fleshy inner rim, and stare straight ahead.

When the elevator doors creak open, he grabs my arm roughly and leads me through a set of metal doors to a tiled room. He shoves me inside. It's not all that different from the way the captain treated me. Although he had much less hatred about him.

"There's a toilet, there," he says, pointing to a water closet.

I go into the tiny room and start to shut the door, but he pushes hard against it.

"Closed doors and privacy are privileges you no longer have."

I consider leaving without using the toilet, but I need to pee, and the thought of wetting myself again is abhorrent.

Thankfully, he turns his back as I relieve myself. My underwear and yoga pants are still quite damp. It's disgusting.

When I go to the sink to wash my hands, Antonio wrenches me away and brings me to an open shower stall.

"Take off your clothes," he demands.

I want to say something. To explain myself. To make him understand my untenable position. My desperation. But his body is tight, and the dark cloud around him is even thicker now than it was at the pier.

As I take off my clothes, I do my best to conceal my naked body. Not just from him but from the cameras that I'm sure are all over this place.

Even now I can't let go of my modesty.

A vivid image of my mother pops into my head. Naked, unresponsive, blood oozing from her mouth and throat. Me, covering her with the picnic blanket, tucking it under her chin. Mamai *wouldn't want anyone to see her naked body*. She was dead. Modesty was such an inconsequential concern, much like it is now.

I don't cry, but as I take off my clothes, I allow myself to wallow in grief.

While I'm undressing, Antonio reaches around me into the shower and turns on the water.

"You have five minutes. Use plenty of soap."

I glare at his back, but I step under the water quietly.

It's barely tepid. I shiver, but I don't care that much about the temperature. I'm just grateful to be clean.

The cool water wakes me up, and as I soap my hair, I realize this isn't run-of-the-mill trouble I'm in. I defied Antonio in a very public way. I challenged his power and authority for all to see.

He's not going to forgive this so easily. *He might not forgive it at all.* I'm a traitor in his eyes. Even my father, who wasn't as exacting, would have viewed my behavior as an act of treason.

Traitors are punished by death in this world.

I'm afraid, although not as frightened as I was on the ship. *Because you're foolish. Antonio is going to torture and probably kill you.* He is. But I don't berate myself for taking any of the risks. I had to try.

Antonio turns off the water and shoves a threadbare towel at me. It's nothing like the towels Victor keeps at the house. Although the rough fabric feels good against my skin. It makes me feel alive.

"Hurry up," he barks.

My clothes are gone when I step out of the shower, and in their place is a pair of thin gray sweatpants and an olive-green T-shirt. No panties. No bra. No shoes. *Be grateful for the clothes.*

As soon as the sweatpants are on and the T-shirt is over my head, he grabs my arm, again, and hauls me out the door into a windowless room with concrete floors. Guards clustered in small groups make a path for us as we approach. No one says a word.

Is this the prison he once threatened me with? The one where he said the guards would take turns using me?

You knew this would be the punishment if you ran. You knew it, and you were willing to suffer the consequences. I was.

"I'm sorry, Antonio. I'm so sorry. I beg you for mercy." It's a very public apology, for a very public offense. My punishment will be very public too.

I'll toss you to the guards and let them have at you. When they've had their fill, they'll take you deep into the caves and drop you into a real prison. Those were his exact words.

"I'm sorry," I repeat, more desperately this time. Although in my heart I'm not sorry. And I'm not the one in the wrong here, but this isn't the time to make a point. I won't win. I'll just make my situation worse.

Antonio grips my arm tighter, and I wince. I'm sure there will be a bruise. This time he won't care. I don't care either. It's the least of my problems.

"I don't want to hear another goddamn word out of you until you're interrogated. Nothing," he shouts. The word echoes in the cold room.

The vengeance he seeks makes my eyes water. But I swallow back the tears. I won't cry in front of them. It'll just be one more thing for them to mock. This might be the beginning of the end for me, but I'll leave this earth with at least a shred of dignity.

Antonio hands me over not to Cristiano, but to Lucas, who has always had a rougher edge about him.

"Chain her to a chair in the central cave." He walks away without once looking at me. It's as though he's distancing himself.

There will be no mercy for me.

Lucas leads me forward without uttering a single word. On the way out of the room, I notice Joey and the creepy man from the market. They're not restrained. They're talking with the guards as if they all know each other.

It was a setup.

That bastard. That fucking sonofabitch. He's evil personified.

"It was all a game," I say to Lucas when we're out of hearing range of the guards. "Did you enjoy scaring me half to death?"

"If you think any of this is a game, you're even dumber than I thought you were."

I shiver at the menace in his voice.

With a hand still on me, Lucas drags a metal chair into the

center of a room filled with wooden barrels, lined up in neat rows. This is one of the caves where Huntsman Port ages.

"Sit," he commands, like I'm a dog.

I sit down, and he attaches cuffs to my wrists and chains them behind my back. The binding isn't so tight that I can't move, but the chains are heavy, and this position is going to get uncomfortable soon. Lucas chains my legs too.

Before he leaves, he brings a water bottle to my mouth. I shake my head.

"It's a mistake, but suit yourself." He screws the cap back on. "One bad decision after another."

Moments later, the lights in the room are turned off, except for the one directly over my head.

Lucas is right about one thing. This isn't a game. This is deadly serious. I feel it in my marrow.

It's been more than twenty-four hours since I've slept. It has to be. Despite my attempts to stay awake, I nod off here and there.

As the minutes turn into hours, I have trouble discerning dreams from reality.

My life flashes before me in little snippets. A happy little girl in a purple tutu with sequins that sparkle when I twirl. Parents who love me dearly. High atop Zeus, galloping with my braids flying behind me.

As I flip through the frames of my childhood, I feel my mother's presence. It's comforting beyond measure, but if she's here, it's a sure sign of what's to come.

But I don't need signs.

Antonio is not going to want a woman who defies him at every turn, weakening his authority. *A traitor.* And once the guards are through with me, he won't want to even look at me. *He doesn't want to look at you now.*

But he's not going to just let me go. He's going to make an example of me. That's how it works.

It's over now. He won. But at least I fought this time. *For all the good it did.*

I'm tired. At this point, death would be welcome. My only fear is that it won't be quick. That the torture will go on for weeks, or months.

As I say my silent goodbyes to Valentina and Isabel, I sob uncontrollably. *I'm sorry I brought you into this, but you'll be safe now. I love you. Take care of each other.*

I had hoped for so much more time. I dreamed of watching Valentina graduate and take on the world with her brilliant mind and an open heart. And I dreamed of falling asleep in the arms of a loving man, and for babies who called me *Mamai.* Despite everything, deep down, I always believed in fairy tales —even for me.

You're a foolish girl, Daniela. You were never destined for a fairy-tale ending. Your ending will look very much like your mother's. But this time there won't be a ray of hope that sprouts from the garden of evil.

52

ANTONIO

I sit in the villa and watch her on the screen. Tormented, tears running down her cheeks. We put her through hell today.

Lucas and Cristiano have caught glimpses of her chained in the cave, but the only one who sees her agony is me. *That's how I want it.*

I'm still irate, but the longer I watch her pain, the more the anger dissipates.

I never wanted to break her. I wanted her compliance, her obedience, but it had never been my intention to destroy her spirit.

But even as I relented, inch by inch, she never made the same effort. She pretended to adjust, but she was just biding her time. That's all. Daniela wants to go back to the US, and nothing, not even the possibility of death, is going to stop her.

Aside from betraying my trust, she took a stunning risk. We never lost sight of her, and the situation was never out of our control, but she had no way of knowing it. One misstep on our part. One missed connection. Or just some good old-fashioned bad luck, and things would have ended differently for her.

Cristiano puts a cup of coffee in front of me.

"Thanks," I mutter, never taking my eyes off the screen.

Cristiano and Lucas have been with me through the entire ordeal, and aside from a nap here and there, none of us have had any sleep. We've been focused on Daniela.

Apart from the forty minutes I spent in my apartment—or the brief interlude with Sonia—my attention has been on her. And even when it wasn't, I never stopped thinking about her.

Cristiano and Lucas have been doing double duty, concentrating on Daniela and on the shipment. Fortunately, the cargo wasn't an issue. It arrived in the UK on schedule—and intact.

Daniela, on the other hand, was a conundrum. Although I'm not sure if the biggest challenge was staying one step ahead of her or the thought—*no, the reality*—of her taking such an enormous risk with her life.

Cristiano, Lucas, and I are experienced at high-stakes endeavors, and we're not easily surprised—let alone stunned. But her perilous decisions were astounding.

Stopping Daniela is essentially like trying to stop a terrorist attack. You can thwart dozens of attempts, but sooner or later the bastards are going to be successful, because they're willing to die in the process.

She got lucky because we were tipped off. Chances are if she had boarded a random cargo freighter—rather than the one we lured her to—it would have been an ugly end for her. After they used her like a whore, they would have dumped her body into the middle of the ocean for the sharks to feast on, or sold her into a life that would have made her wish for death every minute of every day.

I don't have time to babysit her constantly, and we can't afford another day like today, where our best minds and too many resources are being used to track a 120-pound woman.

I need to make a pact with her. I'm not one of those men who believes you don't negotiate with terrorists. Never have been. I negotiate to get what I want. Period. The key is to seize control over the situation—and to never, *ever*, let them know they won a single inch.

That's why Daniela is chained to a chair in the cave. She has to be fully broken to know that I've won before I can show her any benevolence.

"How many people know?" I ask no one in particular.

"A handful of staff, although for the most part that can be covered with a simple excuse, and a dire warning not to gossip. We don't need to worry about Victor," Cristiano adds. "There were a few people at the pier whose silence was easily bought, and the captain of the ship—who wouldn't have had any idea who she was if she hadn't told him."

The captain of the ship. Our freighters are all at sea, and on short notice the best I could do was to borrow a docked ship. That sonofabitch captain is lucky he was nowhere to be found when I got there. Otherwise I'd have plunged a knife into his gut. He was told to scare her, but no one said one word about talking to her like she was a whore. Then, to make matters worse, he had the audacity to rub his cock as he left her room.

I have men scouring the docks for him. Eventually that fucker will show up, and when he does, he's mine.

"The guards know," I grumble. "She has to be punished."

"She's been punished enough," Cristiano replies quietly. "But I don't see any other way around it." He says the words, and he knows it's inevitable, but he saw what she went through today, especially once she got to the pier. Cristiano likes her. He was the one overseeing her safety while she was in the US. He's always liked her.

Today hasn't been easy on anyone. *Especially me.* As I watch the fight in her crushed—maybe beyond repair—I remember the fearless little girl on the spirited stallion, eyes twinkling at me from the saddle.

I've had enough. It's time to end this.

"She's sufficiently broken, and she's had plenty of time to ponder her fate."

The time also gave me an opportunity to take the edge off my anger. Two hours ago, I wouldn't have trusted myself to punish her. I'm still not entirely sure if I'm ready—but she's had enough of the waiting.

"It's time to finish it."

"Let someone else handle it," Cristiano suggests warily. "It doesn't matter who punishes her as long as it's on your orders."

Cristiano is right, but she's my problem. And I won't allow anyone to lay a finger on her.

"I'll do it," Lucas says, getting up.

"Sit down." I glare at him.

Cristiano and Lucas know something that no one else does: I'm not giving her up. *Ever.*

Her life will not be what it could have been, because I'll never trust her. But I made a promise to her father, and I intend to honor it. What my friends don't know is that it's about more than a promise. *I want her.*

Maybe I've always known it—at least since the morning I spent with her after Manuel died. But it became crystal-clear that first night we had dinner. When she turned up her nose at the inferior grapes, or the way her eyes lit up when she tasted the special young Port, or how her face glowed with excitement and happiness, *genuine happiness*, at the prospect of a vintage year for the entire valley—I knew then she was made for me. Her beauty and her good heart are a bonus.

But none of this gives her a free pass. Not in our world.

I look from Lucas to Cristiano. "She betrayed me, and I'll exact the punishment."

"Do you think you're calm enough for this?"

After her reckless behavior, I don't think I could be calm enough if I waited ten years. "She gets what she gets." I turn off my screen.

"I want all surveillance shut down in the cave during the interrogation. Nothing is to be recorded." I stand and push my chair in. "I'll let you know when you can send a few guards in close enough so that they can hear the punishment. Send the ones more likely to spread the warning that no traitor is spared." *Not even a beautiful woman who will be my wife.* "It was a public betrayal, and it will be a public punishment."

I stop before the doorway and turn. "Do me a favor. Find out everything, and I mean *everything*, you can about Isabel."

"We've looked at her pretty close," Lucas says, eyeing me.

"Not close enough. Comb through what we know about her relationship with the D'Sousas. Go back as far as you can into her family history. Something doesn't add up. No one risks what Daniela risked today for a maid."

"Antonio," Cristiano pleads. "Let Lucas or me handle Daniela."

I leave the room without another word.

53

DANIELA

In the distance, a door creaks, rousing me from a dreamlike sleep. The perimeter of the room lights up, softly, and the light directly overhead is dimmed.

I listen carefully as the footsteps approach. *One set.* This is reassuring. Not that one guard can't do a lot of damage, but not the same kind that two or more could do.

Like something out of a movie, Antonio appears from a dark aisle, flanked with wooden barrels.

He positions a metal chair a few feet from me and straddles it. His expression is unreadable—at least to me.

The ancient cave is eerily quiet, as though the spirits have melted into the stone walls, to await news of my fate.

Antonio observes me intently but doesn't say a word for several moments, and I don't dare say anything either.

"What do you have to say for yourself?" he finally asks.

While his voice is neither warm nor forgiving, the hatred seems to have lessened. Or perhaps a bit of sleep, as little and disturbed as it was, has given me a renewed sense of strength.

I can't just give up. I have to appeal to his sense of humanity—for Isabel and Valentina. *And for me.*

Be humble, Daniela. Above all, be humble and contrite.

"I'm done," I croak. "You won. I'll marry you, and we'll live in Porto."

"You'll marry me? This must be my lucky day." He's sarcastic, but not caustic. "I always win, Daniela. Always. I thought you would have learned that by now."

"I'm sorry I ran."

"I don't believe you."

"I made a mistake."

"Just one?"

"I wanted to be with Isabel and Valentina. They'll have a hard time surviving without me until Valentina is old enough to work."

"You *wanted* to be with them? I don't believe it's a thing of the past. You're never going back to the US."

I feel a lump forming in my throat. "I wanted to be with my family—what's left of it. That's a normal thing. I won't run again. But you're right. I'll never stop missing them."

"Your maid and her daughter are not your family."

I need to make him understand that they are family—it's true.

"They are my family, Antonio. In the same way Cristiano and Lucas are yours. If either of them were in trouble, you would risk everything to help them."

"I would never take the kind of risk you took today."

"I don't believe you," I say softly, and respectfully. "They're like your brothers. Not all family is blood."

Antonio's phone buzzes, and he gets up and disappears down the aisle he came up before. The door opens and closes seconds later. One set of footsteps approaches.

I hope it's him returning. My best chance for survival is with him. No one else can make that decision.

When he comes back, he's holding a small plate with a mug and some tea biscuits. He places it on his chair and unchains my wrists, briskly rubbing his palms over my arms and shoulders. I soak in the warmth of his hands—the humanity I so desperately need right now.

Before he sits down, he hands me the cup of tea and the biscuits.

I'm overwhelmed by the small kindness. *Maybe he's not going to kill me.* I start to cry. I'm leaking from my eyes and my nose, and no amount of sniffing can stop it from dripping off my face and onto my shirt.

He gets up and comes back, holding a wet facecloth and a clean T-shirt. He hands me the warm cloth. The heat feels so good against my face.

"Take off your shirt, and put this dry one on."

I don't bother to ask if there are people watching, because it almost doesn't matter. Despite my tears, I'm numb inside.

"The cameras are off," he murmurs.

He remembered my fear of being watched. I almost start to cry again.

"You've had a hellish twenty-four hours, and I'm sure there are people who feel you've been punished enough. I'm not one of those people."

I nod, the hope evaporating.

"Aside from being reckless, your actions were traitorous. You attempted to dishonor me, and your father, by subverting our blood oath. I can't have my enemies, your father's, or anyone else, believe that kind of behavior will be tolerated, even from you."

The last sliver of hope sinks into a cavernous abyss. I hear the thud as it hits bottom.

Not that I'm surprised by his decision. Deep down, I knew he would need to make an example of me. I grew up in this world. I was too young to be privy to all the dreadful details, but I've always known that traitors are punished by death.

"I have two favors to ask before you punish me."

"You're in no position to ask for favors, and I'm in no mood to grant them. But let's hear it."

"When my mother died, Isabel was there for me, every hour of every day," I begin, a slight wobble in my voice. "In the aftermath, when I didn't think I would survive, Valentina was born. She brought sunshine and happiness back to my life—to all of our lives. Isabel let me help care for her, and every day I got stronger. Even if you can't understand it, they're my family."

I lift my chin and meet his eyes. "I was disloyal and dishonest, and I accept your punishment, but please don't let them suffer for my behavior. If I'm gone, they have no way to pay the rent or to eat. Please send them some money. They don't require much, just enough to live decently. You don't have to do it for me, but do it for my mother. She was your mother's best friend, and took her in when it wasn't safe for her to be around your father."

His brow furrows, not like he's worried, but as though he's parsing through my words, trying to make connections. I can't afford to make those connections for him—not even as my time runs out.

"You said there were two favors." His gaze narrows. "What's the second?"

"Instead of giving me to your guards to do as they wish, put a bullet in my head. Preferably when I'm unaware. You don't need to torture me to make your point. Simply murdering Daniela D'Sousa will send a resounding message through the valley."

He eyes me carefully. "If I'm going to grant you just one favor, which should it be?"

"Send money to Isabel and Valentina." I don't hesitate, because really, every sacrifice I've made in the last six years has been for them.

A single tear runs down my cheek. He tips his chair forward and catches the drop on his thumb.

"You will not die by my hand, or at my order. I'm not done with you," he says quietly. "You're mine, Daniela. I'll never be done with you."

His voice is soft but resolute. For the first time, I notice the black circles under his eyes. *He's been up all night too.*

"Giving you to my guards...I made that threat in anger—and I was wrong," he concedes without apology. "But even if I toss you to the guards, they won't lay a finger on you. The men I allow to be anywhere near you would never rape a woman. I'd stake my life on it."

I take a sip of tea. My head is spinning and my emotions are a snarled morass. I can't even begin to process everything he just said. But I'm not going to die. I'm not going to be raped by the guards. Although I'll never go back to the US—*maybe one day, though, they'll be able to come here.*

"You may continue to have money sent to Isabel and her daughter for rent and food and other necessities. That's up to you. I already agreed to that, and I don't go back on my word." He pauses for a long moment. "On our first wedding anniversary, if you don't make my life hell, I'll fully fund a college trust for Valentina. I know you have an account set up for her, but at five dollars a paycheck, it will never be enough."

I don't think about the price I'll have to pay for his generosity—not right now. If Valentina goes to college, she'll have life-changing opportunities. It's what I've always hoped for her. "Thank you," I reply, my heart filled with true gratitude.

"We are getting married," he continues, more forcefully than he's been. "We will live as husband and wife, with everything that entails, and you will never, never take the risk you took today, or betray me in any other way. Is that clear?"

I nod. "Yes."

"But there will be punishment. Here, today, at my hand."

"I understand." I don't know what it is, but I don't care. I just want it over with, and the humiliation behind me. My life won't be what I'd hoped, but Isabel and Valentina will be taken care of, and things could be worse for me. I'm sure many women would love to be married to Antonio.

Just not me. Not under these circumstances.

"I have a proposition for you," he says, his dark eyes glimmering.

I eye him suspiciously, because any deal he makes will be for his benefit, not mine.

54

ANTONIO

"Since you like to run and hide so much, I'm going to give you an opportunity to test your skills. If you're successful in evading me in the dark cave, there will be no punishment. Remain hidden for twenty minutes, and you win. I'll even give you a five-minute head start. But if I catch you before the time is up, I'll do with you as I please."

"Because you haven't hunted me enough in the last twenty-four hours."

There's a hint of sass in her voice. A spark among the ashes. Maybe she's not irreparably broken. That should concern me, but instead it makes my dick hard.

"I'm going to spend the rest of my life hunting you, *Princesa*. And every time I catch you, you're going to worship my cock. Get used to it."

"I won't win," she says softly, defeat in her voice. "You have cameras to track my movements."

"Every camera, every microphone in this room, is off right now, and it will stay that way. I'll set the timer on my phone. What have you got to lose?"

Daniela gnaws gently on the inside of her cheek.

She's thinking about it.

"What about making an example of me?"

Oh, I'll still make an example of you. There's no chance I won't find you before the timer goes off. I'm greedy for you. Drawn to you in ways that are inexplicable. You can't hide from me, Princesa.

"This is my city, my valley, and I make the rules. If I want to give you an opportunity to work off your punishment, I will. What I won't do is let you off the hook for nothing."

She tips her head to the side, studying me carefully. "Isn't a game of hide-and-seek letting me off the hook?"

I feel the edge of my mouth curl. This is *not* a child's game, and she's going to feel the pressure as soon as the timer starts.

"When the stakes are high, it never feels like a simple game." I shrug. "It's up to you. I'm prepared to go forward with the punishment."

She lifts her head, and her eyes flare.

She's going to do it.

"Fine," she says with a ring of defiance in her voice. "But you better not cheat."

I don't need to cheat. "I give you my word."

I use my phone to turn out the main lights. The walkways are illuminated by strips of lighting on the floor. It's dark, but not pitch black. Although the casks stacked on the aisles make it difficult to see anywhere but directly in front of you.

"I'm going to set the timer on my phone for twenty minutes. I'll start searching for you after five minutes—until then, I'll remain right here."

"You won't cheat?" she asks again.

"I already gave you my word."

She nods.

I hold up the phone so she can see me press the start button, and then watch her disappear.

As I listen for the rustle of clothing or a misstep, I imagine her raspy breath as she slinks through the dark. *Is her skin damp yet? Her heart thumping? Is the rush of adrenaline coursing through her veins?* My cock thickens with every salacious thought.

She's light on her feet—that's to her advantage.

I'm enjoying this little game more than I should be. Not hide-and-go-seek, but hunter-and-prey. The hunter has all the advantages—although he doesn't always win. But in this case, it's inevitable.

Even before I worked here, I played in this cave as a young child. I know it intimately. Every corner, every hiding place, all the passageways that lead to dead ends. I could give her a fifteen-minute head start and still find her.

I slip off my shoes while I wait for the time to pass. And I listen. I synchronize my watch to the timer. And I listen.

I hear her turn left at the end of the center aisle. *Right would have given her a better chance.*

My pulse begins to race as I wait for the chase to begin.

When the five minutes are up, I proceed stealthily, pursuing her one step at a time, my bare feet silent on the stone floor.

I don't follow her path. That's what she expects. Instead, I advance toward her, staying some distance away. And I listen.

There's a telling squeak, and a scrape. She's wedged herself between two casks. I would wager my last dollar on it. *Oh Princesa, you're trapped, and I'm coming for you.*

My heart is hammering. My dick is aching for her tight little cunt. *I want her more than I've ever wanted anything.*

I step heavily onto the stone floor. I want her to know I'm searching for her—that I'm not too close, but not too far away either. I want her rattled. I want the pulse in her neck thrumming strong.

If I close my eyes, I can almost smell her fear. Almost taste the salt on her skin.

When only a row of casks separate us, I check my watch. *Three minutes*. I won't risk taking it down to the last seconds, in case she runs. I'll want a minute to chase her.

I hope she runs. God, I want to end this hunt with a run.

With a minute left, I slither around the corner and grab her shoulders from behind.

She screams. It's the shaky scream of someone caught by surprise. Her pulse is pounding, and I feel the surrender in the slump of her shoulders.

The timer echoes in the cave.

"I captured you," I murmur near her ear. "You're mine."

She whimpers, and it takes everything I have not to fuck her on the cold floor.

With the lights off, I drag her into the aisle, snake my fingers into her silky hair, and claim her mouth. She doesn't fight me.

Her surrender is glorious.

I brush the hair off her flushed, damp skin. "You're beautiful, and there are so many other things I'd rather do to you than punish you."

"Please, just get it over with," she pants.

I turn the timer off and slide the phone into my pocket.

It's quiet now. The only sound is her labored breath.

I take her by the hand, threading my fingers through hers, and lead her to a barrel deep in the cave. A barrel that's the perfect height, where her toes will dangle just above the floor.

55

ANTONIO

When we're deep in the cave, beside the wooden cask that holds my prized Port, I pull out my knife and slice through her shirt, exposing her luscious tits. The tips are beaded tight, and it takes everything I have not to lower my head and suck one into my hungry mouth. But if I do, we'll never get the punishment behind us, because I won't be able to stop with just a small taste.

"Lie over the barrel," I murmur into her hair. "With your gorgeous ass in the air."

She shudders but doesn't hesitate.

Her rank obedience feeds my need for control, striking a chord deep in my soul. It both soothes and energizes me in ways that I can't begin to quantify.

There's only a small whimper as I yank off her pants and rub my hand over her smooth skin. "So soft. Flawless. But it won't be like that when I'm through."

She whimpers again, soft and throaty. My cock burns for her.

Without taking a hand off her sexy little body, I text Cristiano that the punishment is about to begin.

I slowly remove my belt.

Restraining the pent-up need, I glide the thick leather across her skin, tapping lightly, coaxing the nerve endings closer to the surface.

She mewls as the soft cowhide trails up and down her back and thighs. The mewls get louder when the strap pauses for a small bite of her flesh. *Just a nibble to prime her for the feast. My feast.*

"I'm going to enjoy turning your skin red. Do you know how hard my cock is just imagining the gorgeous welts?"

Her breathing is shallow and quick as I step between her legs, nudging them apart. My fingertips trace her spine, trailing lower and lower into the hollow of her lower back and over her fine ass.

She's quiet as I explore her body, trembling when my fingers find a sensitive spot. My thumb glides down her crack, stopping to press on the tempting rosebud.

Every muscle in her body contracts. I smile.

"Not today," I murmur, my hand slipping between her legs.

She's aroused, soaking wet, and her clit is hard and swollen when I run my fingers over it. I could stroke her all night. First with my fingers, then with my tongue. "You like this, don't you? My fingers on your pussy?"

When she doesn't answer, I take away my hand and sink my teeth into her ass. Not enough to break the skin, but enough to mark her.

She yelps, pressing her pelvis into the barrel, grinding her pussy on the smooth wood.

I almost toss the belt aside and slide into her, pounding that mound against the barrel until she screams.

My hand is shaking as I force myself to step back. Before I change my mind about the punishment, I fold the belt in half and let it fly over her bare skin.

When the leather strikes her ass, a tortured scream echoes

through the dimly lit cave, and a sense of satisfaction rushes through me. It's the retribution I've craved since the moment I learned she was headed for the docks.

My belt sails again. *Whack*. She cries out. The scream is muffled now, but it's heady, nonetheless.

I picture the captain's hands on her and let the leather fly again. I want to do it again, and again. But it's feeling too much like a drug. Too much like a punishment dealt from an undisciplined hand. *Too much like vengeance.*

I'm a second away from surrendering to the thirst for revenge, and I no longer trust myself with the belt in my hands.

I toss it aside and draw a clean breath, letting my fingertips graze her red, welted skin.

She clutches the barrel and groans with the contact. But I show her no mercy as my hand comes down on her. *I can't.*

Crack.

Crack.

Crack.

My palm stings from the impact—it feels safe, grounding me and reminding me that this vulnerable woman is under my protection. The belt provided too much distance. It made it too easy to spin out of control.

I rub her bruised skin and slide my fingers between her legs, over the slick flesh. She moans softly. Her mewls curl into my consciousness, driving me forward to an end.

With one hand stroking her pussy, I bring the other onto the raw skin. *Hard.*

She screams. It's a tortured cry, but she presses her pussy into my hand for the pleasure she needs to drown the pain. And I give it to her. I swirl my fingers around her clit until she begs for more.

I spank her again, and again, sliding two fingers into her tight little cunt. She moans, loud and sultry, humping my hand, and when I pull it away, she humps the barrel.

Jesus, fuck.

While she grinds into the smooth wooden cask, I almost come in my pants like a schoolboy.

Her face is flushed and sweaty. She's panting loudly. Struggling to finish. *She's close. So close.*

I grab my phone and call Cristiano. "Get everyone the hell away from here. Now," I bark, tossing the phone aside.

I lift her up and off the barrel. Cradling her head while capturing her mouth with mine until I can't breathe.

"I want you to straddle the barrel," I murmur, helping her astride.

Her eyes are glazed, and she doesn't fight me. If I were a good man, I would stop this right now. But I'm not, and I don't.

"Spread your legs nice and wide. That's it, ride it like you would ride me," I instruct when she's safely astride, her palms clutching the edges.

She looks up at me as if uncertain.

I smooth back her hair. "Trust me. I'm not going to hurt you. The punishment is over."

She pauses, then nods. I stroke my cock through my pants as she grips the side of the barrel and lists forward, canting her hips back and forth.

"My prized Port is in this barrel. The one I gave you to taste. Rub that pussy all over it. Make that wine sweeter than it already is."

She rides with abandon. Jaw slack. Eyes dilated and shining. Head tipped back. I can't take my eyes off her. But watching isn't enough. *I need to touch her.*

Without wasting one more goddamn second, I pull off my pants and straddle the barrel behind her, my feet firmly on the floor.

"I'm right here," I whisper into her hair. "Move any way you'd like. I won't let you fall. Do whatever feels good."

"Mmmm."

It's all she says as she rubs her ass against my hard cock.

My thighs are grazing hers, not enough to hinder her movement but enough to stabilize her so she doesn't fall.

I roam her body while she rides. My fingers find her nipples. I stroke and pinch the hard little points.

"Ahhh," she gasps, gliding over the barrel. "Antonio," she whimpers.

My dick gets harder and longer when my name tumbles from those plump lips.

I wrap her hair around my hand and tug her head back to see her face.

"You're beautiful. So beautiful, *Princesa*. Are you going to come for me?"

She purrs, inching forward and rubbing her pussy against the smooth cork stopper. I'm not even sure she's aware she's doing it.

My dick is weeping. I can't wait a second longer.

"I'm going to fuck you," I murmur, holding her hips. "My cock is throbbing for you. I want to feel your pussy around it. I need you to milk it real good. Will you do that?"

Her head bobs up and down. "Yes," she says in a loud, clear voice. "Yes. Now," she gasps. "I need you inside me, please."

A part of me knows I should wait. Knows that this is the pent-up anxiety, desperate to uncoil. A clawing need to be pushed over the edge. The yearning to feel alive. She needs it. She wants it. In the way a junkie craves a fix. I need it too.

I won't deny her.

I won't deny myself.

I gently push her shoulders forward and grasp her hips, lifting them until my cock is notched at her entrance. She tries to squirm onto the fat head, but I don't let her take control.

"You take what I give you," I whisper into the thick air while I slide balls-deep into her.

Daniela groans, and a grunt escapes from my chest. She moans, wiggling into me. Her pussy is hot and tight.

I'm not going to last. I've wanted this too much, for too long.

I reach around her, using one hand to steady us both, and stroke her clit, pressing into the swollen flesh while she whimpers my name. I don't let up until I feel her body tighten, and then I pinch the bud until she bucks, caught between my hand and my cock.

She begs and pleads—and calls God's name and mine as the orgasm rips through her.

I sink my teeth into her neck and own her pussy until I'm empty.

When I can move again, I lean over and drop a small kiss on her shoulder—on the spot where my teeth marked her. She's limp as a rag doll, her body folded over the cask.

"Hold on tight, Daniela. Don't let go of the barrel."

I throw on my pants and pull my shirt over her head so that she's not naked when we leave here.

She hasn't moved a muscle.

"Are you okay?" I ask gently.

She nods. *"Mm-hmm."*

Running a soothing hand over her back, I call the villa. Cristiano answers immediately. "Shut down all surveillance between here and my apartment. *Everything.* Give me fifteen minutes, and then turn it all back on."

She begins to lilt to one side. I tuck the phone into the crook of my neck and lift her off the barrel.

"Everything okay?" Cristiano asks.

I look down at the sleepy woman in my arms. "Yeah," I say softly.

A part of me actually believes that everything just might be okay.

56

DANIELA

The sound of Antonio's stern voice wakes me.

"Daniela D'Sousa is in my bed. And if you like your job here, my mother will not hear a word about it unless it's from my mouth."

Where am I? My eyes scan the dark room for something familiar, but there's nothing. The sheets are crumpled beside me. *I didn't sleep alone.*

"Maria Rosa's daughter?" a woman asks, as if it can't possibly be true.

"Alma, don't test me. I am not playing."

Alma. Oh God. She knows I'm here, in Antonio's bed. I throw my arm over my eyes, trying to remember everything that happened last night—trying to remember *anything* that happened.

A sliver of light shines on the ceiling as the door creaks. Antonio turns on a lamp in the corner and shuts the door.

Although the room isn't bright, I blink several times, adjusting to the light.

"Good morning," he says softly, sitting on the edge of the

bed beside me. His features are relaxed, his expression almost gentle. Something I've rarely seen in him.

I'm still confused about where we are and how I got here. More than just a little confused. It's unsettling.

"Good morning. Where are we?"

"My apartment at Huntsman Lodge."

I nod, trying to remember how I got here.

"How are you feeling?"

"A little achy. But otherwise okay."

"That's from being in bed for so long."

"What time is it?"

"Seven thirty."

He's dressed in a suit, like he might be going to work.

"How long was I asleep?" I ask, somewhat guarded. The memory lapse is making me uneasy.

"About forty-eight hours."

"What?" I gasp, sitting up. "There are huge gaps in my memory. Was I drugged?"

"Absolutely not. Tell me the last thing you remember."

I sift through my memory, trying to piece the fragments together. *I got in the truck. I remember the market and the pier. And a ship, and then Antonio coming into a room where I was shackled to a wall. He was so angry.*

I examine his face for clues, but there are none. Although the wrinkles on his forehead grow deeper with my silence.

"I remember you being angry. Furious, as you dragged me off the ship. And I remember the shower, and everything else is fuzzy." I touch a small round bandage in the crook of my arm.

"The doctor was here yesterday."

"A doctor?"

"I couldn't get you to stay awake long enough to take fluids. I was concerned that you were dehydrated. The doctor gave you an IV and did a little blood work."

I remember the IV going in. A prick. I also remember the

doctor saying he wouldn't advise any more punishment. *"Mind your own goddamn business," Antonio replied.*

Punishment.

"It's not that I have no memory—not exactly. It's that things are choppy and hazy. Just bits and pieces. I'm not sure what parts I dreamed and which are real."

"Give yourself a little time. Eventually you'll remember everything."

"You punished me?" I ask as I remember the bite of the belt on my skin.

He nods. "I did."

His words and his expression are devoid of emotion. I don't know what to make of it.

We had sex. And there was a barrel. And begging. And an orgasm. What if it wasn't a dream? *Oh my God.*

"Did we have—sex?" I ask, swallowing the embarrassment.

His expression is hard now—or maybe serious. "We did."

Public betrayals don't warrant private punishments. "Were people watching?"

He shifts on the bed. "The punishment was heard by anyone in the vicinity. Including your screams. But no one saw anything," he adds quietly.

"They heard us having sex," I mutter under my breath, trying to remember what anyone might have overheard.

"*No.* No one heard us having sex. I had the area cleared before we had sex." He reaches for my hand, running his thumb over my knuckles. "The sex had nothing to do with the punishment."

I nod, cringing inside as I remember more and more about the sex. It might be easier to digest if he said it was punishment, but I know it wasn't.

I remember wanting him inside me. *No.* That's much too mild to describe what I was feeling. I was *desperate* to have him fuck me. *Desperate* for release. I was out of my mind with need, and I would have done anything to make it happen. The truth sits painfully in my chest, elbow to elbow with the unbridled shame.

He doesn't say anything. He sits quietly, his hip against my thigh, letting the memories tumble back.

"Did you use a condom?" I ask, staring at light peeking through the shutters so that I don't have to look at him.

"You're on birth control," he replies, fingering the tiny insert under my skin.

"That's not the only reason to use a condom. I can't believe you would take the risk. And how do you know I'm on birth control?" I ask, glaring at him.

"I have your medical records. In case of an emergency."

"How?"

"Medical records aren't difficult to access." He pauses. "I'm clean, and I'm very careful about using protection. I don't intend on using a condom when having sex with my wife. But you need to know, I'd never take that kind of risk with you. *Ever.* I might be a monster, but I'm not that kind of monster."

I don't know if it's true that he would never risk my health, but I don't respond. As my memory starts to slowly return, I have so many questions. I don't want to talk about condoms anymore.

"How did this get here?" I ask, tugging on the nightgown I'm wearing. It was in my closet at the house a few days ago. I'm positive.

"I sent someone over to the house to pick up a few things for you. Paula packed a bag. After you ran, her weekend off was canceled."

My stomach churns. I gave her the weekend off so that she wouldn't be there when they found me missing. I thought it would be easier on her.

"Alma's here," Antonio says. "Do you remember my mother's cook?"

Yes, I remember Alma. She would sneak me extra treats whenever we visited the Huntsmans. "The one who makes the mouthwatering caramels?"

He smiles. "The very same. She'll make you breakfast, and then you can have a shower, and when you're ready, someone will drive you back to the valley."

Victor and Paula. I betrayed them too. Especially Paula.

"I need to go, but there are a couple things I want to talk to you about."

Although I don't have a clue about what he's going to say, my stomach clenches.

"First, the race is Saturday, and the ball is on Saturday night."

The race and a grand party take place every year in Porto, on a Saturday around the time the camellias are at peak bloom. On Sunday, the vines are blessed, and everyone prays for an abundant harvest. "It's Camellia Weekend?"

He nods. "You'll sit in my box during the race. I'll send someone over to make sure you have the appropriate clothing. Buy what you want. It won't come out of the money you send Isabel. Be extravagant. It's your reintroduction into the world you walked away from six years ago."

The last time I attended the race, my mother was alive. I've never been to the ball. Although when I was a little girl, my parents always went. My mother promised that one day I would go too. Sadness unfurls inside my chest every time I think about my mother. Time hasn't made it any easier.

"While the stylist is there," Antonio adds, "talk to her about a wedding dress. Now that more people know you're here, I don't want to wait to get married."

A lump forms in my throat, making it harder to breathe. "When is the wedding?"

"One week from Saturday. I'll have the wedding planner get in touch with you too."

My stomach is turning somersaults, and if I have to hear too much more, I'm going to vomit all over the luxurious comforter.

"When you get back to the house, call Isabel and calm her down. After what happened, I'm sure she's beside herself. I can't have her skittish. She could create problems. You might want to let her know that there is a guard stationed at the house around the clock. They'll ensure her safety and that of her daughter."

I grab Antonio's wrist. "Are they in danger?"

"We left a guard on the ground as a precaution when you came back to Porto. Isabel and Valentina are not in any danger that I'm aware of." He studies me carefully. "Do you have any reason to believe they're in danger?"

I shake my head, but I'm not entirely sure. "No. Nothing aside from the usual danger that comes from living in an impoverished city."

"The guard should ease your mind."

"What should I tell her about us?"

"Tell her that you've decided to honor your father's wishes, and you're going to marry me."

She's never going to believe that.

"You can also tell her that you'll be in regular contact, including video chats, and that we'll be visiting Fall River as part of our wedding trip."

I stare at him, searching for some sign that he's taunting me. But there's nothing, and a sense of excitement starts to bubble up inside me. "Do you mean it? The contact, and the trip? Because they'll be so disappointed if we don't go."

"What about you? Won't you be disappointed?"

I nod. "Heartbroken. But I can take it. Isabel's fragile, and Valentina is a child. We don't make promises to her we can't keep."

"*Princesa*, unless you've pushed me to the brink of insanity, I never say things I don't mean."

He inches closer, and for a moment I feel like he might kiss me, but he pulls back. "I have a meeting. It's been days since you've had any food. Make sure you eat breakfast before you leave."

"Will I see you tonight?" I ask.

"I'll be out of the country until the end of the week, on foundation business. You can call Cristiano if there's a problem. I'm running a day behind schedule, and I'll be difficult to reach."

When he shuts the door behind him, a wave of disappointment breaks over me. Not a heart-wrenching surge, but a ripple. Still, it takes me by surprise.

As I get out of bed and into the shower, I don't think about Antonio. I don't think about how much I wanted him to kiss me. And I don't fret about the wedding. It's merely a vehicle to get me back to Valentina and Isabel. Not forever, but for a few days.

I'll take it.

57

DANIELA

"*Bom dia*," I say to the older woman bustling around Antonio's kitchen in a colorful bib apron, with her hair coiled into a tight bun. I'd recognize her anywhere. Not as the Huntsmans' cook, but from Santa Ana's, where she sings like an angel on Christmas Eve.

"Look at you," she cries. "So beautiful, like your mother."

I want to leap into her arms, but I squeeze her hand instead. "Every Christmas I think about you, Alma, singing in the church. You were my favorite part of Midnight Mass."

She laughs, but her eyes are wet. It seems more like sadness than nostalgia.

"What's wrong?" I ask gently.

"Were you the woman whose screams were heard coming from the caves?"

Public betrayal. Public punishment. The words are tattooed on my brain, and I knew my screams were heard by God knows who, but the reality still stings. I draw a large breath and nod. My head is so heavy it barely moves.

Alma places a hand over her heart. "Was my son involved?"

She knows the answer, though I'm sure she hopes I'll prove

her wrong. I won't lie to her, but I soften the blow. "Cristiano has shown me as much leniency as he can."

"Lydia will be livid. She will never allow this."

"Antonio isn't a boy. His mother doesn't have control over his decisions. My father and Antonio entered into a betrothal agreement before my father died."

"Your father?" she asks, skepticism in every syllable.

"My father," I reply, my tone tinged with disgust.

"That would have never have happened if your mother was alive."

My mouth curls into a sad little smile. "That's for sure."

"How can I help you?" she asks.

My heart clenches at the sincerity of the offer.

"You can pray for me, but please don't interfere in any way. That will only make matters worse for me. It was not my agreement, and I was appalled when I first learned about it. But I've decided to marry Antonio, and to make the best life for myself that I can." I say the words with as much dignity as I can muster.

"You've decided," she mocks, mostly to herself, knowing full well I never had a choice.

"That's my decision." I take her hand. "If you want to do something for me, you could make me some caramels."

She smiles. "I loved your mother. She had so much spirit. I'm always here for you. Lydia isn't going to be happy about this. If you change your mind, I can call her. Don't forget that."

The punishment for going behind his back to his mother would be enormous. At the *very* least, there would be no wedding trip to Fall River. Lydia won't be able to stop the wedding, and the risk isn't worth it to me.

Victor answers the door when I get back to the valley. "*Senhora* Daniela," he says, greeting me with a smile.

"Hello, Victor." As much as I'd like to hide, I look straight into his eyes. "I'm sorry about any trouble I might have caused for you, or the staff."

He waves me off. "We all do what we need to do in life to survive. Those of us in power need the pushback the most."

I smile softly at him. He's not talking about himself. He's talking about Antonio.

"Is Paula upstairs?" I ask. "I need to apologize to her too."

"I honored your wishes and gave her a couple days off. It wasn't the weekend, but she was still very happy. She'll be back tomorrow."

"Thank you. I'm going to go upstairs and settle in. I'll come down for dinner."

On my way upstairs, I avoid looking out the second-floor window. My hope is to start fresh. To accept my fate, even if I don't like it.

I open the suite door, and everything looks the same. The phone Antonio had given me is on the desk. I pick it up and take it over to the chair that overlooks the garden, and I call Isabel, bracing myself for the sea of emotions she's going to unleash.

"Hello," I say, the guilt from what I put her through hitting me hard.

"Daniela," she says breathlessly. "What happened?"

"First, I'm fine. My plan to escape was never going to work."

"I was so worried about you going down to the docks. Young women disappear from there all the time."

I'm sure Isabel was haunted by her own memories as she thought about my plan. I should have never given her the details.

"Where are you now?" she asks.

"I'm at Antonio's house in the valley. I made a decision to

honor my father's wishes and marry him." It doesn't hurt as much as I thought it would to say the words out loud. Maybe I'm already resigned to the idea. Or maybe, after being on the run, it no longer seems as dreadful as it once did.

She starts to sob quietly, and my heart breaks.

"Isabel. I've done everything I can to get back there. Marrying him is the best thing for *all* of us."

"What have you told him?"

"Just that. That I'm going to marry him. Sometimes saying less is more." This conversation is probably monitored. I hope she gets the hint. "You'll have money to live, and if all goes well, we'll have enough to send Valentina to college when she's ready."

"What did you give up for this?"

I hear the grief in her voice.

A lot less than I've given up in the past to hold on to secrets.

"I need you to remain calm. Stop fretting about me. I'm safe." My safety is the one thing I'm sure about. Antonio's not going to kill or maim me. But I'm not sure whether to tell Isabel about the guard, although I can't see how it can hurt.

"You and Valentina are also safe. There's a guard watching the house at all times. You don't need to worry. It's merely a safety precaution."

"My English," she says. "How am I going to raise Valentina alone in a strange country?"

"Listen to me, Isabel. We fight the battle one hill at a time. What I haven't told you yet is that after the wedding, we'll be coming to see you. I'm not sure how long I can stay—probably just a few days. Please don't tell Valentina about the marriage until I get there. I'd like to tell her myself, and it might be easier if she meets Antonio first."

"Do you think it's a good idea to bring him here?" she asks with some trepidation. The Huntsmans will always be the enemy. She'll never forgive them for what they did to my mother. Not even Antonio, who wasn't there.

"I want to see you, and I don't have a better idea about how to do that. I'm hoping after he gets to spend some time with both of you, he'll want you to come back to Porto. Let's see. I know it's not fair to ask you to keep the secret from Valentina, but I'd like an opportunity to break the news to her." I have no idea how Valentina's going to react, but I'm convinced I can smooth things over better than Isabel can.

"When is the wedding?"

"One week from Saturday," I say softly.

"Your mother," she cries, "she wanted so much for you."

"I have so much. Marrying him is a small trade-off for all of us to have the things we need. It's our best chance to be together again." I say the words, and to some extent I've come to accept marrying him, but it's not a small trade-off, and we both know it.

She sighs.

"I love you, and I'll call you often. I'm going to give you my new phone number, and we can talk every day."

"Can we video-chat again? It was so good to see your beautiful face."

I smile. It's funny to hear Isabel talk about video-chatting. "We can. Antonio has agreed to allow it. A big hug to you, my friend. And give Valentina one from me too."

58

ANTONIO

The driver pulls up to my mother's London apartment. Instead of getting some work done like I promised myself as I boarded the plane, I spent the entire trip indulging in my favorite new fantasy. The one that involves me fucking Daniela on a Port barrel in a dimly lit cave. Her eyes rolling back in her head as she comes all over my dick.

Christ. I'll never get another damn thing done if I don't stop thinking about how amazing her tight little pussy feels around my cock.

I refuse to beat myself up over whether or not I should have let things get that far after the day she had. Although I won't deny that I'm an asshole. I am.

But the one thing I was absolutely right about is that passion burns hot inside that woman. She needs to be freed from the mindset that holds her back. *And I fully intend to be the man who frees her.*

What bothers me most about that night is when she asked for two favors: money for Isabel and the kid, and a quick death. When she could choose only one, she chose Isabel and Valentina.

Faced with what she believed was repeated rape and death, no one—*no one*—would have made that choice. That sacrifice was too big to make for someone who isn't a close relative. I don't care what she says about family. It doesn't add up. *I need Lucas to step up his research on Isabel.*

I ring the bell to my mother's apartment. I'm not looking forward to breaking the news about Daniela to Lydia Huntsman, or Lydia Huntsman Taft as she's now known.

Several years after my father died, my mother married the former British ambassador to Portugal, to everyone's delight. The British and the Portuguese have a special relationship, established around Port, that dates back to the mid-fifteen hundreds. Many families in Porto were created around that relationship. My mother's family is Portuguese, and my father's ancestors are from England. I'm a mongrel.

"Antonio, my love," my mother cries, opening the door, "I don't know if I'm shrinking, or if you're getting taller." She throws her arms around my shoulders, holding me tight.

There isn't a day that goes by that I'm not grateful she's safe and happy.

"How was your trip?"

"Uneventful."

"Just the way it should be. Take off your suit jacket. The queen's not joining us for lunch.

"I had dinner with Rafael on Friday," she continues while hanging my jacket. "He doesn't seem too broken up about Abel."

"I can't say I blame him."

"It's heartbreaking, really."

"Edward at work?" I ask, changing the subject to something far more pleasant. Her husband couldn't be any more different from Abel, or my father. Edward treats her like a queen, which keeps him on my good side.

"He's going to try to sneak away to see you, but he didn't

want to promise. Come into the kitchen while I put the last touches on lunch."

"Don't you have a cook to prepare lunch?" I ask, following her into the spacious kitchen.

"And let an opportunity pass to fuss over my handsome son? If you had given me more notice that you were coming, I would have prepared all your favorite dishes."

"I didn't come to eat. I came to see you. How's Samantha and her family?" I ask, glancing at the photograph of my mother with Lexie, my stepsister's child. Samantha is two years older than me, the daughter my mother happily inherited when she married Edward.

"They're doing well. Lexie is getting to be a young woman. As much as I love having a son, it's fun to have the girls." She sighs. "I miss girl time."

I know she's thinking about my aunt Vera, and maybe Daniela's mother too. My stomach is starting to rebel at the thought of breaking the news.

"I heard cargo was missing," she says, glancing over her shoulder at me from the stove.

I glare at her, trying to keep my anger in check. "Sonia told you?"

"I speak with Sonia regularly. But I speak to a lot of people regularly."

Fucking Sonia. "I allow you some leeway into my personal life, because you're my mother. But you will stay out of my business matters." I say it pointedly and firmly, and even Lydia Huntsman knows not to cross me about this. "The cargo doesn't concern you—missing or not. And if Sonia doesn't learn to keep her mouth shut, I'll cut her loose fast enough to make your head spin."

She starts to say something, and I hold up my hand. "Not one more word about it."

"You can get more honey if you're nice to the bees, Antonio."

"Or you can get stung. And the saying is 'more flies with honey.'"

"Flies are dirty little creatures. I'm not a fly, and neither is Sonia."

It's hard not to laugh, because she means well. "I don't see you anywhere near enough, and I didn't come all this way to argue. Besides, whatever you're cooking smells delicious."

She smiles. "Pour some wine, please. It's a nice day. We'll sit on the terrace and catch up until lunch is ready."

She grabs a small dish of olives and another of nuts, and I carry the wine outside. The apartment is at the top of a steep hill, and the view of London from the terrace is beautiful, especially on a day like today.

My mother is barely seated before she starts. "Why are you here?" she asks, plopping an olive in her mouth.

"I'm traveling in Europe this week, representing the foundation. I don't have appointments in London, but I wanted to see you."

"A visit, out of the blue, in the middle of the week. Antonio, don't lie to your mother. It's a sin that will send you straight to hell."

I'm already going. But I don't say that because I know it'll upset her.

"Monday isn't the middle of the week." I hedge for a minute, thinking about how I want to start. "I'm planning to add to your security detail. I don't want the change to alarm you."

"Why?" she asks warily, her body tightening.

As much as I'd prefer to focus on the snacks, I meet her gaze. "I'm getting married."

She's startled for a long moment, and then a smile blooms on her face. "Oh, Antonio, another girl in the family. I wasn't sure you'd ever settle down. Every time I see you in the paper with some starlet"—she shakes her head—"I've always wished for something better for you." Her brow furrows. "Is it one of *those* women?"

I scoff. "*Those* women aren't so bad. But no. She's not an actress or a model—if that's what you mean."

She narrows her eyes. "Tell me about your future bride. Do I know her? Why haven't I met her? I was just in Porto. Is she pregnant?"

"Are you expecting answers, or are you just going to ask questions?"

My mother eyes me like she's beginning to think that this isn't the happily ever after she wants for her son.

"To answer your questions, in no specific order: She's not pregnant. You didn't meet her when you were in Porto, because she was not there at the time. No, it wasn't sudden. Yes, you know her."

Her shoulders ease with every answer I provide.

"Sonia?" she asks hopefully.

I roll my eyes.

"Am I supposed to guess?"

59

ANTONIO

"Daniela D'Sousa." I just lay it out there. I don't put a shine on it or provide an explanation of any sort. I won't lie to her.

"Daniela D'Sousa," she repeats, blanching. The wheels are turning, and I see the confusion swirling in her eyes. "Maria Rosa and Manuel's daughter?"

I nod. "Yes."

"What's this about, Antonio?" she asks in a tone not much different than she used to question my behavior as a teenager. "Surely not love." Her mouth puckers like she's tasted something sour, because she already knows the answer to the question.

"Not love. But perhaps we'll grow fond of one another as the years pass." I shrug. "It happens." *Although right now I don't see it.*

"Why would you do this?" Her voice is as tortured as her expression. "The vineyards? You don't have enough money? Or power? I want to know how this happened." She bangs her index finger on the table. "Everything."

"I didn't go to Manuel. He came to me about an arrangement."

"A betrothal contract?" She gasps in horror.

As much as I'd like to assure her it's not the case, I nod.

My mother jumps out of her chair and wraps her arms around her midsection, moving across the terrace with her head down.

When she gets to the edge, she slams her hand on the railing and scowls at me. "How could you do this? Maria Rosa was my best friend, like a sister. When Vera went missing, she was the one who risked everything to help me find her. Do you know how many times I cried on her shoulder because the man I was married to was a monster? She saved my life. And this is what you do to her daughter?"

I'm willing to take my lumps—to a point. "We both know that arranged marriages are not some unique phenomenon in our culture. As I said earlier, Manuel approached me. I didn't go to him."

"You couldn't say no? Is there something wrong with your tongue too? Because clearly your brain isn't firing on all cylinders."

"I couldn't say no."

"It's not that you couldn't." She marches over to the table, an arm's length from me. "It's that you wanted those vineyards. And you were willing to sell your soul for them. Don't treat me like I'm a fool."

"The vineyards were part of it. I don't deny it." Although it makes the agreement more despicable in her eyes. "But Manuel treated me like a son. You know this. He steered me to the top on a path that Hugo would have never taken." *And he saved my life.*

"I'm begging you not to do this."

"It's done."

"You're married?" She pulls her sweater tighter, as if the temperature plummeted suddenly.

"Less than two weeks."

"I want to talk to her. I'm going back to Porto with you."

No fucking way. That's all I need.

I shake my head. "Absolutely not. You can speak to her after we're married. Not before. It will only make matters worse."

"Let me tell you something, big man," she says, inching closer to the table. "I've been in her shoes. My sister was in her shoes. I assure you there is *nothing* that could make matters worse. But since you don't want me to speak with her, I assume she's not thrilled with the arrangement. Imagine that?"

"She'll get comfortable. I won't give her a choice." My tone is far more flippant than it should be, and her eyes widen, flaring with a rage I haven't seen in years. Not since my father died.

She takes a long stride in my direction and raises her arm.

I see it coming. I can catch her wrist and prevent the impact. But I let her land the swing.

The slap across the face isn't hard enough to make me flinch, but the significance isn't lost on me. I expected her to be upset by the news, but it's worse than I anticipated.

My mother took endless beatings for me. When I was a young boy, she stepped between my father and me more times than I could count.

"You're going to get his," my father would yell when she intervened, "and then I'm going to turn you black and blue for interfering."

When I was nine, I forbade her from intervening. I warned her over and over. But she didn't listen. Shortly after I turned eleven, after Hugo fractured her jaw in a drunken rage, I told her that the next time she stepped between my father and me, I would run away, and she'd never see me again. It worked, but it caused her great anguish to sit back and do nothing.

My mother never once raised her hand to me before today. Not even when I deserved it. No, the significance of that slap is not lost on me.

"I am your mother. And no matter how important and powerful you become, you will show me respect. What you're doing to that young woman is an atrocity."

Church bells ring in the distance. It seems to go on forever, like the silence between us, growing louder with each chime.

"I love you, Antonio—with all my heart and soul. You're the best thing that's ever happened to me. Bar none. I would go back and relive it all over again, because it meant having you. But what you're doing—it's beyond what I can understand. It doesn't have to be like this."

"It does," I say calmly. "We signed in blood."

"So what? You might lose your position on the foundation? Maybe some euros. A woman's life is worth more than any of that. Surely something can be done to make this right."

"Manuel made me promise to protect her. He was worried about her safety for reasons he refused to share with me. I promised him I would marry her and protect her with my life, if necessary. I will keep that promise."

"Like they protected me," she says softly, sitting on the edge of her chair.

They were there for her when I wasn't. I reach for her hand. "This has nothing to do with you."

She presses her lips together. I know she doesn't believe a word of it.

"I came today because I wanted to tell you myself, before you heard rumors. I'm keeping the news under wraps, for the most part, until after Camellia Weekend. That's when everything will become public."

"You expect problems when it's announced?" she asks before pulling her lips into a thin line.

"I always expect problems. But this will come as a huge

surprise to everyone. That's why I'm asking you to take the extra security without an argument, and not to come to the wedding." I don't know why I even waste my breath with the last part.

She sits back and folds her arms. "Put that idea right out of your head. My only son is marrying my best friend's daughter, even under these circumstances, and you think I won't be there? *Pfft.*"

I think you'll be there, trying to help the bride escape before she gets anywhere near the altar. But that's not my real concern. "It's not safe for you."

"I'm an adult, and I decide what's safe for me. And what risks I'm willing to take. Not my son. Or any other man."

She lifts her chin, and I swallow my plea. No sense arguing with her right now. I'll co-op Edward and Samantha in helping me to convince her to stay home. And if that doesn't work, I'll ground every goddamn plane out of London for a week, if I have to.

"Tell me about Daniela. I haven't seen or talked to her since shortly after her mother died."

Why didn't I know this? *Why would you have known? Daniela was a little girl, not even a blip on your radar.* I assumed they'd stayed in touch until my mother remarried and moved to London. "I'm surprised you didn't stay in contact with her after Maria Rosa died."

She sighs. "I kept in touch with Manuel—for years. He would visit when he was in London. But he only let me see Daniela once after her mother died. He believed that spending time with me made it more difficult for Daniela, because I reminded her of her mother. She had some kind of breakdown a few months after the funeral. He was worried she would commit suicide to be with her mother, so he sent her away to recover, and rest. I never saw her when she got back."

"Where did he send her?"

"Somewhere up north, and then she stayed at the ocean for a while. They had a cottage there."

"He didn't go with her?"

"Manuel had a lot of responsibilities. He couldn't leave everything behind. That's how men are. He visited her."

He sent his young princesa *up north and then to the beach, right after her mother was murdered. Not a chance. He sent her away to protect her.*

"Daniela seems afraid of Abel and Tomas. Do you know anything about that?"

She shrugs. "Nothing you don't know. Manuel was worried because Maria Rosa and I were searching for Vera. Even though we suspected she'd been murdered—we had to try. Daniela might have overheard something between her parents."

"Would they have killed Maria Rosa?" I'm not sure why I ask. Something doesn't feel right to me. But I can't put my finger on it.

She shakes her head. "No. They found the man who did it. Besides, Abel has always been too calculating to do something so brazen. If they were caught—it would have been war. Remember, your uncle was never as powerful as your father, and Manuel had lots of power. Killing Maria Rosa would have been the end of Abel and of Premier. Even your father couldn't have protected him."

"Why was she without a guard?" I ask, gauging her reaction to see if this feels as strange to her as it does to me.

"Why are you asking now?" she asks defensively.

"I'm about to marry her daughter. Humor me."

She rolls the stem of her wineglass between her fingers. "Manuel did business in the city on Wednesdays. He always spent the night." Her voice is soft, mired in sorrow, as she tells the story. "Maria Rosa and Daniela would picnic when he was gone. In the living room, when it was cold, and when the weather turned, there's a meadow just off the property where wildflowers grow. It's such a beautiful spot. Like a private oasis."

"You've been there?"

"I went with them while I was staying at Quinta Rosa do Vale."

"Did you ever tell Hugo about it?"

"Of course not."

She says it like I'm crazy. But just because she didn't tell him doesn't mean he didn't know. I'm sure he tracked her every move while they were separated.

"Why wasn't Daniela with her that day?"

"She was sick."

Nothing about this adds up. "Maria Rosa left her sick daughter home to go have a picnic in the meadow? Does that make sense to you?"

"Daniela had cramps. She wasn't bedridden with a fever."

"Did Manuel tell you that?"

She glares at me. "Do you actually think Manuel talked to me about his daughter's menstrual cramps? He was much too old-fashioned and proper for that. Isabel, Daniela's governess, told me. And yes, for your information, it makes sense to me that she would steal an afternoon alone. It doesn't make sense to you, because you've never been a woman who isn't permitted to come and go as she pleases. He wasn't anything like your father, but even in Manuel's house there were rules."

I want to know more about Isabel, but I've already asked too many questions. She'll get suspicious.

I nod. "Everyone lives by rules. It's the life we were born into. But I agree. It's infinitely worse for women."

"It doesn't have to be like that. But things will never change for women until powerful men like you say *enough*. Until then, every girl born into that world is vulnerable to the nightmare I lived. You have the power to make it right, Antonio."

"You have an inflated sense of my power. More than me,

even," I tease, before catching her eye for a more serious discussion. "I hope you don't think I'll treat Daniela the way Hugo treated you."

The words give me pause when they reach my ears. In many ways, I've already behaved a lot like Hugo Huntsman.

"You're not your father."

I used to think that, too, but I'm not so sure anymore.

60

ANTONIO

Lightning delayed my flight home for several hours last night, and when the phone vibrates on the nightstand before dawn, I groan. *Cristiano*. Not a name I want to see on the screen at 5:37.

"Yeah."

"We have a situation with your car."

My car. Today is the camellia race. I can't afford a problem with my car. I'm wide awake now, sitting up in bed. "What kind of situation?"

"When Roberto got to the track this morning, he noticed that the workbench where he keeps his equipment was moved, and some of the tools were not as he left them. The lock doesn't appear to have been tampered with, but we have a guy looking at it."

Roberto has been the head of the pit crew since right after I started racing. He's meticulous about the car and his tools. It's almost an obsession. If he says something is out of place, it is.

"The entire crew has been with me a long time."

"I don't suspect them either. But I'm talking to everyone,

just to be sure—including the guard, Joaquim, who was on duty last night."

He's been around forever too. "What about the cameras inside the place?"

"They were hacked. Entire segments have disappeared."

Fuck. We don't have any of our own surveillance inside the track. It would violate the rules, and we'd be disqualified from today's race, and I'd be banned from ever entering another. We comply with the rules because I'm not ready to say goodbye to racing yet.

"So we've got nothing."

"Not exactly. Lucas and his team are combing through the feeds we set up outside the track. But we might not have a solid lead until after the race. You might want to consider sitting this one out."

"Like hell. I'm not a fucking coward."

"We don't know if the car was tampered with—or the track, for that matter."

"Roberto will figure it out. The race doesn't start for four hours." I don't mention a possible sabotage of the track, because that's largely out of our control.

"I have great faith in Roberto too. But he doesn't have much time to determine whether there's a problem. Getting behind that wheel today, without a clearer picture of what happened, is a big risk for someone with your kind of responsibilities."

Cristiano knows the best chance he has to sideline me is not to point out the danger but to prick my conscience. *Fucker.* It's why we're friends.

"I'll be racing today. I'd rather die than live as a coward. If I can be intimidated that easily, I'm useless to anyone. They might as well just take my balls."

He doesn't say another word. Although I'm sure I haven't heard the last of it.

"After I get dressed, I'm going to the track," I tell Cristiano as I turn on the water in the shower. “On my way over, I’ll contact the head of the racing commission. He needs to know about the breach. We don’t know how widespread it might be. That place needs to be swept carefully without alarming everyone. If I call him personally, he’ll be discreet.”

“Good idea.”

“I’ll see you there.”

“*Bom dia*, *Senhor* Antonio.”

“*Bom dia*, Roberto. Not a cloud in the sky. Beautiful day to take this girl out for a ride.” I slide my palm over the sleek hood of the car that’s served me well for years. “Talk to me.”

He nods. “When I went home yesterday, I left my tools on the bench, nice and straight, like I always do before a race. I came in early to go over everything one more time before the crew arrived.” He points to the rolling workbench. “The bench was moved back from the car, maybe six inches from where I left it, and the tools were not lined up straight. It’s almost like someone moved the thing without unlocking the wheels, and the tools shifted. Not a big shift, but it’s not how I left them.”

“Were you the last one to leave last night?”

“Always. I locked the door and took the key with me.” He pats his pocket. “Cristiano said you’re still set on racing today.”

“I am.”

He nods with a sober expression.

“Any signs of tampering?”

“Not yet. But it’s too early to tell. I have a checklist—more thorough than the one we would normally use on race day. The crew is on their way, and we’re going to go through the car methodically. We’ll drain the fuel, replace the lubricants, and do a visual. We’ll also run some analytics.”

“If you find any problems, let Cristiano know right away.”

Roberto has a nerve-racking job under the best of conditions, but the pressure is ramped up high now. It'll earn him a nice bonus, whether I win or not.

"Am I going to die today?" I ask in jest.

"Not on my watch."

I pat him on the back. "I have complete confidence in you, Roberto. As far as I'm concerned, you're the best in the business."

We both glance toward the door as Cristiano comes into the garage. His body is so tight I can see the tension from here.

"I'll let you get back to work," I tell Roberto, before turning my attention to Cristiano.

"Anything?"

"We've swept the place twice for recording devices, fingerprints, and explosives. Other than the bench, nothing seems amiss. Only fingerprints on the car are from the crew, and yours. We're running some fibers we picked up in the sweep, but they're likely to lead nowhere." He pauses for a breath. "We do have one lead. A woman brought the guard dinner last night and gave him a blow job before she left."

I hope he enjoyed it, because if he let someone into my garage, it'll be the last time he gets his dick sucked. "Does *she* have a name?"

"We don't know her real name. He met her a week ago at a bar where he hangs out after work, and she gave him an alias. We're running facial recognition on her, but it was dark, and she stayed away from anything that would illuminate her face. She knew what she was doing."

"Distracting that stupid fuck."

Cristiano nods. "What do you want us to do with him?"

"Are we sure he wasn't involved?"

"Right now I'm not prepared to say anything for certain. But I doubt it. He was shitting his pants when I showed up at his door this morning. He was a stooge."

"Probably. But there's no way we can have him work the race today."

"I already took care of it. He called in sick, and we have a guy on him until it's over."

"Someone was in here. I don't believe for a second that it's someone who wants me to back out of the race so they have a chance to win. This is a charity event with bragging rights for the winning port house. That's it."

"Agreed."

"This was either an attempt to scare me—or kill me. But it could also be a diversion. The big bang could come while we're chasing our tails."

"Word's starting to leak out that Daniela's back. This could have something to do with Quinta Rosa do Vale."

"Maybe. Although, even without that, I have plenty of enemies. I want security on her doubled. And I don't want her on the road today. When it's time, bring her here by helicopter. Triple-check everything before she boards."

"I was going to send Alvarez to escort her. He's totally trustworthy. I need to stay on top of things here."

"Not happening. I want you with her from the second she leaves my house, through the race, until you drop her off safely, when it's over."

Cristiano's nostrils flare. He doesn't like it one bit. Big surprise.

"I'm not going to try to talk you out of getting behind that wheel," he says, taking a new approach. "But if you don't push the vehicle too hard, you have a better chance of staying in control of the car if something goes wrong. It's not foolproof, because we don't know the extent of the problem. But it's something."

"I race to win. Otherwise, why bother?"

61

DANIELA

From outside the kitchen, I hear Cristiano and Victor talking in hushed tones. Something about Antonio's car being tampered with last night.

"You know Antonio," Cristiano says with more frustration than I've ever heard from him. "We advised him against racing, because of the danger, but he's so damn stubborn."

A chill runs through me. *Why would he risk his life for a race that's essentially meaningless?*

When I step into the room, the conversation stops.

"You look lovely," Victor gushes, as though he wasn't just contemplating Antonio's death. He's wily like the rest of them.

I want to ask about the tampering, but I decide to wait until Cristiano and I are alone. There's a better chance he'll let something slip if it's just the two of us.

"Are you ready?" Cristiano asks.

"Yes."

As soon as we're outside, the need to know more gets the better of me. "What happened with Antonio's car?"

"I don't know what you mean."

I grab his arm at the elbow. "Don't lie to me. Why is it dangerous for Antonio to race today?"

"You're perfectly safe," he assures me, completely ignoring my question.

Oh, no, Cristiano. You will tell me what I want to know.

"I didn't ask about my safety. But I'm not getting on that helicopter unless you tell me what's going on."

"My back is a bit sore today. Don't make me carry you onto the chopper." Cristiano has a way of softening a real threat—at least that's how he behaves with me.

"You can do that, but then you'll have to carry me off at the other end, and then to the Huntsman box. I've been subjected to a lot of humiliation lately. My tolerance is high. Don't think for one second that I'm not prepared to make a scene. If you don't think Antonio wants that, then you better tell me what happened."

I brace myself for Cristiano's brand of restrained anger, but there's a spark of amusement in his expression.

"There isn't much to tell right now. Someone was in the garage where Antonio keeps the car. A workbench was moved. It could have been anyone. There's likely an innocent explanation."

"But you don't believe that."

He shrugs. "It's my job to treat everything out of the ordinary like a threat, but most issues that catch my attention are benign."

"Thank you," I say as we approach the landing pad. Although I'm not convinced he's told me everything.

The helicopter is over the top, like all things Huntsman.

It's been a long time since I've been on one. My father owned one, and we would take it to the apartment in the city, or when we were traveling a distance and the rural valley roads would make the trip too long.

But even a fancy helicopter doesn't stop me from worrying about Antonio.

I turn to Cristiano while he can still hear me over the chopper. "Given the circumstances, why are you escorting me when you could be doing something more important? I'm not going to run, if that's what you're worried about."

"You are important. The only person who doesn't seem to realize that is you."

THE MOMENT I set foot on the ground, I'm surrounded by burly men—with guns concealed under their jackets, I'm certain. It feels unnecessary, but given the issue with the car, I'm not surprised.

The guards shuttle me to the Huntsman box with only moments to spare before the start of the race.

Cristiano stands directly behind my seat, and even when I turn to ask him about Antonio's grid position, he doesn't take his eyes off the crowd.

"One," he replies, watching intently for any sign of trouble. "He won last year."

Why am I not surprised?

While waiting for the race to begin, I look to the area where my family's box had been. It's been twelve years since I was last here, and I can't tell one box from another.

As I scan the seats, I notice spectators gawking in my direction. I'm sure the gossips are having a field day with my sudden return—sitting in the Huntsman box, no less. *Let them have their fun. It's not something I can control.*

The announcer's voice booms over the intercom, urging the dawdlers to be seated.

He welcomes everyone, reminding the crowd about all the weekend festivities, and he makes a wish that the vines planted this year grow fertile and lush, bringing sweet, juicy fruit when they reach maturation in a few years.

The new vines are the future of the region.

"Now for the presentation of the camellias," he announces in a cheery voice, to much whooping and hollering.

Porto is known for many things, but in the spring it's the city of the camellias. Before the race starts, each participant will do a lap around the track, stopping his car in front of the stands and presenting a camellia to a woman of his choosing. Unless this year is different, the drivers are all men.

The recipient of the flower isn't always a love interest. She can be a friend, a relative, or a random spectator minding her own business.

When I was a girl, like many others, I waited with bated breath to see who would get Antonio's flower. He always presented a white camellia, signifying adoration, never a red one that represents love and passion. He always gave his flower to his mother, or to an elderly woman, or to a young girl no older than five or six. I always prayed he would stop the car in front of my family's box and present me with his flower. But he never did.

While everyone claps and cheers, their eyes focused on the track, or on the big screens that amplify the exchange, I can't help but wonder if Antonio will give me a flower, or if he'll continue his tradition of offering it to someone too old, or too young, to provide fodder for the gossips.

Antonio's car begins to take the lap. He passes the Huntsman box without a glance. I hate that my heart sinks a little when he drives past.

I keep my eyes glued to the car as he takes an unusual second lap. They don't stray from him, not for a second. Not when he stops the car. Not when he takes the steps, two at a time, to the box where I'm seated. Not when he stands in front of me with quirking lips.

His eyes shimmer with mischief as he hands me a red camellia *and* a red rose. After a curt bow of his head, he turns and jogs down the steps.

I hold the stems tight, embarrassed by how happy I am.

The crowd cheers as he makes his way to the car. Before he gets in, he looks up to the stands, right at me, and smiles adoringly. It's all for show, of course, and the crowd eats it up. My cheeks must be as red as the rose.

I lower my eyes to the flowers so that I don't have to see my flushed face on the screen.

Leave it to Antonio to present a rose *and* a camellia. *Always bucking tradition unless it suits him.*

Pinned to the rose, securing it to a lovely grosgrain ribbon, is a gold crown. The Huntsman logo.

I'm captivated by how the crown pierces the rose, right where it buds. I swallow hard. Thankfully, the race begins before I can overthink the connection between the rose and the crown, and what it all means. Because it means something. Antonio does nothing without purpose.

As I watch the cars circle faster, and faster, I hold my breath and clench the padded armrests on the seat. What kind of fool would risk his life for this? *One who won't be cowed.*

Cristiano leans over, whispering so that only I can hear. "You don't have to worry about him. The problem with the car has been resolved. He'll be fine."

I want the details, but I know better than to ask about them here. I look up at him. "I wasn't worried."

A small smile plays on his lips, but he has the good grace not to call me a liar.

Before the afternoon is over, there's a small crash, a flat tire, and countless other harmless mishaps, but none of them involve Antonio's car.

At the end of the long race, my attention is on the large screen as the trophy is presented to the winner. I see the boy I used to dream about. The one who would give his kisses only to me. The joy on his handsome face is palpable, even from where I sit.

And for now, I give myself permission to revel in his happiness.

62

ANTONIO

As soon as I step off the winner's platform, I hand the trophy to Roberto. "Add it to your collection. You've more than earned it this year."

Two hours before the race, he discovered that the steering mechanism had been tampered with. It was a slight modification, hard to spot, but it had the potential to cause serious damage. *Maybe death.*

"Last race?" he asks, like he does every year. One day he's going to be surprised by my answer. But not today.

"*Pfft.* I'm just getting started."

He grins and shakes his head before lifting the trophy so the entire crew can get a good look.

"Congratulations," Lucas says from behind me. "Even though no one in their right mind would have gotten behind that wheel today."

"I never claimed to be sane. Anything on the break-in?" I ask when we're far enough away from the crowd not to be overheard.

"Plenty."

I look into the stands, searching for Daniela, but the

Huntsman box is empty. "Before you start, did the helicopter take off?"

"Momentarily. Cristiano's with her," he says, as if he can read my mind. "Do you want me to tell them to wait?"

As much as I'd like to taste that silky mouth right now, she's safer at the house. "Nah." *I'll see her tonight.* "Tell me what you found."

"We located the woman on the feed, but someone got to her before we did. It wasn't a happy ending for her."

I stop and turn to face him. "They killed her and left the body for us to find?" That's not sloppiness. It's a message.

"They left the body for *someone* to find. I don't think we're prepared to conclude that it was left for us."

"What are we prepared to conclude? That our hands are cramping from holding our dicks for so long?"

He ignores my frustration.

"She had a Georgian passport in her purse. It's a fake. A good forgery, but a forgery. If the body was left as a message for us, someone wanted to make it seem like the Georgians were behind the sabotage. That's something we can safely conclude."

Tampering with my car is an act of war. I could have died.

If we go after the Georgians for it, the small war would cause just enough upheaval for someone else to sneak in under our noses and grab a foothold. It has the Russians' signature all over it.

But it's too easy. I never trust easy.

63

DANIELA

I spoke with Isabel and Valentina when I got back from the race. They were planning on spending the afternoon at a baseball game in the local park. Normally I would take Valentina and her friends—and pretend to look the other way when they flirted with boys. Isabel won't be so patient.

After the call, I slid into a scented bath, lingering until right before the stylist arrived. It was indulgent, but a much-needed escape before the Camellia Ball tonight.

I adjust the ruby-and-diamond necklace that matches my gown. A small piece of my heart crumbles as I glance at it in the mirror on my way to meet Antonio.

My mother had a beautiful ruby-and-diamond necklace that my father had given her as an engagement present. It was one of the last pieces of jewelry I sold. The necklace wasn't as elaborate as the one I'm wearing, but it would have been a better complement to this dress.

You did what was necessary. I did, but it doesn't make me feel any better.

I turn off the light and shut the suite door behind me.

Antonio is waiting in the upper hall, near the staircase. I

haven't spoken to him since he left his apartment on Monday. I text him, *done*, every morning, but he never responds to those texts. Victor did let it slip that each time they speak, he asks about me.

"God, you're beautiful," he murmurs. His eyes darken as he takes me in, and I know the compliment is genuine.

"Thank you. You clean up pretty well too." And he does. The tux he's wearing fits like a glove, accentuating his broad shoulders and narrow hips. "Congratulations. You were impressive today. Although it's not always wise to spit in the face of danger."

His smile fades. "Cristiano spoke out of turn."

"Cristiano didn't have a choice."

He snickers as he slides his hand into his jacket pocket and pulls out a square velvet box. He holds it in his palm and pulls back the lid. "For you," he says quietly. "Now that the word is out about our engagement, everyone will expect you to have a ring."

"I never knew you were such a romantic," I quip.

"It's a gorgeous ring," I add softly, not taking it from him yet. It appears to be an heirloom. *I hope it's not his mother's.* The thought of wearing a ring Hugo Huntsman picked out makes me nauseous.

"It belonged to my maternal grandmother. Her marriage was also arranged, but my grandparents had a very long and mostly happy life together. They died within a week of each other. My mother claims my grandfather couldn't live without her."

I feel my mouth curl, but I still don't take the ring. "Tell me what happened with your car."

"Cristiano told you plenty. You don't need to bother yourself with the details. They're not important. We need to go."

He inches the velvet box closer to me, and I take a small step back.

"I can be a tame bird, kept in a gilded cage, lavished with riches and stroked occasionally, or I can be a strong ally. But I can't be both." I pull back my shoulders. "Before I accept the ring, I want to know if you want a loyal partner or a pampered pet."

"I think you can be both," he says after some contemplation. "Although not a pet. A *princesa*. And I can't imagine you tame."

It's not perfect, but from a man like him, it's the best I'm going to get. I take the ring and slide it on my finger while he watches. It shines brightly, but it's heavy, dimming the joy that ordinarily surrounds an engagement.

"That ring comes with my promise to take care of you, and to keep you safe, at any cost."

But it doesn't come with the promise of love. The one thing I always dreamed I'd have in a marriage. "We're going to be late," I say quietly without looking at him.

"Someone tinkered with the steering mechanism on the car," he mutters as we descend the stairs. "The problem was fixed before the beginning of the race."

I stop on the landing and turn to him. "Do you know who? Or why?"

"We're still working it."

I nod and slide my arm through his as we head out the door. It's a small gesture, but it surprises him. If we're ever going to live civilly, he needs to know that his efforts are rewarded.

Perhaps it's not a great foundation to build a marriage on, but it's the scaffolding our marriage will need to prevent it from imploding and destroying everything around us.

64

DANIELA

From the moment we walk into the grand ballroom, all the attention is on us.

While this afternoon I saw hundreds of people I hadn't seen in years, it was from a distance. Now I'm face-to-face, bombarded with questions from all sides, while women of all ages gush over my ring.

"When did you arrive?"

"How is your aunt?" Oh God.

"When is the wedding?"

"What are your plans for Quinta Rosa do Vale?"

The fate of my family's vineyards interests the owners of the port houses far more than our wedding plans.

I smile coyly in response, when I can, avoiding the land mines. Without any guilt, I explain that Antonio and I never lost touch while I was abroad. That's mostly true—on his part, anyway. And I assure everyone that the wedding plans are going splendidly. But in truth I've given the arrangements so little thought.

Antonio never leaves my side but lets me handle the barrage of questions, only stepping in when I need to be rescued from someone who pushes too hard. I give everyone more leeway to prod than good manners require, but Antonio has no qualms about telling the nosy old biddies to mind their own business. Although he handles them deftly, without offending anyone.

By the time we were seated at the table, I'm overwhelmed.

I turn to Cristiano's date, Mia, who isn't an actual date but one of my guards for the evening. "I'm going to the ladies' room," I mouth from two seats away.

She nods, and we excuse ourselves, making a beeline to the nearest exit so that I'm not bombarded with more questions.

We're gone only ten minutes, but it's been a peaceful ten minutes, away from probing eyes. As I'm reapplying lipstick, a young woman enters the ladies' lounge.

"Hello," she says. "You're quite lovely."

"Thank you," I reply. "That shade of blue is gorgeous on you." It is. She's stunning, and the strapless gown shows off her curves and makes her eyes dance.

"I don't know if Antonio has mentioned me, but I'm Sonia," she says, sending my antennae up when she uses only her first name. Something about it doesn't sit well.

"I don't think he has, but we've been so busy with the wedding plans. I'm Daniela, by the way. It's nice to meet you." I grab my clutch, and Mia follows me out. Before I can ask what she knows about Sonia, Tomas Huntsman appears out of nowhere.

"It's been a long time," he says, the menace sitting just below the surface. "I thought you'd left for good."

My heart hammers, and my first instinct is to flee, but I see Mia in my peripheral vision, and that calms me.

"It has been a long time." *Not long enough, though.*

"I assume she's your guard, but I need a word alone with you."

"Antonio won't like it," I say, taking a step back.

"Do you think I give a damn what Antonio likes?"

If you don't, you're not just a monster, but an idiot too.

"Did you enjoy living in New Bedford?" he asks, gauging my reaction.

But I didn't live in New Bedford. It's a city not too far from Fall River, where I did live. It also boasts a large Portuguese population.

"I understand New Bedford is a wonderful place," I reply. "But I lived with my great-aunt in Canada." I don't say a word about Fall River—where Valentina and Isabel still live.

He smirks, stepping closer.

Mia is instantly at my side. "We should go back to the table," she says, "before they get worried that we've been gone too long."

"The next time I'm in New Bedford, I'll look up your maid and her daughter. What's her name?"

You sonofabitch. I turn to Mia. "Just give us a moment. But don't go too far. I won't be able to find my way back."

"I'll be right here," she says, mostly for Tomas's benefit.

"What do you want?" I hiss.

"Have you told him about his father?"

I shake my head, the bile rising.

"I'm next in line to become president of the foundation. My revenge will reach all the way to New Bedford if it doesn't happen because you couldn't keep your mouth shut. Do we understand each other?"

My palms are sweating.

"I haven't ever breathed a word about any of it to anyone. I'm certainly not going to start now."

"Aren't you going to ask about my father? Have you lost your manners living in the US? By the way, I tracked you all the way to New Bedford."

He's trying to intimidate me with talk of New Bedford—or he's probing. The skin on the back of my neck prickles. "How's your father?" I ask, steering the subject away from where I lived.

"Sweet of you to ask. He seems to enjoy being pushed around the gardens. But it's hard to tell. He doesn't communicate much."

Does he really think I care?

From the corner of my eye, I see Antonio approach. Relief rushes through me, like water through an open dam. It leaves me light-headed.

"Tomas. Congratulating the bride-to-be?" Antonio asks, pulling me close to him.

I lean into his body, not to stay upright, but to feel safe.

"My congratulations to both of you. Your father is somewhere right now, delighted to see her at your side. I can almost see his big grin. God bless his soul."

Antonio tenses, and within seconds I feel the rage vibrating off him.

"Daniela, go back to the table with Mia. I'll join you shortly."

I glance at Lucas and Cristiano when I turn to leave. Then at the men I suspect are with Tomas.

I draw a large breath to steady my nerves.

I'm not ready to bring Isabel and Valentina back into this world. But Tomas knows where they're living. Not the exact location, but he's close. *They can't stay in Fall River.*

I'll be there in a week, and we'll make other living arrangements. Valentina's going to be unhappy about leaving her friends, and I'm sorry about that, but I won't let them be in danger.

Thank God they have a guard.

I look over my shoulder as we walk into the ballroom. From this distance, Antonio doesn't seem any more relaxed.

65

ANTONIO

"I've been wanting a word with you," I tell my cousin, although I'd rather put my fist in his face than talk to him. I can't believe he had the nerve to corner Daniela. Mia was smart to text Cristiano.

"You know how to reach me."

"I've reached you now. Let's go out on the balcony where we won't be overheard. Just you and me."

"I'm not going anywhere with you."

"You always were afraid of your own shadow. And of me. You worried I might steal your lollipop?"

"Fuck you."

"Fine. You want me to say it here, where anyone can hear. My pleasure."

He's wavering. Tomas knows I'm capable of anything. Including saying something that will diminish him in front of his men. Not that they hold him in such high esteem.

"Just you and me," he says, in a tone that he hopes will save face.

Daniela has bigger balls than this guy.

When we step onto the empty balcony, he immediately turns to me. "What the fuck do you have to say to me?"

"It's quite simple, actually." I keep my voice even and low. "If you bring the Russians in, I'll destroy you. The company, your house, everything you care about will be rubble."

He raises his hands in surrender. "Don't look at me. I don't want those greedy bastards here any more than you do. I'm fully aware that they have no regard for the valley. But you might want to take a closer look at Viera. I hear he's been courting the Bratva."

What a fucking liar.

"I'm looking at you," I growl, stepping closer and forcing him back toward the building. "And the next time you so much as breathe on my fiancée, it'll be the last breath you take."

He snickers. "Never pegged you for the kind of man who enjoys leftovers. I hear the *princesa* spreads her legs for anyone who asks nicely."

I slam my open hand into his face, smashing his head against the stone. Before he can react, I pull out my knife and hold the blade to his meaty throat.

"Not here," Lucas cautions, grabbing my wrist, but not before I pierce the bastard's throat with the knife tip, drawing blood.

"Your days are numbered," I warn before releasing him.

66

DANIELA

I don't see Tomas again, and the rest of the evening goes smoothly.

Better than smoothly. It's wonderful, like something straight out of a fairy tale. Although I know at some point I'm likely to lose a shoe, or encounter a pack of wolves—*perhaps just one*. But I don't dwell on that part of the story.

Antonio is relaxed, smiling more than I've ever seen him smile. And he's attentive. My wineglass is never empty, and when I discover I don't have a salad fork, he gives me his before signaling for the waiter. It all happens seamlessly, without discussion, like we've done this dozens of times.

Even when he's chatting with someone who stops by the table, Antonio drapes his arm across the back of my chair, or squeezes my hand under the table. He's the perfect date.

At the end of the night, when Thiago pulls the car up to the house in the valley, Antonio gets out and then helps me out. He doesn't let go of my hand as we go inside.

Several lights are on, but it's after midnight, and the house is quiet.

"Thank you for tonight. It was a lovely evening. When I was a little girl, I dreamed about going to the Camellia Ball."

"I'm glad you finally had the chance." He presses his lips to the top of my head. It feels like an intimate good-night kiss, not at all threatening. "Do you want anything before we go up?"

Before we go up? "You're staying?"

"It is my house." His mouth twitches at the corners, and his eyes glimmer with a hint of playfulness.

"It's—it's just that you don't normally stay the night. At least not since I've been here." I shrug, trying to cover my surprise with nonchalance.

"Is my staying a problem?" he asks, but as he turns out a light and moves toward the stairs, I know he's staying regardless of my feelings.

At the bottom of the staircase, I gaze into his handsome face, and even though I'm a bit nervous of what *staying* means for me, I shake my head.

He motions for me to go up ahead of him, and I do, squeezing the railing as I climb.

When we get to the third floor, he lifts my chin and peers into my eyes. "Tell me what Tomas said to you."

The butterflies swirl madly inside, like a storm is headed my way. *He'll know if you lie.*

"It was strange," I begin, trying to keep as close to the truth as possible. "He kept mentioning something about me living in New Bedford. I'm not sure if that's what he believes, or if he was trying to get me to confirm it. He said he tracked me there."

Antonio's eyes flare, and his expression hardens as I watch. "Did he say anything else?" He releases his hold on my chin.

"Just some nonsense about his father enjoying being pushed in the garden. Then you came."

He nods, studying my face carefully. I didn't tell Antonio everything, but I didn't lie. "I'm worried about Isabel and

Valentina," I continue. "New Bedford is not that far from Fall River."

"Why would he want to harm Isabel?"

He's probing.

I shrug. "Something about his behavior tonight—I can't put my finger on it. But it gave me goose bumps." I grasp his arm. "Would you consider putting more security on them? *Please.*" My voice wobbles as I plead—it's not a manipulation. The more I think about it, the more worried I become.

He takes out his phone and places a call. "Double the security on Isabel and Valentina," he instructs the person who answers. "Make sure there's a guard on each of them at all times. Do it tonight."

Without a thank-you, or a goodbye, he ends the call and slips the phone into his jacket.

"Thank you," I murmur.

He sweeps a lock of hair behind my ear. "I want you in my bed tonight. And I don't want you preoccupied with anyone's safety but your own."

67

DANIELA

His voice is low and rough.

I swallow hard, but I don't respond.

I'm a bundle of nerves, but I do want to be in his bed—although it's still so damn hard to admit it—even to myself. *Especially to myself.*

Antonio runs his fingertips down my cheek. "I'm not Josh. Even when you haven't pushed me to the end of my rope, even when I'm not enraged by your reckless behavior, I'm not the kind of man who'll take you gently. I'm rough. Demanding. Selfish."

His voice is coarse as gravel. His eyes are dark, danger dancing in the shadows.

It's a warning.

"I don't want you preoccupied with anyone's safety but your own."

I'm not afraid of him. Not really.

Just admit it. You want him.

I do.

I want him to do unspeakable things to me. The kinds of

things that aren't discussed at afternoon tea or at formal dinner parties. The kinds of things men whisper about in dimly lit lounges over a tumbler of whiskey and a cigar, using words like *whore* and *sweet little cunt*.

I capture his gaze and hold tight. I don't say what I should say. I say what's in my heart.

"I don't want Josh. I want you."

With a low growl, he lifts me into his arms and takes me to his lair.

The full moon bathes the room in a soft glow. It's deceptive, because nothing about this man is soft.

Antonio sets me on my feet. My knees wobble as he lowers the zipper on my dress, his lips on my throat. The arousal builds as I step out of the gown.

"Beautiful," he murmurs. His fingers work the hooks on my strapless bra until my breasts fall free.

He presses his mouth to mine. It's not a gentle caress, but a bruising battle of lips and tongues.

His mouth is hungry, and it takes everything he needs. The tender caress only comes when he needs to breathe—and then it's gone, as if it never happened.

As we explore, the curl of desire twists low in my belly.

My pussy aches for him. It sways against his cock, brushing wantonly over the hard bulge, inviting him in.

Antonio groans and pulls away, tugging off his jacket and tossing it aside. His tie is next, and a few shirt buttons are freed, then his full attention is back on me.

"Get on your knees," he murmurs. There's something depraved about him—something sinful.

I freeze, lost in his face. Except for my panties and my shoes, I'm naked. *The necklace and earrings are merely adornments that cover nothing.*

"Have you ever had a cock in this sassy little mouth?" He

runs his thumb over my bottom lip, pinching lightly before he drops his hand.

Oh God.

"Have you?"

His voice is gentle, and it calms me. Although I'm still a bit embarrassed.

I nod. "But I'm not—I don't have a lot of...experience. Hardly any at all."

"Get on your knees," he repeats softly. "Use me to steady yourself."

I do as he demands. Clutching first his arms, then his muscular thighs to lower myself to the rug. It's not easy in high heels, but I manage without falling on my butt.

When I'm on my knees, I peek up at him. He's beautiful as he looks down at me with unfettered lust whirling in his eyes.

"Take out my cock," he instructs, his tenor seductively smooth.

My hands tremble as I tug at the hooks at his waist and wrestle with the zipper. He doesn't utter a word. He doesn't move a muscle. He just lets me fumble my way through, learning as I go.

After long moments, his cock is free—inches from my face.

I take a breath, and I stare—probably for too long. But he lets me look, not saying anything to embarrass me.

His cock is long and thick, the skin pulled taut, smooth and shiny, with a bead of precum on the crown. This time I'm not afraid to lean over and lick it.

He grunts softly as my tongue glides over the head, lapping the milky pearl until it disappears.

When I'm through, Antonio threads one hand into my hair and takes his cock in the other. He slides the crown across my lips until they part for him.

"Use your hands," he instructs in a tight voice. "Your mouth, your lips, your tongue. Suck my cock. Swallow me into your throat."

I shiver, opening my mouth wide and letting my jaw go slack as I explore his cock and balls.

For several minutes, with his hands fisted tightly at his side, he lets me set the pace. He lets me learn him—the ridges and edges, the dips and valleys. But when I take him deeper into my mouth, his hands find my hair and tighten slowly around my scalp. His hips cant forward as he feeds me more of his cock.

"For years I've fantasized about your sweet little mouth around my cock. I've jacked off more times than I can count thinking about it."

His words imbue me with a heady sense of power, and my jaw relaxes, welcoming more of him inside.

"*Princesa*," he gasps, thrusting deeper and harder. "Your mouth is heaven."

Soon I can't keep up with his movements, and I gag when he hits the back of my throat.

He pulls out—to the tip—and gives me several seconds to catch my breath.

"Breathe," he commands, pushing his cock deep. "Swallow. Yes, that's it."

I gag, again and again. Tears spill onto my cheeks.

Antonio pulls me from the floor, pressing his mouth to mine, until I can't breathe. "Sit at the edge of the bed," he says, removing his clothes. "Wait quietly for me."

I don't question him. I just do it, because right now, I'd do anything to have his hands and mouth on me.

He strides toward me, naked, his cock hard and proud. Pushing my thighs apart, he lowers his mouth to mine in a long, sensuous coupling that makes my toes curl. Before I'm ready for it to end, he drops his head and sucks a rosy nipple into his mouth. I gasp at the sensation—at the way my pussy throbs as he plays with my breasts. He lifts his head and lavishes all his attention on the other tight furl until I'm squirming with need.

I pant softly as he removes my shoes, one at a time, and then my thong. Antonio's eyes never leave mine as he takes everything but my jewelry—and even when the need to shy away starts to overwhelm me, I don't surrender to it.

When he's through, he slides a pointed tongue down my seam, grazing my clit. I cling to the bedcovers, taking handfuls of the soft fabric and gripping tight.

"*Princesa*, you're so wet. Did you enjoy sucking my cock? Did you like choking on my big dick?"

Yes. And I need more. I wriggle closer.

Antonio stands and flips me onto my stomach. "On your hands and knees," he commands. "I want that gorgeous ass in the air."

Before I can think too much about it, he spreads my legs, licking my pussy from back to front until the pleasure is coiled tight.

"Please," I beg. Although I'm not sure what I want most from him.

His tongue circles my most private place, licking the tiny rosebud. I squeeze my eyes shut and tense my sphincter as a wave of shame and fear swells, almost ruining my pleasure.

Without warning, Antonio sinks his teeth into my ass. It comes as a surprise, and I yelp loudly.

"You're mine," he chides. "No part of you is off-limits to me. Do not tighten your muscles to keep me out."

My emotions are all over the place. I'm aroused—maybe more than I've ever been, maybe more than I can take.

"Shhh," he whispers, as though he can hear the voices in my head. "Don't think. Just feel."

He's behind me, nudging my legs farther apart, his fingers dipping into my wet flesh and swirling around my clit without ever touching it.

I'm out of my mind when I feel his cock at my entrance, and my walls relax to let him in.

A long, low groan escapes from my chest as he fills me. He feels enormous as my body stretches to accommodate him.

"This pussy is going to be my downfall," he mutters in a tortured breath, stilling inside me while I get used to him. When he begins to move, the zings of pleasure are heavenly. I arch my back and buck into him. He grips my hips and slides, in and out, long and hard.

I want more.

More. More. More. It's all I think about until he reaches around me and holds my throat in his large hand. My breath catches as his fingertips tighten.

Antonio leans forward and drops a small kiss on my ear. "Are you afraid?" he asks, like he hopes I'll say yes.

"No," I gasp. Although I am a little afraid. "Are you going to hurt me?"

He pulls his cock all the way out, then fills me with a long, brutal thrust. "Definitely," he murmurs, his breath hot against my skin. "But not tonight."

His free hand skates over my back and around to my belly, moving lower and lower until his fingers are stroking my clit.

"You've been such a good girl I think you need a reward." He moves his fingers in quick, clever ways, his cock unrelenting. "You're going to come nice and hard all over my dick."

Antonio's hand tightens around my throat, and I gasp for air as he pounds me with long, punishing strokes until my body tightens and bucks as the orgasm consumes me.

"*Princesa*," he groans, in a prayer. "*Princesa*."

His movements are jerky, desperate, and with a few agonizing thrusts, I feel the rumble of his release.

Antonio presses a kiss to the back of my neck and pulls out of me. I collapse on the bed, shivering. He gets up and returns with a soft blanket, draping it over my body.

"Do you need anything?" he asks, lying beside me and brushing the hair off my sweaty face.

"Stay with me," I say, even though I'm in his bed. "Don't leave tonight."

"Sleep, *Princesa*. I'm here." He brushes his lips over my forehead. "You're safe."

68

DANIELA

When I awoke on Sunday, Antonio was gone without a goodbye. Not even a scribbled note or a hasty text. *Nothing.* It hurt, but as I reminded myself the entire day, it's just sex to him. The sooner I get comfortable with the idea of *just sex*, the happier I'll be.

I haven't seen or spoken with him since. We've texted a few words here and there, mostly about wedding details. That's it.

He's been staying in the city, and Victor says he's swamped, trying to take care of business before we leave on our trip. Sometimes I wonder if he'll continue to spend nights in the city without me, after we're married. I shouldn't care, but I do. I care about all of it.

"I have something to show you," Nelia says, reaching into a tote bag that says, *I Make Dreams Come True.*

Nelia, the wedding planner Antonio hired, and I have been in the library for the last two hours, reviewing last-minute preparations. The wedding is less than two days away. Thirty-nine hours, to be precise.

At first, I had no interest in planning the ceremony or the reception. But after the Camellia Ball, it hit me that most of the wedding guests would be people who knew my parents, some who knew my grandparents. If for no other reason, I got involved to ensure that the wedding wasn't some gaudy show.

Nelia hands me a small mesh bag with a few candied almonds. "It would be a nice touch to hand everyone a favor as they leave the church. All the extra security means lunch might be a bit delayed. Your guests will enjoy a little something to snack on if they missed breakfast. Since it's spring, this seems perfect."

I glance at the pastel nuts peeking through the white gauzy sacks. The cost of this wedding is starting to feel staggering. "Have you checked with Antonio?"

"Whenever I ask Antonio anything about the wedding, he tells me it's up to you."

I'm not surprised. Since my initial contact with Nelia, which went smoothly, he seems to defer to me on all things wedding related. Although the venue and the guest list were in place before I got involved.

The *small affair* includes three hundred guests. I was free to add to the list. But I didn't.

The ceremony will take place at Santa Ana's, and a luncheon will follow here, at his estate. Antonio put together a guest list that includes the mayor of Porto and the owners of all the port houses and their spouses, along with those who own the most prominent vineyards in the valley. People he does business with. Other than *Sonia*, relatives and friends are in very short supply.

But I suppose the guests reflect the occasion. After all, our marriage is nothing more than the sealing of a business deal, uniting a well-established port house and important vineyards.

"Can I keep this?" I ask Nelia as she's packing up to leave. I'll give it to Valentina when I tell her about the wedding. I don't want her to think I kept it from her, but I also don't want her to know that I was forced into the marriage. I haven't settled on how I'm going to approach it with her.

"Of course. I was planning on keeping a few aside for you. The day goes so quickly"—she snaps her fingers—"and it's gone. But don't worry. I'll take care of you."

At the door, I place a kiss on each cheek before pulling her in for a warm hug. "In case it gets too crazy on Saturday and I forget, I want to say thank you for everything. You've been wonderful." She has been. In addition to pulling this off in little more than two weeks' time, Nelia knows that marriages like mine and Antonio's are arranged for convenience—and not the bride's. She's been incredibly supportive without ever mentioning a word about it.

"You've been a delight to work with. Saturday is going to be perfect. I promise."

It's almost nine, and after I say goodbye, I go up to my suite to shower.

Paula is coming out of the bedroom when I arrive. Our relationship is almost back to normal after my escape. I apologized for pulling her into the ruse, and at first she seemed a little nervous around me, but things are better. Her face lit up when I invited her to accompany me to the church the morning of the wedding. She agreed immediately.

"Paula, it's late. You don't have to turn down the bed every night, especially on nights like this when it starts to get late. I'm not helpless."

She smiles. "I left something on your bed. It's from *Senhor* Antonio."

God help me.

"It's a wedding gift," she adds with a small giggle.

It's so charming that I laugh too. "Thank you, and good night."

"Good night," she says, shutting the door behind her.

A gift from Antonio? That could mean anything. He's a complicated man.

I stop in the bedroom doorway, gaping at the leather case on the bed. It's similar to the one he left in my closet, perhaps slightly larger. The one with the *toys*.

Maybe he's not so complicated.

This case also has a gold lock, but unlike last time, the key is in the lock.

When I see him, I'm going to murder him with my bare hands for giving this to the staff to deliver.

I'm tempted to toss it out the window. But I'm also curious. In truth, the toys have been—amazing.

I sit on the bed and stare at the case for several minutes. *Just open it. You know you want to see what's inside.*

When my curiosity doesn't subside, I turn the tiny key. I hesitate before lifting the lid, because each time he gives me something, I'm newly reminded that this is a sham marriage, and our vows will be sealed not with love, but with kinky sex. It hurts my soul every time.

I glance at my engagement ring. *Now that the word is out about our engagement, everyone will expect you to have a ring. That ring comes with a promise to take care of you and keep you safe, at any cost.*

I sigh and pull back the lid.

Time disappears as I stare into the case, taking it all in, one section at a time.

When I can breathe again, I lift a charm bracelet off the velvet lining. It was my mother's. Each charm represents something significant in my life. *"It doesn't matter where I am. When I look at my wrist, all I can think about is you."* I hold it for several minutes before putting it back. My fingertips gently caress the small gold cross my parents gave me on the day of my First Communion. I was so proud that day.

I can't take my eyes off the case. Every piece of jewelry, *every single one*, mine and my mother's, that I sold to survive, is in this case.

The tears fall in a deluge.

I don't know why I'm crying. I'm thrilled to have the jewelry back, especially my mother's pieces. But I'm also stunned. It's as though the boat has capsized, and I'm adrift in the middle of the ocean, surrounded by a dense fog.

My emotions are twisted, tied in knots so tight they'll never be disentangled. I don't know what to feel. Or even how I should feel. I'm a mess, and I can't seem to find my out.

I hate myself for not hating him. That's the bottom line. The one I've been loath to admit. I hate that he controls my mother's vineyards. I hate that he's forcing me to marry him. And more than anything, I hate that he's separated me from Isabel and Valentina. But I don't hate him. *And I never have.*

The light on my phone screen catches my eye. It's a text from Nelia, something about flowers.

I should call him. It's the polite thing to do.

Before I lose my nerve, I place the call.

"*Princesa*," he murmurs. "I've been thinking about you."

"Thank you," I whisper. "My mother's jewelry is one of the few things I have left of her. I can't tell you how much it hurt me to sell it."

"I can't take credit. It was Cristiano's idea to buy the pieces back as you sold them."

"But you agreed. Otherwise, it wouldn't have happened."

He doesn't respond.

"This means so much to me."

"It's not the only things you have left of your mother. Now that everyone knows you're back, after the wedding Cristiano will take you to your parents' house. Alma packed away anything of value. We did some upkeep of the property, but most everything is as you left it."

"I'm having a hard time understanding you," I say, fighting

back a sob. “Every time I think I have you figured out, you do something that surprises me.”

“Don’t spend too much time trying to understand me,” he murmurs into the silence. “You won’t like the answers you find. I told you once that I was everything you thought, maybe worse. That hasn’t changed. You’re marrying me because I’ve given you no choice. Don’t be wooed by a box of trinkets and a trip to visit Isabel. You’re smarter than that.”

I’m not sure I am.

69

ANTONIO

From the anteroom, I gaze out into the church. White flowers and satin ribbon grace the altar and every pew. The greenery adds some warmth to the vast stone structure.

Guests are beginning to arrive, and the security we have in place to protect them melds seamlessly into the fabric of the ancient church.

Rafael, Cristiano, and Lucas are attending to last-minute details, and I'm happy to have a few minutes alone to digest the weight of the moment. I've been busy the past week, putting out small fires as the concerns of the individual port houses bubbled to the surface.

Daniela returning on my arm sent a seismic surge through the valley, just as I expected.

I haven't had a minute to think about—to *really think about* —what this marriage will mean for me, not from a business perspective, but personally.

My life is about to change in ways that I don't pretend to fully understand. Only a fool would believe that everything will remain the same.

I always knew I'd eventually marry—fulfilling my duty to

produce a legitimate heir. But I expected to feel more hesitant, some wistfulness or regret when the time came. While I don't love Daniela, I have no regrets.

There's something about her—something beyond her beauty and my carnal attraction to her—something that calls to my better angels.

"Antonio." *My mother.*

I had zero success in getting her to stay away. As did Edward and Samantha, although I'm not convinced Samantha tried very hard, because she insisted on coming, too, much to her husband's dismay. William understands the threat better than most.

"You're here early." I place a small kiss on each of her cheeks. "You look lovely."

"And you look so handsome," she says, her hand cradling my face. "I want to see the bride."

And so it begins.

"You'll have plenty of time to chat with Daniela after the wedding. I expect her to be around for a long time."

Cristiano must have seen her approach the anteroom, because he's at the doorway, waiting to save me if it becomes necessary.

"I want to see her now," my mother demands. "You've managed to keep her away from me with the promise of *amanhã*. Well, tomorrow has come. I'll find her myself," she adds in a huff.

My mother knows better than to make demands of me in public. She's fully aware it puts me in a dangerous position. I don't believe for one second she doesn't see Cristiano in the doorway. Yes, she knows it's safe to talk around him. Still, the tic in my jaw is relentless.

"Cristiano, give us a minute."

"Don't undermine me in front of my men," I warn when he steps away.

"I won't be seated until I've spoken to her."

I could threaten to have her removed from the church, but she's my mother, and there's no sense in making a threat I'd never carry out.

"Do not make this more difficult on Daniela than it has to be. Upsetting her changes nothing. I need your word before I let you see her."

"Is my word enough, or do you require a drop of my blood to seal the promise?"

My father did his best to destroy her spirit, but he never did. I gently take hold of her face and drop a kiss on her head. "Behave yourself," I say before turning to Cristiano.

"Please escort my mother to see the bride. They have only ten minutes to chat, so that Daniela has time to finish getting ready before the ceremony."

My mother touches my cheek. "I love you just as you are. But until I take my last breath, it's my job to make you a better man."

"Go, before I change my mind."

"Ten minutes," I repeat as Lydia Huntsman slips her arm through Cristiano's and murmurs something that makes his mouth curl.

I'm going to regret letting her go to Daniela. *I'd stake my fortune on it.*

70

DANIELA

The bride's parlor is beginning to feel suffocating. Along with Paula and Nelia, there's a seamstress in case there's a problem with the dress, and a makeup artist. I can't spend another minute in here with people I barely know fussing over me.

In a perfect world, Isabel and Valentina would be here.

In a perfect world, my mother would be here. *I miss her.* The hole in my heart is especially raw today. I need her to reassure me as she adjusts my veil, or to squeeze my hand and tell me how much she loves me. *Doesn't every bride want this?*

I need to get out of here for a few minutes.

"I'm going across the way to the bride's chapel," I tell Nelia.

"Shall I come with you?" Paula asks, handing me a small white Bible that I requested for the ceremony. The Bible my mother carried on her wedding day is at Quinta Rosa do Vale. I could have sent someone for it, but it didn't feel right to carry it today. Just like it didn't feel right to wear my mother's veil—or her jewelry. My parents loved each other, and comparing their wedding to this is to make a mockery of their love.

"You don't need to come. I'd like to spend a few moments

alone before the ceremony. But could you please keep this for me?" I ask Paula, handing her my bouquet of creamy white garden roses with a sprig of myrtle, a nod to Antonio's British roots and my family's stature in the valley. I especially love the silk wrap at the bottom, held in place by pins with pearl heads. The arrangement is beautiful in its simplicity, unlike the complicated arrangement I'm about to enter.

When I open the door, Pinto, the guard stationed outside the door, is talking to Sister Maria Gloria, an elderly nun who attends the bride's parlor.

"Put the lid back on the kettle," she chides. "Otherwise, the water will be too cold for tea."

"I'm sorry, Sister, but I need to take a quick look inside before you can take it to the bride."

I shake my head—everyone's suspect, even an elderly nun.

"Sister Maria Gloria," I say, giving her a small smile. "Is he giving you a hard time?"

"It's your wedding day. Don't worry about me, dear. I can take care of myself." She winks at me. "I've brought some more hot water, if you'd like a cup of peppermint tea before the ceremony begins. I also brought some biscuits to settle your stomach. Brides get very nervous while they wait to walk down the aisle," she whispers around Pinto's shoulder.

"That's very sweet. Thank you. I'm going to say a small prayer in the chapel, and then I'd love some more tea."

She smiles as Pinto holds the door, giving her plenty of space to roll the small cart into the room.

As I wait for Pinto to assist her, I hear the organ and Alma's sweet voice. Alma singing at the wedding was the one thing I insisted on. This reminds me of Christmas Eve Mass with my parents. Today, everything reminds me of them.

I turn to Pinto as he shuts the door. "Would you mind unlocking the chapel for me?"

It's not a strange request, and he doesn't hesitate. The tiny sanctuary was built specifically for this purpose. For women like me, who need the strength of prayer before they promise their life to a man who will never love them. As the world has become more enlightened, it's not used in this way so much anymore, just for special *princesas* like me, forced to marry men their fathers chose for them.

Pinto nods to another guard, several feet away, before leading me to the chapel. He unlocks the door and sticks his head into the windowless sanctuary before allowing me to enter.

"I'll be right outside the door," he says kindly, "if you need anything."

Pinto has been a gem today. I'm sure he has sisters, or daughters, or cousins he wouldn't want to see in this situation. "Thank you."

When I enter the chapel, I go directly to the statue of Santa Ana and kneel before her. Like so many mothers, she, too, gave up her daughter to an arrangement. Only her daughter Mary's arrangement was made by the Heavenly Father himself. I wonder if it made a difference.

My father won't be here to walk me down the aisle, but with every step I'll feel his betrayal—betrayal that I still don't understand.

It doesn't seem like I've been here very long when the door opens behind me. I'm sure it's time to go. I don't open my eyes. I'm not ready.

I feel a small hand on my shoulder. "Just another minute, please."

"Daniela, *querida*."

I turn toward the woman's voice. *Lydia Huntsman.* I knew she'd be at the wedding, but it surprises me that she's here now.

I stand, careful not to tear my dress. We stare at each other for a moment before she wraps her arms around me, pulling me tight. "I know the circumstances are unconscionable. But you're a beautiful bride. Your mother—"

"Please," I plead softly. "I miss my mother. I'm a heartbeat away from melting into a pile of tears thinking about her."

"Me too," she whispers. "Me too."

I take her hand and lead us to a narrow bench, where we sit with our backs against the wall. She doesn't let go of my hand.

Lydia starts to cry. "You look so much like her—I can't help myself. I want you to know that even when your father said it was too hard on you to see me, I never stopped thinking of you, sweet girl."

My father made one decision after another to protect me. At least that's what he said at the time. Looking back at it now, Lydia would have brought me great comfort at a time when I was scared to death.

"Your mother isn't here to tell you this, but I can speak for her, because I know exactly what she'd say. You don't have to do this." She holds my hand between both of hers. "My son is so much more than he shows the world, and I would be honored to have you as a daughter-in-law, but you have a choice here."

Oh, Lydia. I don't have a choice—any more than you did. "We both know that there are no choices. Not now. Maybe a month ago—maybe—but not now."

"I'll help you," she says firmly. "I'm not afraid of my son."

But I am. I shake my head. There are things bigger than me that I need to protect. "You can't help me. Maybe you can protect me today, or tomorrow, but if I walk away now, I'll eventually be punished in ways that make my heart bleed."

"Oh, sweet child."

"But please don't be a stranger in my life. I'm so happy to see you—"

Boom.

Boom.

Instinctively, I fling my body over Lydia's to shield her from flying debris.

We cling to each other as the explosion shakes the centuries-old walls, crumbling one section of the chapel and collapsing the bench under us. Isabel's and Valentina's faces run through my head in slow motion, like frames in an old silent movie.

The statue of Santa Ana topples to the floor.

Is it an earthquake? A bomb?

71

DANIELA

Cristiano barrels in, gently pulling me to my feet and helping Lydia, who is bleeding from her forehead.

"Have you seen Antonio?" I ask, coughing.

He drags us to the center of the room, away from the walls.

"Antonio and Edward?" Lydia cries. "Samantha's here too." She tugs on Cristiano's jacket. "Find them."

"Antonio can take care of himself. He has Lucas and Rafael with him, and others. I'm staying here with you. That's what he would want. He'll make sure they're protected."

The words are barely out of Cristiano's mouth when Antonio storms into the chapel. "What the hell happened?" he yells in Cristiano's direction.

I release a loud sob I've been holding back.

"Are you hurt?" he asks me softly, taking the handkerchief square from his lapel pocket and holding it to his mother's bloody forehead.

I shake my head. "No."

I glance at Cristiano. "Your mother?" I see the worry in his eyes, but he doesn't respond.

"Edward and Samantha?" Lydia mutters.

"Everyone inside the main church is fine. Including Alma," Antonio adds. "They're in the process of being evacuated. The explosion occurred in this part of the church."

In this part of the church? Who would do this? Maybe it was an accident. This is the oldest part of the building, and it's vulnerable.

Another piece of the wall crumbles. Antonio glances at Cristiano. He's calm, but I see the trepidation.

"We need to stay here until it's safe to leave—just a few more minutes. This could be a diversion to draw us out."

A diversion? Cristiano doesn't believe it's an accident.

I glance at stones on the floor that were once part of the wall and then at Lydia. She's not young, and if we need to get out quickly, she won't be able to—not like the three of us. "Maybe we should leave the building."

Antonio runs a palm over my bare arm. "Right now, this is probably the safest place. Are you sure you're not hurt?"

"I'm sure."

"What happened?" his mother asks in a shaky voice.

"We're figuring that out as we speak."

Each word vibrates with an intensity that makes me shiver. If this was done on purpose, whoever is responsible is going to experience hell at Antonio's hand. I'm sure of it.

"Tell me everything you remember," Cristiano says to me, "starting right before you came into the chapel."

I try to remember exactly what happened. I know the details are important, and I struggle to get them right. "I wanted a few minutes alone, and I gave Paula my bouquet to safeguard."

My eyes dart from Cristiano to Antonio. "Is everyone in the bride's parlor safe? Where's Pinto?"

"Who else was in the bride's parlor?" Antonio asks without answering me. "That information is important."

"Paula and Nelia. The makeup artist, Monica, and the seamstress, Lourdes. That's all."

"You handed Paula the bouquet," Cristiano prods. "Then what happened?"

"I opened the door and the guard, Pinto, was talking to Sister Maria Gloria. He lifted the teapot lid that was on her cart, and she scolded him to hurry up so the water wouldn't get cold."

"Who the hell is Sister Maria Gloria?" Antonio asks, as if exasperated that there's something he doesn't know.

"She takes care of the bride's parlor and brings refreshments on the day of the wedding."

"Refreshments?" Antonio asks suspiciously.

"She's been doing it forever," Lydia replies, dismissing him. "She brought me tea and biscuits when I married your father. She must be eighty years old."

"Eighty-two next month," Cristiano clarifies, seeming to placate Antonio a bit. While he didn't know anything about the elderly nun, Cristiano knew plenty.

Alvarez rushes into the room. "All clear," he says before saying a few quiet words to Cristiano.

"One minute," Cristiano says quietly, sending Antonio a look that I don't understand. He leaves the room and returns without his jacket.

"It's safe to leave, but cover your mouth and your eyes. It's smoky out there, and we don't know what kind of chemicals might be in the air."

I lift the outer skirt of my dress, trying to cover my face the best I can.

Antonio gives his jacket to his mother. "Take my shirt," he says, tugging at the buttons.

"This is fine. Better," I assure him. "Maybe you can use your shirt." But he doesn't.

Antonio wraps an arm around his mother, steadying her,

and he reaches for me with his free hand, holding my fingers tight as we leave the chapel.

Outside the chapel there's still smoke, and even with them partially protected, it's enough to make my eyes sting.

When we approach what was once the bridal parlor, I freeze. It's hollowed out, like something in a war zone. No one inside that room could have survived. My stomach twists and the tears begin to flow. I can't move.

There's a man on the floor nearby, a suit jacket covering his face. I'm sure it's a guard. *Maybe Pinto.*

"We need to keep walking," Antonio chides, tugging on my hand.

"Were they still inside?" I ask Cristiano over my shoulder.

"We don't have many answers yet," he replies quietly.

We go through a door and onto a side portico, where an older man and a younger couple are waiting. The area is surrounded by guards.

The man lunges for Lydia as soon as he sees her, and they embrace. *Edward.*

"I want you on Edward's plane," Antonio tells his mother in a voice that leaves no room for negotiation, "along with Samantha and Will, as soon as possible. A doctor will meet you there to examine you before takeoff."

"Our things are at the house," she says defiantly.

"Not a concern right now. We'll collect everything and ship it to London. You need to go home and stay put until you hear from me."

Sirens are getting closer.

A man I believe is Will steps in. "I brought plenty of security with us," he tells Antonio. "You need all your people here."

"I don't think it's me you need to be worried about," Lydia says to her son, while she squeezes my hand.

"I'll decide who I need to worry about," he replies, pointedly.

Lydia bristles, but Antonio is not going to indulge her. She's going to have to do exactly as he says.

He turns to Edward. "Do not let her out of your sight until you hear from me."

"You have my word."

I almost ask if I can go with them, but if I do, Antonio might be angry, and the trip to Fall River will be off.

"Let's go," Will mutters impatiently, when Lydia and Samantha are taking too long to say goodbye.

"Will," Antonio calls. "Take Rafael with you. Call me if he gives you a hard time."

"I can manage Rafa," he replies. "Don't give any of this"—he indicates an orbit around his wife and in-laws—"a second thought. You take care of business here, and let me know if you need reinforcements. My wife was in that church."

Antonio nods.

I've never laid eyes on Will until today, but I can tell from the way he and Antonio communicate that the man has plenty of his own power.

"Antonio," I plead as his mother gets into a car. "Who was in the bride's parlor when the explosion happened? There's nothing left of the room." I can't wait any longer for answers. Everyone in that room was there because of me. My insides are shaking. In my soul, I know they're all dead.

"It might be awhile before we know who was in the room." He wipes a smudge off my face with his thumb. "You weren't there. That's all I care about."

"Who would do something like this? Why?"

"At the very least, someone wanted to embarrass me and to stop the wedding. But that's not happening," he growls, dragging me inside to the vestibule at the front of the church, where the priest is gathering vestments and oils used in holy rituals.

"You need to marry us now," Antonio demands as soon as we set foot in the chamber.

"I'm preparing to administer the last rites."

"They're dead, Padre. It can wait."

"Antonio," I gasp, but he ignores me.

"We came to be married in God's house. We'll leave married."

The priest gawks at him like he's insane. But he doesn't dare go against him.

"You can do an abbreviated version. Just the essential parts," Antonio instructs him. "God will forgive you under the circumstances."

He's lost his mind.

"Outside." Antonio continues his demands, like this is his church.

72

DANIELA

On the church steps, ringed by armed guards, with death looming, we say our vows.

Father Aguiar asks the first of the three questions that characterize Catholic marriages. "Daniela and Antonio, have you come here to enter into marriage freely, and without coercion?"

Antonio scowls at him before he says, "I have."

The priest's eyes are on me as he waits. My chest constricts as Antonio gazes at me with an abundance of patience, but says nothing. He's more confident of my answer than I am.

"I have," I submit softly, knowing I'll have to make my peace with God later.

"Do you promise to love and honor each other, vowing fidelity, for as long as you both shall live?" the priest asks.

"I do," we say at the same time. And as long as we're married, I will honor this promise. But I have no opinion, only a prayer, as to whether Antonio will be faithful to me.

"Are you prepared to welcome children into this marriage?"

"I am," Antonio says in a clear, unwavering voice.

"I am," I also promise. *If it's safe for them. That's up to you, God.*

Father Aguiar gestures for us to face each other. Antonio reaches for my hands as the priest asks us each to give our final consent before God.

"Antonio, do you take Daniela for your lawful wife, to have and to hold, from this day forward, for better, for worse, for richer, for poorer, in sickness and in health, to love, honor, and cherish, until death do you part?"

Antonio reaches over and gently brushes a lock of disheveled hair off my forehead. "I do," he says unequivocally. His sincerity makes my heart clench. While I might not be loved, I'm wanted.

Father Aguiar turns to me. "Daniela, do you take Antonio for your lawful husband, to have and to hold, from this day forward, for better, for worse, for richer, for poorer, in sickness and in health, to love, honor, and obey until death do you part?"

I gaze into Antonio's eyes, searching for the boy I fell in love with as a girl. The one who visited me in my dreams, lavishing me with sweet kisses—and later passionate ones. Each kiss sealed with a declaration of love. While I don't see that boy now, I pretend. Because it's the only way I can find the courage to promise my life to this man.

"I do."

Almost before the words are out, Lucas presses the rings into our hands. The priest is still blessing the marriage when Antonio grabs my wrist and yanks me into the vestibule and out the side door to a waiting car. Cristiano is in the passenger seat.

"This is a well-protected vehicle," he assures me. "You'll be safe.

"Take her directly to my apartment at the lodge. Other than you," he orders Cristiano, "no one in or out of the apartment. I don't give a damn who it is."

I reach for his arm and grasp tight. "Please be careful." Even as I say the words, I know he's not going to be careful. Antonio is out for vengeance, and men with that kind of hatred in their hearts are never careful. "Please don't take any chances with your life."

His brow furrows as he traces my jaw with his fingertip. "You're a beautiful bride," he murmurs. "Don't give my men a hard time. They're here to protect you," he adds as he pulls away and shuts the car door. He taps the rear of the car, and we speed away.

When I turn around, Antonio's on his way inside the church. There will be more death today. I'm sure of it.

By the time I turn to face the front, the privacy screen is raised before I've had the chance to ask a single question.

I look down at my tattered dress, covered in dust and soot. *Somehow it seems apropos that I got married in a dirty dress.*

For the remainder of the ride, I think about the four women who were with me in the room. Four lives lost because they were there to serve me.

I hold my hands near my mouth to catch the vomit as I retch.

73

ANTONIO

Daniela, my mother, and Cristiano—mere feet away from a deadly explosion. Whoever is responsible will be pleading for death before I'm finished with them.

Lucas is headed in my direction. He should be back at the villa, studying feeds and overseeing the lab analysis and the forensics as they come in. That's what he does best, and he is the best. Cristiano should be running this operation on the ground, but I need him with Daniela.

"How the fuck could this have happened?" I bark when Lucas approaches. "We've had people on the church since the wedding announcement went out. We swept the entire place yesterday, twice, and again this morning."

"We found what appears to be a small timer in what was left of the bridal bouquet," he says, the venom reverberating in every word. "At least we think it was the bouquet, but we won't know until we've done the forensics. It's probably not the entire story, but it's definitely a piece."

"Have someone pick up the florist, the delivery driver, the cleaning staff, and anyone else who might have even glanced at that bouquet. Put them in separate interrogation rooms in the caves. I want you back at the villa, running those forensics."

"We're still collecting evidence here."

"I'll run the operation here. I don't know a fucking thing about running forensics."

"Cristiano can come back after he makes sure Daniela is tucked in. The lodge is impenetrable."

"No. I don't want that. If the bouquet was rigged, or if a bomb was detonated in the bride's parlor, it was meant to kill her. It wasn't a fucking warning," I growl, the lust for revenge growing with each passing second.

"Maybe," Lucas says carefully. "The explosion did a fair amount of damage, but all in all, it was contained. Bombs are notoriously finicky, even in the hands of an expert. Until we learn more, we won't know if the damage was intentional or something gone awry. The one thing for sure is that whoever is behind it was willing to take a risk that it would kill her—and hundreds of other people too."

"Any word on the women inside the room?"

"Paula is the only one accounted for. She was in the bathroom when it happened."

"We lost one guard. Anyone else?"

"So far Pinto is the only confirmed casualty. Although I don't have high hopes for the women in the room."

I don't, either, but it's hard to hear. "Daniela said that some nun went into the room shortly before the explosion."

"Sister Maria Gloria. I just tried to talk to her. She's completely distraught. I'm going to talk to her again when she's coherent. She's been the caretaker of the room and has served every bride who's been married in the church for the last fifty years."

My phone rings. *The Porto police captain.* No surprise. His men were sent away when they arrived on the scene. "I need to take this."

"Santa Ana's is an important piece of our history, not to mention a church." The captain doesn't even say hello before he begins the lecture. "You have some balls sending my people away. The culprits need to be brought to justice."

Stupid fuck.

"The culprits will be brought to justice. Don't you worry your pretty little head about that. The explosion occurred mere feet away from where *my* mother and *my* bride were standing. Justice will be done—and swiftly. Count on it. This is mine. Keep your people the hell away."

I hang up, and seconds later the phone rings. *The mayor's chief of staff.* Fuck him. If the mayor has something so damn important to say, he can contact me himself.

After I block the chief of staff, I call Cristiano.

"Everything battened down there?" I ask as soon as he picks up.

"Yeah. I can come—"

"No. Have you talked to Lucas?"

"A couple of times."

"Contact the rectory and tell *Senhor* Padre we'll make a large donation to rebuild the damaged areas of the church, but first get Pinto's wife on the phone for me—and make sure there's a deposit in her bank account before the sun goes down. He was a good man, always loyal. His family should want for nothing."

"On it."

"Is my mother airborne?"

"Not yet."

"Let me know as soon as it happens."

"Not to get too far ahead of ourselves, but are you going to want to do anything for the families of the women in the bridal parlor?"

"Not until we're absolutely sure that they weren't culpable in any way. What do you know about Paula?"

"What do you mean?"

"She was in the bride's parlor when Daniela left, but she was in the bathroom when the explosion happened."

"She was checked out pretty thoroughly before we brought her into the house, but I'll take another look."

"Do that. Sooner rather than later. What about the nun?"

"An unwitting accomplice, if anything. Because my mother sings at the church, I've known her my whole life."

I grunt out of frustration, because he's probably right, which puts us no closer to a culprit. We're going to question everyone associated with the florist, but they were heavily vetted too.

"I understand you're running the operation on the ground."

"You got a problem with that?"

"Since you asked, yeah, I do. If you don't want me to run it, let Alvarez do it. The main part of the church has been cleared, but the area where it occurred is still smoking, and we can't know for sure if everything's been detonated. You shouldn't be back there."

"I'll take my chances." I hang up, because if I wanted to be nagged, I'd call my mother.

After quickly checking my messages, I go to the scene of the explosion. The air is still thick with smoke, and someone hands me a mask. "Watch yourselves," I caution. "We don't know if anything else is going to blow."

No one in the bridal parlor survived. I don't need a forensics report to tell me that.

Were they after her, or did they go after her to get to me? That's the question.

It takes someone *special* to set a bomb in an iconic church like Santa Ana's. I'm not a religious man, and even I wouldn't stoop so low.

Someone was desperate to stop the wedding.

Tomas would love to see me embarrassed—or even better, dead. But I don't believe he has the wherewithal to orchestrate something like this himself. Or the balls to blow up Santa Ana's. Besides, he was sitting in the pews when it happened. He's too much of a coward to risk his life, even to get to me.

This was done by someone who doesn't care about what the old church means to the people of Porto. *Or someone determined to prevent us from going through with the wedding.* I keep coming back to that.

"Hey," Lucas says. "I'm going back to the villa to get started on the forensics, but you shouldn't be back here."

I glare at him. "Don't you think it's convenient that she wasn't here when it happened?"

"Who is she?"

"Daniela."

He raises a brow, and I recognize the look—he thinks I'm nuts.

"I'd never underestimate her, but no, I don't think she would have set a bomb in Santa Ana's, and killed innocent people. Besides, she had no opportunity."

He's right, of course. But I don't trust my judgment when it comes to her.

"Did Cristiano tell you that, when he went into the chapel after the explosion, Daniela had thrown herself over your mother to protect her from the falling debris?"

No. He didn't mention it. I shouldn't be surprised. She has a good heart and a clean soul. It seems she's always protecting someone other than herself. *It's your fucking job to protect her, especially now that she's your wife.* So far, I'm doing a helluva job.

"I'll catch up to you at the villa in a little while. Lucas?"

"Yeah?"

"I want the sonofabitch who did this. Don't stop turning over rocks until he's ours."

74

DANIELA

I glance at the television screen. They're talking about the explosion at Santa Ana's. The report claims that old electrical wiring caused the blast. "Fortunately, no one died," the newscaster claims.

It's a lie, of course, because I saw a dead man on the ground, covered with a jacket. *And there will likely be more.*

Antonio texted earlier to tell me that Paula had been located. I haven't heard another word from him, and it's nearly midnight.

The waiting is killing me. I've taken a bath, eaten some crackers, and tried to read to take my mind off what happened today. Off how close I came to dying. Off the innocent women who still haven't been accounted for—surely Antonio would have texted me if they had been found alive. Or Pinto, the man who stood outside the door to protect me.

What about Sister Maria Gloria? Did she make it out of the room?

I hope Antonio isn't so thirsty for vengeance that he's reckless with his own life—or the lives of others.

Who would do something like this? Tomas? I don't think so.

There would be other ways to kill me. Maybe it wasn't meant to kill anyone. Maybe it was intended to intimidate me—or Antonio.

The questions pop into my mind, one after another. Nothing is engaging enough to get my mind off the horror.

I should call Isabel. She's alone tonight, and I'm not sure if the explosion will make the Portuguese news in the US. She'll be beside herself with worry that something happened to me.

I place the call, then pace the room as I wait for her to answer.

"Hello?" Isabel says, as though she's not sure it's me calling.

"Hello."

"Daniela. Are you married?" she whispers.

"I am." I don't allow the emotion I'm feeling to control my voice, but it doesn't matter. Isabel begins to cry.

"It's okay," I assure her. "He's not so bad. Not like his father." I wait for her to blow her nose. "Is Valentina at her event?"

"Yes. But I don't like it. When we got to the school, there were so many boys."

Valentina was so excited about the dance-a-thon tonight. The kids are locked in the school gym for the entire night to raise money for homeless teens. Isabel hates the idea of girls and boys mixing for the night, but Valentina and I managed to wear her down. It's a good thing too. She doesn't need to sit around all night watching Isabel grieve.

"I can't wait to see you," she says. "Even for a few days."

I have a feeling that Antonio won't leave Porto until we know who was responsible for the explosion. I need to prepare Isabel without alarming her. "There's a possibility that our trip might be delayed by a day or two. But I promise I'm still coming. I'll know more in a few hours." *I hope.*

"Is everything all right?" she asks, her tone suspicious. She doesn't trust Antonio.

Isabel hasn't heard about the explosion, and I'm not going

to tell her. If she sees it on the news now, she'll have already spoken to me, and she'll know I'm not hurt—*or dead*.

"Everything's fine. Antonio has some pressing matters to attend to before we can leave. But we're coming."

After we hang up, I lie on the couch with a book. Before I even finish reading a page, the elevator dings.

I toss my book aside and rush the elevator, praying that it's Antonio and not someone bringing bad news.

75

DANIELA

The doors open, and Antonio steps into the apartment. I draw a long, ragged breath.

He looks haggard, and worn, and I can almost see the weight of the world on his shoulders. *It's bad. It has to be.*

"Is there any news?"

"We're making progress. But it's slow."

He's wearing sweatpants and a T-shirt. Somewhere along the way, he lost the dark bespoke suit—his wedding suit.

I'm relieved that he doesn't seem injured.

We stand in the hall, perfectly still, gauging each other.

"How are you?" he murmurs.

"I'm doing better. But I wish there was news on the missing women."

He steps closer to me and cradles my cheek.

I tip my face into his warm hand.

"I don't expect the news to be good."

I know this, but a tear trickles down my cheek anyway. "Any chance it was an accident?"

He swallows hard and shakes his head.

"Any clues as to what happened?"

"Someone almost killed you. My mother was nearby. Do you know how to humiliate a man? How to destroy him?"

I nod. "You take his women. His wife. His mother. His daughters. His sisters. You kidnap, rape, torture, kill them—any one of those atrocities will do."

He studies me. My response surprises him. It's a lesson I know deep, deep in my heart.

"No clues at all?" I ask before he prods me to tell him more.

"The bridal bouquet was rigged with a tiny plastic device that managed to get through our security. Someone from the florist left the door of the shop unlocked last night."

There is hatred in his voice. I'm beginning to feel hatred well inside me too. That decision cost people their lives. *I was lucky.*

"Who did he leave the door unlocked for?"

"He didn't know. He was contacted anonymously. A large sum of money was deposited in his account yesterday. My men picked him up at the airport in Lisbon."

"I'm surprised whoever paid him didn't kill him after it was done."

"I suspect they hadn't gotten to him yet. They were sloppy."

"Do you think they'll still try to contact him? Maybe you can—"

He shakes his head. "The devil is the only person contacting him now."

Antonio killed him—or it was done on his order. I don't feel any regret. None. It's chilling. "He's dead?"

Antonio takes my hand and leads me to the kitchen. "Daniela—no more questions tonight." He pours himself a big whiskey and downs it in one gulp.

"I'm sure this wasn't the wedding night you were thinking about, but I need you—now." With one hand, he sweeps the candlesticks and flowers off the table and onto the floor.

The pain in his face eats right through me.

He reaches for me and rips the nightgown off my body. His eyes swirl with dark emotions that I've never seen. I'm not even sure what to call them.

"I'll take care of you, but first I need this," he mutters, lifting me onto the table.

As I watch him pull down his pants with trembling hands, the ice inside me cracks—it begins with a small fissure.

His cock is hard and angry, jutting straight out from his body.

A shiver runs through me as he notches at my opening. But he doesn't push inside.

He wraps my legs around his waist and lowers his mouth to mine in a bruising kiss. "They could have killed you," he whispers, a low growl twisting from his chest.

His eyes are black—and lost, drowning in despair. I pull his face down and kiss him, sliding my tongue into his mouth.

"Fuck me," I say softly.

He presses a small kiss to my forehead. "I don't deserve you," he murmurs as he takes me ruthlessly.

I squeeze my walls around him, pulling him into my body.

His thrusts are merciless, wanton. I reach up to cradle his jaw as he ruts deeper and deeper and deeper.

My body revels in the punishment, demanding everything he has to give. His frustrations, his fears, his emotion, his pain —I want all of it.

His gaze never leaves mine, not even as he roars his release.

Before either of us can catch our breath, Antonio carries me straight to bed. Laying me on the cool sheets, he crawls between my legs, licking my pussy until I scream. And then he does it again until I'm thrashing on the bed, my legs quivering.

He slides up and hovers over me. And without apology or permission or anything at all, he fucks me long and hard, as though he's trying to convey what's in his soul, using not his words, but his body. When I'm teetering at the edge, he reaches between us and rubs my clit between his fingers, and another orgasm rips through me.

I'm shaking, but I dig my heels into his ass, urging him to find peace inside me.

He rears up and plunges deep one last time, emptying himself inside me with the tormented growl of a wounded animal. It makes my heart weep.

We lay like that, skin to skin, until Antonio rolls over, pulling me with him.

As my head rests on his chest, I don't think about how he forced me to marry him, or about anything, really, except his beating heart and strong arms wrapped around me.

For the first time today, I feel safe.

76

ANTONIO

The phone vibrates. *Lucas.* I told them to call with anything new. "Hold on," I whisper, going into the bathroom and closing the door behind me so that I don't wake Daniela. It wasn't much of a wedding, but we made the most of the wedding night.

"What do you have?"

"Isabel is dead. Our man on the ground was killed too."

For several seconds, I grapple with the information. I brace my hand on the wall, wondering how I'm ever going to tell Daniela.

"When?"

"Last night. Around nine or ten Eastern Daylight Time."

"The daughter?"

"From what we know, she's alive."

"Do we have her?"

"She's at some overnight school event for several more hours."

"The guards?"

"We lost one," he says, anger rippling through his voice.

Fuck.

I hang up and wonder if I should let Daniela sleep. There's nothing she can do right now. Yesterday was a nightmare of a day, and I used her hard last night.

I can't. She's going to want to talk to the kid.

I go back into the bedroom and watch her sleep. She looks so peaceful—and she's had so little peace that it kills me to shatter it.

"Anything on Nelia?" she mutters, half-asleep.

She's such a light sleeper. Maybe one day she'll feel safe enough around me to sleep soundly.

I dim the bedside lamp before turning it on. She closes her eyes.

I'm about to break her heart—again. It's the last thing I want.

I sit on the bed beside her and take her hand. She's wide awake now. "Nelia's dead," she whispers into the dimly lit room.

"We still don't know anything about Nelia." I suck in a long breath, then blow it out slowly. "Isabel was killed last night."

Her face is blank. And she's still—eerily still and far away. I feel like I've lost her.

"Daniela," I prod gently, tightening my hold on her hand.

"Someone killed Isabel?"

I nod. "Yes." The word twists from my chest, and I watch, helpless, as it lands in her heart like a poison dart.

"Valentina?" she asks, blinking rapidly. "Did someone kill Valentina?"

Daniela's body is here, but her affect is off, *way off*, and her mind is somewhere else entirely.

"As far as we know, she's safe."

She pales as a burst of light flashes in her eyes. "No!" she shrieks. "No!"

She pulls her hand away and leaps up, standing on the bed, clutching the sheet. She's trembling when I reach for her.

"You're going to fall. You need to come down."

She shakes her head vehemently, clutching the sheet closer.

"Daniela." I say her name much too firm and loud, because I don't know how to bring her back, so I go directly to my default setting.

As callous as it is, it seems to work.

She lowers herself to the bed and stands, her feet firmly planted on the floor.

"I need to go to Fall River. Right now!" she cries when I don't move.

I take tight hold of her upper arms. "We can't. Not right now. Someone tried to kill you yesterday, and now Isabel. You can call Valentina."

"No!" she screams in my face. "I need to go. Right now."

I've seen her frayed at the edges and downright terrified, but I've never seen her like this. Not even when she thought I was going to throw her to my guards and kill her when they were done using her.

"You can't go right now," I say with as much compassion as a man like me knows. "It's too dangerous. Isabel's daughter is not your responsibility."

Daniela's face tightens, as though in agony.

Her dark eyes scour my face, rifling through my soul, searching for something she desperately needs. That's how it feels.

"How can I help?"

Her eyes are still glued to my face, but she doesn't respond.

"Let me help you." I step toward her, and she stumbles back, a lone tear trickling down her cheek.

"Valentina," she whimpers. "Valentina is . . . isn't." Her voice is a wobbly, hoarse whisper, as though she's trying out the words for the first time.

Daniela's shoulders roll forward as she cups her elbows.

I want to comfort her. But every time I inch toward her, she moves farther away. Forcing her into my arms isn't the answer. Even I can see that.

"What about Valentina?" I urge, keeping my voice low and steady. Although it's not easy, because I feel powerless right now. And I despise that feeling more than *anything*.

She tips her head back and squeezes her eyes so tight her beautiful face contorts into someone almost unrecognizable. Not Daniela but a haunted young woman with despair and agony woven into every line, every crease.

A mournful wail twists from her body as the demons are exorcised from the darkest corners of her soul. "Valentina isn't . . ." She draws a ragged breath.

"She isn't Isabel's daughter."

THANK YOU FOR READING GREED! Read more of Daniela and Antonio's story **HERE**

ABOUT THE AUTHOR

After being a confirmed city-girl for most of her life, Eva moved to beautiful Western Massachusetts in 2014. She found herself living in the woods with no job, no friends (unless you count the turkey, deer, and coyote roaming the backyard), and no children underfoot, wondering what on earth she'd been thinking. But as it turned out, it was the perfect setting to take all those yarns spinning in her head and weave them into sexy stories.

When she's not writing, trying to squeeze information out of her tight-lipped sons, or playing with the two cutest dogs you've ever seen, Eva's creating chapters in her own love story.

Sign-up for my monthly newsletter for special treats and all the Eva news!

Eva's VIP Reader Newsletter

I'd love to hear from you!

eva@evacharles.com

MORE STEAMY ROMANTIC SUSPENSE BY EVA CHARLES

A SINFUL EMPIRE TRILOGY

Greed

Lust

Envy

THE DEVIL'S DUE (SERIES COMPLETE)

Depraved

Delivered

Bound

Decadent

CONTEMPORARY ROMANCE

THE NEW AMERICAN ROYALS

Sheltered Heart

Noble Pursuit

Double Play

Unforgettable

Loyal Subjects

Sexy Sinner

Made in the USA
Las Vegas, NV
25 June 2023